ALSO BY EMIKO JEAN

Tokyo Ever After

Tokyo Dreaming

Mika in Real Life

THE
RETURN OF
ELLIE
BLACK

A Novel

EMIKO JEAN

SIMON & SCHUSTER

New York   London   Toronto   Sydney   New Delhi

Simon & Schuster
1230 Avenue of the Americas
New York, NY 10020

First Simon & Schuster hardcover edition July 2024

SIMON & SCHUSTER and colophon are registered trademarks of Simon & Schuster, Inc.

Simon & Schuster: Celebrating 100 Years of Publishing in 2024

Interior design by Wendy Blum

Manufactured in the United States of America

ISBN 978-1-6680-2393-8

To G & M.

Thank you.
I am shaken, but I still believe.

PROLOGUE

THIS IS HOW IT BEGINS:

With a girl running through a forest, her veins tight with adrenaline. She exhales in short, even bursts. There is dirt under her fingernails, fresh mud stains on her jeans, blood on her sweatshirt, and vomit on her breath.

Soon.

Soon she will be home.

Images surface. The one stoplight on Main Street. The chipped green shutters of her house. The weathered flooring of her father's commercial fishing boat.

In the distance, a horn blares and she ducks, covering her ears, the sound slicing through her skull like an anguished scream. The world shrinks and becomes abstract, too colorful and too bright. The horn recedes and the trees slowly refocus.

She counts her breaths as her heartbeat steadies. One. Two. Three. Then she counts her steps. Four. Five. Six. How many will it take for someone to find her? Seven. Eight. Nine. Her bones are heavy, her feet tired. She has traveled a long distance. Her shadow stretches ahead of her, as if she's chasing it—come and catch me. Ten. Eleven. Twelve. Her body wavers. Maybe she should sit down. Thirteen. Fourteen. Fifteen. She pushes herself to keep going. The sun rises higher behind the gray clouds. The air smells of pine and resin. Like water and moss. Like life itself.

"Hey! Are you all right?" A pair of hikers—father and son—appear, rounding the corner of the trail. They wear overstuffed backpacks, rolled sleeping bags at the top, a pot hanging from the bottom of one, two metal cups from the other. The girl slows her pace and draws closer to them.

Sixteen. Seventeen. Eighteen.

The father places an arm across his son's chest to shield him from the girl, and she falters, caught in the chokehold of their gazes. The son's eyes are brown with tiny flecks of gold, and they remind her of someone she used to know. Her mind tumbles and trips back in time.

Tell me, what would you do for someone you love?

Anything. I would do anything.

The father clears his throat. "Miss, are you all right?" He studies her.

She imagines what he sees. Filthy skin. Tangled hair. Bony body. Bloodstained sweatshirt. She is something the world has chewed up and spit out.

The son's nose twitches.

"Miss?" the father says with more force this time. He takes a single, tentative step toward her.

The girl licks her dry, cracked lips and works to keep her voice steady as she answers, "Yes?"

"Are you all right?" the father asks again.

The girl blinks. Shakes her head. Stares into nothing. "No, I don't think I am."

"What's your name?"

"My name?" Who is she? What has she become? A vessel. To be carried. To be kept. To be filled.

"Yes, what's your name?" The father drags the words out.

The girl hesitates. Her name is stuck somewhere inside of her. Down in the deep, deep dark where she hid it. To be safe. Don't remember. Never forget. She squares her shoulders and reaches for it.

"Elizabeth," she says on a whoosh of breath.

She has not spoken those four syllables in forever. Her name. Her *real* name. The name her mother picked because it was classic and royal and carried all her hopes and dreams for her daughter—college, career, a family, happiness. Once, the girl had worn her name proudly, like a crown. Once, someone whispered her name back to her, love on their tongue.

With a final twist, the girl wrenches her whole name free. "My name is Elizabeth Black. I think I'm missing."

ONE

CHELSEY WAKES TO HER PHONE ringing.

"No," her husband, Noah, groans. "Make it stop." The mattress squeaks as he shifts away from her.

Rising on an elbow, Chelsey fumbles for her phone on the nightstand. It's a little after midnight. She silences the ringer and peers at the screen. "It's work."

"Somebody better be dead," Noah mutters.

Chelsey smiles at Noah's wry sense of humor. She is a police officer, a detective. Most likely, somebody is dead.

"Detective Calhoun," she answers, switching on the light and moving to the edge of the mattress, a shiver racing up her spine. Spring in Coldwell Beach is always frigid. Summer, too. Residents are lucky if there are a few days above sixty-five degrees. This stretch of coastline in Washington is situated between two rocky bluffs and is known for its temperamental weather. Lewis and Clark marked it on their map as uninhabitable.

"Chelsey." It's her boss, Sergeant Abbott. She no longer blinks when he uses her first name. It doesn't matter that he addresses her male counterparts by their last names. Doesn't matter at all. "Got a call. A girl has been found." Sergeant Abbott waits for a beat. "She identified herself as Elizabeth Black."

1

At this, Chelsey does blink. Ellie Black. Alive? It's been two years. She stands abruptly and switches the phone to speaker.

Noah flicks on his bedside lamp. A gold chain with two pendants hangs from his neck—twenty-one, his old basketball number, and a saint medallion. Chelsey doesn't remember which, some spiritual warrior in the battle of good versus evil. "What?" He sits up and scratches at his beard.

She presses a finger to her lips and then fishes a pen and paper from the nightstand drawer while Abbott rattles off information. Hikers in the Capitol State Forest found Ellie Black. He gives her their phone numbers. Ellie has been transported to Legacy Memorial. No word yet on her condition. Chelsey googles the location. Olympia. Two hours southeast of Coldwell. "I want you at the hospital."

"I'm on my way." She yanks on her jeans.

"I've got Douglas heading toward the trail she was found on."

A slow, hot pause. Douglas. Sergeant Abbott's son. She has known him since they were children. Both their dads were cops. Chelsey's had been higher ranking, the police chief. And Doug's dad, still a uniform, not yet a sergeant, not yet Chelsey's boss. Doug is a couple years older than Chelsey. He fucked around for a few years before following in his father's footsteps. Abbott recently promoted his son to detective, same as Chelsey, though she'd logged more hours. Chelsey had no problem with it. Really. They rarely crossed turfs, anyway. She works in Family Services, and Doug in Narcotics.

She flashes back to one of the precinct picnics. Back when they'd been young. When Lydia, Chelsey's sister, had been alive. Doug had been in a group of boys making fun of Chelsey. Asked if she'd arrived in a bento box. Chelsey was adopted. Full Japanese. The rest of her family was fair-haired and milk-skinned. Even now, thirty plus years later, the memory is visceral. Watermelon spoiling in her stomach. Clouds covering the sun. Laughter bleeding away to tears shed quietly under an oak. After that, Chelsey walked with her neck bent, gaze pointed at the ground. A boyfriend once made fun of her for it, mimicking how she stooped. Chelsey has come a long way since then. Still she remembers

Doug, her ex-boyfriend, and other people like them in the world, as arms trying to hold her down.

"Chelsey, you there?"

She swallows twice. "I'm here."

"If this is Ellie Black, I want the guy responsible found. I want an arrest, and I want it soon."

Chelsey bristles against the command but pushes the feeling away. "Got it." She punches her arms through her shirt, keeping the phone in one hand.

"Media is going to be all over this," he continues. "They're going to be watching closely. I will be, too. No mistakes."

"I'll keep you posted."

"Do," he says.

Chelsey hangs up, finishes dressing, and ties her hair back in a tight low ponytail. Shoes. Where are her shoes?

"Did I hear right? Ellie Black has been found?" Noah follows her through the apartment. It is a nice place. Temporary. The walls are white. The ceiling popcorn. A couch. A dining table. Mostly Noah's stuff. Including two framed *Battlestar Galactica* posters—one with a fist raised to the air with the words SO SAY WE ALL underneath and another a silhouette of a beautiful woman, a Cylon, that states NEVER FORGET WHO THE ENEMY IS. Chelsey and Noah are both sci-fi geeks.

"Hasn't been verified yet," she tells Noah.

It doesn't happen often, but there has been a time or two over the course of Chelsey's career when someone came forward, professing to be a missing child, all in the hopes of defrauding some grief-stricken parents out of their money. Ellie's parents mortgaged their house to offer a fifty-thousand-dollar reward a few weeks after Ellie disappeared. The timing isn't right for fraud, though. Ellie hasn't been gone long enough to be physically unrecognizable. Two years, two weeks, and one day to be exact. Chelsey keeps a calendar with the anniversary marked.

"Jesus, what are the chances?" Noah pauses by the fireplace. On the mantel are photographs—one of Noah in a cap and gown the day he graduated with his master's in Education. Another of him and his family at the rodeo—parents and all six kids in jeans and cowboy hats. A wedding picture from the courthouse where he and Chelsey eloped. And last, one of Chelsey as a teen, head to toe in camo, rifle slung over her shoulder, dead deer at her feet—her first kill. Her years at Coldwell High School had been filled with buckshot, stripping hide, and using a compass to navigate home.

Chelsey crosses the room to the kitchen, where remnants of the curry they had for dinner still spice the air. A safe sits atop the laminate counter. She spins the dial; nestled inside are her gun and holster. Noah rubs the back of his neck. He's uncomfortable with firearms. Even though he grew up on a farm, shooting coyotes on the weekends. Even though he married a detective.

"I guess we won't be looking at houses tomorrow." He scoops her keys from the counter and hands them to her.

She fists the keys. "Sorry." The apology is half-hearted. They dated for a year and a half. Have been married for a little over six months and searching for a house since then. A place to settle down. Chelsey has found something wrong with each property.

"It's all right. I get it." But disappointment lingers in his eyes. *When you're married to a cop, there are hundreds of you in the relationship—you, him, and all his cases, their families,* Chelsey's mom used to say.

"I don't know when I'll be able to reschedule," she says.

He scratches his brow. "Don't worry about it." Again, a flicker in his expression. Is he tiring of this dance? Chelsey stepping back while he's stepping in. When they met, it had been the same way. Noah chasing Chelsey.

Peet's had been crowded that night two years ago. It was the eve of Chelsey's promotion to detective. Ellie Black would disappear the next day. Cops pounded her on the back, offering congratulations, asking to buy her a beer, but she'd refused. She'd already stayed too long. Noah bellied up to the bar, squeezing in next to her. *I'm Noah*, he introduced himself. *I just finished my master's in Education. I'm subbing at the high school but looking for something full time.*

Chelsey was always suspicious of someone who gave too much information.

I want to teach gym, physical education, he shouted over the noise.

Chelsey signaled Tim, the bartender, for her tab.

Noah pressed a hand against his chest as if offended. *You're leaving? Was it the gym teacher part?*

Nope, nothing against teachers, Chelsey said, scribbling her name on the check. Tim slipped a plastic bag of takeout in front of her.

Tell the chief I said hi, he said, eyeing Noah.

She thanked Tim, then slid her gaze to Noah. *I have to get dinner to my dad.* Her father was midway through chemo and sicker than a dog. Crankier than a donkey. Almost everything tasted like metal to him. He could only stomach hot wings and Sour Patch Kids. She shoved her way through the bodies, Noah on her heels.

Let me come with you, he'd said outside, breath fogging in the evening spring air, hands jammed into his pockets.

She paused and leveled him with a stare. *I'm flattered, but I'm not interested in dating right now. My job is busy. My dad has cancer . . .* She waited for the C-word to do its work. Scare Noah off.

He puffed up with a smile. *Let me come with you*, he repeated. *I'll help.*

She scoffed. *Does it look like I need help?*

Nope. But those are usually the people who need the most help.

She did not want to like him. *You got some weird kind of savior syndrome?*

Only when it comes to pretty girls. He grinned then, white teeth flashing against his beard.

Fine. She let him come with her. Made him leave his car and drove them both, making sure her gun was visible. He whistled low when he saw the house. *Nice place*, he said, peering up at the gabled roof.

Come on. She unlocked the door. Her dad was on the couch, *Homeland* on the television.

Who the hell are you? her dad whistled out, seeing Noah. All his hair was gone, his cheeks sunken in, and his skin pallid. An oxygen tank rested nearby, the nose cannula discarded on a rose-colored cushion. Her mom had loved that couch.

Dad, she chided. *You're supposed to be wearing this.* She fitted the hose back around his head.

I asked a question, her father ground out.

This is Noah. He followed me home.

Her dad refused to shake Noah's hand. *Cancer, huh?* Noah said, dropping his arm back to his side. *The farm I grew up on, we had a horse with cancer. She liked these CBD pills the vet prescribed. Maybe that'll help.*

You comparing me to a horse, boy?

Chelsey didn't try to intervene. She waited to see how Noah would handle it. If he would ask for a ride back to the bar. She kept her coat on.

No, sir, Noah answered, straight-faced and stoic. *The horse was much nicer.*

Chelsey's dad gave a startled laugh, coughed up some blood, and offered Noah a seat.

Chelsey blinks away the memory and stares at Noah, keys loose in her hand now. "I have to go."

He pecks her cheek. "Be safe." It's what he always says. A futile request. As if she could stop a bullet or a fist or a car with a heavy-limbed drunk behind the wheel.

She jams her feet in her shoes and jogs down the stairs into the cool night. Noah waits at the top, leaning against the doorjamb. She keeps him in her line of sight as she climbs into her car, an Oldsmobile she inherited from her father. On the back window is a *Firefly* sticker. Noah had brought it to her on their third date. Over that dinner, she'd opened up to him about the responsibilities of being a cop. She'd unburdened herself.

They'd brought the leftovers to her father. Then, while her father slept, lost in the ether of pain medication, Chelsey walked Noah to his truck. He kissed her. The night was still, calm, satin black. She unbuttoned her blouse. He opened his car door. They climbed in, shed their clothes, ground their hips.

She'd fallen in love with him quickly.

For the most part, Chelsey shares everything with Noah. He knows about Lydia, her dead sister. He knows about her parents' divorce. He knows the day after Chelsey's eighteenth birthday, her mother skipped town to Scottsdale. He knows about her father's death, because he'd been there, standing by her as the cancer took him. And Noah knows about the house she inherited after he died, a place full of forty years of outdated furniture and bad memories.

But he does not know everything.

Behind the wheel, Chelsey gives Noah a wave, swallowing against the guilt, the fear. The slow drip of dread. She doesn't want to lose him but can't seem to hold on to him without letting go of something else. She starts the car, puts it in reverse, and backs away, Noah caught in the snare of her headlights.

Chapter

TWO

CHELSEY IS THIRTY MINUTES INTO the drive to Olympia before she unclenches her hands from the wheel. There isn't any traffic, save for the occasional semi. There aren't any streetlights on the two-lane road either. She flicks on her brights and settles deeper into her seat. This narrow strip of land is the only way in and out of Coldwell. One side is dark trees and gray cliffs glistening in the silvery moonlight, and the other a white-capped ocean guarded by a thin twist of metal. Someday a tsunami will wash out the road, and Coldwell will be stranded. She takes a breath. She knows the way by rote and can allow herself to sink now. To let go. To be lost in memory.

Ellie Black.

She remembers the initial call two years ago, the day after she met Noah. The radio's crackle and the dispatcher's scratchy voice announcing a seventeen-year-old girl didn't come home from sleeping over at a friend's house.

Chelsey had immediately pulled a U-turn onto Main Street and headed straight for the Blacks' house, winding through emaciated Coldwell. Chelsey couldn't recall when the town started to change. The erosion was slow, the act of water whittling away at rock. First, the staff at the schools was cut by thirty percent. Then the library closed. After that, the rec center. Once, when Chelsey was young, it had been bustling. Kids swam in the pool during the summer. Soccer in the fall. Played basketball in the winter. Crafts in the spring. Now, the building was boarded up, slowly succumbing to salt water and storms. And the kids? Forced to go online or into the woods.

The Blacks lived on the north side, in a neighborhood populated mainly by commercial fishing families and cannery workers. Houses crouched behind overgrown junipers, brown lawns, and chain-link fences.

Chelsey had knocked on the Blacks' door, the porch wet and squishy beneath her feet. Doug answered. He'd been in a uniform then, not yet promoted to detective. *Hey.* His smile was wide. He was young and dumb and too excited about the case. About being the first on the scene. *I started to take statements.*

Should have waited for me, Chelsey said.

His cheeks flushed salmon. *Sorry.*

Jimmy, Ellie's father, appeared, edging around Doug to introduce himself. *Jimmy Black.* He stuck out a hand, and Chelsey shook it.

Detective Calhoun, Coldwell PD.

Jimmy squinted at her. *How long have you been with the force?*

Chelsey's face worked against her. Unlined and surprisingly Asian. She saw it in Jimmy's expression, the doubt, the wondering if Chelsey was too young, too foreign. Did she even speak English? *I've served near a decade*, she said, her eyes downcast, then she flicked her gaze up. *I'd like to focus on Elizabeth. Should we talk about her?* Later on, she congratulated herself. She'd been cool. Focused. Even though it was her first case as detective. Even though her heart was pounding, an unnerving reckless beat. Sometimes she wondered at how small she felt. What hands had shaped her, worn her down.

That seemed to be enough for Jimmy. He let her in. *Thanks for coming, Detective.*

Call me Chelsey, she had said, shuffling into their living room. Kat, Ellie's mother, was there, seated on a faded blue velvet couch, an undrunk mug of coffee cupped in her hands. Jimmy sank down next to his wife, close enough to touch but not. Both held their bodies stiffly, as if to brace against a coming squall.

Chelsey settled into a worn-out plaid armchair across from them. *Tell me what's going on*, she said. *Dispatch said your daughter didn't come home.*

Doug posted himself near the door, hands on his belt, feet spread, and chest puffed out.

Kat peered down into her cup. *I tried calling Ellie*, she explained, a hollowness to her voice that Chelsey recognized as shock. You never think it can happen to you. *Then I called India.*

Chelsey could see through to the kitchen, where a recycling bin overflowed with empty bottles—wine, whiskey, tequila. One of the cabinets was smashed in as if a fist had gone through it. Chelsey jutted her chin at the damage. *What happened to your cabinets?*

I put a hole through it, Jimmy offered calmly. Too calmly? *Got pissed.*

Before or after Ellie disappeared? The air in the room seemed to still, then pulsate. Kat hung her head. In shame? Embarrassment? Fear?

Before, Jimmy answered, low. *I got nothing to hide. You want prints? You want to search the house? Have at it.*

All right. I'd like to take a look around. Especially Ellie's room, but that can wait, Chelsey said. She placed Jimmy in the back of the line of suspects. She returned to Kat. *Who is India?*

Kat swallowed. *I don't know her well. Ellie doesn't have many friends. A week ago was the first time I'd heard her name. Thank god I insisted Ellie give me her phone number. Ellie was supposed to be staying the night at India's house. But India said the last time she saw Ellie was at some motel. They were having a party.* Kat placed her mug on the coffee table with an audible thunk. *I feel like I am in some alternate universe. How is this happening?*

There were many things to wrest a person away. But Chelsey decided to keep that to herself. Kat didn't have much more information, and Jimmy had been gone for work.

I'm sure Ellie will turn up. You know girls, Doug offered. *They get crazy ideas and run off all the time.* Chelsey's lips twitched, hating the

11

implication that being born female made you automatically guilty of something.

Jimmy stood, his hands balling into fists. He was a big guy and kept a bat by the front door. *That's not her. That's not my daughter.* He advanced on Doug. *Ellie wouldn't just run away.*

Chelsey had been quick to step between them, all five feet nothing of her blocking the two men. At the same time, she clocked the bat, calculating how many steps Jimmy would need to take to grab it—three, maybe two. *Officer Abbott,* she said, *why don't you take a walk.* It wasn't a question.

S-sorry, Doug stammered, sticking up his hands. *Didn't mean any offense.* He backed out the door and hung out on the lawn, staring at his phone. Doug liked to make videos and post them on social media. Jesus Christ. He was the typical middle child, always eager to please.

Is it true what he said? Hope blazed in Kat's eyes. *Does this happen all the time?*

Statistics were Chelsey's best friend in situations like this. *Regarding girls in Ellie's age group, sixteen to twenty-one, they do come back eighty-one percent of the time.* She didn't add that the odds decreased to half a percent after twenty-four hours. Better to let things unfold as they would. *Now, tell me more about Ellie.*

Kat listed off several nonessential facts: *Ellie is headstrong. Stubborn at times. Her grades aren't great, but she's so bright. Jimmy, remember when she scored high on her writing exam in the fifth grade? She doesn't have a lot of friends, but her boyfriend, Danny, adores her.*

All these details to show how special Ellie was. Proof she deserved to be searched for, to be found. There was no way Kat could know a dollar figure was attached to each case. A careful calculation multiplied by parents' wealth, then divided by race and religion. The poorer and darker a girl, the less funds and time the department allocated to her rescue—after all, the public is a little less outraged when those types of girls go missing. Maybe Ellie's mom could sense it—some daughters were worth more than others.

This was not a viewpoint Chelsey subscribed to. But it was a reality, even if she didn't want to believe it.

Chelsey searched Ellie's room and left soon after, promising to call when she had more information. It wasn't an emergency. Not yet. Ellie's shoe, cell phone, and blood hadn't been found yet. Kat hadn't cried yet, the type of gulping and sobbing that overtakes your whole body. And the Blacks' entire existence hadn't been distilled into a life lived one day at a time yet.

Still, Chelsey moved quickly through the regular procedure, interviewing everyone who had seen Elizabeth last. Starting with India.

Listen. Ellie and I have only hung out a couple of times. We had fun together, but we're not close, India had said through a rickety screen door. She had pale blond hair, the kind from a box, and a tiny silver nose ring that glinted in the light. Chelsey smelled booze on her, not fresh, but oozing out of her pores. India was hungover. *It was all Ellie's idea anyway,* she went on.

What was? Chelsey prodded. A seagull shrieked and landed in the yard.

The party. I provided transportation, that's all. I'm not her keeper.

Got it. The girl was more concerned with the possibility of being in trouble than the fact of Ellie's disappearance. *I don't care about the party. If you drank. Did drugs,* Chelsey assured her. *I just want to find Ellie.* That had mollified India enough for her to send Chelsey photos of the party. Chelsey pieced those photographs together to establish part of the timeline. Eleven thirty-one p.m. was the last moment Ellie was captured on film in the motel room. By eleven thirty-nine, she was gone. She was there, and then she was not, a butterfly dragged away in the wind.

Next, Chelsey questioned Daniel Partridge, Ellie's boyfriend. *I was home sleeping,* he'd stated, leg bouncing. They were in his house, at a little built-in table with wooden benches, stalks of wheat carved into the sides.

Is there anyone that can vouch for you? Chelsey stared at him without blinking. Lydia, her sister, used to call this her fox face. Most crimes are perpetrated by someone the victim knows. Danny seemed nice. But it was

13

the nice guys you had to watch out for. The mean ones, they wore their crimes on their sleeves, carting them around with all their messy emotional baggage. Nice guys buried things deep.

Daniel's leg stilled. His eyes narrowed. *My folks were working, but my mom dropped off some dinner.* His parents owned a bar and restaurant on Main Street. A few months earlier, Chelsey remembered, the Fishtrap had been vandalized, the words REDSKIN and GO BACK TO THE RES sprayed on the front windows in neon orange paint. The Partridges were Chinook. They cleaned up the graffiti, installed security cameras, and hung their tribal flag in the windows.

I'd like to give your mother a call if you don't mind, Chelsey said. *Verify your story.*

Danny jumped from the bench and yanked open kitchen drawers until he found a scrap of paper and a pen from the local bait and tackle shop. He scribbled his mom's name and phone number and threw the paper down on the table like a gauntlet. *Have at it.*

Chelsey had offended him. But everyone was a suspect. She'd even tracked Kat and Jim. The way they gripped their cups. Too tightly? Too casually? What kind of details did they offer? Were they too verbose or too vague? The truth tiptoes on a thin, narrow line.

Turned out, Danny had a reason to be defensive. He hadn't been home all night as he'd stated. He'd been lying. Hiding behind his outrage.

Then she'd interviewed the kids at the party, the teachers at Ellie's school. Reports vacillated about Ellie, from worse to worse. *She was such a fake, pretending to be rich*, a classmate said. *That girl? I always thought she'd get herself killed someday*, a teacher said, so self-righteous it made Chelsey want to vomit.

Rain splatters the windshield, and Chelsey jolts back to the present. She clicks on her wipers. She is closer to Olympia now. Closer to Ellie. Thirty minutes and she will be at the hospital. The knowledge tightens around her chest like a lasso. The highway widens into three lanes. There are more cars, semis, fast food restaurants, assorted motels, and gas stations. She glances at her phone, discarded on the passenger seat. She should call Jimmy and Kat.

Jimmy kept in touch with Chelsey. The last time she saw him was five months ago. He'd made a habit of visiting the precinct every now and again. Meandering in right when they opened, a carafe of coffee and a dozen donuts from Cottage Bakery in his callused hands. Last time, he'd presented them to Suzette at the front desk while making small talk, asking about her husband and grandchildren. He'd straightened when he saw Chelsey, and she led him back to a private room and closed the door. They sat across from each other, a table between them, and began their ritual. It was always small talk at first.

How are you doing, Jim?

All right, he said.

And Kat?

Oh, you know, she has her good days and bad days. Sam and her family will be moving here soon, and that's cheered her up a bit.

Ellie had an older sister, Sam. They'd been born ten years apart. Not close. Not like Chelsey and Lydia had been. She and Lydia may not have shared blood, but they shared everything else. *You're like two peas in a pod*, their mother used to say.

That's nice, Chelsey remarked.

What about you? How's that man of yours? I saw him quoted in the paper, taking his team to states. Noah had finished his first year teaching at Ilwaco High School and coaching basketball, leading the team to the 2A state championship. He was devastated when they lost. Had gone with his brothers to his parents' cabin to brush it off.

Noah is good. Chelsey paused, knowing the question Jimmy had come to ask. Might as well get it out of the way. She viewed these conversations as akin to putting down an old dog. Why delay? *There haven't been any new leads, Jim*, she said gently. *You know I'd call you.*

Jimmy sighed and removed his baseball hat, cupping the bill between his palms. His hair stood up in little tufts of gray and brown. *Can I see it?*

Of course. Chelsey stood and retrieved the twelve-by-twelve corrugated box from evidence. She placed it on her desk and reminded Jimmy not to open any plastic bags. *It's still an open case.*

Jimmy nodded once. He knew the rules. It was always the same. First, he read the police report. Then the witness statements. Looking for anything Chelsey might have missed. Any scrap of information that could be the key to breaking Ellie's case wide open. Last, he peered at the physical evidence, handling each piece like a crumbling relic—one of Ellie's shoes, her cell phone with a cracked screen, gravel with blood on it, CCTV footage photographs pulled from the motel and the Pentecostal church next door, all of the parking lot where Ellie's things had been discovered. Semitrucks and scattered cars blocked any view of Ellie. Chelsey had chased down every owner of each license plate she could make out. Nobody had seen anything.

Just tell me you still believe she's out there.

Chelsey began to place the contents back in the box. Were these the last things Ellie held? What would these objects say if they could speak? What secrets might they whisper?

The case is still open. I won't stop searching until Ellie is found, she promised, because she did believe—it may have been silly, but she had to believe. She cut herself up on the razor's edge of hope.

Jimmy nodded solemnly and excused himself on a tremble. Chelsey let him go without another word. She'd learned enough to know Jimmy Black, like most men, required privacy when he fell apart.

Chelsey inhales, swimming free of the memories as she rolls to a stop at a red light. A sign for Legacy Memorial is posted at the intersection. It is time. She picks up her phone and dials the Blacks. It rings and rings. Two years. Two weeks. One day.

Ever since Ellie Black's disappearance, Chelsey has volunteered for any case involving violence against women. She always has plenty of work to do. All those beaten, all those bruised, all those maimed women are welcomed on Chelsey's shores. It is a type of atonement, Chelsey understands. She could not save Lydia. She could not solve Ellie's case.

The ringing stops, and the line picks up.

"'Lo," Jimmy answers. A television blares in the background, but his voice is sandpaper rough with sleep.

"Hey, Jim, it's Chelsey. Is Kat around? I have some news." She waits for Jimmy to awaken Kat, and she thinks of their daughter. Sees Ellie in the spiral of her mind. There she is, standing in the shadow of a hollow curve. Silent. Waiting for her turn to speak.

Yes, it is time.

wanted. The scheme had good profit margins, enough for me to buy a refurbished phone. I wanted Danny to stay the night with me. There's that word again. Want. Was that the problem? Did I want too much? I think a lot about how all of what happened is my fault.

"I'm sorry, I can't," he said. The hall was clearing. Classroom doors slammed. Danny rested his forehead against mine. "I love you."

I didn't say the words back. Withholding love was a power play. I had a mean streak a mile wide.

Danny sighed. "Are we really going to fight about this?"

"Depends on you, I guess."

I frowned. He kissed the corner of my mouth. It was our last kiss. I wish I had known. I would have lingered against him. I would have held his hand a little tighter. I would have told him goodbye.

At 1:03, 2:30, and 2:55, a flurry of texts passed between Danny and me. The contents are embarrassing, but suffice it to say, I was trying to make my boyfriend feel like a piece of shit for working and skipping out on me. There are lots of moments I'm not proud of. This is one of them. But I was selfish. I was that girl—the one who persuaded other people, Danny in particular, to do things they shouldn't do. What I should have said was that I would miss him. I should have said never mind, it's a stupid idea. A phone isn't that important. Let's go to the movies instead. But I was stubborn. Selfish. Foolhardy.

By 3:07, I was late again, but it wasn't my fault this time. Our substitute English teacher held the whole class captive two minutes past the final bell to finish a poem about a snowman and a moor.

India waited for me in her car. We pulled out of the school parking lot right as the last bus left, around 3:20.

By 3:45, we were outside of Coldwell. I tapped out a text to my mom: REMEMBER, I'M STAYING AT INDIA'S TONIGHT. I included India's number. Then another to Danny: WILL GUNNER WILL BE THERE. It was a last-ditch effort to get Danny to come to the motel. I dated Will before Danny. He'd graduated the previous year and then gone to school on a partial baseball scholarship. He visited during breaks and frequently tried to hook back up with me.

"You want one?" India offered me her pack of clove cigarettes. I scrunched up my nose and shook my head. She shrugged, tapped one out, and held it in her teeth. Keeping one hand on the steering wheel, she lit the cigarette with the other, the maneuver oddly graceful. "Aw." She squeezed my thigh. "Cheer up, chickee. Danny will come around."

I'd told India everything. Except I'd left out the part about Danny working. And I'd added in a part about him being too tired. Maybe called him a pussy. So what if I'd cast myself in a more sympathetic light? Every story needs a villain. I checked my phone. No word from Danny. BE HOME EARLY TOMORROW MORNING, my mom had texted back. REMEMBER, IT'S SAM'S DAY.

India yawned, and I stuck my finger in her mouth. She swerved off the road and back on. Horns blared. A sedan whizzed past. India held her chest and laughed, righting the car.

We drove awhile, over a bridge and into Astoria while listening to a song about how the night can break your heart. India pulled over into the Riverbend Motel parking lot, right under their sign advertising hourly and nightly rates. "This good?"

"Perfect," I said.

India was already texting the address to people. She stubbed her cigarette out in the ashtray. "All right. Let's do this."

The night would be long, with many moving parts. I rented a room using Sam's ID, then India and I found a grocery store with a stocked liquor section, and I cleared the shelves. The bottles jiggled in plastic bags as I exited the store. India waited in the car behind the wheel.

"Hey," a woman called out to me. I stopped. She was pretty with long dark hair, an open face, big eyes angled down and cheeks stung red by the wind. "Do you think you could give me a hand?" She stood by her car door, a banged-up SUV, arms full of a baby carrier and grocery bag.

i

I USED TO OBSESS OVER stories about missing girls.

The headlines were always so provocative. So irresistible. Like watching a car wreck in slow motion. Back then, I didn't think of the girls as actual people. Not living, breathing humans who had been tortured, pushed beyond their breaking points. That could never be me. Never. I'm ashamed to admit that a small, secret part of me was smug. I thought I was invincible.

But then, I learned. I learned that I didn't need shackles or chains to keep me bound. All I needed was four walls of pristine forest. And fear. The kind that festers and blisters, makes your limbs twitch. Yes. The best prisons are the ones created in our own minds.

—

When a child goes missing, the first forty-eight hours are crucial. Time is of the essence. Facts are cataloged and filed in a report. Where did the child go? Who did the child see? What was the child doing?

Let's make it easy. Here's the timeline of my abduction. This is what you probably already know.

The day started like any other. Around seven in the morning, India picked me up for school. I was in the kitchen, eating cereal standing up. A honk rippled through the neighborhood. I shoved one last heaping spoonful of colorful loops into my mouth.

Mom wandered into the kitchen. She looked sleepy and small, wearing one of Dad's sweatshirts and pajama pants dotted with Christmas wreaths. It was May. She leaned against the counter and palmed her head. The day before, she'd made me come to work with her. Then stay after closing while she drank with her friends. I had to drive us home because she'd been tipsy. She rubbed her face and narrowed her eyes at my bottom half. "Christ, Ellie."

I'd doodled on my jeans with a Sharpie—shooting stars, arrows piercing hearts, a human body with a horse head. "What?"

"What do you mean what? Those are brand-new jeans. I just bought them for you."

Mom was always worried about money. About how much things cost. How much *I* cost. Sometimes I wondered if I hated her. Which hurt to think of. Then I wondered if she hated me. Which hurt even more to think of. "I'll buy my own jeans next time." I also planned to buy a new phone. That's what started it all. A phone. My current phone was old and had about two hours of battery before dying. I'd inherited it from my mom. I was a girl who wanted something and would go to great lengths to get it.

She leaned against the counter. Right below the cabinet my dad busted a week ago. He'd been angry at me. "With what money? Ellie . . . you're missing the point."

Beep. Beeep. Beeeeep.

Mom covered her ears. "Christ," she said again. "Is that Danny? Please tell him to lay off the horn."

I rolled my eyes and dropped my bowl and spoon into the sink with a clatter. Mom winced. The old porcelain sink was original to the house, and we broke more dishes in it than we washed. But the dish didn't break, and I remember thinking: my lucky day. I feel like a fucking idiot now.

I dashed from the kitchen, grabbing my backpack. "It's not Danny. It's India. I'm staying at her house tonight." The lie slipped easily off my tongue. I had something much bigger planned than sleeping over at India's. Bending the truth was a special talent of mine. Say anything with enough conviction, and you can even fool yourself. "Remember?" I challenged my mom. "I told you last night."

"Oh, right. I should probably meet her sometime. Send me her number, please?"

"Sure," I promised, leaving the kitchen.

"Be back early!" Mom shouted as I headed for the front door. "We're shopping tomorrow with Sam for maternity stuff."

India's horn blared again. "Yeah," I hollered over my shoulder, backpack in hand. "I can't wait." Mom kept shoving us together, Sam and me, hoping we'd become best friends. But we had nothing in common, most of all age. The problem was . . . I thought Sam treated me like a baby, and Sam thought I acted like a baby. The last time I'd seen Sam, she accused me of stealing her ID. *I can't believe you'd even think I'd do something like that*, I told her, spreading the indignation thick.

Sam had crossed her arms, resting them on her protruding belly. *It was in my wallet when I came over last night, and now it's gone. It didn't just disappear, Ellie.* Then she softened up. *I won't tell Mom if you give it back, okay?*

But I'd insisted I didn't have it.

Outside, India's hatchback idled at the curb. I dove in the front, shoving my backpack at my feet. David Bowie played on the speakers. India's white-blond hair practically glowed in the morning light. The inside of her car reeked—must, clove cigarettes, stale coffee. I flipped down the visor and applied eyeliner. We sped off, our smiles wide and contagious, so careless, so free, not knowing how little time I had left.

At 7:24, we arrived at school with one minute to spare. The morning hours blended together. Biology. English. Gym. I was present and accounted for in all my classes. Jeremy Davis, Lindsay Jackson, and Steven Laurier probably even remember slipping me twenties between periods.

At 12:09, I scarfed down a vending machine sandwich on the school steps. The words SAFE, RESPONSIBLE, AND RESPECTFUL stenciled in yellow on the risers. An arm caught me by the waist. Startled, I spun around.

"El."

There he was. Brown skinned, a boyish face, tender eyes, the kind that couldn't hide emotions very well. Dark shiny hair scraped his shoulders. Danny. Boyfriend. Best friend. Love of my life. Have you ever felt that way about someone? As if the two of you invented love?

Danny grinned at my half-gone sandwich. "Egg salad from a vending machine. Brave girl."

I lifted a shoulder. "I like to live on the edge."

"I know you do. How does it feel to be free again?"

Did I mention I'd been suspended the week before? For possession on school grounds. I had a tiny bit of weed in my locker. Not illegal in Washington. But I was underage. Cops were called. My parents had grounded me, which was why I'd been to work with my mom the previous day.

"Great." I gave Danny a salute. "I'm totally reformed. Ready to walk the straight and narrow."

"That sucks. I kind of have a thing for bad girls."

We kissed. Right in front of the school. The one-minute bell rang, and Danny and I broke apart. "You're still coming tonight, right?" I asked. I had a roll of twenties and my sister's ID burning a hole in my backpack.

Danny's lips twitched. He wouldn't meet my eyes. "Yeah, I meant to tell you. I can't. I have to work at the restaurant tomorrow morning. I need to get some sleep. I have to be up early."

"Seriously?" I pushed out.

"C'mon, El."

"C'mon, D. It's important."

It wasn't, really. I wanted a new phone. I'd stolen Sam's ID and planned a motel party, charging kids twenty bucks to drink as much as they wanted. The scheme had good profit margins, enough for me to buy a refurbished phone. I wanted Danny to stay the night with me. There's that word again. Want. Was that the problem? Did I want too much? I think a lot about how all of what happened is my fault.

"I'm sorry, I can't," he said. The hall was clearing. Classroom doors slammed. Danny rested his forehead against mine. "I love you."

I didn't say the words back. Withholding love was a power play. I had a mean streak a mile wide.

Danny sighed. "Are we really going to fight about this?"

"Depends on you, I guess."

I frowned. He kissed the corner of my mouth. It was our last kiss. I wish I had known. I would have lingered against him. I would have held his hand a little tighter. I would have told him goodbye.

At 1:03, 2:30, and 2:55, a flurry of texts passed between Danny and me. The contents are embarrassing, but suffice it to say, I was trying to make my boyfriend feel like a piece of shit for working and skipping out on me. There are lots of moments I'm not proud of. This is one of them. But I was selfish. I was that girl—the one who persuaded other people, Danny in particular, to do things they shouldn't do. What I should have said was that I would miss him. I should have said never mind, it's a stupid idea. A phone isn't that important. Let's go to the movies instead. But I was stubborn. Selfish. Foolhardy.

By 3:07, I was late again, but it wasn't my fault this time. Our substitute English teacher held the whole class captive two minutes past the final bell to finish a poem about a snowman and a moor.

India waited for me in her car. We pulled out of the school parking lot right as the last bus left, around 3:20.

By 3:45, we were outside of Coldwell. I tapped out a text to my mom: REMEMBER, I'M STAYING AT INDIA'S TONIGHT. I included India's number. Then another to Danny: WILL GUNNER WILL BE THERE. It was a last-ditch effort to get Danny to come to the motel. I dated Will before Danny. He'd graduated the previous year and then gone to school on a partial baseball scholarship. He visited during breaks and frequently tried to hook back up with me.

"You want one?" India offered me her pack of clove cigarettes. I scrunched up my nose and shook my head. She shrugged, tapped one out, and held it in her teeth. Keeping one hand on the steering wheel, she lit the cigarette with the other, the maneuver oddly graceful. "Aw." She squeezed my thigh. "Cheer up, chickee. Danny will come around."

I'd told India everything. Except I'd left out the part about Danny working. And I'd added in a part about him being too tired. Maybe called him a pussy. So what if I'd cast myself in a more sympathetic light? Every story needs a villain. I checked my phone. No word from Danny. BE HOME EARLY TOMORROW MORNING, my mom had texted back. REMEMBER, IT'S SAM'S DAY.

India yawned, and I stuck my finger in her mouth. She swerved off the road and back on. Horns blared. A sedan whizzed past. India held her chest and laughed, righting the car.

We drove awhile, over a bridge and into Astoria while listening to a song about how the night can break your heart. India pulled over into the Riverbend Motel parking lot, right under their sign advertising hourly and nightly rates. "This good?"

"Perfect," I said.

India was already texting the address to people. She stubbed her cigarette out in the ashtray. "All right. Let's do this."

The night would be long, with many moving parts. I rented a room using Sam's ID, then India and I found a grocery store with a stocked liquor section, and I cleared the shelves. The bottles jiggled in plastic bags as I exited the store. India waited in the car behind the wheel.

"Hey," a woman called out to me. I stopped. She was pretty with long dark hair, an open face, big eyes angled down and cheeks stung red by the wind. "Do you think you could give me a hand?" She stood by her car door, a banged-up SUV, arms full of a baby carrier and grocery bag.

"Yeah, sure." I put my plastic bags down and opened the door for her.

"Thanks." She smiled brightly, clicking the car seat into the base and depositing the bag next to it. The baby made a little noise as she shut the door. Then she dug around in her purse. "Here," she said, offering me a five-dollar bill.

I put up my hands. "It's cool." Then I added. "My sister is having a baby." I don't know why I said it.

She smiled even wider, tucking the bill back into her wallet. "Well, congratulations."

I muttered a thanks and picked up my bags, scooting back to the car. India laughed and called me a Goody Two-Shoes. I cracked open a bottle of vodka and swigged it right there in the passenger seat.

At the motel, a man with small teeth loitered in the doorway of the room next to ours.

"You girls having a party?" He pressed a cigarette to his lips and inhaled. His fingernails were bitten down and bloody.

India straightened. "Just a few friends."

He whistled low and smiled. "Yeah, yeah. If it gets too crowded, you all can extend the festivities to my room."

India stuck out her hand for a shake. "India."

"Brett." He took her hand and looked at me.

"Ellie," I said.

"Ellie and India," he repeated. He flicked his cigarette away. "You girls make good choices." He went back to his room, and we fell into our own room in a fit of giggles.

"Fucking weirdo," India said.

It wasn't long before kids showed up. More money exchanged hands.

By 11:01, the party was in full swing, with forty kids crammed into our motel room. I sipped from a wine cooler and moved toward the bathroom. The door was shut. Will Gunner leaned against the wall. "Hey," he said. "Nick and Lindsay have been in there for twenty minutes. Pretty sure they're hooking up. Or puking. You want me to walk with you to the gas station? You could use the bathroom there. We could catch up." He licked his lips.

I huffed out a laugh, automatically smiling while I turned Will down. "No. It's cool. I'll go on my own."

I didn't think I needed to tell anyone where I was going. I felt certain I was safe. Untouchable. That I had forever.

I headed out. The night was cold and the air stung my lungs. Brett, our small-teethed motel neighbor, hung out in the open door of his room. "You making good choices?" He picked at his face. I hurried away, passing the vending machines with posted signs: ARE YOU A VICTIM OF HUMAN TRAFFICKING? CALL THIS TOLL-FREE NUMBER FOR HELP.

I have a hard time not blaming myself for what happened next. I wish I didn't. I wish this was not a cautionary tale about what happens to girls who wander off in the dark. Who are made to learn there are bad people everywhere. That the truth is these people are not strangers. They are the men who you sleep with, the men you work with, the men you raise. I wish this wasn't what it means to be female—it is not a matter of if something bad will happen, but when.

Chapter

THREE

THE HOSPITAL IS A GRAY cube with vertical slits for windows. When Chelsey arrives, the parking lot is littered with news vans. She wonders who tipped them off. It could have been the hikers who found Ellie. Maybe someone at the hospital. Or even at the precinct. She remembers how the media treated her sister's disappearance. Like a perverse form of entertainment. A bad taste in her mouth, Chelsey keeps her head angled down as she cuts through the glossy-haired reporters and bright lights.

In the emergency room, she flashes her badge to a security guard and then to the front desk attendant. A woman with a heart-shaped face leans against a wall outside the girl's room. She straightens as Chelsey approaches.

"Denise." Chelsey gives a curt nod. "I wish I could say it's nice to see you . . ."

"But we only see each other when something bad has happened," Denise fills in. "I figured you'd show up soon. Thought I'd wait for you. Brought you a coffee." Denise holds two cups. Her bangs are cut straight across, and she wears Doc Martens adorned with tiny skulls. A badge hangs from her neck: THURSTON COUNTY, PUBLIC HEALTH AND SOCIAL SERVICES DEPARTMENT.

"Thanks." Chelsey sips, cup warming her hands. The coffee is tepid and strong. "Anybody in there with her?" She nods at the closed door, noting how dark it is inside, quiet as a tomb. A couple of uniforms are posted at each end of the hallway. A flutter of excitement beats against Chelsey's throat.

"Nope. Elizabeth is alone," Denise responds. "I spoke with the admitting doctor. She's pretty shaken up. Light sensitivity, clear signs of abuse. Hart is on her way." Hart is the county's sexual assault nurse examiner. "Elizabeth hasn't said much except to say her name and ask for her parents."

"They're coming." A siren wails in the background.

"You want to wait for them?" Denise asks.

Chelsey shakes her head. "Elizabeth is over eighteen." Near twenty years old, above the age that she'd need parental consent. "You take the lead?" Chelsey will watch for now. Most assume Chelsey is suited for working with victims because she is a woman. But she is not. She is gruff and distant. *You're just like your dad*, her mom, Marianne, said, the words half accusation, half reprimand. A phantom fist squeezes at Chelsey's heart. Chelsey has spoken to her mother twice in the same number of years. Once to tell Marianne that Chelsey's father, her ex-husband, had died. And then again shortly after to announce she'd married Noah.

"I'll take the lead," Denise confirms. She drops her coffee cup into a trash can. Chelsey takes one last sip and then discards her cup, too. Denise straightens her shirt, inhales visibly, and knocks twice on Ellie's door before inching it open. "Elizabeth?" she calls carefully into the dark. "I'm Denise Little, a victim advocate with Thurston County." She pushes the door open farther. A cone of light floods the room. The girl's eyes are sunken and hollow, fruit without pits, and her hair is matted and crisp—a nest of tangled wires. A shock of recognition runs through Chelsey. Unmistakable. It's her, really her. Elizabeth Black is alive.

Ellie's empty gaze drifts to Chelsey. "Who are you?"

Words have fled Chelsey. She is mesmerized. Ellie Black in the flesh. It is a miracle, and Chelsey wants to weep but does not allow herself to. She wills the tears away until the sensation is a dull ache in her jaw.

Denise glances back at Chelsey. "That's Detective Calhoun. She's the primary on your case."

"Primary?" Ellie's voice is hoarse.

Chelsey closes the door. The room stinks of campfire, sanitizer, and vomit. It's not the worst thing Chelsey has ever smelled. "I work in Pacific County. I'm the lead detective on your case," she says, placid.

Denise smiles. "May I sit?" She drags a chair over and eases into it. "It's nice to see you, Elizabeth. We've been looking for you for a long time."

"Yeah? How long?" Ellie moves gingerly, limbs poking like shards of glass under the hospital sheet. She's thin. Starved, maybe. Her fingers are so filthy they've left marks on the bedding. The clothing she was found in is crumpled at the base of the bed. It is dirty, rust-colored, and wet with mud. Old blood, but new dirt. Chelsey files away this information. It's a puzzle piece, one of many, that she'll turn in her hands, seeking the right fit.

Denise purses her lips. "Well, I don't know the exact details of your case. My role is to support victims of crimes." Ellie doesn't blink. She does not flinch. "But I believe you have been gone for about two years."

Chelsey jams her hands into her pockets and settles against the wall. Seven hundred and forty-six days, to be exact. A lot can happen in that time. Cells divide millions of times over, and it's a miracle, a baby. Another cell divides abnormally, turning a person's insides black, robbing them of life, like Chelsey's father. In seven hundred and forty-six days, the Earth does two complete rotations around the sun, and Ellie Black disappears and reappears like a magic trick. Now you see her, now you don't.

Denise leans a little closer to Ellie. "We have a lot to talk about, Elizabeth. And I am here to offer support. But before we chat, we'd like to have someone examine you. Is it okay if we have a SANE nurse come in and do that?"

"SANE?" Ellie picks at her cuticles. Shiny scars track up her arm where the skin has peeled away. A type of burn, Chelsey surmises. Other than a couple of scraped-knee scars, Kat never mentioned Ellie had any others.

"A sexual assault nurse examiner," Denise clarifies.

Ellie stiffens. "Is that necessary?"

"I understand how uncomfortable it may seem, but time is crucial. This will help with the investigation."

Ellie turns away, jaw locked. "I just want my parents."

"They're on their way," Chelsey says. "But it will take some time."

"Why?" Ellie punches out.

Denise looks heavily at Ellie. "Elizabeth, do you know where you are?"

"At the hospital," Ellie says.

"No, do you know where you are geographically? What city you're in? You're in Olympia, Washington. Two hours outside of Coldwell Beach and Astoria, where you disappeared."

"Olympia," Ellie says to herself while touching her left wrist, an absentminded motion. Is she feeling for the ghost of something? Cuffs? Rope? There are no marks. But Chelsey catalogs it.

"Yes, Olympia." Denise waits a minute or two, content to give Ellie time before pressing her. "Now, how about that exam? Will you consent?"

Ellie hesitates. "They'll stop if I ask them to?"

Denise's nod is decisive, the chop of a knife. Chelsey has seen Denise halt exams. That's it. No more right now. Everybody out. "Yes. Anytime during the exam, you may put a stop to it. I will be present, and a nurse can give you a calming medication beforehand."

"No," Ellie jumps in. "No drugs."

"All right. No drugs," Denise promises. She turns to Chelsey. "Anything else?"

Chelsey shakes her head. "No." She keeps her voice gentle even though her insides are hot, boiling with questions. Chelsey has always been a little impatient when she wants something. She's the first to eat the whole cookie, to wake up at Christmas, to grow agitated in the grocery line when the checker is too slow. When it comes to solving cases, impatience has served her well. She recognizes the cost of time. How much you can lose in a minute. Still. Still. She cautions herself to go slow. Ellie is not a suspect. Ellie needs a day to rest. Time to tend to the slashes in her psyche.

She moves in closer, softening her tone a degree more. "I'm just . . . I'm sorry this happened to you."

Ellie is silent, sitting with Chelsey's statement. Absorbing it. Recognizing the shell shock, as if surviving a flood or bomb. This sacred truth, that something terrible has been done. "Thank you." Ellie touches her left wrist again.

Chelsey nods once, a faint smile on her lips, and leaves. Outside Ellie's room, Chelsey checks her phone. Two calls from Sergeant Abbott and one from Doug, followed by a text from him: AT THE TRAIL.

She calls Doug back first.

"Is it her?" he answers.

Hearing Doug's voice, Chelsey's younger self rushes up, and she feels small. Spiteful. She waits a beat, gathers herself. "It's her." She sees Hart, the SANE nurse, pushing a covered metal cart down the hall, giving her a wave as she passes.

"Ho-lee shit," Doug drags out.

Chelsey stares at her shoes, worn boots with frayed laces. A lump rises in her throat. She mentally chastises herself for being too emotional. She hears her father's voice. *Get it together. If you're going to be an officer, you'll have to be better than a woman.* She forces herself back to attention. "I'm going to stick around here through the medical exam and until Kat and Jim arrive. How are things at the trail?"

"Weather report calls for rain in the next couple hours, visibility is shit," Doug says. "These trails are like spiderwebs. She could have come from eight different directions, and they're all well-traveled—lots of footprints. There are a couple K-9s on the way. Hopefully, we'll be able to get a scent before it's washed out."

Chelsey thinks about how Ellie smelled like vomit and campfire. "I want you to keep looking. Search for any sign of encampments, anywhere someone could have made a fire or dwelling." Through the metal slats of the blinds in the hospital window, Chelsey sees Ellie in the bed, Denise beside her. Nurse Hart is there, too. Smiling, touching Ellie's knee with a latex-gloved hand. Then she reaches for the clothing at the end of the bed and seals it in a plastic bag with **CHAIN OF CUSTODY** written on the front. Chelsey feels a sick drop in her belly.

"All right," Doug says. "What do you think happened to her?"

"I don't know. There's evidence of long-term abuse and neglect." Nurse Hart reaches up and pulls the curtain closed, cutting off Chelsey's view. Chelsey knows what will come next. Ellie's nails will be clipped. Her teeth flossed. Mouth swabbed. All of it placed in little tubes. Ellie Black is a piece of evidence now. Her body will be on trial. "She was too shaken up to talk much."

"That's to be expected."

A series of flashes burst around the curtain. Photographs being taken of Ellie. Chelsey turns. It is one of the most difficult parts of her job, reviewing what has been done to a person, studying the carnage. The depravity. But someone has to look. Someone has to bear witness. "I think she escaped from somewhere."

"Makes sense."

Chelsey blinks, scanning her memory of Ellie in the hospital bed, her body. No deep lacerations on her hands or feet aside from minor superficial cuts, no physical evidence she jumped from a moving vehicle. "Probably on foot." That is why she is good at her job. She notices details. She can read people. Had perfected the art of observation during her childhood, carefully watching her father's moods.

"Got it. What's the perimeter?"

Good question. Chelsey squints up at the fluorescent hospital lights. How far can a person travel if they're running for their life? Chelsey recalls overhearing a fellow detective talk about a case he worked on in Idaho. A girl chained in the basement of her parents' home escaped and walked through her neighborhood, down the freeway, and into the next town before stopping and asking for help. "Make it fifteen miles."

They hang up, and Chelsey's brain spins and spins. A frenetic whirlwind of the same questions that have plagued her for the last two years. What happened to you, Ellie Black? Where'd you go?

FOUR

KAT RACES THROUGH THE HOSPITAL, unlaced shoes squeaking on the linoleum, personnel whipping by her in a blur of blue scrubs and white coats. *My baby. My baby. My baby.* The two words run a loop through her head. Something primal has escaped inside of her. She'd caged it up after Ellie disappeared. Couldn't handle all that love, with nowhere and no one to channel it toward anymore. She rounds a corner, spots Detective Chelsey Calhoun, and halts, suddenly tentative, self-conscious.

"Is it her?" Her vision pulses. If it's not Ellie, it will be okay. Really, it will not be okay. But Kat will pretend it is. She will pretend she is happy some other lost girl has come home.

Jimmy catches up and places a hand on Kat's shoulder. She grips his blunt fingers. He squeezes. They both want it to be, need it to be, Ellie. Of course they do. They want their baby back. They believe she will fix all that is broken between and inside of them.

Detective Calhoun straightens. "It's her."

She grips Jimmy harder, knees weakening, and tilts her chin to him. The bill of his ball cap is frayed and the embroidered American flag is faded—red to pink, blue to gray. "It's her."

He nods once. Kat wishes for more, a sign he is as flayed by happiness as her. "Thank god," she says to Calhoun, straining to hold her emotions back. "I want to see her."

Calhoun points to a door. "She's through there. But, Kat, Jim . . ."

"Yes?" Kat keeps her gaze on the door. Ellie is behind it. It's silly, but Kat thinks she can feel Ellie, her heartbeat, the gentle pull of her.

"It's Ellie." Calhoun pauses. "But she's banged up pretty bad. Skinny. There's evidence she's been abused for a very long time. I want you to be prepared. It can be shocking. She has an aversion to light and doesn't like to be touched."

Kat stills, feels like one of those bugs entranced by blue light, flying high and suddenly zapped. She's had nightmares. Plenty of them these last two years. Visceral images of Ellie trapped somewhere, beaten and bloody, calling for her like she did when she was little. *Mommy, I need you. Mommy, could you help me? Mommy, I can't do it on my own.* She only sleeps if she takes a tiny blue pill before bed. She has consoled herself, thinking it can't be worse than what she's imagined. It can't be worse than the not knowing. But now, she isn't sure. The only word she can mutter is "Okay."

"Can we see her now?" Jimmy's voice is hoarse.

"Of course," Calhoun says. "I'll give you some privacy."

Now Kat moves slowly. Hand splayed on the door, she eases it open. It's dim in the room. Ellie sits up in the bed, her profile turned to the ceiling. Kat remembers running her finger down Ellie's tiny ski slope of a nose when she was a baby.

Ellie shifts to peer at her and Jimmy. Time slows and stretches. Kat takes it all in, digesting her daughter, what's become of her, like a bitter pill.

"Ellie," Kat says.

"I was counting the specks on the ceiling," Ellie says matter-of-factly.

Kat bursts into tight sobs. It's Ellie. An echo of her, at least. A skull with empty sockets. Jimmy shuts the door, finds his feet first, and shuffles to the bedside, his gait slow and heavy, like some sort of penance.

"It's really you," he says. When Ellie was suspended the week before she disappeared, Jimmy had raged. Slammed cabinet doors, put a fist through one. *What about your future?* he'd yelled at their daughter, but then he'd grown silent and pulled away. The next morning he'd taken off on a week-long work fishing trip. Leaving Kat to deal with Ellie. Ellie was grounded, but Kat did not see why she should be locked at home, too.

She'd forced Ellie to go with her to the salon, then hang around after hours with her co-workers and friends. Ellie had sulked, slowly twirling in a ripped stylist chair while Kat and the ladies smoked and drank. Ellie had to drive Kat home. It wasn't a big deal. But Jimmy came back, and Kat was hungover. They'd fought. Jimmy implied Ellie's behavior was Kat's fault. She'd thrown her hands up. Of course, always blame the mother. Kat had said maybe if Jimmy was home more . . . Everyone knew girls with daddy issues rebelled. They'd quit speaking to each other. Hadn't been speaking to each other when Ellie disappeared. It wasn't always this way between them. Once, their relationship and marriage had been formed on a bed of concrete on which tough times broke. But Ellie . . . Ellie had been a jackhammer, chipping away at all they had built. An unexpected storm in the summer of their lives.

"Honey." Jimmy reaches for Ellie, and she recoils.

"I'm sorry." Ellie's smile is warped and fractured—a bird with a limp wing.

Kat inhales. She wipes her eyes and smooths her hair. She stands next to Jimmy and slips an arm through his. Jimmy is stiff and uncomfortable. Unsure what to do, Kat can tell. Sometimes she thinks he's a robot. When they'd been dating he'd been stoic, sometimes mechanical, and she'd liked it. The challenge of him. She'd been young and foolish and too romantic then. Thinking he might open up to her. Thinking she was special. Different. All Jimmy needed was a good woman. But Jimmy was Jimmy. His father had been a career Marine, serving in Vietnam and Desert Storm. He'd been tough on Jimmy. Called him a little soldier. Stuff like that. And Kat often wondered if that had locked something up inside of him.

"Jim." Kat keeps her voice light. "Why don't you find a nurse? See if we can take Ellie home?"

"Yeah, sure." Jimmy lifts a hand as if he wants to pat Ellie on the head like he used to do, ruffling her hair and calling her "buddy." But he just flexes his fingers, as if shocked at the empty spaces between them. "Right," he says, hand gripping the rail of the hospital bed. "Right." He taps the metal, crosses the room, and leaves.

Kat slides the water pitcher to the center of Ellie's tray. Straightens a stainless-steel kidney dish. Tucks the bedsheet under the end of the mattress. "Are you comfortable? Do you need anything?" She wrings her hands. There is nothing left to do but look at Ellie, even though it hurts.

Ellie shakes her head. "I'm fine."

Before Ellie disappeared, Kat would speak to anyone about her daughter—clients, co-workers, people in line at the grocery store. What to do about Ellie. Grounding her did not work. Yelling did not work. Naked disappointment and shame did not work. Kat had been exasperated. Her daughter was unbreakable. Now, Kat sees that she was wrong. Ellie is fractured.

Kat stands next to the bed and whispers to Ellie, "I never gave up hope, you know? I could feel it here"—she places a hand to her chest—"that you were still with us." Kat longs to tell Ellie all the things she has done to find her. Walking into seedy bars to enlist the help of the local motor club. Calling psychics and spending money that she and Jim did not have. Sitting in the parking lot where Ellie was abducted, following truckers for miles and miles. Hunting down Brett Jones, the guy who had rented the room next door to India and Ellie that night at the motel. But he had died of an overdose not long after. And Kat had tortured herself, thinking Brett took the truth of what happened to Ellie with him.

Kat smiles, strained, and stares at Ellie in silence for a long moment. A fly buzzes about in the windowsill. She's flooded with relief when Jimmy reappears, Nurse Hart in tow. The doctors would like to keep Ellie overnight for observation, but Ellie balls up her fists hearing that.

"I want to go home. I want to go home." She pounds her bed.

Kat twists her mouth. "Only for observation?" she says to Hart. "Surely we can watch her at home?"

Nurse Hart hesitates but agrees. She leaves and returns with discharge paperwork. A bottle of pills is pressed into Kat's hands while Hart speaks. Ellie is having acute anxiety. Ellie's pregnancy test was negative. Ellie's blood tests are normal. Ellie should see a counselor, a Dr. Fischer in Astoria.

Then Ellie is released.

Kat walks next to Jimmy wheeling their daughter through the ER and feels daunted. Maybe she shouldn't have been so hasty asking for Ellie to be discharged so soon. This is kind of like when she and Jimmy left the hospital after Sam, their first daughter, was born. They'd been so young. So unsure. Kat couldn't believe the doctors and nurses were letting her take a newborn home. Especially when they barely had a home to bring Sam to, only a studio apartment above the grocery store on Main Street. The ceiling laden with asbestos, the walls with lead paint. Sam had been an accident; Kat never meant to get pregnant at eighteen. Ellie had been on purpose. They'd waited ten years to have another baby. Everything was supposed to be different with their second daughter. Easier.

Soon, they arrive at a set of double doors. Jimmy jogs off to the parking lot to bring the truck around. Outside, the crowd of reporters multiplies, their bodies and voices humming with excitement. Kat grows queasy and protective, and she stands between Ellie and the media, a human barricade. Jimmy returns, and Ellie bows her head and covers her face as they go outside. Voices crest and crash into them:

"Elizabeth, can you tell us where you've been?"

"Is it true that there was blood on your clothing?"

"Elizabeth, who took you and why?"

"Did you run away?"

"Elizabeth, I am from the National News Network. We'd like to offer you an exclusive. One hundred thousand dollars for your story."

Inside the Blacks' truck, the voices of the media are muted. Ellie slumps in the back. And Kat is drained, dazed. The drive home is silent. Awkward. Kat fiddles with the radio and settles on an oldies station. Thick forest gives way to rocky cliffs and a dark ocean about an hour into the ride. Kat glances back at Ellie, she can't stop, has been checking on her daughter every few minutes. Ellie has opened her window a crack, visibly inhaling and exhaling.

Headlights flash in the rearview mirror. A station wagon approaches from behind, drawing threateningly close. What is wrong with the driver? What could they possibly be thinking? Kat swings her body around to face Ellie, a hungry instinct to protect her daughter.

Jimmy speeds up and says, "Probably teenagers. They don't know how dangerous these roads can be."

The wagon keeps pace with their truck, its lights flooding the interior. Ellie clenches, flexes her hands, squeezes her knees, her breathing rapid. "Jimmy," Kat says calmly, "let them pass."

Jimmy sighs. He flicks on the blinker and moves to the shoulder. The blue station wagon flies by, hand heavy on the horn.

—

It's three o'clock in the morning when they walk through their front door. Kat whips around Jimmy and Ellie. The lights are all on, dishes are piled in the sink, and the television blares with a popular news station. Ellie is the top story. A clip of her exiting the hospital plays on loop. Her head is down, her face obscured by matted hair. A news ticker scrolls across the bottom of the screen: **ELIZABETH BLACK FOUND ALIVE.**

Kat finds the remote and clicks the television off, pushing the button so hard it sticks. "Sorry about that," she says to Ellie. Jimmy moves around the kitchen, dumping his keys into a wooden bowl of loose change, miscellaneous screws, and batteries.

Ellie winces, and Kat remembers the lights. She hurries to dim them. "Better?"

Ellie nods. "Thank you."

"Are you hungry? Do you want something to eat?" Kat drifts into the kitchen. "I have some chicken I could make. Or maybe spaghetti?" That had been Ellie's favorite. Noodles with sauce and lots of parmesan.

"I'm not hungry. Thanks." Ellie wanders into the kitchen, smiling feebly as she passes Kat. She stops at the sink and flicks on the faucet, turning the nozzle to the hottest setting. It takes a moment for the water to heat, but then steam rises, and Ellie runs her fingers under the spout. Ellie muffles a groan and closes her eyes. Kat startles and her mouth parts, watching the rapture on her daughter's face. It's as if Ellie is touching hot water for the first time. She glances at Jimmy, alarmed, and he shakes his head—don't say anything. Neither knows what to do. Taut silence is their only option.

Ellie shuts off the faucet and turns to them. "I'm tired."

Kat smiles even as uneasiness twists in her gut. "Let's get you to bed, then."

"Go on ahead," Jimmy says. "I'll lock up."

Kat follows Ellie up the stairs. Photographs in wooden frames line the walls, and Ellie pauses in front of one image. The baby in the photo wears a ridiculous flower headband and sports a gummy smile. Ellie tilts her head.

"That's Sammy's girl," Kat says.

"What's her name?" Ellie asks.

"Mia. After the soccer player. You know Sam, how much she loves the game. I'm sure you'll get to meet her soon. Valerie and Sam live here, in Coldwell, now. They moved home after you had been gone awhile . . ." Kat realizes she is talking too much, that her frayed nerves are showing. "Anyway, they were headed out for a vacation. Just a few days in Seattle. Sam loves the city. But they'll be driving home in the morning, and they want to come right to see you. That is, if you're up to it? I don't know . . ." Kat stops as Ellie turns and drifts up the stairs.

She catches up and finds Ellie standing in the middle of her room. It is exactly as Ellie left it. A sloppily made bed, photo collages all over the walls and on her dresser mirror, tennis shoes, a record player, shirts stuffed into a too-full, disorganized closet, a collection of fairy figurines. Kat could not bear to go inside the room. Other than the detectives, she would not let anyone inside the room either. It hurt to see the empty space but hurt more to imagine someone else in it, cleaning or touching or dismantling all Kat had left of Ellie.

Kat wrings her hands as Ellie walks the room's perimeter, letting her fingers run along surfaces. Ellie stops at the light and switches it up and down—three short bursts, three long bursts, three more short bursts. SOS. Morse code? A chill runs down Kat's spine.

"We haven't touched anything . . ." Kat speaks, a tenor of fear in her force. "We kept everything as you left it. We knew you'd come back and want it exactly that way."

Ellie pauses at the window, parts the blinds, and looks out at the darkened view of the sad brown grass, emaciated trees, and rooftops with peeling shingles. Kat knows Danny used to sneak in through that window. She'd looked the other way. Maybe she let Ellie get away with too much. Maybe Jimmy was right. She was a bad mom. Not fit. She had known Ellie was lying about spending the night at India's. Moms always know when their daughters are lying. But she'd been so tired of fighting with Ellie. Every conversation was nerve-jangling, like walking a tightrope. She'd let it slide. *What's the harm?* she'd asked herself back then. She'd only wanted one day off from Ellie. One night without slamming doors, loud music, or shouting—*I hate this house. I hate you. Why did you even have me?* What was the harm, indeed.

"Tomorrow we could give your hair a trim," Kat suggests. "It's been a while since I've done any cutting." She quit her job soon after Ellie disappeared. Didn't like the way people looked at her. As if what happened to her family was catching. "But I've got my old shears here somewhere."

"No," says Ellie, quick. "I'm not allowed."

Kat waits a terrifying second, letting the words compute. "What do you mean?"

"Mom," Ellie says at the same time.

Kat's insides flare with warmth. "Yes?" Kat recalls the way Ellie used to say her name. As a baby, little girl, teen. *Mama. Momee. Mom.* A spectrum of emotions contained in that one word. Wonder. Joy. Worry. Derision.

Kat could tell how her daughter was feeling by how Ellie said her name. How does she say it now? Hollowed out. Painful.

"I'm going to go to sleep."

The warmth fizzles out. But Kat keeps a punishing smile on her face. "Oh, okay. I'll be up for a bit longer. Just come and get me if you need anything."

Ellie says sure, and Kat is suddenly standing outside her daughter's door, staring at the faux grains of wood. Eventually, she stumbles downstairs. Jimmy is waiting in the kitchen. He's filled two glasses with amber liquid and pushes one toward Kat.

"Thanks," she says, and sips.

"She okay?"

She peers at Jimmy over the rim. Three days after Ellie disappeared, Jimmy abruptly announced he needed to go back to work. Then he'd waited for Kat to say something. All she could do was stare at him blankly and mutter okay. She sensed his relief immediately. Inside, she was so angry, white-hot angry, but it was better than the fear, better than the anguish, so she nourished it a bit. Eventually, fury turned to ambivalence. Sometimes she wonders if she loves Jimmy anymore. If the only thing keeping them together is a black rope of grief and a thin string of red hope. "She wants to sleep."

"That's good. That's good," he mutters.

They sip in silence, and Kat is suddenly crying. She places the glass on the counter, covers her face, her mouth, muffling the sound, the carnage. Jimmy wraps his arms around her, holding her from behind. She grips the counter and pushes away. She can't look at him, at his clouded eyes. She blames him as much as he blames her. "I'm going to clean up."

"She's going to be okay," Jimmy says.

"Of course she is," Kat says. "She's home now."

He nods. "I'm going to head to bed. You come up soon?"

"As soon as I am done," she promises.

Jimmy goes upstairs, and the house is achingly quiet. Kat busies herself, and an hour later, she lies down next to Jimmy. She does not take a blue pill. Again, it is like she has a newborn. That pressing need to stay awake. The knowledge that she must be ready. Alert. She cannot remain still, and finally, she gives in and checks on Ellie. She pads down the hall and flashes to seventeen years ago . . . No, she corrects, Ellie isn't seventeen anymore, she is nineteen, nearly twenty. Time has stood still for two years.

Now, she pauses outside of Ellie's door and listens. All quiet. She turns the knob. The lights are off, but Ellie is not in bed.

Panic surges through Kat. She races through the house, opening doors, peering under beds, readying herself to shout for Jimmy, but then she stops, wide eyed and frantic. There, in Sam's old bedroom, the crawlspace door is ajar. Just as she felt Ellie behind the hospital door, Kat feels her daughter in that unused space. Slowly, she steps around tubs of old clothes and a dusty elliptical machine. She kneels down and pulls the door wide. Ellie is curled up in the fetal position, comforter twisted around her legs. Her daughter's body twitches as if she's caught in a nightmare. This isn't right. This isn't my daughter. This is a stranger. Silly thoughts that bring a burst of bright red shame. But Kat cannot shake it. The idea her daughter has been replaced by a changeling. Somebody else's baby.

Chapter

FIVE

EARLY-MORNING RADIO SHOW LAUGHTER SPILLS from the speakers of Chelsey's car. She is bleary-eyed, and the sun is nearly rising. Her body aches. She should be heading home to grab a shower, eat, freshen up. Instead, she's driving the long winding road to Paradise Glen in Coldwell. To her parents' empty house. To what she cannot share with Noah.

She rolls to a stop at a pair of wrought-iron gates, lowers her car visor, and presses the button on a remote. The gates open with a groan and creak. She keeps the speed slow, passing an arched pathway with rickety stairs that leads down to a private beach and residences with gabled roofs, weathered gray shingled siding, and central chimneys. The Cape Cod–style houses are perched on a bluff and centered around a park with a miniature lighthouse.

Chelsey and Lydia whittled their childhood away in that park, running the spiral stairs to the lookout of the lighthouse to watch for pirates. *Goonies* was a popular movie back then. She and Lydia reenacted their favorite scenes. Always playing the same characters—Chelsey as Mikey, the eventual hero, and Lydia as Andy, the good-girl love interest. When they'd grow tired of that, they'd entice the neighborhood kids out of their homes to play hide-and-seek. They'd chase each other through the streets, devour dinner, and beg their parents to let them sleep in the same bed at night. *We promise we won't stay up late. We'll go right to sleep.* Back then, love was a thing that curled in Chelsey's lap to keep her warm. Back then, her heart had sighed in happiness. It had all been so . . . idyllic. More than anything, Chelsey wishes there was a way to know when you were experiencing the happiest moments of your life.

Chelsey winds a curve and parks in the driveway. She pays to keep the lights on but doesn't bother with the yard maintenance anymore. At the front door, she takes a deep breath and unlocks it. A waft of stale air hits her first. Then other notes as she flips on lights in the foyer, family room, and kitchen: antiseptic, rose potpourri, the ghost of her mother's perfume—Poison by Dior. Unsettling yet soothing at the same time.

Her cell phone rings, hitting all the lonely spaces in the vacant house. "Hey," she answers Doug, stopping in the dining room at a Lucite table with matching chairs and a shell vase on top. The house could be historically registered as a pristine example of mid-nineties architecture and interior design—blond hardwood floors, brass finishes, chunky pastel furniture. "How's the search going? Have you found anything yet?"

"Nope, not a fucking thing. Dogs lost Ellie's scent two miles west. It's like she appeared out of nowhere. No prints to follow. Nothing. And it's raining now. The weather is shit. I don't know . . ."

"Keep looking," she insists, standing at a bay window. The beach is painted in reds and oranges, and wind whips the bare sand. If she cranes her head just right, she can make out the rooftops of Ellie's neighborhood, like toy houses, from this viewpoint. You could buy eight homes in Ellie's neighborhood for the price of the property Chelsey is standing on.

"It would be easier if we knew what we were looking for."

"You know that's not how this works." She rubs an eye with one hand, annoyed with Doug. Even though she's felt this way before, too. Wishing the work was simpler. Wishing for a break sometimes, yearning for a slice of shade from the sun.

"Did she give you anything to go on?"

"Nothing yet. I'm going to visit her in a few hours." Chelsey plans to let Ellie settle in at home and get some sleep. She doesn't want to press Ellie too hard, doesn't want to break more of what has already been broken. "Call me if you find anything."

"Don't hold your breath," Doug says. They hang up, and Chelsey calls Noah.

"Hey," she says when he sleepily answers. "I'm checking in. I'm back in Coldwell."

"You at the precinct?"

She pauses and stares at the beach below again. One of her neighbors has appeared down on the shore with a metal detector, scanning the sand. She thinks of things lost. Of things never found. "No. I'm at the house." It used to be Chelsey's family home. Then it was her parents'. Then it was her dad's. And now, it's just "the house." A lonely, lost place, stuck somewhere between here and gone. It all makes her slightly numb. Her father got it in the divorce. Her mother hadn't wanted it. She had wanted to move to Arizona to make a fresh start.

"Oh yeah?" he says with interest. "You must be close to finishing boxing everything up."

In the garage is a stack of flattened boxes. Nothing is in them. Nothing has been packed. This is what Noah does not know. He believes the house is nearly done. But each time Chelsey went to touch a box or remove an item from a shelf, she was suddenly paralyzed, her chest cold with fear. Hands shaking. Body plunged into some deep dark abyss. She understood it. She was afraid of letting go. Of dispersing the last home Lydia knew. Her father would call her too sentimental. She felt weak—conquered like a deer standing at the end of a rifle. How could she tell Noah all this? She was ashamed. Inadequate.

"It's a big house." She moves to the kitchen and touches a pill organizer on the counter—one of those seven days a week, a.m./p.m. things. It's empty now, but seven months ago, there were so many tablets she couldn't snap the lids closed. Her dad had been taking thirty-one different medications toward the end. He'd refused to have a nurse in the house. Wouldn't let anyone but Chelsey or Noah help. *There isn't any dignity in dying*, he'd told Chelsey. *Let me keep what I have. Don't subject me to a stranger.* She could not refuse him.

"We could hire someone, or you could let me help you," Noah says. Chelsey swallows. *I need to do it on my own*, she's told him. Now, she's quiet. At her silence, Noah says. "Babe?" His voice is low.

"I'm going to try to get some work done here." She deliberately keeps it vague. She leans a hip on the dishwasher. One of the newer items in the house. Her father insisted it be manufactured in America. It was part of his way of thinking. *They don't make things the way they used to, all of these exports from China.* It always weighed on her. And she wondered what he thought of his Japanese daughter. But she kept silent.

"All right." He pauses. "Love you."

"You too," she says. After, Chelsey wanders the house. Lydia's door is open a crack. The contents precisely as she left them. A peeling poster of *Into the Wild* above her desk. Fairy lights strung around her canopy bed. A Tiffany heart bracelet on her nightstand along with a toy VW Beetle, the car she wanted when she turned sixteen. Chelsey can still feel Lydia here. In this small corner of the universe, tucked into the folds of the pink gingham curtains, the group of Beatrix Potter bunnies with frayed ears and a chunky white iPod, Lydia endures. Here Lydia is still fifteen. Here Lydia is still alive.

She moves to her father's office at the end of the hall. The walls are covered in plaid wallpaper and photographs of him, iron-jawed and lionized, with local law enforcement celebrities. As the chief of police for Pacific County, he'd rubbed elbows with sheriffs, mayors, even the governor of Washington. There are also animal heads. White-tailed deer. Moose. Elk. Big-horned sheep. The furniture is substantial. A large mahogany desk. Two leather armchairs. A gun safe with an etching of the American flag carved into the metal.

Chelsey's father had been a bulldog of a man. Not large but imposing, compact, and clean-cut, with red hair giving way to gray. He did not smile often. And when he did, it was reluctant, almost painful, like granite cracking.

Now his desk is littered with Chelsey's open case files. She prefers it here over the precinct. Chelsey's department is filled with men who speak too much about themselves and ask too little about others. Plus, there are other things. The uniforms wear personal T-shirts under their blues. Sometimes sports teams, other times slogans, and, most recently, their favorite: IT'S OKAY TO BE WHITE. They'd had those special made, snickering to each other like frat brothers. Chelsey is used to it by now. She has always been an outcast. A castaway.

She sits in her father's worn leather chair and fires up the computer. The Coldwell PD insignia appears on the screen. She logs in to her email. Only one piece of new mail. Fire season in Coldwell is a few months away. Would Chelsey like to volunteer as a firefighter? She moves to the shared drive. A new report is logged—the evidence collected from Ellie at the hospital.

She clicks it open and scans the doctor's notes. Signs of long-term abuse. Severely underweight. No fingerprints recovered from any of the clothing aside from Ellie's. Not a surprise. A few dog hairs. Had Ellie been kept somewhere with animals? The blood on her sweatshirt is old. From a previous injury? Chelsey shudders as she clicks through the photographs—jarring images of Ellie's body, her legs bent and open to show bruises, a metal ruler against her thin skin. She studies them like a road map, hoping they will lead to whoever did this.

Chelsey's phone chimes with a text from Sergeant Abbott: STATUS UP-DATE.

She writes back with pertinent information. Doug is at the trail working that angle. She's reviewing the evidence and will take a run at Ellie later this morning.

Chelsey clicks out of the file and into her contacts to find Dr. Fischer's number, the counselor Ellie was referred to. They've worked together before on cases—abductions, kidnappings, abuse. She leans back in the chair and rubs her eyes as the phone rings on speaker. It is common for her to touch base with counselors. Chelsey's job is to catch whoever did this and build a profile. Who was Ellie before? Who is she now? How has she been fundamentally changed? The sentence will fit the damage done.

"Detective Calhoun." Cerise Fischer's voice is smooth and alert, despite the early hour.

"Dr. Fischer," Chelsey says. "I'm surprised you answered. I was planning to leave a message."

"I received an interesting referral late last night, which kept me up. I assume you're calling about Elizabeth Black?"

Chelsey finds a heavy silver pen on her father's desk and grips it. He'd thrown it at her mother once. He'd been working a big case. Up early in the morning, then until all hours of the night. She wasn't sure what her mom wanted. But she did recall the sound of the pen as it hit the closing door. How her mother had ushered Chelsey and Lydia away, saying, *Let's give Daddy some space*. Chelsey had spent many childhood years tiptoeing past her father's office. When he finally allowed her in, after Lydia died, she'd felt chosen. Anointed. Chelsey swats the memory away. "I am. She hasn't spoken very much."

Dr. Fischer sighs. "You know I haven't seen her yet, and even if I had, I can't divulge anything."

"I'm not asking that." Chelsey pauses. "At the hospital, she seemed confused. Disoriented. She didn't know what city she was in or how long she'd been gone."

"That is quite possible," Dr. Fischer says quickly. "You know the impact of trauma on memory and recall. Hypothetically speaking, Ellie most likely has disassociated . . ."

Chelsey leans back as Dr. Fischer goes on about how Ellie's mind has been rearranged. How the accounts of what happened may be impaired. How she may have trouble sequencing the details. How her memories will be like flashes in the dark. "In cases like these, the mind becomes a laby-rinth. It's a method of survival, I believe," Cerise says. "Then, as patients begin to heal, their brains are more like a surrealist painting."

Chelsey thinks of melting walls, stairs leading to nowhere, untouched realms, time curling in on itself, warped grief. What is real? What is not? Blood pumps in Chelsey's ears. She renews her vow to find this person, this man. Chelsey can picture him. A figure sliding along the fences of El-lie's mind. Biding his time. Ready to strike.

ii

HERE IS A TIP FOR all the girls out there: Never let an abductor take you to a second location.

And here are some tips for all the parents of girls out there: Make sure your daughters know there are bigger things to worry about than how much body hair they have, or who is taking whom to prom, or how many friends they have online. Teach them never to pull over onto the side of the road when someone flashes their lights. Or to walk into an alley next to a nightclub. Or ride their bike down the street in broad daylight. Or leave a motel room to find an unoccupied bathroom . . .

—

To the left was a church with a neon cross. Gas station lights glowed farther down. But I headed across the street, to an abandoned parking lot—it was closer, and I was cold. Gravel crunched under my feet. Cars zoomed by on the highway. I passed a few vehicles that I barely glanced at. I don't remember what colors they were or if someone was lurking behind the wheel. Within a few feet, I came to a set of scraggly bushes. I squatted and did my business. I finished quickly and stood. A star streaked across the sky. Hands on my hips, I looked up and made a wish. That's when I saw it.

Danny's car parked at the motel. The driver's seat empty. He came. I bounced on my toes and took out my cell phone, ready to text him.

But then.

Hands gripped my shoulders. Alarms blared in my head. A scream built in the back of my throat. One of the hands moved, snaking around to cover my mouth, to muffle my voice. His fingers smelled of dirt and something foul. I gagged.

It's the first time I remember the out-of-body feeling. Do you know what I mean? A part of me broke off, detached, and drifted away. I let myself go. I didn't have a choice. Sometimes, when I think back on that night, I can almost hear my fractured half whispering, "Go away. Go far away. Stay safe. Stay alive." Now, it makes me sad to think about how far I've gone, how far I've traveled from myself. I'm not sure I can ever return. How do we let go of what no longer exists?

I struggled, though. I fought as hard as I could. Black dots sprung in my vision. Cold tears leaked from my eyes. All of my power slipped away. My phone fell to the ground, screen cracking. Something sharp stabbed my upper arm. I struggled harder. But soon, my body felt light and weightless. My eyes rolled back in my head. Above me, the stars shone. Dots of white lights in endless black space—then, nothing.

—

I woke in pitch-black dark and to pain, a sharp kink in my neck—the kind of deep muscle ache that occurs when you sleep too long in the same position. My mouth felt like it was filled with cotton. And there was a strange metallic taste on my tongue, like I had sucked on a mouthful of copper pennies.

The surface I had been sleeping on was cold, and the cold had seeped in through my clothing. I shivered in the dark. My eyes drifted shut. I wanted to sleep more. But I was in pain, and I didn't know where I was. I remembered the party in the motel. India's cackle as I shotgunned a beer. Had I drank too much and passed out somewhere?

I listened carefully. Around me: the sounds of the forest waking up, birds and wind in trees. And yet, there was no light. A sudden jolt of fear raced down my spine. I should have heard the highway, seagulls, the ocean. But there was nothing. Wherever I was, I was far from Astoria. Far from home.

I tried to sit up, but my shoulder slammed into . . . metal encased in soft cushioning? The edge of a seat? I lay back down, pain zigzagging across my shoulder blade. My stomach twisted, and I dry heaved. Stars danced in my vision. Not the good kind I loved to stare at on calm, clear nights, but the bad kind, the kind that signals an imbalance in your brain. A warning light blinked on in my mind. Danger. Danger. Danger. Instinctually my hand went to the back of my neck, then fluttered down to my upper arm. I pressed. Sharp pain flared.

I stood, swaying, nauseous and afraid. I breathed through it. I felt around like a blind person, tapping along the curved edges of seats, a floor, walls, windows. A school bus? Above me was a thin square outline of light—the emergency hatch. Suddenly it didn't matter how I had gotten here. It only mattered that I got out.

Adrenaline coursed through me, my heart raced—I was at the hatch, standing precariously on one of the seats. I pushed against the center of it with all the strength of my wrecked body. The hatch opened an inch enough to let light pour in but not enough for escape. The rounded ed of a padlock came into view. I pushed harder. It wouldn't budge. I st my fingers through the opening. Only cold metal. I pulled my hand b Then I pushed the center of the hatch again. Nothing. I tried agai again. Sweat dotted my brow, and my arms turned to limp noodles

The windows were totally blacked out. But maybe there was ca or paper on the outside. Maybe this was a cruel prank. My mc were clumsy, frantic. It took three tries before I slid the window

But no air passed through, only dirt. I dug my hands into earth and scooped it inside. Dirt spattered the vinyl seat and nose. Soon my hands hit clay and rocks. By this time, they w and bruised.

I had to stop.

I scurried to the back of the bus, to the farthest corner. There I huddled, arms looped around my legs, the weight of the truth crashing down on me. I didn't know how it was possible, but I knew it with certainty: I was underground. Someone had stuck me inside a buried school bus.

Even though I was tired, I forced myself to stay awake. Sleep was terrifying. I bent forward and used my thumbnail to scratch a tally into the back of the seat in front of me. The edge of my pinkie brushed against another mark, one I hadn't made. My hand drifted over it, tracing the images. Circles and lines—someone had made a stick-figure family and crude letters under each drawing. I flattened my hand against the etching. Had someone else been here? Had they been buried, too? Broken-glassed terror rained down.

I screamed and screamed until my lungs dried out. Until all I could produce was a whimper. A whistle squeezing between my tight throat and lungs. Like a little bird in the dark. Singing and singing for no one.

Chapter

SIX

THE PRESS IS AT JIMMY'S house when he wakes up. He parts the blinds and stares, cup of coffee in hand, as they chuckle with one another in the frigid air. He sips and frowns at one of the newscasters who has drifted onto his lawn. He can hear the reporter through the thin pane of glass, practicing his speech. He is lauding Ellie for her resiliency. Jimmy's daughter is the one who got away. People adore a feisty heroine. Ellie is the lucky one. It all makes Jimmy sick—sick and angry. His little girl's name in their mouths. Like most kids in Coldwell, Jimmy grew up ready to fight at a moment's notice. He trembles with the urge to hit something.

A maroon SUV parks along the curb. Sam's car. Jimmy's elder daughter's family wades through the sea of reporters. Sam's wife, Valerie, holds their baby, Mia, in one arm and wraps the other around Sam. Both women hunch and scurry toward the house. Mia wails.

"I said no comment, assholes." Sam slams the door.

Valerie wanders into the corner of the living room, whispering platitudes to Mia. The baby's bawling subsides to a whimper.

"Dad." Then Sam is in his arms, and he's cupping the back of her head while she soaks his shirt with tears. He takes a moment and lets his cheek rest on the top of her head. She does not fit like she did when she was a child, right into the crook of his chest. She doesn't cling like she used to, either. In fact, they don't hug much. Guilt stabs at him; he's enjoying the moment while Ellie is upstairs.

"Where is Ellie? Where's Mom?" comes Sam's muffled voice.

She pulls away and tilts her head up at him, and it is like she's a little girl again. Looking at Jimmy as if he holds the solutions to the universe. It is Jimmy's greatest secret that he knows nothing. He fears someday he will be found out. Fears that someday someone will realize he has spent most of his life up before dawn, just trying to figure out how to get by. *You're the man of the house, Jimmy*, he remembers his aunt telling him, mouth full of potato salad, after his dad died when he was eight. *You take care of your family.* "They're both sleeping."

Sam nods, then her eyes narrow at a pack of cigarettes on the mantel. "I thought Mom quit." Adult Sam is back. Sam was ten when Ellie was born. She'd been excited about a little sister. Had been a little helper, a second mother. And it stayed that way for the rest of her life. It does not escape Jimmy that Sam sometimes tries to mother her own mother, him too. When Sam had Mia, it was clear she planned to do things differently than her parents did. *Better* was heavily implied. He supposed that was the natural way of things, wanting to fix your parents' mistakes. Jimmy is left-handed, and his father had forced him to use his right. When Kat had been pregnant with Sam, Jimmy made a big deal of never asking his kid to change.

Jimmy runs a hand through his hair, surprised at how thin it is. He wonders if he's been asleep the last two years and is only awake now, with the world completely changed around him. "Cut her some slack, would you? It's been a rough night."

"She needs to learn better coping mechanisms," Sam says. "You're enabling her."

Enable. Sam had said something similar about how he and Kat parented Ellie. When Ellie stole Sam's ID, Sam wanted them to report it to the police. *It's identity fraud*, she'd exclaimed. *You have to report her. If you don't, it's enabling. She'll never learn.* Sam's need for control doubled after

Ellie disappeared, then tripled when she had Mia. When Kat watched Mia, Sam brought over typed annotated schedules. *You may let Mia cry for seven minutes when you put her down, then go back in and gently reassure her you are there but DO NOT PICK HER UP. She can have anything organic and nothing with more than 3g of sugar.* This is the ripple. Sam will be strict with Mia. Because Sam always thought they were too soft on Ellie. Maybe being strict will work. But most likely not. He should have taught his daughters that you cannot save yourself from heartbreak. You cannot save yourself from grief.

"How is she?" Sam asks.

"I don't know," is all he says, honestly. The floorboards in the hallway squeak. And then Ellie appears, a specter in the doorway.

Sam gasps and cups her hands over her mouth.

Valerie smiles, bouncing Mia. "Ellie, it's good to see you again. Welcome home. This is your niece, Mia."

Ellie blinks, turns, and walks away. They hear the back door slam. Sam steps forward, but Jimmy throws up a hand. "I'll go."

———

Outside, the garage door is open. Boxes line the walls. Old bikes with flat tires lean on each other; there is a broken shop vac, a dented bumper. Jimmy has a hard time throwing things away, believing someday they may need them. It is always good to have something to sell. It is Jimmy's greatest shame Kat worked at the salon while she was pregnant and after she had the girls. He knew Kat was ashamed, too. She used to tell the girls at the shop she was working to keep herself busy. Then she'd come home and add up her tips, carefully stacking the bills. One pile for formula. Another for diapers. Too many times to count, he's had to go to one of those check-cashing places with interest around twenty percent. He always went late, right before closing, and could never look the teller in the eye.

"Ellie, you in here?" he calls, and finds her at the very back, at the workbench.

"I'm just getting some air," she says. She hasn't showered and wears one of Jimmy's old jackets, the size is too big and the color—sand—washes her out.

He steps forward and picks up a plastic pipe, rolling it around in his hands. It's small, only six inches, with capped edges. It's a remnant from when he fixed some duct work at the house. "You get this down?" He holds it up. The tip of his left ring finger is missing. He'd been out on the boat and alone when fishing wire twisted around his finger, slicing it clean off. Blood soaking the deck, he'd wrapped up his hand and finished his day before stopping by the ER on the way home.

A flush sweeps across Ellie's cheeks. A similar reaction when Jimmy asked her about stealing Sam's license way back when. "No," she states.

Jimmy sighs and decides to let it go. He does not want to cause friction. It's not a big deal. He places the pipe back up high and faces Ellie, crossing his arms. "There is a lot of press outside. Sam is inside. I've got some work to do on the boat, was thinking of heading to the docks." It's how they used to connect, out on the water. Ellie would come with him on short fishing runs and test her dead reckoning skills or chart the stars.

Ellie curls her hands in. "That sounds good."

A rush of relief. Finally, something he can fix. "We can stop on the way and pick up a new phone for you." He already has his phone out and is texting Kat and Sam that he's taking Ellie away.

Ellie shakes her head as if dislodging something unpleasant. Her eyes are dark with guilt, and she glances down. "I don't need a phone."

Jimmy draws in a breath. Now he remembers. They'd fought about a new phone before she disappeared. It was why she had the motel party, Jimmy later learned. It seems like such a small issue now. The most inconsequential thing. Especially because Jimmy and Kat were doing all right then financially. They could have pinched their pennies, gotten Ellie a new phone. Saved her life. Jimmy thinks about choices people make. How a decision cascades. How one event can change everything.

"Sure you do. I bet we can get the same number. We never . . . we never canceled your plan. We'll get you a new phone," he insists, and Ellie doesn't say anything. But she does follow him out of the garage and into his truck.

———

Jimmy's boat is called *Turmoil.* She is forty-six feet of fiberglass, aluminum, and wood. Her paint is peeling, the deck is stained with rust and fish blood, and sometimes the engine smokes. But she is a good boat. Reliable and worthy of trips all the way to Alaska. Ellie stands on the deck next to the cargo hatch, peering into eleven thousand pounds of tuna on ice. Jimmy imagines hundreds of round black eyes staring back up at her, questioning. She has not spoken very much since they left. Only a begrudging thank-you when he pressed the new phone into her hand. She left it in the car.

Jimmy pulls a bag of coarse salt across the deck. He's wearing thick gloves. "Back up." Ellie steps away, and he dumps the salt into the hatch. It will mix with the water to make a brine, which will keep the tuna frozen until he can process and sell it. It also causes moderate to severe burns. Jimmy's arms are flecked with red spots from the brine.

Ellie wanders to the railing, wind blowing hair in her face, and he watches her. "You want to take her out awhile?" he yells over the sound of water pumping into the cargo hatch. Jimmy is a solemn man, but the ocean opens him up. He believes everything is ten times more beautiful when you're on the water. He used to believe the ocean swallowed problems. But he doesn't anymore.

He knew Kat was pissed when he went out on the boat three days after Ellie disappeared. Honest to god, he'd stared into the ocean and thought of throwing himself over. He had failed at protecting his daughter. He deserved to die. He hated himself. But he'd come back. And thought himself a coward because he couldn't do it. He wanted to live. To be with Kat. To fish and remember Ellie and the good times. His baby girl was all over the boat. Standing at the helm, face turned up, laughing at the sea spray. Behind the wheel, tongue tucked in the corner of her mouth as they navigated home by the stars. Dancing on the deck to Motown and singing to the fish. They'd been happy then.

She's gripping the railing now, and her eyes are squeezed shut, and Jimmy can tell something is wrong. Askew. He struggles to find words. He'd been a quiet boy and had a slight lisp when he was younger. Kids at school made fun of him, called him a girl. So he kind of stopped speaking after that. Used the least amount of words possible. While Jimmy is quiet, Ellie darts away.

"Ellie," Jimmy calls, but she's already climbing the ladder and running down the dock. "Shit. Shit. Shit." He rips the gloves from his hands, remnants of the brine burning his fingers, and chases her. He flashes on a memory of Ellie at age four, running from him, lost in a hurricane of a temper tantrum. She hadn't been looking where she was going and ran toward the ocean. A wave came, knocked her down, and he scooped her up before the ocean could take her. He relives that moment now. The sickening dread, the fear you may lose something precious. After he'd rescued her, he'd tossed her up in the air, crying and laughing at the same time.

Now, he slows, seeing her waiting for him by the truck. The tin-roofed cannery is behind her. Once, it boasted hundreds of jobs, and now, only a few, most replaced by machines. Big companies are buying up commercial boats and licenses. Jimmy has had offers for seven figures. But he won't take it. It's his legacy. He is from a long line of laborers, of maimed men, underpaid men. Salt of the earth men. Jimmy believes all of his self-worth lies on the boat. In the blood-soaked planks and peanut butter sandwiches. He lumbers forward and watches as Ellie plucks a white piece of paper from the windshield. She stares at it, face drawn, then crumples it in her palm. Jimmy is still regaining his breath when he reaches her. He feels old. Out of shape. "Jesus Christ, you can't . . . you can't run off like that!"

"Sorry," Ellie whispers. She's shaking. Her lips and chin tremble, and Jimmy thinks he's made her afraid by yelling. Rage explodes behind Jimmy's eyes. Not at Ellie. But at whoever did this to her. His daughter has never been afraid of him before.

A car door slams and they both turn toward the noise. Detective Calhoun steps out of her plain sedan and waves. "Morning." She smiles bright and walks toward them.

The paper falls from Ellie's hand, and Jimmy stoops to pick it up. It's a postcard with birch trees on the front and the number three sharpied on the back. Other cars in the lot are peppered with bright-colored flyers pinned under their windshields, different from the postcard. Odd.

But then again . . . lots of folks come through Coldwell as a stopover on their way to the Olympic National Forest. The woods draw all types. Those who are lost. Those seeking to be lost. Those with something to say. It's not unusual for cryptic flyers to appear on your doorstep or under your windshield or pinned to telephone poles—proselytizations flapping in the Coldwell wind. Jimmy recrumples the postcard and throws it into the back of his truck. It lands near the leaflet someone left last week on his windshield. A plain white folded piece of paper with nine words printed on the inside: MAY YOU NEVER IGNORE YOUR GROWING SENSE OF DISQUIET.

Chapter

SEVEN

"ELLIE." CHELSEY STRIDES FORWARD, GRAVEL crunching under her shoes. Ellie is wearing an oversized jacket, and her face is pale. Jimmy doesn't appear much better. Chelsey has interrupted something. "Everything okay?" Her voice arches with the question.

Ellie's cheeks redden, and she shoves her hands into her pockets. "How'd you know I was here?" Defensiveness caps her tone.

"I stopped by the house. Kat let me know." Chelsey keeps her voice neutral. She places her hands on her hips and stares out at the sea. Noah is terrified of most natural disasters—earthquakes, volcano eruptions, tsunamis. She never much liked the ocean either. Panic inches up her spine every time she peers at the endless horizon. But Lydia . . . Lydia had loved the sea. Chelsey's sister was giddy imagining all the life under the water. Giant squids. Blue whales. Bright coral. Her sister fantasized about worlds beyond her own. Of escaping.

"Chelsey." Jimmy holds out a hand.

Chelsey clasps Jimmy's hand. "Hey, Jimmy. How are you doing?" The morning is damp and cold, skulking. The sky gray, the color of wet newspaper.

"I could do without a bunch of reporters on my lawn and people leaving shit on our porch," Jimmy says. Chelsey nods in acknowledgment; she had to wade through pink teddy bears, candles, and bouquets of flowers to knock on the Blacks' door. Not to mention the news vans. "But other than that, I'm all right. Happy to have my girl home."

Chelsey eyes Ellie. Her dark hair like a curtain as it hangs down her face. "Yeah, Kat said the media showed bright and early this morning. I'll get a few more units to drive by and try to discourage them."

"That'd be appreciated." Jimmy nods and stares expectantly at her.

"I was hoping I might speak with Ellie," Chelsey says evenly with a hint of a smile. A seagull lands nearby with stringy bits of fish in its beak, then gulps it down.

"I don't know, Chelsey." Jimmy scratches the back of his head. There are blood spots on his hands. "But I guess it's up to you," he says to Ellie.

Ellie presses her lips together, and Chelsey sees the no forming. "We can chat wherever you'd like. Your house, or I can take you two out for some donuts and coffee. What's more comfortable?" She looks at them, feeling bad, refusing to take no for an answer.

Ellie winces but finally says, "My house."

———

Seventeen minutes later, Chelsey sits across from Ellie in the Blacks' living room. Chelsey expected Ellie to choose her home turf, a place she feels in control. She once interviewed a victim in their bedroom under a pile of comforters. If Ellie were a suspect, Chelsey might bring her to the station. Have Ellie sit in a windowless room for a while, maybe even turn up the heat. Then she'd bring in a bottle of water, slide it across the table, and make small talk while slipping in the suspect's Miranda rights.

Chelsey sits on the edge of a worn-out recliner—the same chair she sat in while taking Kat's and Jimmy's statements the day Ellie disappeared. Despite her lack of sleep, Chelsey's never felt lighter, more present. It's the adrenaline. A high. She is most alert when she's solving a case. Kat and Jimmy are in the backyard. Cigarette smoke drifts through a cracked window mixing with mandarin candles. The murmur of reporters filters through the thin glass.

Chelsey removes an audio recorder from her pocket. "I'd like to record this. You mind?"

Ellie shakes her head and fingers her left wrist. She's still wearing the oversized jacket, like a blanket covering her from neck to knees. "It's fine, I guess."

Chelsey clicks on the recorder and sets it on the nicked coffee table. Quickly, she lists off the basics. Her name. Ellie's name. The location, date, and time of the interview. "Now," she says to Ellie. "Tell me what you remember. We could start with the night you disappeared?"

It's quiet for a moment. A faucet drips in the kitchen. Ellie's eyes flick to Chelsey, then away. "I was so dumb," she says. Chelsey remains silent. Waits. Ellie swipes under her nose. "I shouldn't have ever left the party," she says, meek.

Chelsey nods. Blaming yourself is common in these scenarios. People are conditioned to believe girls plus bad choices equals bad things. It's a type of inoculation. Lead a good life, and nothing heinous will befall you. But no one is invulnerable. No one untouched.

"The party?" Chelsey inserts.

Ellie gives an angry chin jerk, and her voice is taut. "I had to pee. Someone was hooking up in the bathroom. I'd been drinking." She offers up the detail like a challenge.

Chelsey waves a hand. She remembers picking through Ellie's room, finding joints and booze. Secrets. Every teenage girl is hiding something. The contraband didn't amount to much for Chelsey. It did not condemn Ellie. "You had a few drinks. It's not your fault."

Ellie's arms loosen. She relaxes a bit. "I was going to go to a gas station, but the parking lot was closer . . . I, uh, really had to go."

Chelsey nods. Will Gunner, Ellie's ex-boyfriend, corroborated this story two years ago when Chelsey interviewed everyone at the party. Ellie had to use the bathroom. That's it. "What happened next?"

"I don't know, really. I was grabbed. Drugged with something, I think. After that, it's a blank." Ellie bows her head. "I woke up in the dark." When she looks up, her eyes shine wet.

"Tell me about the dark. What did it smell like? Feel like?"

Ellie trembles and wipes her tears, leaving wet slashes in the wake of her fingers. "It was cold and smelled like mildew, like plastic. Like my vinyl records. I could hear birds, an owl sometimes, dogs howling." She abruptly stops and grips her left wrist.

"You keep touching your wrist. Is there a reason why?"

Ellie jerks and places her hands under her thighs. "No reason."

A lie, Chelsey thinks. She waits a beat, an infinite pause for Ellie to fill in more. But Ellie stays mute, chin trembling. "All right. Let's go back to the dark. How did you feel?"

"I hurt all over, and I was hungry. I was scared." The words come out choppy. Serrated.

"Yes. Of course you were." A short pause. "Were you alone?"

"No. I mean, yes, for a while. I think a few days."

"Then what happened?" Chelsey edges forward.

"I was so hungry. I thought I was dying. Then *he* came."

Chelsey swallows. "Tell me about him."

Ellie's eyes flutter closed. "I didn't see his face. It was too bright. He wore a bandana that covered his mouth and nose."

"Okay. What color was the bandana?" Chelsey asks. Sometimes details lead to other details. An angry voice to a furrowed brow with a scar running through it.

"Red. It was red. It hurt staring up at him." Underground. Ellie was kept somewhere underground, Chelsey realizes.

Ellie's eyes open suddenly. "I don't want to do this anymore."

A sudden sting of disappointment. "That's okay." She forces a smile. "Perfectly fine. We can pick it up again tomorrow or the next day. We'll take our time."

"No." Ellie's nostrils flare. "I don't want to do this at all."

"I'm not sure I understand," Chelsey says, though she does. Sometimes victims decline to participate in the investigation. It's their right. To move on. To not relive the painful memories.

"I don't want to talk anymore. I mean, ever again."

"No. Ellie, please," she says. Breathless with a bit of panic. "We don't need to plan another time to speak. But let's not go through the formality of ending the investigation, of making anything official, until we're absolutely sure that's what you want."

Without Ellie's participation, the ADA won't touch the case. There'd be no prosecution. Chelsey cannot stand the thought. To have come this close to catching whoever did this and have it all slip away as easy as a body in the tide.

"Take all the time you need, Ellie," she says, and it's a defensive move. A tunnel opens inside Chelsey's mind, and she slides backward fifteen years.

She'd heard Lydia's door open that night and swung hers wide right after. *Where are you going?* Chelsey had asked, rubbing a bare foot against her shin. Her toes were painted a dark purple color called Boris and Natasha.

Nowhere. Lydia's hair was crisp and curled, her lips maroon, and she wore a cropped cardigan, a lacy camisole underneath—dressed older but looking young, wide eyed, and fresh, like a mermaid breaking the surface and seeing land for the first time. It had been a harvest moon, and shimmering orange light filled the house. Chelsey didn't budge. Lydia rolled her eyes, and an excited smile lit her face. *I'm going to a party at Oscar's house.*

Oscar Swann was a senior. Lydia was a sophomore, and Chelsey was a freshman. The girls were not allowed to date yet. Their father was a sit-on-the-porch-with-a-shotgun-to-scare-off-boys type.

Can I come? Chelsey had asked. She worshipped Lydia. Had followed her around like a lovesick puppy. Copying her mannerisms. Wearing her clothes. Offering her the last Kudos bar.

No, Lydia replied, sharp and smug. *You should see Oscar. He's like obsessed with me.* She sobered. *Don't tell Mom and Dad.*

Chelsey had been more fragile then, much needier. She desperately wanted her sister's approval. Wanted to be liked, so she'd answered, *Of course not.*

Lydia smiled. *Good, because I'd hate you forever if you did.* Then she stuck out her pinkie. Chelsey had stuck hers out, too. *Swear,* they'd said, hooking their pinkies together and shaking.

Lydia scooted away, pausing at the top of the stairs and pressing a finger to her lips. Shh. Don't tell. Off Lydia went, wild in love.

If only Chelsey had held on to Lydia. Begged her not to go. Or begged to go with her. Maybe Lydia would still be here. Chelsey had waited to tell her parents. Two whole days passed before Chelsey fessed up. She knew where Lydia had gone. Two whole days, Chelsey watched her mother weep. Two whole days, police trudged in and out of her house. Two whole days before Chelsey's family learned what really happened—that Oscar and Lydia were dead.

As a final thought, Chelsey drops her voice and adds, "If you're afraid, we can protect you. There are measures we can take to keep you safe." It is knife-edged in a promise: No one will hurt you as long as you're with me.

Ellie gives a short, mirthless laugh, and Chelsey feels its weight. The heavy message inside of it, the looming threat. No one can help me. No one can keep me safe.

iii

HERE'S THE THING: I DIDN'T have big dreams. No plans for college, no plans to move away from Coldwell. Not like Sam, who grew like a tree, always reaching higher and higher, hoping to catch the sun. I would have probably married Danny. Popped out a couple of kids. It would have been a small life. But it would have mattered. I still matter, don't I?

On the bus, every day, I shrank. Little by little until it was unbearable. The desperation. The longing. I think that was the purpose. Actually, I am nearly positive. Because the moment I felt like nothing, something happened.

—

The second day, I lay crumpled in one of the seats. "It will be all right," I told myself over and over again. I was cold and shaking, my teeth painfully chattering. "Mom will realize you're not where you're supposed to be. She'll look for you. It will take her an hour, maybe two, tops." I dug my hands into my pockets. I usually kept my cell phone there, but it was gone. Rain tap-danced on the roof. Dogs howled off in the distance.

"Mom will call you," I told myself. "When you don't answer, she'll sound the alarm. The police will get involved. Dad will return to shore. Danny will lead the charge."

Have faith.

Keep the faith.

They'll find you. All you have to do is listen. In a little while, you'll hear them calling your name. You'll answer back.

So, I waited. I waited until the light around the hatch faded and the sweat on my brow dried and cooled. I picked underneath my fingernails, where there were little balled-up pieces of skin. Evidence. Had I scratched my attacker? I gathered the skin and put it in my pocket. When I was found, I would present it to the police.

I slept lightly and woke with a start. *Click. Click. Click.* Something was on top of the bus. Animals. A whole bunch. But just in case, I uncurled my body and went back to the hatch. My arms were stiff and slow as I lifted the square metal door. I stuck my fingers out again, tentatively searching.

"Hello?" I called gently. A wet nose brushed the tip of my thumb, and then there was a scrape of teeth against it. Involuntarily my arm withdrew, but I wasn't fast enough. The hatch collapsed on top of my knuckles. I howled in pain. Whatever was on the roof turned tail and skittered off the bus. I returned to my corner, sniffling and sucking on my bruised knuckles.

I slept again and awoke to an aching bladder. It was still night. I paced up and down the aisle of the bus. "C'mon, I have to take a piss." Finally, I couldn't hold it anymore. I squatted over the stairs and let myself go. Humiliated tears burned the backs of my eyes.

After, I retreated to the back of the bus, far away from the stairs and my filth. I stayed awake this time, eyes trained on the hatch. I blinked when the sun started to fill in the outline again. Another day had begun. And I was still stuck in the dark.

—

On the third day, when the light around the hatch was dimming, I heard a thump. And then another. The rhythmic, slow heavy tread of human footsteps.

I was out of my corner in an instant, dragging my body down the aisle of the bus. I climbed onto the seats below the hatch and screamed. The footsteps stopped. I stilled. Metal scraped against metal, and then there was a click. The hatch opened. A person stared down at me, their face covered with a red bandana, their body limned in light. The person had a flashlight and shined it in my face. It stung. I scurried into a seat and shielded my eyes.

"What's your name?" His voice was thick and deep and his skin was white, the color of sheep's fleece. Dogs crowded at his heels. German shepherds that stuck their noses in the hatch and whimpered.

"El . . . Ellie." I shook.

He made a sound. Something dropped into the aisle. He closed the hatch before I could even blink. "No," I moaned. I pounded on the hatch, pain shooting down my arms. "My name is Elizabeth Black." I knew he was still up there, listening. The toes of his boots blotted out the light. I could hear the click of the dogs' claws. "My name is Elizabeth Black. Please, my parents will give you anything." I went quiet, waiting. Nothing. "What do you want? You son of a bitch!" I lashed out. He stepped back off the hatch. "No, I didn't mean that. Whatever you want, please." The thump of his boots grew softer in retreat. The dogs went with him. "Please," I said again and again.

I sank back down, huddled in the dark. I landed on something. It was soft and spongy. I picked it up. Brought my nose to it. Clean, slightly sweet. Bread. I tore into the loaf, jamming fistfuls of it in my mouth.

Then I remembered two things had dropped. I felt along the floor under the seats until I found a plastic bottle of water. I took a long, deep drink. My stomach hurt. I'd eaten too quickly, and now the bread was like a rock in my gut. After I finished, I realized the bread and water could be poisoned. The man could have slipped the same drug he had injected me with into the food. Maybe I should throw it up. But the damage was already done. And slipping back into that dark slumber where everything was forgotten didn't sound that bad. I wanted to forget.

I took the remaining bread and water to the back of the bus and steeled myself for another night. My head fell back and rested on the old vinyl. My hands fisted at my sides. I imagined my family at home. Mostly my mom. When I was still young enough to curl in her lap, the sun streaming through the window. It's painful to think of that now. Back when love felt good.

—

Every few days, the man came, wearing his red bandana. He'd open the hatch and stare down at me. He always asked the same question: "What is your name?"

I always gave the same answer: "My name is Elizabeth Black." And then I would beg, consumed with panic. *Please. Let me out. I'll give you whatever you want. Anything.*

He'd throw me more bread and water, and I would scurry to collect it, a dog diving for scraps under the dinner table. I saved the bread and water and rationed them, tucking them both under the seat at the back of the bus where I slept. I allowed myself a few sips a day, and when it rained, I gathered water from the hatch by cupping my hands and drank until I was full. Sometimes the bread would mold. I could smell it. I ate it anyway. And the loneliness . . . I thought I might die from it. It burrowed under my skin and fed on my blood and bones like a parasite.

When the the man returned, I refused to answer him. "What is your name?" he asked.

I kept silent, tucking my chin into my chest and refusing to move from the driver's seat. He slammed the hatch shut and locked it up. He didn't leave me any bread or water. A punishment for my silence.

—

The man didn't come for five days. It was the longest stretch I'd gone without seeing him. My bread and water ran out. No rain came. Hunger and thirst gnawed, and I pulled down the windows on the bus. Sucking moist dirt through my teeth, searching for a single drop of water until I choked. I ate worms, too. Their bodies squirming and falling still as my incisors cut them in two.

It wasn't the worst thing I did on that bus.

Here's what I learned about the human body: It is hardwired to live. No matter how much you will your heart to cease its gentle beating, it will endure. Instinct kicks in, driving you to extremes—like feeling along your thigh, your arm, thinking of ways to make your appendages bleed, so that you can experience the sensation of wetness on your tongue.

But then . . . then I stopped thinking of my family. I stopped craving food. I stopped dreaming. I don't think I knew how to anymore. More days slipped by.

I lay down on the bench seat at the back of the bus, sure I wouldn't get up again. It was time to give up. Give in. I'd reached my lowest point. My eyes fluttered closed, ready for it. For death, cruel and glorious and sweet.

Footsteps. The hatch opened. I couldn't move. I was too weak. Light flooded the cavernous space. The man's shadow stretched the length of the school bus aisle until it almost, almost touched me.

"What is your name?" he called down, a finality to his words. If I did not answer, he would not return. The dogs sniffed at the opening.

I opened my mouth to speak, but the words got stuck in my throat. What's my name? What's my name? I couldn't remember. Did I even exist anymore? I squeezed my hand into a trembling fist. My bruised knuckles sent a shock wave of pain through me. Yes, I was still there. Still alive. Barely.

"What is your name, girl?" he asked. Girl? Yes, I was a girl. I was a girl who loved a boy. What was the boy's name? My fingers skimmed the scratches in the vinyl. I had etched my name there once. But it was jumbled up. Name, name, name. The word beat like a drum in my head. But nothing followed. I spiraled into darkness.

The man moved, and the hatch closed halfway. He hadn't thrown me any food. I tried to scream, but it came out as a grunt. It was all I could manage. The hatch opened back up, the best gift.

"Tell me your name, girl." He crouched at the edge of the opening. His boots sent specks of dirt fluttering down, a show of glitter suspended in the sunlight. One of the dogs lay beside him and sighed.

I managed to slip from the bench seat. I crawled down the aisle. The grating dug into my hands. The man was patient. I stopped below him, tipping my chin to the light. "I don't know."

"Don't know what?" New words. He had never said so much before.

Please don't go away. My limbs shook, and so did my voice. "My name. I don't remember it."

The man stood. I thought he was going to close the hatch. I resigned myself to a slow death on the bus. I would die on this grating. I was too weak to move back to my safe spot. I was ready. Let my soul rise above my body. In the distance, I heard the phantom voice of my mom calling. In my thoughts, I answered back. I'm coming. Won't be long now before I am home.

But he didn't leave.

He lay down, dipping the upper half of his body into the bus. He reached for me. "Take my hand."

My eyes were wet with tears. I reached back. My hand closed around his wrist. He pulled me up into the daylight, nearly yanking my arm out of its socket. The sun blinded me. Even though I couldn't remember my own name, or the name of the boy I loved, I remembered the name of the feeling sweeping through me. Joy. At last.

Chapter

EIGHT

UNDERGROUND. DARK. A RED BANDANA. Cold. The smell of vinyl.

Beneath the glow of a green shaded lamp, Chelsey sits in her father's office and replays her interview with Ellie Black, listing the facts on a sheet of paper—a loose, nonsequential outline. She clicks off the recording and presses her palms against her eyes until she sees stars. She is stumped. Frustrated by Ellie's refusal to cooperate.

But she has been here before. Standing at the bottom of the well. Staring at the stone when she really should be looking up. Searching for a new angle. She opens Ellie's case file, mouse drifting to the photographs. The images are still jarring. Ellie with her limbs outstretched. Each bruise measured and cataloged. There are pictures of her clothing. Items laid out on a steel table. A dingy white bra and pair of thin underwear with pin holes from overuse. A pair of unlaced shoes. Jeans. A sweatshirt with a University of Washington Volleyball insignia. The bloodstain is smeared as if wiped. A transfer, then. Not from a gunshot or other spatter. Could the sweatshirt have been used to clean blood off of something or someone?

A small square of fabric has been cut from the center of the stain to be submitted for analysis. It will be run in CODIS, the Combined DNA

75

Index System, for a match. If the blood isn't Ellie's—and if Ellie's abductor has priors—it will show up. Blood always tells.

Chelsey leans forward and rubs her lips until the letters blur together. What had Ellie been wearing when she was taken? She slides back in time, recalling her initial conversation with Kat the day after Ellie disappeared.

It was midmorning. Ellie had been missing for less than ten hours. Kat had peered up at the ceiling. *What was she wearing? I don't know.* At that moment, Kat was pale and blank, the physical manifestation of the word shock. *You know, I lost Ellie once when she was a toddler. We were in Seattle at the Children's Museum. One minute she was there, and the next, she was gone. You turn your head for one second . . . Anyway, we found her in the next exhibit. One of my girlfriends said I should start carrying a photograph of Ellie, just in case. I'd forgotten about that until now.* Kat wrung her hands, too distraught to continue. She squeezed her eyes shut, then forced herself to carry on. *We fought about her jeans yesterday. She'd written on them with a Sharpie. Did you and your mom ever fight?* she asked Chelsey.

No, Chelsey replied, thinking of her teenage years after Lydia died, how she and her mother orbited each other like binary stars, never crossing paths. You couldn't fight if you didn't speak to each other.

That's good, Kat said with a furtive smile. She shook her head. *I can't remember her top. I should have told her she couldn't go out last night, but I didn't want to fight again. It's been rough with Ellie. Much rougher than with my first. We got pregnant with Sam when I was eighteen. And I waited to have Ellie until I was older. I wanted to do it right, you know? All the things with Sam I got wrong. But Ellie . . . she's so different than I imagined. So much harder. I can't help thinking she's somewhere and needs my help. In my head, I keep hearing the words Ellie needs me. Ellie needs me.*

Chelsey sucked in air through her teeth, feeling a kinship with Kat. It haunted her, too. The voice she could not hear. Often, she wondered what Lydia's last moments were like. How much blood she'd lost. What she saw. What she said. If she'd begged. Asked for her mother or for Chelsey. Enough. Chelsey shook it off. *It's no problem you don't remember what Ellie was wearing*, Chelsey had said to Kat, flipping her notebook shut. *I'm heading to India's after this, and I'll ask her. See if she has any photographs.*

India did have a picture of them drinking wine coolers and flashing peace signs in the cheap motel room. Chelsey opens that photo now. It takes a moment to load on her father's old Dell computer. The image revealing itself one static inch at a time. There. Ellie was wearing a maroon crop top with a flannel over it.

These are not the clothes Ellie was wearing in the forest, not the clothes stripped from her body in the hospital, not the clothes laid out on the metal table. These—this University of Washington sweatshirt, jeans, and tennis shoes—are new clothes. Not surprising; it's been more than two years. Her abductor could have bought them. But maybe Chelsey could trace them. There is a lightness in her chest. A lead.

She narrows in on the sweatshirt. It's a popular school. Could Ellie's abductor be an alumnus? She zooms in. The emblem is the UW logo with the word **VOLLEYBALL** underneath. She clicks to the next photo of the back of the sweatshirt, a number fifty-five. She opens her browser and searches UW Volleyball. Rosters date to 2011. No players with the number fifty-five. Huh. She clicks back to the photograph of the front of the sweatshirt and zooms in on the tags—**ONE OF A KIND CUSTOM COLLEGE APPAREL**. She searches the company online and phones customer service, perching on the edge of her seat while the line rings.

An answering service picks up. "Thanks so much for calling One of a Kind Custom College Apparel. You've reached us after business hours . . ."

She leaves a message with her details. "This is Chelsey Calhoun. I'm a detective with Coldwell Police Department. I have a question regarding a sweatshirt purchased from your company. Please give me a call back as soon as possible."

Disconnecting the call, Chelsey flexes her hands and rubs her eyes. She's tired now. Her body achy. When was the last time she slept? She cannot remember. Never a good sign. She stumbles to the couch in her father's office and collapses.

She dreams of the beach.

Of Coldwell's rocky bluffs. And it is no longer a dream but a flood, an infinite sleeping memory, a loop she lives in. Of a car mangled and crumpled, perched precariously on a wedge of basalt, tipping in the wind. They'd been driving around Coldwell searching for Lydia when they got the call. Her parents told her to stay put in the backseat, but Chelsey had followed them, past the uniform vomiting in the sand reeds, down the path in her pale pink puffer jacket. Below, she recognized the blue sedan as Oscar's car. The driver's door was open, Oscar's body sprawled half out of it. A gouge in his forehead, watery blood leaving a trail down and pooling in his open eyes. One of his K-Swiss shoes was a foot away, lodged on a sharp rock. His fist was full of Lydia's hair. The yellow strands bloated with sea foam, a chunk of her scalp weighing it down. Chelsey's mother screamed and went as if to fling her body over the edge, but a cop held her back. Chelsey's father could not move. His face was white. Bleached completely of color. A murder-suicide, police ultimately determined. Oscar killed Lydia, then himself.

A shrill ring rends the memory in half, and Chelsey bolts up. She finds her phone on the carpet. "Detective Calhoun," she answers. It is light out now, and she's suffering a faux hangover. Her mouth full of cotton, her eyeballs sticky and dry.

"Yeah, this is Gino from One of a Kind Custom College Apparel. We received a phone call from you?" His deep voice curls into a question.

"Yes." Chelsey scrambles to the desk and pounds the computer awake. The sweatshirt photos are still on the screen. "I'm a detective working a missing person case and have a piece of evidence, clothing purchased from you. I'd like to track down who made the order."

"All right, I'm not sure if I'll be of any help. We ship around five hundred units a week. But let me pull up the records. Wait." He pauses. "Maybe I should check with my manager. Do you need a warrant for this?"

"No. I don't," is all Chelsey says, and there is quiet on the other end of the line. "You could help me find a missing girl's abductor." She stops. Waiting for the idea to take root and blossom. Gino could be a hero.

A short beat. "You got a style number? I need all eight digits plus what comes after the dash. That'll help me figure out the year."

"Where is it located?" She zooms in on the tag. No numbers, only the company name and size—small.

"Inside of the sweatshirt, left-hand seam."

"I don't have that." Chelsey rubs the bridge of her nose.

"Without that—"

"The sweatshirt is gray with a University of Washington Volleyball insignia and the number fifty-five on the back," she says, sharp, insistent but calm. "Can you search using any of those parameters?"

"Hold on. Let me check if any orders came in with a special request for that number. It'll take a minute. But you know, this computer system only goes back five years. Anything before that isn't accessible anymore."

"Give it a try," Chelsey prompts.

There is tapping in the background. "Got something," he says. "An order from 2018 for a custom sweatshirt, University of Washington Volleyball, number fifty-five." He whistles low. "Man, this is lucky. Did I say we ship out over five hundred units—"

"Name? Name on the order, please." Her palm is sweaty. This could be something, or this could be nothing. But the chance, the promise of it, makes Chelsey salivate. She has a tree to shake now. A fight to win.

He sighs. "Althea Barlowe." Chelsey takes down the address and hangs up on Gino mid-sentence.

She types the name into the computer. A headline appears: MISSING GIRL FOUND DEAD. Althea's name is highlighted as the grandmother of Gabrielle Barlowe—a sixteen-year-old girl last seen five years ago in a University of Washington Volleyball sweatshirt. And found . . . found about a year and a half ago deceased. The story unspools around Chelsey. Gabrielle's body was discovered on Spencer Island, a marshy park area northeast of Coldwell. She'd been strangled. No other details but the date. There is a photograph of Gabrielle. She is roughly the same age as Ellie. Same dark hair. White. Big eyes and lips puckered for the camera.

Chelsey sits back, unanchored and adrift but happy to let the tide take her. What new island will she wash up on? She does the math while gnawing on her cheek. Gabrielle Barlowe disappeared years before Ellie but was found six months *after* Ellie was abducted. Their timelines over-lapped. What does that mean? Could they have been at the same place at the same time? Held somewhere together? Adrenaline surges through Chelsey's body, and she shoots upright to stand.

She gathers her coat, her keys, and gets in the car. Her hands flex around the wheel. She is still deep in the well, but instead of looking up, instead of staring at the stone, she is digging now. What was Ellie doing wearing a dead girl's clothes?

Chapter

NINE

A BABY CRIES ON THE other side of the door. Chelsey checks her phone to make sure she has the correct address. The Tacoma detective had texted it to her an hour ago, saying SURE, WE CAN TALK ABOUT THE BARLOWE CASE. I'M ON MATERNITY LEAVE, YOU MIND COMING BY MY HOUSE?

After finding Gabrielle Barlowe in the MUPS directory, Chelsey called the lab tech. *I need a rush on the blood samples from Ellie Black's sweatshirt. See if it's a match against Gabrielle Barlowe. Case number . . .* Then she'd called the detective in charge of Gabrielle's case in Tacoma, only to learn he'd retired. A junior detective had inherited Gabrielle, and here Chelsey is, on her front doorstep.

She raises her hand and knocks sharp and loud. A dog barks. The door opens. A woman answers in a tank top, open flannel shirt, sweatpants, and a burp cloth slung over her shoulder. A perky golden retriever noses his way past her, spins a circle around Chelsey's legs, then prances back inside.

"Hi." She smiles. Her face is plain, makeup-free, her complexion ruddy. "You must be Detective Calhoun. I'm Detective Ross."

"Call me Chelsey." Chelsey sticks out a hand.

"Brielle." She shakes Chelsey's hand and swings the door open. "Come on in. Thanks for agreeing to visit me at home. I'm technically on maternity leave, but you know the job . . ." She trails off and peers over her shoulder. "Would you mind . . . your shoes?"

Chelsey toes off her boots. Her socks are Noah's, too big with gray toes and heels. Brielle shows Chelsey into the living room. Some sort of contraption is moving up and down in a slow, steady motion, and inside it is a swaddled baby that resembles an old man. "Cute," Chelsey says.

"Yeah, I think I'll keep her." Brielle smiles in the way all moms do when talking about their children. "You got kids?" Brielle slumps down into a large armchair and gestures for Chelsey to sit. The golden retriever settles at her feet, resting his head on his paws.

"Nope." Chelsey posts herself on the edge of a lumpy couch. There is a breast pump on the coffee table, yellow with tubes and suction cups, an alien-looking device.

"Well, my only advice is not to have one until you're ready. And even when you feel like you're ready, you're not ready. Oh, and make sure you have some sort of help lined up. I don't know what I'd do without my mom and sisters."

Chelsey smiles uncomfortably. She doesn't think much of having children. She's discussed it with Noah before but in a far-off, distant future sort of way. She's made no plans. No promises. Lydia had been the one who wanted children.

Time erodes, and Chelsey is lying in bed with Lydia. Lydia is eight. Chelsey is seven. Down the stairs, their parents have guests over for the New Year. It's merry, but there is an undercurrent of dread. Y2K. Chelsey's dad doesn't believe it, but her mother made him buy a survival kit. Just in case. But Chelsey and Lydia are oblivious. They huddle together under Lydia's Barbie sheets. It doesn't matter Chelsey was adopted or Lydia was the Calhouns' biological child. They were like twins, absolutely enchanted with each other. It is the only time, besides being held by her mother, Chelsey has ever felt perfectly loved. In the dark, under a canopy bed, they whispered their dreams to each other. Lydia's dream was to get married and have kids young. *Like Mom and Dad*, she said with a soft, expectant smile, confident the world would be hers. Later, the dream changed. *I hate Coldwell,* she announced at thirteen. *I can't wait to get out of here.*

"Coldwell PD, huh?" Brielle's question cuts through Chelsey's thoughts.

"I've been a detective there two years now." She keeps her voice low for the sleeping baby.

"You don't have to whisper." Brielle smiles. "She'll sleep through anything—vacuums, dogs barking, you name it." She sighs. "When I entered the force, I imagined I might be a sergeant someday." She smiles. "But now I'm not sure. I have the baby and am one of four women in the precinct. And two are front office staff."

Chelsey softens a fraction. She understands what it is like. To be a woman and considered defective. How often has she been told by a fellow officer they'd rather have a 240-pound man watching their back than a slight woman? It did not matter Chelsey could shoot better than most. Or that she was smart, too. She was a liability. "I'm the only woman in my precinct. I mostly keep to myself." She liked her sergeant fine. In some ways Abbott reminded Chelsey of her father. Stoic, inflexible.

"I don't know why I stay."

"My dad was an officer," Chelsey volunteers, and she's not sure why.

"It's in your blood, then."

Chelsey does not correct Brielle. She just nods politely. It is something thicker than blood, she thinks, though. Her father had been dubious about his children in law enforcement. But then Lydia was killed, and everything changed. Her father had passed her the baton. *Do not let what happened to Lydia happen to you. Do not let what happened to Lydia happen to any other girls.* There had been pride in his eyes when she graduated from the academy. He'd patted her back right between the shoulder blades. Sometimes she could still feel it. The thwamp-thwamp-thwamp. Everything was illuminated in that bright moment.

Silence reigns. Then Brielle says, "So, you want to know about Gabrielle Barlowe?"

Chelsey nods. "A sweatshirt with her initials was discovered on a victim a day ago."

Brielle's mouth hitches up. "I've seen the news. Elizabeth Black, right?"

"I think she was wearing Gabrielle's sweatshirt. What can you tell me about the case?" Chelsey flips open a notepad.

She rubs her knees. "I'm not sure how much help I can be. After the detective originally assigned retired, I inherited the case two years ago, along with about forty others."

Indignation curls in Chelsey's abdomen. All these girls lost twice over. First, to unknown circumstances. And then, to the chain of command— to retirees, to shifting political landscapes, to budget cuts.

"Anything will help," Chelsey says, trying to hide her frustration.

"Gabrielle's parents weren't around. She lived with her maternal grandmother." Brielle pauses. "Grandma waited almost thirty-six hours before reporting her missing. The original detective thought the old woman might be good for it. Neighbors said they'd heard Gabby and her grandma fighting all the time—yelling, slamming doors, that kind of thing."

"But never anything physical?"

"Nothing reported. No calls to police for domestic disputes. No visits to hospitals. Teachers said Gabby was always clean and well taken care of. They dropped the grandma thread. Then they found Gabby's car on the side of the road. There was evidence of a struggle. The driver's-side window had been broken, and her blood was on some of the shards of glass found. There were marks in the dirt, too, like she'd been dragged to a vehicle." The baby's mouth opens in a mew of discontent, and Brielle's attention shifts. She turns away from Chelsey and leans down to change the setting on the contraption. Now it zigzags. The baby quiets. "This thing cost three hundred dollars, and it is the best money I have ever spent." She taps her thigh. "What else? What else?" She snaps her

fingers. "CCTV footage caught a station wagon following Gabby but no license plate."

Chelsey's breath catches in her throat. "A station wagon." An image of the Pentecostal church's CCTV footage springs to Chelsey's mind. She remembers seeing a station wagon sandwiched between two semis.

"Yep," Brielle tells her. "The wagon followed her through a stoplight. But like I said, no license plate. The old detective tried to run it down but didn't have the manpower to check all the registrations. You know how it goes . . ." She trails off, letting Chelsey fill in the blanks. Unfortunately, Chelsey does know how it goes. All these dangling threads and not enough people to pull them. "Anyway, that's about it. All efforts to find Gabrielle were exhausted. The case had gone cold."

"Then her body was discovered?"

Brielle nods. "Near a popular equestrian trail. A horse bucked its owner, and they found the animal nudging at the body. She was naked. Had been strangled. No ligature marks. They used their hands." Chelsey flashes on Ellie. She'd been bruised, but not around the neck. Still, she could have escaped . . . or been left for dead. It tracks. Is that why E is so frightened? She isn't supposed to be alive? Could she be scared abductor will return to finish the job?

"Any fingerprints, DNA?" Chelsey asks, although she kno answer.

Brielle's lips flatten. "Nope. The medical examiner said she' there about a month. She wasn't killed there, though. It wa been dumped. We were lucky to determine the cause of de was smart and carefully timed when he got rid of the body. her deep, far from the trail. A flash flood came through an slide, washed Gabby up. Pure chance she was even foun

"What else?"

"There was wild game in Gabrielle's stomach. Dee lace was found in her bloodstream."

"Queen Anne's lace?"

"A plant that looks like a weed. I pull it out of my garden every year. Gabrielle was probably eating it. Her teeth were bad, near rotten." Brielle stops and wrinkles her nose.

"That all?"

Brielle shakes her head. "There were bite marks on her bones, her legs."

Chelsey stills. "Could you tell what kind of animal?" She remembers Ellie mentioning hearing howling. The dog hairs found on her clothing.

"Canine, dogs specifically," Brielle confirms. "Lab says most likely inflicted before she died," Brielle says, and Chelsey shudders. She shakes her head. "It's hard to think about, especially after having kids. I'll have all the files forwarded to you, and you can see for yourself." She pulls herself from the chair. "If you want to confirm the sweatshirt, you'll need to talk to Gabrielle's grandmother."

"Okay if I contact her?" Detectives could be touchy about their cases. Possessive. Chelsey stands, too.

Brielle whips out her phone, and Chelsey's dings with an incoming text. "Here's the address. I spoke with her this morning. She's expecting you."

TEN

DR. CERISE FISCHER SURVEYS THE legal pad balancing on her lap. On top a single line is written. **ELIZABETH BLACK. 05.24.2022.** She glances up. Elizabeth sits so still on the sage-colored couch that someone could be painting her portrait. Rain splatters against the thin-paned windows. Outside, the ocean is a violent clash of waves.

Cerise's office is on the top floor of a converted Victorian mansion. The doors are heavy and swell shut in the summer. She liked the idea of patients entering a place resembling a home. Of traveling the spiral staircase to her office in the turret. There was something whimsical about it that called to Cerise as well when she rented it. A fanciful notion of princesses in castles.

"Elizabeth?" Cerise says. Her voice is smooth and low. Inviting. She's been told the tone is reminiscent of her great-grandmother's, who'd immigrated from Jamaica and been a nanny. She loved singing to her charges. Her favorite lullaby was "Swing Low, Sweet Chariot."

Ellie blinks. "Everyone calls me Ellie."

"Okay, Ellie." Cerise smiles. She is a middle child. A people pleaser. A helper. Some clichés are true. "Since this is our first session, I thought we could get to know each other. Chat a bit. How does that sound?"

Ellie doesn't answer. Her eyes land on something over Cerise's shoulder. Cerise shifts to see what has captured Ellie's attention. "Have you seen one of those before?"

Ellie shakes her head.

"It's a Newton's cradle—it demonstrates the conservation of energy." Cerise reaches and pulls back one of the spheres and lets it drop. It collides with the others and sends the sphere on the opposite end swinging out. The pattern continues, keeping a steady beat like a metronome. Delicate clinking noise fills the office. Cerise settles back to peer at Ellie again. "And that's about all I know about physics."

Ellie's lips twitch with the beginnings of a smile, but it's quickly wiped away. "I like it. It's kind of comforting." Her gaze stays trained on it.

Cerise inhales and regards Ellie with a tilt of her head. "How are you doing right now, in this moment?"

Ellie's hands flex, and she bites her lip.

"Are you nervous?"

"No." Her denial is quick, and her eyes flick everywhere, all over the office.

The brain is always vigilant, always assessing for danger, searching for threats. But when something happens to someone, something traumatic, the brain becomes hyper-vigilant. Thinking isn't possible. Cerise wonders if this is happening to Ellie. If she's reverted to some primal state.

"Yes, actually. Kind of nervous," Ellie admits.

"Okay. Let's go with that. What is making you nervous? Are you nervous to be here?" Cerise perches at the edge of her chair, ready to receive, to listen without judgment.

Ellie shrugs. "Here. Anywhere. Alive." She laughs, but it is dry. No humor in it.

"Are you not supposed to be alive?"

Ellie's mouth forms a firm line. Cerise senses she's lost Ellie again, to some hollow space.

"You've been home for a few days now. The hospital report stated that you were having acute anxiety triggered by lights and noises. How has that been?" Cerise pretends to leaf through the file underneath her notepad. She's memorized most of the details of Ellie's case. But she wants to give Ellie a moment.

"Fine. The headaches are better. I don't feel . . ." Ellie trails off.

"You don't feel . . . ?"

"Anything," she says, her voice raspy all of a sudden. "I don't feel anything. It's like I'm wrapped in cellophane."

Cerise's heartbeat slows. "That's understandable."

"It is?"

"Yes." Cerise nods. "I don't know what happened to you." She waves a hand at Ellie's open mouth. "And you don't have to tell me right now. This is all conjecture on my part, but when someone becomes . . . overwhelmed, a person may disassociate. It's a survival response. And it can manifest in many ways—amnesia, identity confusion or alteration, depersonalization . . ."

"What's that?"

Cerise grips her notes, thinking. "Let's see. How to explain? Depersonalization is a kind of detachment. When you say you feel as if you are wrapped in cellophane, that would be depersonalization. The world is more dreamlike or unreal in that state."

Tears pool in Ellie's eyes. Cerise has struck a target.

"Identity confusion is a loss of who you are. A struggle of sorts. And identity alteration is a change. Like something in your behavior is fundamentally different." Such as refusing to shower or sleeping in a crawlspace or turning the lock on your bedroom door over and over again, or not eating but hoarding food. Over the last few days, Cerise has had long conversations with Kat. *She reacted strangely when I wanted to cut her hair. Said she was not allowed.* Cerise knows what Ellie is like now, or at least, she has a good idea. But she would like to know the Ellie before, too. That is how healing starts, bandaging those past wounds. When you study what you've been through, what happened to you, it loses its power, and then you have a choice: stay or move on.

Ellie cups her knees. "That makes sense."

Red and blue lights flash against the window, slicing up the neutral room. An email circulated last week about increased traffic in the area. Ellie tenses. "The governor is in town," she explains, hoping to calm Ellie. Sweat has formed on Ellie's brow and she compulsively rocks. Cerise shoots up from her chair and closes the curtains with a swish. They are flimsy and near see-through but help filter the brightness. She sits back down. "Sorry about that. Better?"

Ellie inhales long, exhales long. Repeats, flexing her fingers. When she opens her eyes, they are bloodshot, ravaged with terror. "Bright lights are still bothering me." Her voice is rough as sandpaper.

"Do you want me to dim the lights? Or would you like to sit where I'm sitting, with your back to the window?" She aches for Ellie. What happened to this girl?

"No. Sorry, I'm so jumpy." Ellie musters a smile, won't look at Cerise. The clock behind Ellie is near the top of the hour. They have fifteen minutes left in the session. "It's fine."

It's quiet for a moment. Rain patters against the window. "What are you thinking about, Ellie?"

Ellie picks at her fingernails. "How does the doctor-patient confidentiality thing work?"

"Oh." Cerise purses her lips. It's not an unusual question. People are always afraid of telling a stranger their secrets. "As your physician, I am legally and ethically prohibited from disclosing our conversations."

"So, whatever I say, you can't tell anyone?"

"With some minor exceptions, of course."

"Exceptions like what?"

"Well, if you posed a threat to yourself or others, I would have to disclose that. Or, if you were being harmed by someone—your parents, boyfriend, etcetera—I would be legally obligated to tell the authorities."

"Huh."

"This is a safe space, Ellie," Cerise reassures her. "Now, do you want to share what you're thinking?"

"I was thinking about forgiveness," she half-whispers.

Cerise sinks back. She is not religious anymore, but she grew up attending church. "What about forgiveness?"

"How sometimes people do things that make it impossible for the world to forgive them."

Curiosity strikes, and Cerise feels a little chill. Did Ellie do something bad? She immediately rejects the idea. Victims often blame themselves. "That's interesting." The clock clicks forward. It's one minute to the hour. Cerise wishes she could go on with Ellie. She makes a note that their next session should be longer. Ninety minutes. But she's got another patient in the lobby. A yellow light, placed discreetly in the corner, lets her know when someone is in the waiting room. "Let's pause here and pick this up again next session?"

Ellie leaves. And Cerise makes quick notes about their session. *The patient seems to be suffering from disassociation. She is visibly frightened and hyper-vigilant.* Cerise inhales and exhales deeply, takes a few seconds to compose herself, to think of Ellie Black, maybe even say a little prayer, not necessarily to God, but to the world, that Ellie will find only kindness from now on.

Then she rises. Gets ready for her next patient. She opens the curtains. The governor's security detail is pulling away—black sedans and police cars with red and blue flashing lights. The color catches in the water on the window, the droplets sticking to the glass like blood spatter.

Chapter

ELEVEN

ALTHEA BARLOWE, GABRIELLE'S GRANDMOTHER, IS a soft breeze of a woman. Stout with gray hair piled high on her head. She busies herself around the kitchen, placing a cup of coffee and a bowl of unshelled peanuts in front of Chelsey; a ruby on her right middle finger is dull in the light.

"Thank you." Chelsey sips and works to keep her brow from wrinkling. The coffee is terrible. Too sour.

"Sure, sure," Althea says. A scar bisects her top lip. There is an album in front of her, blue, embossed with a pair of baby shoes. "I was surprised to get the phone call this morning." She seems nervous, apprehensive. Behind her, in the dining room, hangs a wall-to-wall tapestry of *The Last Supper* and, underneath, a silk arrangement of flowers. "I really didn't expect to hear anything. After they found Gabby, Detective Ross reopened the investigation, but there wasn't enough evidence . . ." She curls her gnarled fingers around the album. "She said all leads had been exhausted. Never thought I'd hear that phrase twice in my lifetime. First when Gabby went missing and then after her body was found. Anyway, I've put it all to bed. She's buried now. At rest."

Althea flicks a hand behind her, where two kids hang out in an open doorway, unabashedly watching them. "Kayden"—she means the younger

93

one, the boy with dark eyes—"was four when Gabrielle disappeared, and Courtney"—the older lanky teen girl with a sulky appearance—"was just ten. They're nine and fifteen now. Kayden has lived more years without Gabrielle than with her." Althea pauses suddenly in her explanation, as if winded.

"Do you mind if I ask about their parents?" Chelsey asks, filling the silence. "I mean, how you came to raise your grandchildren?" Chelsey places the coffee down and slides it away with her pointer finger.

"Their mother, my daughter Crystal, is . . . troubled. I don't like to say too much in front of the kids." Althea drops her voice to a whisper. "Alcohol. I got custody of them when Gabby was eight. Their dad didn't want them. Can you imagine? Not wanting your own children? Never imagined I'd be raising kids again at my age." At the exhaustion in Althea's voice, Chelsey nods.

"I see. And what about Gabby? Can you tell me a little about her?" Chelsey opens a notepad, pencil poised.

Althea gives a shallow sigh. "Gabby didn't like all the responsibilities that came with being the oldest. I always told her she'd enjoy having siblings when she was an adult. I used to fight with my sister, but now we're best friends." Althea shrugs. "Perhaps I asked too much of her. The detectives thought we'd fought, that she'd run away. But that wasn't the truth. Gabby was happy. She loved her life." She flips through the album to the back. "Here she is." She rips a photograph from a sticky page and scoots it to Chelsey. "My Gabby. Taken a few days before she disappeared. Wasn't she gorgeous?"

In the photograph, Gabby stands with her sister and brother, his thumb in his mouth. She splays a hand on each of their chests, bent down between their two dark heads. "She'd spend hours making these friendship bracelets. That was the thing then."

Chelsey nods. When she was in high school, it was hair feathers, fishtail braids, and Silly Bandz. Noah says now it's white eyeliner and flannels.

The nineties are back. "Gabby was always bubbling up with new ideas about something to do, someplace to go. She was the kind of person girls liked and boys loved . . . maybe a little too much. She was a pain in the ass, but I loved that little girl."

She was the kind of person girls liked and boys loved. Chelsey notes Althea's affectionate tone. Lydia had been that way, too. Chelsey remembers that precinct picnic again. The boys teasing Lydia but in a different way. Smiling, flirting.

"Detective Ross told me you waited a while before calling the police," Chelsey says, steering the conversation back toward Gabby's disappearance.

Althea stiffens, and Courtney steps forward to place a hand on her grandma's shoulder. "I did," Althea says. "Her grandpa wanted to wait. I shouldn't have listened to him. But I called her friends. I called the neighbors. I even went outside and shouted her name—like I used to when telling her to come in for dinner."

"Why did your husband want to wait?"

"He figured she'd come back on her own. Gabby always ran late. I used to joke that she'd be late for her own funeral." Her laugh is rueful, edged with regret and anger. "He didn't want to be stuck paying for the police fees."

"Is he here now? Can I talk to him?"

"No." Althea sips her coffee. "He lives in Texas now. After Gabrielle disappeared, we . . . we couldn't stay together. He came home for the funeral, though."

Chelsey understands. Lydia's disappearance was like a knife scraping out the insides of their family until only a delicate shell remained. Was it any wonder it shattered? Chelsey's parents divorced shortly after the funeral. Her mother had wanted to move on. Her father could not. And truthfully, neither could Chelsey. They'd been left behind, living on the jagged edges of never knowing. Yes, Chelsey has had a place to bury her sorrow, but her sister's last days are still a mystery to her.

Althea waves a hand, and Chelsey blinks away the memory. "Anyway, that's all water under the bridge, as they say," she says. "I shouldn't have listened to him. I should have called the police. At the time, I thought it would be okay. I trusted Gabby. I trusted the world would bring her home." She shifts her gaze, staring down into the bottom of her coffee cup. "I guess the truth is, I didn't want to call the police either."

"Why not?"

"I don't know," she says. "Maybe because that would make it *true*."

They sit in silence for a moment. Visits like these, with the parents of the missing, always make Chelsey less lonely. Their lives bound together by tragedy. The knot so tight, near undoable. Chelsey clears her throat. "I don't know if Detective Ross explained the recent situation—"

"She said there was some new evidence," Althea says.

"A girl was found two days ago who has been missing for two years. She was wearing a piece of clothing we believe may have belonged to Gabby."

Althea straightens. "She was wearing a University of Washington sweatshirt the day she disappeared."

"That's how I traced it. Through One of a Kind Custom College Apparel. There was a number on the back—"

"Fifty-five," says Althea. "Her lucky number. She wanted to play volleyball at University of Washington. That was her dream."

"I've brought it with me today, and I'd like you to verify it if you can." Chelsey had checked it out of the evidence locker before setting out to Tacoma.

Althea nods somberly. "I'll take a look."

Outside Althea's house, Chelsey pops the trunk of her car, closes it, and places the plastic-wrapped sweatshirt on the hood. It's folded backward, number showing. Something flashes in Althea's eyes, and she pales.

"Gabby," she says, reaching for the sweatshirt, intent on unwrapping it.

"Sorry," Chelsey says, intercepting Althea's hand. "It's evidence. You can touch the plastic but not the actual garment."

"Is it hers?" Courtney is outside on the stoop, arms looped around Kayden. A couple of crows land in the yard and peck at the brown grass.

"Take your brother inside," Althea shouts.

Courtney looks ready to argue.

"Now!" Althea snaps out like a rubber band. At that, Courtney grabs her brother's hand and drags him inside.

"Althea?" Chelsey steps closer to her.

Althea's eyes, her whole body, are fixated on the sweatshirt. "We bought it for her for Christmas. She wanted it so bad. That night, we had turkey for dinner and a salad with oil dressing." She thumbs the sleeve, where there is the faintest dark spot. "It stained the sweatshirt, and I tried to get it out." A tear trails down Althea's cheek. "It's hers."

Adrenaline courses through Chelsey, and her arms prickle. She has to remember to be patient. To be calm. To stay in control. "You sure?"

"I'm sure." Althea glances at Chelsey. In the afternoon light, all the lines on her face are perfectly cast, the makeup gathered in the creases.

Chelsey plucks up the sweatshirt, ready to put it away.

"Wait." Althea stops her. "The blood—is it Gabby's?"

Chelsey squeezes the sweatshirt, plastic crinkling. A square of fabric is missing right under the W from the logo, where the lab cut it out to test the blood. "We don't know. The lab is processing it. I've asked for it to be expedited and run against DNA collected from Gabby's case. It's also being tested against Elizabeth Black's DNA—the girl who was found wearing it."

Althea looks up. The sky is cold and shot through with wisps of gray clouds like a piece of marble. "Listen, if you find out, I don't want to know. I don't want to know what happened to Gabby. I don't think I can handle it. She was alive for years, wherever she was. Lord knows what she endured. I can't . . ." She breaks off with a shudder. Then comes back resolute. "I've buried her now."

"Understood," Chelsey says. That was Althea's right. "But I believe these cases are connected, and this investigation is only starting." Chelsey hesitates to say more. "It's a promising lead."

Althea fixes Chelsey with a stare. "I want him caught." She tugs at her ear. "But I don't want to know what he did to her. I want to remember her as she was before. Does that make me bad?"

"No," Chelsey says. "It makes you human."

iv

I NEVER SAW THE BUS again.

Sometimes I would think of it, wish for it—the quiet dark, the smell of dirt and vinyl and metal. If given a choice between the bus and where I went, I would have chosen the bus.

But I didn't know that then. All I knew was that I had been freed from a dark prison. I had escaped. Only I hadn't. It was a reprieve at best. Where I went was hell on earth. But he called it "paradise."

—

Humid heat slapped me in the face, and daylight burned my eyes. My throat was dry, and I coughed. The kind of hacking that rattles your whole body. I staggered, hands on my knees, and steadied my breathing. Did I even remember how to speak? Consonants and vowels came to me, but my tongue couldn't shape them. There was pain, sharp and intense, like a thousand tiny paper cuts all over my body. A rock dug into my shoeless foot, its point angled right into my arch.

The man thrust a plastic water bottle in my direction. I palmed it in both hands, water sloshing over the side, and guzzled. I coughed, and my stomach cramped. The water burned as it came back up. The man stepped

99

back, narrowly avoiding the splash of vomit. He yanked the bottle from my fingers. One of the dogs darted forward and licked my feet.

"Sip it," he said. He held the bottle within my reach. I grabbed for it, but he pulled it back. "Sip it," he ordered again before finally handing it to me.

I did as I was told, studying him over the curved edge of the plastic. He'd seemed so tall, staring down at me from the hatch, but now I realized he had only a couple of inches on me. A red bandana covered the lower half of his face. It reminded me of a photograph I'd seen of May Day protestors in Seattle. They wanted to put an end to capitalism. What did this man want?

"Follow me," he said, and started walking, the panting dogs loping alongside him, one of them with a bulging stomach, pregnant.

But I stayed put.

Giant Douglas firs and redwoods sprung up around me. The forest was thick, so dense that you couldn't see beyond two or three feet in any direction. We weren't on a trail. Tall grass, shrubs, and thorny bushes brushed against my calves. The air was stifling and stagnant, aside from the bugs. It was summer. When everything bakes. Rots.

The man stopped when he saw I wasn't following him. My legs wouldn't work. My muscles spasmed and ached.

He stomped back and ducked, so his face was in my line of sight. "There is only one rule. Listen carefully, because I will only say it once. I tell you to do something, you do it, or you go back in the hole." My body trembled at the mention of my prison. "Do you understand?"

"I don't think . . . I—I can't move," I said, keeping my gaze trained on the ground. A shiny beetle crawled under a leaf and then around my pinkie toe. My stomach screamed. I wanted to eat it.

"Look at me," he said. I brought my head up. His eyes were blue and empty, like an irradiated lake. I couldn't hold his stare, so I averted my gaze. Over his shoulder, a woodpecker pounded on a tree oozing sap. "You'd be amazed by what the body can do under the right amount of pressure. Now let's try this one more time. Follow me, or you go back in the hole." He wore army fatigues, camo pants, and a sand-colored shirt. He clucked his tongue and shook his head. "Smile. You should be happy. That's the problem with women today. Never happy."

He started walking again, his heavy footsteps trampling the undergrowth. A shiny black gun was tucked into a holster around his waist.

I couldn't feel my legs, and I was hyperventilating, but my body was moving. For a moment, I was grateful. The fresh air in my lungs was hot but sweet and the earth beneath my feet felt solid. There was life all around me. I didn't even mind the mosquitos biting the thin skin under my eyes.

I bet you're wondering if I tried to escape. That's what everyone wants to know, right? Why didn't she try to escape? I thought about it. My eyes were wild, darting all over that forest, considering what direction I should run. How far would I make it? But I was physically outmatched. The man was stronger, better rested, and nourished. In the distance was the rush of water. I remembered a survival show I watched once. What did it say about water? Find the source and follow its banks—eventually, it will lead you to a road.

The man sighed. "I know every inch of this forest—every tree, every rock, every stream," he said. "There is nowhere for you to hide." He turned but kept talking, voice as steady as his pace. "If you run, I'll send the dogs after you." There were five dogs in all. Sleek German shepherds with black eyes and sharp teeth. He snapped his fingers and the dogs' ears perked up. "I whistle a certain way and they attack." He stopped, grew quiet, and I was too afraid to speak. The idea of the escape worn down to a nub.

We walked for hours following a marked path, trees bound with orange ribbon. My jeans snagged on thorny bushes, and my ankles brushed against poison oak. The next day, I would develop a rash and scratch it until it bled. The man stopped once and let me have more water.

"Who are you?" I licked my lips and handed the bottle back.

He dipped his head. "Michael. You can call me Michael." I counted the famous Michaels I knew. Saint Michael. Michael Jordan. Michael Jackson. Michelangelo . . .

"Why . . . why are you doing this?" I kept my eyes trained on a fern sprouting from a decaying log.

"Me?" He tucked in his chin, surprised and offended. "I'm not the problem." He started walking again. "None of this is my fault." He went on. I only remember snippets. Words that filtered through the pain and numbness. Men were being abandoned. Left behind. He had no other choice.

After that, we fell silent. I promised myself I wouldn't ask him any more questions. Ever. I folded my arms around myself and pretended all of this was a bad dream. I pinched my upper arms, but I didn't wake up. There was no escape. To live meant to follow.

—

Blisters formed on my heels. The skin on the bottom of my bare foot split open. Pain shot through my calves. I almost fell over twice. But I stayed upright, my legs moving as if answering a call. The dogs wound through the forest, and overhead, a plane glided through a bank of white clouds. I looked up, stunned to see something so ordinary when everything felt so extraordinary. Waving my arms or calling for help would be useless; the plane was a speck of dust in the sky. I watched it disappear.

We walked through a creek, water flowing like a silver string. The trees thinned and dissolved into a clearing. A meadow came into view. I saw buildings, all desperately in need of repair—rusted, weathered, in danger of crumbling. Later I'd have nightmares about earthquakes—the walls collapsing, pinning my legs, crushing my skull. Who would find my body? Weeds and vines curved around the bases of the structures. Evidence of human activity was everywhere—piles of garbage, blue tarps sagging with water and dirty leaves, a rusted car without its wheels, a row of dog kennels caked in feces.

Michael led me to the center. We passed a silo, the door padlocked, then rooms set into the ground like a bunker. Through the bars on the windows, I glimpsed dirty mattresses and crumpled sleeping bags. We finally stopped at another building, with thick plastic sheeting covering the windows and door.

Michael parted the plastic and gestured for me to go inside.

I kept my head down and didn't budge. Michael kicked my knees from behind, and I fell through. The dogs yipped and howled. The plastic sheeting fell into place behind me with a whoosh as I landed hard. The packed-dirt floor felt like concrete. Plumes of dust rose up, almost choking me. The air was humid with heavy breathing and body stink.

I wasn't alone.

TWELVE

A FEW HOURS LATER, CHELSEY is back, winding Coldwell's familiar streets. She parks near a garbage can with black bags piled against it, slams her door, and shakes out her clammy hands. The anticipation is making her dizzy. The questions, too. She confirmed that Ellie was wearing Gabrielle's sweatshirt. Plus more. A station wagon. Dog bites. She knocks on Ellie's door, bouncing lightly on her heels. The day has grown cold.

Kat answers, and Chelsey is hit with the aroma of onion, garlic, and warming spices. She promised Noah she'd be home for dinner tonight. He's making something, he'd told her on the phone, but now she cannot remember what. She'd been too busy wondering about what had happened to Gabrielle Barlowe, whether Ellie had known her.

"Detective Calhoun," Kat says, surprised.

"Hey, Kat." Ellie appears behind her mother like a wraith. There is an emptiness in Ellie's gaze that startles Chelsey. "Hey, Ellie. I know I'd said we'd take some time off the case, but there's been a recent development, and I have a couple of quick questions."

"We're having dinner soon." Kat's brow dips. It is the first time Chelsey has felt like an unwelcome presence at the Blacks'.

"It won't take much time. Promise." She polishes her statement off with a bright disarming smile.

Kat looks back at Ellie, and Ellie jerks her chin up. "It's okay," Ellie says.

"I'm going to finish dinner," Kat says. She floats back to the kitchen. And Ellie curls up in a chair. It squeaks as she rocks back and forth. Chelsey perches on the couch and leaves her jacket on. "How are you, Ellie?"

"What's the new development?" Ellie's voice is raspy.

Chelsey's gaze drifts to her neck, to the white unmarred skin. She has Gabrielle's autopsy report now. Brielle sent it over. She peeked at the photographs while driving, nearly getting into a collision with a semi. Not one of her better moments. Gabrielle had marks all over her neck. Had been choked to death. There was a bald spot on her head, too. From her hair being pulled? Some bleeding in her ears. Nails jagged and broken as if she'd fought. The usual stuff. Then the bite marks. Torn flesh. Chelsey blanched and had to pull over, roll down the window, breathe deep before starting again.

Chelsey looks at Ellie's clasped hands. The nails are even. Neatly filed. She makes a mental note to go back through the photographs of Ellie to check if her nails were broken during the exam. Maybe Ellie hadn't been left for dead. Maybe she'd escaped before he had a chance to try anything? As if sensing Chelsey's thoughts, Ellie tucks her fingers under her thighs.

Chelsey clears her throat. "I was reviewing the evidence from your case. I'm still waiting on forensics, DNA, that sort of thing. But I noticed something on the clothing you were wearing." She stares hard at Ellie, searching for anything, a tell—of discomfort, fear, annoyance.

Ellie stops rocking and pulls her legs up to her chest to hug them. "Yeah?"

"The University of Washington sweatshirt you were wearing had a number, fifty-five." Chelsey senses another body in the room and glances up. Kat is leaning in the doorway, kitchen towel in hand. Chelsey returns her attention to Ellie and catches her flinching. No, not flinching. Spasming. "The clothing came from One of a Kind Custom College Apparel. It was special ordered by Althea Barlowe for her granddaughter." Chelsey gives Ellie a long, measured look. Ellie puts her hands to her ears and begins to rock back and forth.

"Ellie?" Kat says, then focuses on Chelsey, warning in her eyes. "Detective Calhoun."

Chelsey ignores Kat, lasering in on Ellie. Digging. Digging. Digging. "Does the name Gabrielle Barlowe mean anything to you?"

Ellie stands abruptly, pushes past her mother, and darts into the kitchen. Chelsey rises and finds Ellie doubled over the sink, vomiting, while Kat rubs her back. Ellie wretches again. Violent tremors wrack her body. Kat holds a dish towel to Ellie's mouth. She looks up from her trembling daughter and right at Chelsey, radiating hostility. "I think you should go."

Chelsey shakes her head, refusing to cede this ground. "Did you know Gabrielle?" She's caught in an avalanche and cannot claw herself from it. "Please, tell me. Anything." Outside, rain starts, heavy and fast, and the wind picks up, rattling the windows like bones clicking together.

Ellie takes the towel from her mother and wipes her mouth. She grips the edge of the sink. "I don't want to talk to you anymore." She over-enunciates the words. Each one tumbles from her mouth like barbed wire, cutting into Chelsey. "I'm done with this. With you. The whole thing."

Chelsey freezes, realizing that she has lost herself for a moment. And now she's lost Ellie. She tries to regain her composure. "You're declining to participate in the investigation?"

"Yes. Whatever." Ellie heaves. Tears stream down her face. "No more, okay? Just no more."

Chelsey hangs her head.

Kat shuffles to the counter to a bottle of pills and shakes one out. She presses one to Ellie's mouth along with a glass of water and murmurs to her. Then she glances over her shoulder at Chelsey. "You can see yourself out."

Chelsey puts her hands up. "Of course." The words scrape against her throat.

Outside, she lingers in her car, rubbing at a pinch in her chest. Ellie does not want to talk. Ellie does not want to help with the investigation.

Chelsey sighs, unsure what to do now. How to proceed. She fires up the ignition, and a body in the Blacks' window catches her eye. Ellie is there, the curtain pulled back, head tilted. Staring at Chelsey. Watching her.

THIRTEEN

"SO THAT'S IT, THEN." NOAH uses the flat edge of a chef's knife to squash garlic cloves and then sets to mincing them. His sleeves are rolled to his elbows, and thick veins creep up his arms like ivy. Music plays, Pearl Jam. Noah is obsessed and has driven three times to Seattle to watch them in concert.

Chelsey leans against the counter, glass of red wine in hand and real estate flyer loose in the other. She is giving the townhome a half-hearted appraisal. She places it down along with her wine and reaches for a jar of pickles tucked in a cabinet. "I don't want to share a wall with someone." She pauses. "What do you mean, that's it?"

He throws the garlic in a pan, and it sizzles in the oil. "The vic—"

"Ellie," Chelsey corrects.

"Doesn't want to cooperate."

"Declined to participate," she corrects again. She twists the jar's lid, and it doesn't budge. A growl of frustration. "Why do you always close jars like you have something to prove?"

Noah stops stirring the garlic and saunters over to Chelsey. Gently, he pries the jar from her and cracks the lid, the scent of pickle juice wafting. "I'm making dinner." He hands it back.

"This is an appetizer." She crunches into a pickle.

Noah resumes his position at the stovetop. "All right. So, Ellie has declined to participate in the investigation. I may not be a cop, but I do know you have to have a complainant for a case."

He's right. The ADA won't even look at it. The case is too weak. There's no prosecution. But . . . "I thought about that. I don't need Ellie. I have another victim. Gabrielle Barlowe." Chelsey has sunk her teeth into this, and she will not let go. It doesn't matter if Gabrielle Barlowe is outside of Chelsey's jurisdiction. She's in pursuit.

Noah shakes his head, equal parts exasperated and affectionate. As he reaches up for some spices in the cabinet, Chelsey admires his back, the way the muscles flex. He is four years her junior and went to a school nearby in Ilwaco. He admitted six months into their relationship he'd seen her back then at football games with her father. Sitting high in the bleachers under the stadium lights. That's why he approached her at the bar. He'd recognized her. *I always thought you were so hot*, he stated.

She watches in silence as Noah makes the rest of dinner—boiling noodles and finishing the sauce. They plate up and sit at the table. The lighting is low and warm, and there's a muted baseball game on the television.

"What exactly is Ellie so scared of?" Chelsey says between bites of noodles. "What did he do to her?"

Noah rubs his head. "Chels," he starts, and she knows he's trying to steer the conversation in another direction. Away from work. Away from missing girls.

"C'mon," she cajoles. "Play detective with me." It's been a while since they've done this. Noah acting as a sounding board for Chelsey's cases.

He balls up his napkin and stares at her for a second, quietly pondering until he comes to a decision. "You want to profile him?"

"Yes." Chelsey pounds her fist against the table, excited.

Noah grins, and suddenly it's like old times. When Noah had been fascinated by Chelsey's career. Back then, he'd wanted to know all the details. He'd listen for hours and hours, lending his ear and thoughts. He tops off Chelsey's glass and then his own, skirting the edge of the bottle with his thumb and licking off an errant droplet of dark red wine. "All right. So, he snatched two girls."

"Gabrielle Barlowe and Elizabeth Black." Chelsey nods. "Originally, I thought she'd been left for dead, but she doesn't have the same injuries as Gabrielle Barlow. No signs of a struggle. No bruises around her neck. Maybe she escaped before any major physical damage could be done? Still, I wonder if this guy uses parks as a dumping ground." The search of the park and trail where Ellie had been found didn't yield anything. No campsite. No primitive dwellings. But they hadn't been looking for bodies . . .

"It's a good theory." He chews slowly. "But are you positive it's the same guy?"

She arches a brow. "What do you mean?"

"It could be two different perps. One offs Gabrielle, gets rid of her clothes, and the other picks them up."

Chelsey shakes her head. "Too much of a coincidence." Plus, there is the station wagon. The dogs.

Noah sighs. "Okay, so it's most likely the same guy. What do you know about him?"

Chelsey's forehead crinkles as she thinks. She doesn't have much. Loose facts jangle around in her mind. "Well," she starts. "He strangled Gabrielle Barlowe. That's angry and intimate. On the other hand, how he dumped her body suggests planning and caution. According to the detective that took over the case, it was 'pure chance' Gabrielle's body was discovered. He's smart, controlled when he needs to be."

Noah twists the stem of his wineglass. Chelsey has a flash of Noah's hand holding her by the neck, his grip tightening, anger burning in his eyes. Silly. She dismisses the image. That's what this job does. Makes you question the people you love, ask yourself whether you really know them, whether you can even trust them. But of course she can trust Noah. He is a good man. They have a good marriage.

"To strangle someone . . . you have to look at your victim, look them in the eyes," Chelsey continues. Did Gabby's killer stare at her while he did it? And why did he leave her naked? To humiliate her? Because he'd been humiliated? Both? "There was evidence of sexual assault on both Ellie and Gabby," she adds.

"Maybe he thinks he's in a relationship with them . . ."

Chelsey bobs her head. "He kept Gabby for years." Does he think he loves them? Does he fear being abandoned? It makes sense. Men like this, misogynists, disempower women. Strip them of self-confidence. Security. Until they are reliant. Too weak to leave.

Noah swipes a hand down his face. "He kept her for years . . . and *then* murdered her? What happened? Did she get too old?"

"I thought about that. Maybe he takes one when the other no longer fits his preferences."

"What are his preferences?" He pushes away his plate, the spaghetti forgotten. Chelsey isn't eating anymore, either. The discussion is feeding her now.

"It's hard to tell with just two. Young. Ellie was seventeen, and Gabrielle was fifteen." Chelsey pauses. "There was wild game in Gabrielle's stomach. Ellie has an aversion to unnatural light. This probably means they were kept somewhere without electricity, rural, maybe off the grid." An encampment of sorts? A farm?

"He's a loner."

"Yeah."

"Narcissistic."

"Hostile towards women," Chelsey finishes. They are not smiling anymore. Sexual assault is less about the act and more about domination. Chelsey thinks of Ellie and Gabrielle. Of rings of bruises around the soft flesh of necks. Of jackals roaming the streets. Making nests in the woods. "What makes a man a monster?" she whispers.

"Didn't cry enough as a kid," Noah says. It's a joke but not a joke. Research correlates a man's inability to show emotion to violent behavior. Silence falls again, and the air around Chelsey and Noah snuffs out.

"Maybe mommy issues," Noah says finally.

"Or daddy issues." Chelsey casts Noah a grim smile. How many times has Chelsey heard from men who beat their wives that they saw their fathers do the same to their mothers? Why are women most often the target of bitter men?

"Well, I have officially lost my appetite." He stands and clears his plate. He flicks on the sink faucet and the garbage disposal, dumping slimy noodles down the drain.

Chelsey approaches Noah, hugging him from behind. He goes still for a moment, then lays his wet hands over hers. "Thank you. I'm sorry I've been distant lately." She rests her chin between his shoulder blades.

He turns, and his eyes catch hers, locking in. He cups her cheeks. "I know it's hard not to bring the work home, but you've got to try. It's just a job, babe."

But not to her. And herein lies the problem. This is Chelsey's *life*. The darkness that swallowed Lydia touched Chelsey, too. This is where she lives now. She is drawn to the shadows. Every case is personal. Chelsey stays mute, folds that charcoal part of herself up, and puts it away. She gazes at him with all the love she feels but cannot say. She smiles.

He raises a brow, then lays one on her. And she presses her body into him. His eyes go hazy and dark, and she leads him to the bedroom.

They fuck long and slow with all the lights on. Afterward, they lie next to each other, bodies slick and sticky. "Hey, we can go check out that townhouse." Chelsey stares at the ceiling and holds the sheet to her chest.

Noah shifts and hovers over her. She takes the medallion he always wears between her fingers, the metal cold. She touches his face, his beard. She always jokes that if he shaved, she wouldn't be able to pick him out of a lineup. His eyes crinkle at the corners. "Yeah? You think it looks good? It has a nice backyard. We could get a dog," Noah says. All he wants are simple things. A wife. A home. Maybe tickets to a ball game.

She makes a mew of agreement, resolves to try again. To open a box in the garage, carry it to the living room, place a vase or picture frame inside of it. It cannot be that hard. She becomes aware of her hands, suddenly clammy.

He smooths the hair from her face. His eyes are glazed, blissed out. He kisses her once. Twice. She kind of nuzzles into him and inhales. Noah smells of summer, freshly mown grass, time inevitably moving forward. "I'll set it up. Tomorrow good? We could go after I get off."

"Yeah, tomorrow is good. I'll make time," she promises, but feels a tiny pinch, the unbearable idea of packing up her father's house. And it's compounded by the fact that Noah and Chelsey need the money from the sale of her father's place for a down payment on a new one.

Noah lies back and drifts off to sleep. Ever so discreetly, Chelsey shifts and clicks on her phone. She jots down notes, ideas from the conversation with Noah. Noah rustles, throws an arm over his head. But his breathing is steady. His chest rises and falls, the saint medallion glinting in the emaciated moonlight.

She goes back to her phone and clicks open the photographs of Ellie's exam, finding the snapshots of her hands. There. Ellie's fingers are spread on a piece of white cloth. Underneath her fingernails is dirt, but the nails themselves are clean-cut. Not like Gabby's. Whose nails were ragged, ripped off. Lost in a fight.

V

TO ANSWER YOUR QUESTION: YES, I knew her. Yes, I knew Gabby. Yes, I remember her.

I remember her in the forest. In the summer. Smiling, her body suspended in warm light like honey. I remember her by the campfire, body quivering from the relentless cold. I remember her in the dark, screaming, feet digging into the ground. I remember her.

The world called her Gabby. But I . . . we called her Hope.

—

I was in the room with plastic sheeting. On my hands and knees, coughing up dust. Footsteps, and then someone was in front of me. Someone new. Their shoes were white, unnaturally clean. My fingers curled against the dirt. I eyed a rock and thought about picking it up.

"I'm David," said the new person. His voice was pleasant, almost kind.

I lifted my chin.

Later, as the days passed, I studied his profile, trying to locate it in my memory. Did I know him? Had I met him on the street? Could he have worked with my dad at the docks? Always, I came up blank. He was thin but strong, with a sleek runner's body and the type of face that was unremarkable and easily forgotten. Had I seen him before? No, I did not know him.

"Would you like something to eat?" David asked. Music played on a battery-operated stereo. The song "You Are My Sunshine" on loop.

"Please," I said. There are so many different meanings a single word can have. Please don't do this. Please help me. Please let me go. "I just want to go home."

David smiled widely, weirdly. "You are home."

"I want my mom." I was going to die. I was sure of it.

He hung his head. "I understand."

Pale hands grazed my shoulders—not David's, someone else's, a woman with frizzy hair. David called her Serendipity. She reached for me, her expression tender despite her haggard, rough look. She grasped my hand. Too stunned to move, I let her help me up, accepting her embrace as I stood. Her arms were sinewy and strong. I'd been alone so long that I leaned in. A natural human instinct, to seek affection, gravitate toward shelter. I rested my chin on her shoulder. A piano was in the corner of the room, glossy and ridiculous in all the filth.

She pulled away from me and held my cheeks in her dry, cracked hands. Then she moved in close again. Not for a hug, but to say, "It's an exciting day." One of her bottom teeth was missing. Her breath smelled of must, decay. I stared into the dark pit of her mouth as she christened me with a new name. A secret name. A fate to be fulfilled.

When she finally stepped away, I saw the others. They huddled together. One was slender, white, and tall, with a sturdy build and a square dimpled chin—beautiful. The other was white, too. But shorter, with fuller hips. I imagined all of our faces were shaded by the same look—hurt and hungry, cornered by fear.

David smiled, and it was the smile of a man who believed too much in his own greatness. He introduced me to my sisters—Charity and Hope. "You'll love them as much as I do," he promised. But David didn't love things. He owned them. He was a collector of sorts. A man always chasing the one woman who would not love him in the way he wanted.

Serendipity said my new name, and her eyes darkened, like a piece of cloth doused in water. "You're a very lucky girl." She hugged me again. My face was shoved into her bony shoulder. I inhaled. Wet wool. My body went limp.

"Let's celebrate." David clapped.

A plastic cup of red liquid was pushed into my hand. Over David's and Serendipity's shoulders, Hope made the slightest movement. A tense, single shake of her head. I was too terrified to speak.

"Not thirsty?" David said. "You need to learn to appreciate what's been given to you. Nothing in this world is free. That's what my dad used to say." He touched my cheek. The cup dropped from my hand. Red bled into the dirt. "Clumsy," he said. "We're not off to a great start. It's my birthday, you know. You haven't even wished me happy birthday."

"S-sorry," I stammered. "Happy birthday."

David chuckled. He kissed my cheek, touched the small of my waist, and whispered, "You're a temptress. Dance with me?"

My body shook with refusal. But I felt Hope's and Charity's eyes willing me on.

His palms were soft and moist on my hips. We swayed to the music. I was all locked up inside. I could only see myself from the outside. Like I was peering down from some towering height, a mighty windswept ledge.

"Tell me about your old life. The one you left," he said.

I didn't answer. His fingers bit into my skin. "I'm from Coldwell. I have a sister," I choked out. I don't know why I thought of Sam in that moment. "She's older."

He stopped. "How much older?"

"Ten years."

"Ouch." He screwed up his face. "Sounds like you must have been a mistake." David found our insecurities and nibbled away at them. Like a rat. "Hope and Charity are your sisters now. You'll never speak of your other sister again."

I tucked my chin down and started to weep.

"Poor thing," David said. He hummed the lyrics to the song. *You are my sunshine, my only sunshine. You make me happy when skies are gray.* It gets hazy after that. I don't remember leaving the room with the plastic sheeting. But I do remember David lifting a key from a metal hook. Remember him fitting it into a rusted lock. Remember other doors in the corridor with similar locks—Charity's and Hope's rooms. Remember him following me in.

Next, there are still shots, like photographs or a slideshow. A metal frame with a thin stained mattress and crumpled sleeping bag. A small window cut into the upper part of the wall, big enough for me to peer out. Silver moonlight shone in the room. The air was still and sickly sweet, humming with insects.

I looked down at my hands and spread my fingers apart. The nails were bitten down to the quick; I'd eaten them on the bus. My cuticles were caked in dirt. My pinkie on my right hand had a single chip of red nail polish, a final splash of color from Before.

David touched my shoulders. Slid the shirt from my body. Pulled down my pants. What kills me the most . . . I didn't even say no. I couldn't. I just lay there murmuring, over and over again, "I'm not sure if this is okay. I'm not sure if this is okay."

When he was done, he touched my cheek and stood by the bed. I lay there staring at the wall, at a crack, retracing it again and again with my eyes. "Did you have a happy childhood?" he asked.

"Y-yes," I stammered out, eyes flickering shut, sucking at the marrow of my memories. My bed, curling under a warm blanket. The smell of the house when my mom dyed her hair. Making wishes on birthday candles. I shook in anguish at the sorrow of it all.

"Me too. I had a perfect childhood." He rustled behind me, the sound of putting his clothes back on. "Sleep well." He dropped a kiss to my temple, tugged on a lock of my hair. "Your hair is too short. I don't like it."

When he left, I propped myself up to stare out the window. The night was overcast, but through a break in the clouds I caught a glimpse of Sirius, the Dog Star. When I'd been taken, it hadn't been visible. Too early in the season. Based on its brightness and location, I'd been held captive in the dark for nearly two months.

———

The next morning, I huddled around the fire with Hope and Charity. The air was hot and thick, the cloak of summer. David plopped down next to Hope, his thigh rubbing against hers. She shifted away. My eyes watered. The U and W emblazoned on her sweatshirt blurred together.

David smiled, perfectly charming. "It's a beautiful day."

None of us spoke.

Serendipity served us some type of meat. Deer or elk. A hoofed carcass was strung up near the watchtower. Its stomach had been split open, its red guts littering the ground beneath it. The dogs chewed on the scraps, muzzles bloody. My stomach heaved. The outside of the meat was charred, almost black, but the inside was still pink.

David sighed. "You're all in moods today. They're all in moods today," he called out to Serendipity.

A blue station wagon with wood-paneled sides drove onto the compound. Face covered with a red bandana, Michael opened the door and stepped out of the driver's seat. He rounded the wagon and popped open the back doors. He often left for long periods and returned with supplies. I didn't know David but maybe I knew Michael. Was that why he always kept his face hidden? Would I recognize him? Did I find the low notes of his voice familiar?

"David," Serendipity called, walking toward the wagon. I watched her for a moment. Wondering about her. The ease with which she moved. How had she come to be here? Was she taken like us? Or was she here because she wanted to be?

David cupped Hope's knee, squeezed, and stood. "Duty calls." The pregnant dog trotted over and lay down, panting and hot.

I stared as David joined Serendipity. Then transferred my gaze to about fifty feet away. To the break in the trees where Michael had driven through, the branches still in the wavy heat. There could be a road on the other side. I could be a few feet away from freedom. My body tensed, ready to explode into a run. I'd find somewhere to hide, wait out the day, and use the night as cover. The stars would show me the way.

"Don't do it," Hope whispered.

I swiveled to her.

"You won't get very far," she said. Then she addressed Charity. "How many girls since you came?"

Charity's thumbs rubbed the edge of her plate. One of them bent a little backward. She told me later it was from being broken. Multiple times. "Two."

"There were three before her," Hope said. "Five total. And who knows how many others. Only a few make it off the bus."

My stomach plummeted. I thought about the bus. The relentless dark. The bone-chewing loneliness. "All five of those girls ran. They didn't come back."

"They could've gotten away." The words were unbelievable, sour on my tongue. "Someone could find us."

Charity and Hope shared a look. They pitied me—my optimism, my blind faith. "Girls like us don't get found," Hope said. I didn't know what she meant yet, but I would learn over the next few months. David took us because of all the things we weren't. We weren't rich. We weren't remarkable. We wouldn't be missed, other than by our families.

"What about her?" I jerked my chin to Serendipity.

Hope snorted.

Charity leaned in. "Don't ask Serendipity for help. Don't run. Don't talk back. And don't eat the meat." Charity glanced over her shoulder. David and Serendipity were distracted. She dumped her plate into the fire.

The meat sizzled and the fat popped. Hope did, too. They both cast me expectant looks. I followed suit.

Silence stretched. "I'm scared," I whispered into my metal plate.

"David won't visit you for a while," Hope said. "He rotates through us. Now that you're here, he'll only come every four nights."

I started to cry. Hyperventilate.

Hope scooted closer and pressed an old soda can into my hand. I remembered the punch from the night before. "Water," she said. "It's water."

I sipped, and the liquid was cool and gritty going down my throat.

Charity's hand touched mine, and I gripped it. "You'll be okay," Charity said. Okay. I used to repeat it to myself. It's okay, I would say. Two words I could whisper a thousand times in one hour.

"Take these." Hope thrust a handful of hairy brown seeds at me.

"What are they?"

"Shh, keep your voice down," Hope hissed. She jerked her chin at Charity, and Charity turned, keeping a lookout. The fire crackled. Smoke drifted into the bold blue sky. The little brown seeds were stuck in the crease of her palm. "It's Queen Anne's lace," she said. "It will keep you from having a baby. It's what he wants."

I closed my eyes, my vision swimming. "I don't want to—"

"That's fine," she said, a little huffy. "I don't have very many. David knows what it's used for, and he's cleared the compound and everything within a mile radius." She started to close her fist.

"Wait." The single syllable tumbled from my tongue. I grabbed the seeds from her and shoved them in my mouth.

"Chew them," she said. "I'll give you more tomorrow. It will make you cramp a bit. Maybe make you bleed, but it's better than—"

"Thank you." My mouth tasted bitter. I swallowed back a gag.

That was the moment. The turning point, I suppose. Those seeds. Who knew? They would be our downfall.

Chapter

FOURTEEN

THE FISHTRAP IS BUSY. THE dinner rush started at six and hasn't let up. The restaurant hums with conversation, the clink of silverware and rattling glasses. It smells of the ocean: fresh fish, mussels, cooked seafood. Danny is behind the bar, leaning against the shelves of liquor. He stares at his phone. A text chat is open, and Ellie's number is at the top. He's done this before. When Ellie was gone, he read their old text messages over and over. Stared at her number, even called it to listen to her voice.

Out of the corner of his eye, a regular in a members-only jacket raises his glass and taps it, motioning for a refill. Danny ignores him. His thumbs hover over the keyboard. He knows Ellie is back. He has seen her on the news and driven the streets of her neighborhood, but he'd been too much of a coward to call her. Until now, until he saw her dad at Ray's, the grocery store, this morning. They'd hugged and made small talk. Then Jim had mentioned Danny should come around. See Kat. Ellie. *She has the same phone number,* Jimmy had casually slipped in.

All day Danny has been figuring out what to say. How to say it. Fuck it, he decides, and taps out: HI. I'M THINKING ABOUT YOU. He immediately feels like an asshole. I'm thinking about you. It sounds weak. Cliché. With none of the intimacy they once shared. He wipes down the bar and fills a few drinks. His phone lights up with a call. The name Ellie flashing on the screen. His heart pounds. Jesus, he's nervous.

"I'm taking a break," he yells at the barback, pushing through the kitchen doors and out the back. He's in the alley and out of breath when he answers. "Hello? Ellie?" He's frantic, afraid he's missed her again.

He'd gone to the motel that night. Driven all the way to Astoria and sat in the car berating himself, calling himself a pussy because he couldn't stay away. The whole party was all because Ellie wanted a new phone. It had been a dumb idea. He'd called her a stupid girl in the car, whispering it to himself. He was tired of her. How she didn't take life as seriously as he did. It was the first time he ever thought of Ellie as bad. As a bad person to have around. Then he hated himself after she disappeared, as if he'd manifested it. For two years and two weeks, Danny has lived on a highway of regret.

"Ellie, are you there?" Goosebumps break out over Danny's arms. The dumpster he stands next to stinks of fish guts.

"I'm here."

He slumps against the wall of the methadone clinic next door. "It's really you," he sighs, feeling the air rush back into his lungs. It's the first time in two years that he is completely at peace.

"That's what everyone keeps saying." A small, self-deprecating laugh. Her voice is husky, lower than he remembers, but it's Ellie.

"I can't believe I'm hearing your voice right now." Danny wishes he was a smoker. He'd like to light up. Do something with his hands. Time stretches between them. The only sound is Ellie's breathing.

"I was about to go to sleep," she blurts.

"Oh." He cannot keep the disappointment out of his voice. The dull pang from echoing in his chest. "I'll let you go, then."

"No, I mean, it's okay. I wanted to talk to you."

His face heats up, her words mingling with his marrow. "I want to talk to you, too."

"Do you want . . . are you busy? I mean, do you want to come over?"

"You sure?" He is already heading back to the bar to grab the keys to his shitty car.

"Yeah," she says, and he has to work to hear her over the hustle of the restaurant. "Park down the street," she tells him. "Don't let anybody see you. There's a bunch of press. You remember the way?"

Through Mrs. Johnson's yard, over her fence, and up the tree into Ellie's window. He used to sneak in all the time. They'd have sex in her bed. They couldn't get enough of each other. "I won't let anyone see me," he promises. "I'm on my way."

—

Ellie's bedroom window is cracked open, and Danny jimmies it the rest of the way. He climbs over the sill and shuts it behind him, cutting off the gusts of wind. No lights are on in her room. But he can tell by the outline of the furniture that everything is in the same place. He finds Ellie in the center of the carpet. Clothes hang loosely from her frame, like she's a twisted wire wrapped in fabric. In her hand is a phone and on the screen there is a picture of a girl. One he does not recognize. She has dark hair, a stack of friendship bracelets loops her wrist, and her mouth is puckered, a typical selfie pose. Ellie places the phone down and clicks on the bedside lamp.

They stare at each other. She looks . . . not good. And he wonders if she is thinking the same about him. Sometimes he's surprised when he sees himself in the mirror. It all shows on his face, a lifetime of grief doled out in the span of a couple years.

"Danny," Ellie says, and their relationship, the entirety of the past, comes back to him, curling around him like a wave and sweeping him away.

Before they dated, Danny had seen Ellie around the halls at school. Coldwell was a small town, the high school even smaller. Everyone knew she slept with Will Gunner freshman year, and everyone knew she lied sometimes. Especially the whopper about her family being wealthy and only living in Coldwell until their mansion was done being built in Seattle. They didn't have a class together until chemistry, junior year. They'd sat next to each other. She was wearing a plastic choker around her neck and smiled mischievously at him, dropping a note on his desk during the lecture. It was a doodle of their chemistry teacher with a dick for a head. Danny had coughed into his fist to avoid laughing.

After school, Ellie approached him at his locker and laid a hand on his chest. *Bonfire on the beach*, she said. *You should come.*

Danny thought of all the reasons he shouldn't go to the beach. Knew what happened there at night. What kind of kids hung out there—druggies and flunkies. But he'd grown up working evenings and weekends at his family's restaurant. He'd missed most of his childhood. Ellie was fun. Danny wanted to have fun, wanted to be a kid. She'd been frustrating and fascinating and fucking mercurial in her moods. And when she'd kissed him at the bonfire, he'd been a goner. He'd insisted on walking her home, and she'd told him to fuck off.

I don't need you to walk me home, she'd said, slurring her words, drunk off her ass and pushing at his chest. After that night, they were going out. They called each other. Texted each other. Then he was in love with her. And all of it, all of it was blown away as easily as smoke.

Now Danny opens his hands. "I feel like I should have brought you something." He smiles, but it is grim.

"It's okay."

"I don't think any reporters saw me." His arms twitch at his sides, and he reaches for her. "Ellie," he says.

She ducks away and backs into a corner, a shadow crossing her face. "I don't like . . . I don't like to be touched." She huddles into herself.

A rubber band tightens around Danny's stomach. "All right." He shifts on his feet, tucks his hands into his pockets, thumbs out. "You okay with me standing here? Or do you want me to back up a little?"

Her chin trembles. And Danny kind of hates himself. "You can stay there," she rasps out. "Just don't reach for me again."

"I won't."

The tension in Ellie's body eases. Danny keeps his distance.

"This is my fault. If I'd come to the motel party . . ." He straightens, as if facing a firing squad. He wants Ellie to rail at him. To blame him. But she doesn't. She stays silent. So he does, too. Finally, he gathers himself. "Is there anything I can do? Anything that will help you?"

Danny is aware he's always had a bit of a hero complex. What man doesn't? he thinks. Maybe that's what drew him to Ellie in the first place. The idea that she needed to be saved. Then, when she called him out on it—*I don't need you to walk me home*—he'd felt stripped, completely naked.

"I don't want to talk about anything," Ellie says now.

"Okay."

She throws him a relieved smile, and Danny wants to fucking die. To flay himself. He wants to tell her to ask for more. Money. Blood. His life. "Can I sit?"

"Sure."

He sits right where he is, keeping his eyes on Ellie the whole time. There are three feet between them. Enough distance to whisper but not to touch. If this was two years ago, they might have tucked themselves into Ellie's twin-size bed. She might have thrown her arms around his neck.

"What other rules do you have?" he asks as Ellie sinks to the floor. He notes she is careful to keep space on both sides of her. Notes that her eyes flutter to the windows and doors, to the exits.

She swallows. "Just the things about touching and talking. And no asking me questions like, how are you feeling? Are you all right?"

"Got it," he says in an even, calm voice. He lets his body relax. "So, what do you want to talk about?"

She draws her legs up and rests her chin on her knees. She looks at her feet. "Sam came over a couple days ago. She brought Valerie and the baby."

"Yeah?" Danny shifts and leans back, catching his weight with his hands.

"Sam called the reporters outside assholes," she says, a smile in her voice.

Danny chuckles. "That sounds about right. What else happened?"

Ellie's record player sits in a spot where the light doesn't reach. She glances at it. "Do you want to listen to some music?" she asks, ignoring his question. Once upon a time, she'd told him she saw her future in the spinning vinyl and in between the lines of lyrics.

"As long as it's not David Bowie."

"Still not a fan?" Does she remember that Danny secretly loved hair bands? How they had fought, which was really thinly disguised flirting, over music?

"I maintain his music does not have a single redeeming feature."

"We agree to disagree." Another smile and Danny's chest is light. His world turning lazy and slow. Perfect. "No Bowie, then. You pick."

Danny moves to the record player. He rifles through the albums and chooses Johnny Cash. He puts the record on. The vinyl spins, and Johnny's deep, melodic voice starts up. He sings about a man coming around and living like a bird on a wire. Danny leans his head against the wall and closes his eyes. The song changes. "You are my sunshine," Johnny sings. The music abruptly stops and Danny opens his eyes. Ellie is crouched by the record player, the vinyl gripped so hard in her hands it's warped near to cracking. "I don't like this song," she states, and it startles him, the way she says it.

He's not sure what to say, if he can ask why, so he answers with a simple, "Okay."

"Choose something else." She replaces the record back in the sleeve with a tremble.

Danny waits a beat for Ellie to settle back against the wall. Then he sorts through the records again. "Dylan okay?"

She nods once. He puts on Dylan's greatest hits. And Ellie's eyes flutter shut. He closes his eyes too and wonders about the Johnny Cash song, "You Are My Sunshine." She never hated it before. Then he thinks, and it's deeply disturbing, that he might not know Ellie anymore. For two years, it is as if she's been frozen in time, trapped in amber, forever seventeen. But that is not the truth. The truth is something happened to Ellie.

The air shifts around him, and he opens his eyes. Ellie is standing next to him. He waits. Doesn't move. Holds his breath. She melts down and sits beside him. Their legs both outstretched, not touching, but still.

"I'm sorry I freaked out. I'm also sorry if I smell," she says so quietly, so softly, the sound is just a smudge in the dark, a tear to be wiped away. "I threw up earlier."

"It's fine," he says. The smell reminds Danny that she is here. She is alive. Whatever happened to her during the two years she was gone doesn't matter, he tells himself. She is still the person he fell in love with. The only person, the only girl in the world, capable of destroying him.

FIFTEEN

"YOU WANT ME TO PULL every available unit I have and put in calls to Thurston and Lewis Counties to look for a blue station wagon?" Sergeant Abbott cuts an elegant shape as he leans back in his chair. Today he is dressed in a suit and tie, badge hanging around his neck. His skin is pale, near translucent, and his cheeks dusted pink, salmon colored. His office is sparse. A single clock on a bare wall, five minutes past eight and ticking. A file cabinet with a frame on top. The sergeant, as a younger man, on his boat—because everyone in Coldwell has one—the *Good Fortune*, named for his then-wife, who eventually changed both her monikers, first and last, after she left, after she peeled the skin of Coldwell from her body.

Chelsey is standing and leans down, fingers splaying on top of the sergeant's desk. "Thurston, Lewis, *and* Grays Harbor," she qualifies. In front of Abbott are two black-and-white photographs from Ellie Black's and Gabrielle Barlowe's missing person files—the lot full of cars where Ellie was abducted, a red circle around a station wagon, and the CCTV footage of the same station wagon following Gabrielle's car.

She straightens and notices Abbott's lips twitch at something above her shoulder. Glancing back through the window, she sees a television on in the bullpen. They can't hear the sound. Abbott's door is closed. It's a newsreel of Governor Pike. Previously Mrs. Abbott. She charted a meteoric rise from councilwoman to mayor to governor and has been outspoken about her private life. Her lousy marriage, hinting at domestic abuse, with no choice but to flee with nothing. Even leaving behind her children, who sided with their father.

"Sir?" Chelsey prompts.

Abbott's attention returns to Chelsey. The salmon of his cheeks a shade darker. She remembers that precinct picnic again. How Abbott had been there with his wife, the now-governor, and their kids. Before Doug asked Chelsey if she came in a bento box. Before the watermelon had been sliced. Before the deviled eggs had been consumed. Abbott had been sipping from a Gatorade bottle, his breath and skin reeking of cinnamon.

He stopped drinking around the time Lydia was murdered. Her death had sobered up the entire town. The chief's daughter killed by Coldwell's golden boy. How could this have happened? His wife had left him by then, and he'd showed up on the Calhouns' doorstep with a casserole from the frozen aisle at Ray's two days after Lydia had been found.

I'm so sorry, kid, he'd told Chelsey while she stood on the doorstep, blank and empty. Her father and mother would not come to the door. Could not handle the stream of constant visitors. It had been up to fourteen-year-old Chelsey to field the calls. To make the funeral arrangements. To insist on peonies, Lydia's favorite flower. To accept hugs from strangers. *This never should have happened. You let your parents know I stopped by? That I send my condolences?*

Since, he'd turned his life around. It had been a slow thawing with a few spots of relapse. A few years back, Chelsey was working late, and she found him in his office, smelling of cinnamon again. Turns out he liked Goldschläger. This was around the time his ex-wife announced her run for governor. *She was the love of my life*, he'd blubbered to Chelsey.

Let me take you home, sir, she'd offered.

He'd waved her off. And the next day, he'd been sober and told Chelsey he was leaving early to go to a meeting. They never spoke of it again. But

Chelsey respected Abbott. He was trying. He'd been a drunk, Chelsey thinks, but an abuser?

Now, he regards her with a frown. "Thurston, Lewis, and Grays Harbor. That's a lot of manpower."

She keeps her voice from wavering, though her insides are buzzing. "It is."

The muscle in his right cheek flexes. "Where are we with the other evidence, the blood on the shirt? You get a match on that to Barlowe?" Even if the blood is Gabby's, it wouldn't be much in terms of a lead, Chelsey thinks. It would only solidify that Gabby and Ellie may have been taken by the same person, strengthening the tie binding the two girls together. Chelsey needs the wagon. "It's not in yet. The wagon—"

He stands, cutting her off. "It's not enough, Chelsey. It's too much of a coincidence. Bring me something more solid, and I'll go to bat for you." His tone is not angry. It is matter-of-fact.

Chelsey's jaw locks. "I strongly disagree. The wagon is our best lead." In truth, Ellie was their best lead, but she's no longer an option. Chelsey flashes back to the expression on Kat's face when Ellie vomited upon hearing Gabby's name. A lioness protecting her cub.

"Noted," Abbott says, rounding the desk and tucking his keys into his fist. He stops in front of Chelsey and smiles patronizingly. Sometimes Abbott makes her feel like a child. Like they're still standing on the stoop of her parents' house, when he'd offered her a casserole and called her kid. It rankles even more that she wants his approval. To see his eyes glint at a job well done. "I'm on your side here."

Chelsey forces the corners of her mouth up. "I know you are," she says.

"Let me know when the blood is in," he says, the door swinging shut behind him.

—

It is strangely quiet at the Blacks' house as Chelsey parks alongside the curb. The reporters have fled, off to chase a new story. All that's left are muddy teddy bears, wilting flowers, and soggy cards on the Blacks' front porch. Chelsey thinks about the girl inside. What are you afraid of, Ellie Black? What are you hiding? Chelsey frowns at the question. At the inference she's making. That Ellie may be willfully concealing something. She shakes it off. And yet . . .

The front door opens, and Kat emerges with her purse tucked under her arm.

Chelsey swings open her car door. "Kat," she calls out, flagging her down and jogging across the street.

"I'm on my way to the grocery store," Kat says, rounding the hood and opening the driver's door. Kat has never given Chelsey the brush-off. She has never been cold.

"How's Ellie?" Chelsey's voice curves with concern. "She okay?"

Kat's eyes skip to the house. Chelsey glances over her shoulder, and one of the curtains swishes in the window. Ellie. She's watching again.

A siren wails. Every first Monday of the month, there is a tsunami drill. Chelsey looks to the sky, waiting for it to pass. As soon as it does, she says, "I'm sorry about what happened the other day. I pushed Ellie too hard. I know that now." Chelsey draws a little closer to Kat. All she wants to do is help. Why can't Kat see they are on the same team? "But I know you know what it's like. Those two years, wondering what had happened to Ellie. Remember when Jim would come to my office?"

Kat startles. "Jimmy came to your office?"

Chelsey's brow furrows. Jimmy never told Kat? Why? "Yeah. He'd come and bring the precinct donuts, ask to go through the evidence."

The keys jingle in Kat's hand. "I didn't know."

"There's another family," Chelsey presses, sensing an opening. "Gabrielle Barlowe's." Her grandmother, Althea, might not want to know the details, but she wanted justice. Chelsey does, too. There isn't anything she wants more. She will spend her whole life pursuing redemption. "Gabrielle is dead, and Ellie is our best lead to finding out what happened to her, to catching this guy. Anything you can tell me about

Ellie, anything she shares . . ." She stops, voice suddenly choked with emotion.

Kat heaves a deep sigh. "She barely talks, but I'll let you know if anything comes up that feels relevant." Kat clutches the edge of the car door, ready to go, but then she pauses, looks at Chelsey, and thinks for a minute. "Danny came over last night. Snuck in through her window." Her face changes and turns wistful. "I recognized his voice through the walls. Maybe she said something to him."

Chelsey backs up and nods gratefully. "Thank you." She watches from the sidewalk as Kat drives away.

———

Late that afternoon, Chelsey moseys into the Fishtrap and steers herself toward the bar. There are a few scattered patrons, the die-hard daytime drinkers. A row of slot machines sits against the back wall. Chelsey recognizes Charlie immediately, a regular in the drunk tank, feeding dollar bills into one. Danny is behind the bar, a white towel slung over his shoulder. Her muscles tighten as if readying for a fight. She takes a seat, and Danny's jaw flexes when he lays eyes on her.

"Cup of coffee, please," she says.

Danny grunts and pours her one. Sliding the mug in front of her, he says, "That'll be twelve bucks."

Chelsey sucks in her cheeks. "Must be a good cup of coffee."

"It's about eight hours old," he deadpans. Above him is a sign that says: NO ASSHOLES. Along with another that advertises the special tonight: RIBEYE, TWO FOR ONE.

Chelsey isn't surprised by Danny's chilly demeanor. She thinks back to the first time she met him when Ellie was reported missing. When she was busy chasing down every possible lead. Camera footage from the motel showed Danny's car entering the lot. He'd lied about being at home when Ellie disappeared.

Chelsey had hauled him down to the station, courtesy of a cop car, and made him sweat it out in a box for an hour before interviewing him.

Do you have a temper, Danny? She hovered over him while he fidgeted. *Ellie was a bitch that day, wasn't she? I totally understand. She made you feel like shit because you had to work.* She'd laid into him, until he quaked uncontrollably and slammed his fists on the table.

I was there, he wildly spat out. *I went to the motel. And you're right. She had picked a fight with me that day. I sat in the parking lot, got out of my car, got back in, and drove home. And I thought, fuck this, fuck her.* He started crying and wiped the tears furiously away. *Oh god, oh god*, he'd hyperventilated, his whole body lost in a shudder. *Forgive me. If she had been with me, none of this would have happened.*

Chelsey had broken him that day. Ripped part of his boyhood away. And that's what he'd been. A kid. A confused, sorry kid who blamed himself. Still, she could not bring herself to apologize. In quieter moments, she had examined what drove her to such desperation, and the answer quickly became clear: Oscar Swann, Lydia's killer. Everyone thought Oscar was such a nice guy, that he couldn't harm a fly, that he couldn't be capable of such a heinous act.

Chelsey's eyes flick to Danny as she pours creamer into her cup. Yes, two years ago, she'd changed him. She deserves all of his ire. His blame. "Heard you saw Ellie last night."

"So?"

"So . . ." Chelsey repeats slowly, tapping the spoon against the cup. "I'm wondering if she said anything to you." She pauses. "And I'm wondering if you might be able to keep an eye on her for me."

"You want me to spy on her?" Danny snorts. "You're a piece of work, aren't you?" He settles his elbows on the bar until he's eye level with Chelsey. "I know all about you." He stares at her long and hard. "Your sister went missing when she was in high school." Usually, when people mention Lydia, their eyes glitter with pity and sympathy, but Danny's sharpen with anger. "Your parents offered a half-million-dollar reward.

What was it like having all that money? All those resources? Precincts at your disposal?" He straightens, using his towel to dry some glasses behind the bar. "A statewide search? Helicopters canvassing the forests? A national press conference?"

Another stab of guilt. It is true. Lydia benefited from everything Ellie and other girls did not. Lydia had been young and white *and* well-off. Her father had set up a command center in his office, tugging on all his political connections to find Lydia. Money poured in from anonymous donors. News reporters created moving biopics of Lydia's life. Forty-eight hours of constant coverage ending in a helicopter hovering over the crash site. The story after that centered on Oscar Swann. The boy next door turned killer—how could no one have seen this coming? Ellie's case hadn't received one-tenth of the attention Lydia's did. No benefactors. No political favors.

Chelsey faces off with Danny, keeping her expression purposefully blank. Just then, her phone flashes with a text. It's Noah: I'M AT THE TOWNHOUSE. ARE YOU ON YOUR WAY?

Shit. Her promise to Noah. She'd forgotten. She taps out a quick text: I'M SORRY. COMING RIGHT NOW.

"You know, this coffee is terrible." Chelsey pushes the mug back toward Danny, liquid splashing over the rim.

"You still have to pay," Danny says, dumping the coffee into the sink behind the bar.

Chelsey's phone buzzes again. Not Noah, this time, but the lab. "I have to go." Chelsey pulls out a twenty and leaves it on the bar.

"Don't be afraid to be a stranger," Danny calls out.

"Detective Calhoun," she answers her phone, the wooden door of the Fishtrap swinging shut behind her.

"Detective Calhoun. Tech Kinsley here."

The coming evening is laden with cool, wet air. Main Street is quiet. A plastic bag blows down the sidewalk. "You got the blood DNA from the sweatshirt?" Chelsey pauses next to a maroon sedan with an old VOTE FOR PIKE election sticker on the back windshield.

"Yeah." The tech draws out the word. "A mixture of DNA was found, actually, male and female. Neither are a match for Gabrielle Barlowe."

"No?" Chelsey's mind spins. Not Gabby's blood. She'd been so sure. If not Gabby's, then whose? Another victim? Their abductor?

"Nope," Kinsley says. "But we got a hit on an inmate at Riverbank Correctional in Philadelphia. He's on year fifteen of a twenty-year sentence. His name is Timothy Salt."

"He's been in for fifteen years?" She's unable to conceal her distress. Her confusion. That the ground feels as if it's giving way beneath her. All these tiny earthquakes, and she cannot help but picture a pair of ghost hands holding Chelsey like a rag doll and shaking. If Timothy Salt has been incarcerated for fifteen years, he can't be responsible for Gabby's death, for Ellie's abduction.

"Yep, but it's only a partial match," Kinsley adds.

Someone related to him, then. "Send me the full report," Chelsey says, and hangs up. Family, Chelsey concludes. She needs to look at Salt's family.

She closes her eyes for a beat, letting her body reset, allowing the coldness of the air to recharge her. In her mind, the investigation shifts, a new form taking shape, another tunnel to be dug, another cavern to be explored. Noah will have to wait.

vi

TIME AS I'D KNOWN IT ceased to exist. We measured the days by the sun inching across the sky. The nights by the changing moon. The hours by David. He liked "his girls" to be on a schedule. We bathed in the creek every morning and spread peach lotion from a glittery bottle onto our limbs. We were allowed to use the bathroom three times a day. David did not let us cut our hair. He made us keep our nails nice with a file. He told us to smile, to say thank you, to be happy. Joyful. Content. He had rescued us from a world that did not want us. Weren't we lucky girls? Wasn't he a lucky man?

"It's my turn with David soon," I said to Hope. We were on our knees, scrubbing the dog kennels. I wiped my brow with my forearm. Even in the shade the heat was stifling. Every fourth night, David visited me. He liked for me to say certain words while I softly scratched his back. Whispers into the night. No, I would never leave him. Yes, I would always stay. I learned to go away in my head. We all had our ways of coping. Hope would refuse to eat or would throw up her food. Charity would scream in the middle of the night and keep us awake. "I need more seeds."

"We're running out," Hope said, bending and using a bristle brush on the side of a metal kennel. "We won't last the rest of the summer."

I hung my head and touched my stomach, thinking about a baby in there. Hope said another girl, before me, got pregnant, but the baby got stuck and they didn't make it. I inhaled and stared at the grounds. At the silo where David kept his guns locked up. At the garden we'd planted a few months ago. Not much had come up. A few thin carrots. Heads of lettuce that some creature immediately ate. A patch of strawberries consumed by a swarm of bugs. David fancied himself an outdoorsman. The truth was he was a terrible survivalist. We ran out of food often. Nobody knew how to start a fire without a lighter. And all the shelters leaked when it rained. Michael came and went. Sometimes we wouldn't see him for a few days, and I wondered if he had another life. A job. A wife and kids somewhere whom he kissed goodbye, lunch box in hand before going off to work, to torture us. He'd bring back canned food and gasoline for the generator, and once, a deer carcass. David said he'd shot the animal with a bow and arrow.

"We could try growing them," I offered. One of the dogs lay with her pups under a maple tree. She'd had the litter a few weeks ago. She'd nipped at David once, and I thought he might shoot her. But he'd smiled. *She's just doing her job*, he said. *Mothers are supposed to protect their young*.

Hope mopped at her brow. She refused to stop wearing the University of Washington Volleyball sweatshirt, even though we had other clothes. It was soaked in the armpits, but it kept her skin safe from the sun, from cooking like an egg yolk in a hot pan. "Too dangerous."

I dumped a bucket of water from the creek on my kennel. "We can make it look like they're growing wild."

"Too risky—"

I stopped. "Just listen—"

"No." She moved down to the next kennel. Minutes ticked by. "How would we do it?" she asked quietly.

I hurried to answer. "We can make it look like they're growing wild," I repeated. "If we work together, we can plant them, and then we'll have seeds for the whole winter."

"Yeah." Hope stilled, head down. "Yeah, okay. Let's try."

I nodded gravely. So did Hope. By the end of the day, we'd finished the kennels, and we had a plan.

The next day, Charity and I gathered kindling, and we scoped out places where we could scatter the seeds. A meadow. At the base of a copse of trees. Farther down the creek, seeds could be folded in among the rocks, where the water would trickle and drench the roots.

The day after, we set to secretly planting. One of us keeping a lookout while the other loosened the soil to place one of the precious seeds in the ground.

Then we waited. We checked them as often as we could. Nothing grew near the copse of trees. Or the meadow. But one day . . . one day, Charity returned from washing at the creek, a grin twitching at the corners of her mouth. "They're growing there," she'd whispered in an excited rush. That night, we all shared secret smiles during dinner. It was easy. Almost effortless. Like stepping from a cliff into a free fall.

—

Near the end of summer, there were full blooms.

As soon as one sprouted its lacy head, we plucked it up and harvested the seeds. By the time the trees had changed colors and lost their leaves, we had enough seeds for the winter and to save for planting again. We built a big fire that night to ward off the cold.

Charity rubbed her arms and leaned into the fire. "I'd do anything for some of that generator heat." David slept on the other side of the compound, in a room that overlooked everything. I could see it from my prison at night. He and Serendipity had electricity up there. A heater and television. David liked Western movies. Cowboys and Indians, that type of thing. There'd be popping sounds, horses neighing against the black of the night, mingled with our weeping.

"I'd give anything for some real food," I volleyed back. Across the way, David and Serendipity ate separately. Sometimes Michael brought food from a deli. Serendipity would serve David, hovering over him. Making sure his plate was full, a napkin within reach. That night, I salivated, watching the two of them share it. Teeth ripping into cold chicken. Nibbling on macaroni salad. Lips greasy from a buttery, flaky roll.

Charity stirred her gray porridge. Keeping her gaze downcast, she whispered, "We did it." She smiled into her food. "We actually did it."

A thrill stabbed at my chest.

Hope grinned, tucking her chin into her shoulder. "I made us something. To celebrate." She pulled up the sleeve of her shirt where there were little pieces of rope braided and tied around her wrist. She untied two and handed one to each of us. "Friendship bracelets."

Friendship. The word looped around my throat, and I blinked away fresh tears. I hadn't had many friends back in Coldwell.

"I used to have like fifty of them stacked up to my elbow," Hope said as we tied them around our wrists. Warmth crept into her voice. "My sister and I made them for each other."

"I had a sister, too," I offered solemnly. "She was pregnant." Sam had probably had the baby by then. I wondered if my family still thought of me. Or if I'd been forgotten. It was easy to think that I had been. I was so far removed from the world. David had said I was a mistake. *Don't you think if your parents wanted you, they'd have found you by now?* he'd said one night.

"I'm an only child," Charity said. "But I always wanted a sibling."

Hope sat in the middle of us, and she put her hands down on the log, palms up. "Sisters," she said, wiggling her fingers. Charity and I placed our hands in hers. We held on for a moment. Fingers intertwined, thinking we might survive if we had each other. We didn't stay like that for long, though. We couldn't. David and Serendipity didn't like it when we acted too close. One of them would swoop in to separate us. So, we released each other, but the sensation stayed like a warm blanket had been draped over us.

That's how it started. For ten whole minutes, we shared our old lives. Charity's dad was a musician, her mom a cocktail waitress, but they couldn't look after her, so she'd been in foster care for a long time. Because she was tall and athletic, people thought she should play basketball or run track. "But I wanted to dance," she said. She'd watch tutorials online and practice steps, twirling in a shared room at her group home. Sometimes she'd watch reaction videos. She liked the one where a guy heard Bruce Springsteen for the first time and he cried. Or the cop who rapped while patrolling the highway. Hope and I had seen him, too. It was good to remember the girl I was. I'm not sure what girl I am now.

Hope lived with her grandmother, a house cleaner. "I hated my grandma because we were poor. Like, why agree to take us in if you can't afford us?" she said. And on it went. The day's events had made us feel brave, made us cling to our pasts with both hands, made us forget the bone-deep sadness. We waded into dark waters with triumph in our eyes. And finally, we whispered our real names to one another, the words standing like monuments between us.

Gabrielle.

Elizabeth.

Hannah.

"If someone always remembers your name, speaks it out loud, you're never really gone. That's the real afterlife," Gabby said. Then we said all the things we'd do when we were free. Hug our families. Eat whatever we wanted. Travel. We would cast our nets wide, pulling up friends, lovers, maybe even children. All that we would have had in a lifetime if only given the chance again. Does that sound like a bad country song? What we crooned by the fire, wrung out from the lungs of small birds trapped in long-abandoned mines.

Gabrielle. Hannah. Elizabeth. When I'm alone, I still repeat our names sometimes. I thought it was dangerous to trust them. But I was wrong.

They never should have trusted me.

Chapter

SIXTEEN

CHELSEY IS IN LACEY, A rural town outside Olympia, in the passenger seat of a cop car winding through the quiet tree-shaded streets. She flexes and unflexes her toes inside of her black tactical boots. It's one of those rare spring days, cold but clear.

"We're nearly there," Montoya says. Chelsey forces her attention away from a burned-out bus on the side of the road and refocuses on Montoya. He is a detective, too. And has too many accolades to count, including an impressive stint in the capital's counterterrorism unit. But he's best known for his work on the White Mountain serial killer case. He's smart. Savvy. And handsome in a boy-next-door type of way. He also loves Creedence Clearwater Revival. "Born on the Bayou" is his favorite, with "Have You Ever Seen the Rain?" a close second. He clicks off the music. His fingers are slender, with clean round nails. He has admitted to her that he gets a manicure once a month. Nothing too fussy. Just a clip, file, and buff.

Chelsey has learned all this over the last twenty-four hours, working closely with Montoya to chase warrants, debrief the team, and set up the raid. Chelsey holds photographs in her hands—a picture of Lewis Salt and drone footage of his property.

Lewis Salt is an unemployed construction worker. He is the son of Timothy Salt, the inmate serving time at Riverbank for rape and armed robbery, whose DNA was a partial match for the blood on Gabrielle Bar-lowe's sweatshirt. Lewis Salt has had three run-ins with the police, all involving spats with his girlfriend. But none of these infractions led to any arrests or convictions. His DNA isn't in the system. Lewis has a license to carry a concealed weapon. He lives in a two-story house on fifteen acres in the middle of the woods. A busted-up barn is also on the property. The roof is partially caving in, the boards cracked and splintering. It is a place he could have kept Gabby and Ellie, Chelsey thinks. And the final nail in Lewis Salt's coffin: he drives a blue station wagon.

Chelsey rubs her hands together and focuses on the car in front of them. All in all, there are ten police units and one SWAT van. She'd wanted something a little more understated, but Abbott opted for flashier. A joint task force between Coldwell, Tacoma, and Olympia PD, co-led by Calhoun and Montoya. Once they get him, Chelsey hopes Ellie won't be so afraid. That she'll come to Olympia for a lineup. That she'll be able to raise her arm and point to Lewis Salt through the glass. That's him. He's the one. Maybe then she'll lose the haunted look in her eyes.

"What's his MO?" Montoya dips his chin to the picture of Lewis Salt, one hand on the wheel. "I always wonder what makes these guys tick."

Chelsey swipes a thumb over the photograph of Salt, right over his scraggly beard. "That's what we're going to find out."

"Yeah." They pass a splintered wooden sign with Smokey the Bear stating FIRE DANGER IS LOW TODAY. "Sometimes there is no method to the madness."

It often seems that way. But Chelsey knows that violent men are not inevitable. They are not a matter of course. Of nature. Of being born. Violent men are forged. They are made. All of this . . . all of it is preventable.

The cars drift to the side of the road, mowing down brush to park. Doors slam and officers don flak jackets and helmets and fit microphones into their ears.

"North road is secure," Chelsey hears on the radio. Then another voice: "South entrance secure."

Montoya speaks into his earpiece. "Copy." He looks at Chelsey. "Your call. We strike at your command." The team draws black masks around their mouths, places helmets on their heads, shifts their shields into position, readies their guns.

Chelsey inhales, her skin abuzz. She closes her eyes and gathers herself. For a moment, she is fifteen again, one year after Lydia's funeral. She's with her father in a GI Joe's, a store now out of business, but it had specialized in outdoor recreational equipment. They're buying camouflage for Chelsey, a bow and arrow, a rifle. After Lydia, there were no more ballet recitals or Barbies on the weekends.

Instead, Chief Calhoun drove his last daughter to the woods Friday through Sunday, someplace Chelsey could stay out of trouble, and if trouble did find her, she'd know how to handle herself. The first time he lectured Chelsey, his mouth was full of shoulds.

Lydia should not have gone out that night. Lydia should not have met up with that boy. Lydia should have known how to defend herself. Lydia should still be here. I gave you girls too much freedom, he finally finished with a swipe of his hand. *No more.*

It had been a relief, getting away like that, escaping to the woods with a gun. Her mom was a wreck. And the kids at school stared at her. She'd felt so alien. Lydia had been Chelsey's home planet; without her sister, Chelsey was adrift. But often, Chelsey wondered if her father, if people in general, should spend less time protecting daughters and more time worrying about sons. The dangerous things boys do. How they might be raised differently. She'd mentioned something similar to her father once, and he'd gazed at her hard, then said even harder, *I don't have any sons.*

Now, she opens her eyes and surveys the street, the team, the perfect day about to explode. "I'm ready," she says to Montoya.

He grins, dimples popping in his cheeks, and touches his earpiece. "All teams go."

—

Anticipation loose in her chest, Chelsey and the team pile into and around the edge of a BearCat, a black SWAT van, holding on to metal handles bolted to the sides. Lights turn on along with a siren, and they swarm the farm. The BearCat speeds onto Salt's property, swerving and stopping short of the front door. Teams of five dart left and right to surround the building. Chelsey and Montoya follow SWAT to the front door, rolling up the steps and onto the rotted porch.

An officer pounds his fist against the thin wood of Salt's door. *Bang-bang-bang.* "Lewis Salt. Olympia PD. We have a warrant for your arrest and DNA." Nothing from the other side of the door. Not a sound. A single light flickers above him. Cobwebs and dried-up moths hang from it. There's a soggy couch on the front lawn, haphazardly covered by a blue tarp—mosquitos swarm above water that has collected in the drooping plastic. Half the roof is nearly caving in, and the paint is peeling off the house. Blackberry vines snake around the foundation. All utterly still. Too quiet. Chelsey's nerves ratchet up a notch.

The team uses a battering ram, and the door splinters as it bursts open. Lewis Salt stands in the middle of the living room. He's as dirty as the house. Stained Grateful Dead T-shirt. Threadbare holey jeans. Greasy hair and yellow teeth. Chelsey grimaces, seeing him. "Hands behind your head," the front officer shouts, gun raised.

"I didn't do anything," Salt spits out in a slight southern accent. He folds his arms behind his head. He glances down at his midriff, where a dozen police have trained the red dots of their automatic rifles. "I didn't do anything!" he repeats.

Another team arrives through the back of the house. Salt is completely surrounded.

"On your knees," says Chelsey. She steps forward, fast food wrappers and cigarette butts crunching under her foot.

"I can't . . ." Lewis Salt sways and visibly pales. "I didn't do anything . . . I swear. Oh my god, I'm going to be sick." Then he spews all over the dingy carpet, and vomit splatters Chelsey's boots.

"Ah, shit. You want to cuff him?" Montoya asks Chelsey, keeping his rifle trained on Salt.

Chelsey nods. "I got him." She lowers her gun and sweeps into action, reading Salt his Miranda rights and zip-tying his hands together. The room reeks of puke. The team stands down, and Montoya directs them to start searching the house.

Chelsey squats next to Lewis Salt, wipes her forehead with her forearm, and stares at him. She tilts her head. This is him? This is the guy? Chelsey is . . . unimpressed, disappointed.

"I want my lawyer," Salt huffs, tears streaming down his face. It does not make Chelsey feel sorry for him. She wonders how many times Ellie wept while she was held captive. If Gabby cried while he had his hands around her throat. How many tears did Lydia shed before she died?

"You can have one soon as we get to the station," Chelsey says. "But first, I'm going to need to collect your DNA." She motions a lab tech forward. "Go ahead, be a good boy and open your mouth for me."

He draws up and purses his lips, ready to spit near Chelsey's feet. Chelsey darts forward and squeezes his cheeks. Good thing she's wearing gloves. "Go ahead," she says to the tech. The tech steps forward and circles around Salt's mouth with a sterile swab.

Chelsey straightens and picks through the house. Not much to see. A brown couch with a slice through one of the cushions, stuffing spilling out. A clunky coffee table from the seventies. The walls are bare and stained yellow. She wanders into Salt's bedroom. There is a mattress on the floor with a dingy white sheet twisted at the bottom. She opens a closet door. A belt hangs from a hook. A red bandana is next to it. All the hairs on Chelsey's arms stand up. She flashes to interviewing Ellie in her folks' living room. *I didn't see his face. It was too bright. He wore a bandana*, Ellie had said, then added, *Red. It was red.*

Chelsey shouts for a tech, warmth spreading through her chest, the slow burn of excitement, the heat of relief. She's got him. It is almost over. The tech appears in a white hazmat suit. "Bag this up," she says, pointing to the bandana.

Chapter

SEVENTEEN

"HOW ARE YOU TODAY, ELLIE?" Dr. Cerise Fischer scrawls a heading at the top of her notepad. *Ellie Black, session 2.* It's a bright day, and Cerise has closed the curtains, anticipating Ellie's aversion to lights. A single lamp is on in the corner, its bulb casting a warm yellow glow.

Ellie shifts and lifts a shoulder. Her hair is dirty, unwashed. She has not showered, Cerise mentally notes. "The same."

She smiles at Ellie as if she is an old friend. "Do you still feel as if you're wrapped in cellophane?"

Another shrug. "Sometimes."

She jots a note down on her pad. *Client notes she still feels physically shut down and detached.* "And other times?"

Ellie laces her fingers together, gripping them so tightly that the flesh around her knuckles turns white. "Trapped. Afraid. And that other thing," she slides out. "You know, when you don't know who you are anymore."

"Loss of identity?" Cerise writes another note and underlines it. *Unable to render sense of self.*

"Yeah, I don't know who I am anymore." Ellie covers her eyes with her hands. Cerise has seen this before with other clients, other victims, a gesture of meekness. Shame, utter despair. "I . . . I tried cutting my hair the other day."

"And?"

"I don't know . . . I held the open scissors to my hair and couldn't do it. I just couldn't. I stayed like that until my hand cramped up."

"You mentioned to your mother you weren't allowed to cut your hair," Cerise ventures. "Why is that?" Ellie's jaw works, teeth clenching. She stays mute. Cerise decides to change course. "Your parents tell me you've been seeing more people."

"Just Danny," says Ellie. Quiet ensues once more.

"How did that go?" she gently presses.

"Okay." Ellie pulls the sleeves of her sweatshirt down and fists them. "I mean, not okay. He tried to touch me. But not like that." Ellie's eyes flick, startled, to Cerise.

"Like what?" Cerise carefully controls her expression. She waits patiently for Ellie to elaborate.

"He wanted to hug me, I think. That's all. But I felt totally freaked out." She stops.

"Go on."

"I don't know." A shake of the head. "I want to be touched, but I can't stand it."

"That will come in time. Perhaps you're not ready yet for physical affection." Ellie winces at the last two words. "Be patient with yourself." Cerise pauses to gauge Ellie's reaction.

Ellie squeezes her eyes shut. "New topic, please."

Cerise inhales. "Sure. You haven't seen any other friends since you've been home? Why not?"

Ellie shakes her head and gazes out the window at the endless ocean. The water is calm today. "Um, I didn't have many friends. From before," she qualifies.

"Got it," Cerise says. She sets her notes aside. "I thought you might enjoy some art therapy today. No talking required. Would you be open to that?" Cerise hopes drawing may be easier than speaking. That Ellie will be able to show what she cannot tell.

Ellie pushes hair away from her face. "Sure. I guess."

Cerise beams. "Great."

"You're easy to please," Ellie blurts. Then covers her mouth, horrified. "I shouldn't have said that. Sorry, sorry, sorry," she says, rapid-fire, body tightening as if she's about to be struck.

"Hey, hey," Cerise says. And Ellie calms. "It's okay. That was funny."

"It's just that since coming home, I feel like I'm letting everyone down," Ellie tells her.

"There isn't a right way to heal," Cerise says, and busies herself pulling out art supplies and placing them on the coffee table. Stubby sticks of charcoal, sharp colored pencils, a row of bright oil pastels, a large drawing pad.

"It's nice to feel like I'm doing something right."

"You're doing everything right. I'm going to put some music on, okay? While we listen, I'd like for you to draw something."

Ellie picks up the thick pad, holding it with two hands. "What should I draw?"

Cerise considers for a moment. She thinks about what Ellie said and follows her instinct. "How about what friendship looks like?" Ellie said she did not have many friends before. But what about after? What about those two years she was missing?

"Yeah, okay, I can do that." Ellie takes a jittery breath, picks up a piece of charcoal, and starts to draw.

The hour passes in a blur. Cerise pretends to work on her computer, but she's watching Ellie closely, the way she seems to be lost in memories, almost in a trance. At five minutes till the hour, Cerise clicks off the music, and Ellie jolts upright, pastel loose between her pointer finger and thumb.

"All right, Ellie. Our time is up. Let's see what you've done." Cerise opens her hands, inviting Ellie to show her work. Ellie rips two drawings from the pad and places them on the coffee table.

Cerise uses a finger to rotate the art toward her, careful not to smudge anything. Ellie rubs her hands together, staining her palms with blues, purples, blacks, greens, and yellows from the oil pastels. The colors of bruises and the forest.

Cerise delicately picks up both sheets and puckers her lips. "A field?" She focuses on the drawing in her right hand. Ellie has sketched a line of birch trees, a bloody sunset behind them. "And a . . . ?" Beneath the birch trees is a black void.

"A hole." Ellie scrapes the pads of her fingers. Bits of pastel peel from her skin and fall onto the sage couch.

Unease skitters up Cerise's spine. "This represents friendship to you?" she asks. This picture resembling a grave?

"Um, I guess more love than friendship." Ellie peers down at her knees, then up at Cerise, the word love hanging between them, an empty noose in the air.

"I see," Cerise says. She places the drawing to the side and braces herself for the next. Ellie has used only charcoal on this one. And she's depicted four girls. Three are tall, and one is short. Younger? On the bigger girls, Ellie has drawn a loop around each of their wrists. Chains? Rope? The smaller girl's wrists are bare. The loop noticeably absent. Lastly, all of the girls are depicted with two X's for eyes and a frightened oval for a mouth. Because they are dead? "Is one of these you?" she says, voice low.

Ellie wipes her sweaty palms on the knees of her jeans. "I'm there."

Cerise lets loose a breath. Maybe not dead? But hurt? "And the rest, do they represent real people, too?" A slight crack in Cerise's voice, fear slipping through.

Ellie bobs her head. "They do."

"Will you tell me their names?" Cerise points at the bigger girls.

Ellie's eyelids twitch. She flexes her hands. "I'm . . . something is happening," she rasps, clutching at her chest. The beginning of a panic attack.

Cerise's clinical training kicks in. "Breathe, Ellie. You are safe. You are here, with me, in this room. Come back to me. Ellie?" Cerise says again.

No use. Ellie shakes her head, won't open her eyes. She is lost in a horrid memory.

"Let's try a grounding technique. Can you follow my instructions?" Cerise keeps her tone even and low, her voice seeking to pull Ellie from the dark water. "Push your feet hard into the floor." Cerise sees Ellie's toes flex through the thin fabric of her shoe. "Good. Feel the couch beneath you." Ellie's hands skirt the couch, and the trembling in her body eases. "That's it. Notice your spine and how it supports you. Acknowledge that you are struggling. Perhaps you are anxious, sad, or reliving a painful memory . . . but just as you feel pain, there is a solid body around that pain that you can control. Now open your eyes." Ellie does. "Tell me five things that you see in this office."

"Chair, yellow sticky notes, a lamp with a gold base, a silver pen . . ." Ellie trails off and focuses on the drawing on the paper. Her mouth moves but no words come out.

"What is it, Ellie? What would you like to say?"

"My friends, I see my friends." She reaches out and thumbs the girls' images, sadness on her face. The kind reserved for things loved and lost—people who are gone.

"They were your friends?" Cerise asks.

"No, better than friends." Ellie touches the loops around the girls' wrists, then her fingers skirt to the fourth girl, the shorter girl, reverence in her touch. "Sisters. They were my sisters."

Chapter

EIGHTEEN

CHELSEY FOLDS LEWIS SALT INTO the back of a squad car, then shuts herself up front next to Montoya. The engine purrs to a start, and lights flash. Montoya glances back at Salt and says, "You like CCR?" Salt doesn't say anything. His hands are cuffed and pinned behind him. "Creedence Clearwater Revival? The greatest band of all time," he clarifies. "You a fan?"

"Not my first choice," Salt spits out, snot trailing from a nostril, hair hanging in his face.

"That's too bad. You're going away somewhere where you aren't going to have a lot of choices. Better get used to it now." He switches on "Have You Ever Seen the Rain?," adjusting the fade to blare on the back speakers. As they drive off, Chelsey grins to herself. Thrilled at her well-executed plan.

———

At the Olympia PD station, Chelsey eyes Lewis Salt through a two-way mirror.

"Still not talking?" Montoya stands beside her, a paper cup full of yellow liquid in his hand—he prefers Mountain Dew over coffee. He's changed out of his tactical gear and is back in his T-shirt and jeans, badge hanging from his neck by a chain. Chelsey is in her civilian clothes, too—a flannel shirt and jeans with her badge clipped to her waist.

"Hasn't said a word other than he didn't do anything." Chelsey crosses her arms. Her patience is wearing thin. It's been five hours. She wants a full confession. Nothing less will do.

"Well, I've got more bad news," Montoya says.

Chelsey glares at him. A muscle under her eye ticks. She is tired. That is all. "What?"

He sets his cup down and holds his phone out to Chelsey. "They didn't find anything after raiding the rest of Salt's property." Grainy body cam footage plays on his phone. The police sweep the dilapidated barn. A flashlight beam crosses a rotting hayloft, a dirt floor, and then settles on a trapdoor.

"Here," the officer shouts. Another officer comes into view and yanks the door open. Guns poised, the police rush down the dusty stairs into the room.

"Empty," the officer announces, camera spinning around. "Nothing down here except some shelves and an old jar of . . ." He picks it up. ". . . pickles. No evidence of human inhabitants." A pause. "Hey, Bo. I'll give you fifty bucks if you eat one of these pickles . . ." Montoya shuts off the phone.

"He could have cleaned it," Chelsey says. Might make sense. Ellie escapes; Salt is spooked, scrubs his property.

"He could have," says Montoya evenly. "Dogs are on their way. They'll pick up if your girls were there."

She reviews the evidence in her mind. The blue station wagon. The red bandana. The homestead in the middle of nowhere. "Salt could have a second piece of land. Somewhere else where he kept them," Chelsey thinks out loud.

"I'll see if I can dig up anything."

Chelsey tilts her head. Her instincts scream Salt is involved. It's a hunch. Like the one that cop followed two counties over. A three-year-old kid went missing from her mom's house. The parents were fighting over custody. They searched the dad's place. Nothing. But then . . . the cop noticed some floorboards that didn't seem to match the others. They'd found the little girl stashed under there, curled up with an iPad and headphones. "The DNA isn't in yet," she says. No point in folding now, not when Chelsey still has some cards to play.

"Welp." Montoya glances at the clock on the wall. "DNA will take a couple days. Your best hope right now is getting him to talk. We've got enough to hold him for forty-eight . . . scratch that—forty-three hours."

"Good." Chelsey lifts her chin at Salt through the glass. "I'm not done with him yet."

———

The defense attorney assigned to Lewis Salt doesn't show until five p.m. "Sorry," she says, buzzing into the precinct, introducing herself to Chelsey and handing off her card in a whirl. "Full day in court," she finishes. She wears ivory pearls in her ears, a simple brown blazer, a matching skirt, and nude heels. She stops at the two-way mirror and peers through it at Lewis Salt. "You have him in there this whole time?" She checks her watch. "The raid was at ten a.m. Seven hours in restraints?"

"We gave him some food and water and a bathroom break," Chelsey defends.

A frown. "What's the charge?"

"He was brought in on suspicion of kidnapping, rape, and murder . . ."

The attorney arches a carefully plucked eyebrow. "And?"

Chelsey sighs and scratches her forehead. She has to tell it all. "His property didn't turn up anything, but we did find a red bandana that matches descriptions from a vic. Plus his car, the make and model, are the same as the one seen on CCTV footage of the crime scenes."

"Coincidental," the attorney pushes out.

"Maybe." Chelsey shrugs. "Dogs are combing the property right now.

And," she adds with emphasis, "we found DNA connected to a body found a year ago on a sweatshirt the victim was wearing. The DNA was a partial match for Salt's dad, who's serving time. We took a sample from Salt. The lab is running it right now. If it's a match . . ." Chelsey makes it sound like she's more confident than she is.

The defense attorney pinches her nose. They both know what will happen if the DNA comes in as Salt's. It's all pretty much a done deal—a trial with a guilty verdict, a lengthier sentence.

"You get him to talk and I'll put in a good word with the ADA," Chelsey says. She needs Salt to talk. This is true. And she will speak with the ADA if he does. Also true. But not for Salt. For Ellie. For Gabby's grandmother. If the DNA is a match, if the case is open and shut. Chelsey won't push for a courtroom; she'll push for a plea deal. To spare Ellie and Gabby's grandmother. Who don't want to relive it. *Your girls*, Montoya had said earlier. But he had it wrong. Ellie and Gabby do not belong to Chelsey. Chelsey belongs to Ellie and Gabby.

vii

HEAVY RAIN FELL AGAINST THE plastic sheeting; the outside was blurry but distinguishable. In the sky, a bird flew. A bald eagle I recognized from its flight pattern, its glorious wingspan. So high the eagle could see everything. The concrete buildings we inhabited spread across half an acre. A bunker where we slept. An armory resembling a silo. The battery that David occupied with its shell room and officer quarters. The compound had been erected during World War II in the event Japanese submarines made it to shore.

Inside, David held a Bible flipped open. He read from Psalms. "'My closest friend whom I trusted, the one who ate my bread, had lifted his heel against me.'" He shut the Bible with a thump. The air was hot and humid with twice-breathed air. "We have a traitor in our midst."

Charity, Hope, and I kneeled next to one another, silent. Serendipity stood off to the side, her arms crossed. A faint glimmer of fear on her face. I'd never seen Serendipity afraid before. My stomach dropped.

The plastic sheeting opened, and Michael stepped through. He sauntered to David's side. I kept my eyes downcast. I only remember seeing the tips of his dirt-crusted boots and the seeds as they sprinkled onto the hard earth near my knee. I felt Hope shudder beside me. Our precious seeds.

"Did you think I would not know? That I would not find out?" David ground out. "Look at me!"

Michael pinched my cheeks and forced my gaze upward. I tasted blood in my mouth. "Whose idea was it?" David asked, eyes darting back and forth between us.

Nobody spoke. I made a choking noise. Michael let go of my cheeks. David peered down at me. "Speak."

I hung my head.

Then David laughed. A sick chuckle. "I see," he said. "Pick them up," he commanded, nodding at the seeds. I glanced at Hope, and I shouldn't have. Michael's hand flashed out and connected with her cheek. "I said pick them up," David repeated.

Hope held her cheek as we gathered the seeds. Once they were in our palms, David marched us outside to the fire. "Throw them in," he commanded.

One by one, we cast the seeds into the fire. Some of them stuck to my hand, and I had to scrape them off. David watched us, shadows and darkness ricocheting off his face. "Foolish girls," he said as the seeds turned black and into ash. "Foolish, foolish girls."

I squeezed my eyes shut, wishing myself somewhere else. Wishing to be a bird or a bug and just fly away. Warmth brushed my wrist. David had hooked his finger under the bracelet Hope had made for me. "Pretty," he said. "And matching." His gaze drifted to Hope's and Charity's wrists. "Those go into the fire, too."

Tears began to slide down my face as I worked on the knot. I dropped the friendship bracelet into the fire. Hope and Charity did the same with theirs. More tears came, a gentle heaving as we watched it all burn.

It's hard to remember the in-between spaces. What happened next, some of it is a blank. The tick of a second.

A blink.

I was curled up on my bed when the metal door creaked open, and

David entered. Michael was with him. The room seemed to shrink, and my body tightened.

David sat on the edge of the bed and patted the seat beside him. His knuckles were bruised and bloody. I scooted forward until my legs dangled off the side. Michael guarded the door, dogs at his feet, tongues dangling. A puppy was there, too. One I named Star because of the white mark on her forehead. Michael had taken the rest of the pups away one day and had come back alone.

"Whose idea was it, the seeds?" David asked quietly, softly, like the hiss of a snake. "And before you answer, I already know. Tell me the truth, and then we will move on."

My nails bit into my palms, almost drawing blood. What had Charity and Hope said? That it was my idea? I hung my head, unsure what to do. What game was he playing? What vile trick? Or maybe he spoke the truth. I was so confused. David liked to set little traps for us, and when we fell into them, he would be there at the rescue.

"I'm hurt. I give you all of this. Food. Shelter. And how am I repaid?" He squeezed my knee. Hard. "Michael found the seeds in your room. Are you surprised? Did you believe we wouldn't be keeping an eye on you?" His words wrapped around my neck, a noose growing ever tighter. "My father used to sweep my room. And it was for the best. I am looking out for you. My job is to ensure you do not stray from the path." He sighed. I wrapped my arms around my middle, unable to stop shaking. "I have seen the way you smile at each other. You like Charity and Hope." His touch softened. "It's not your fault. You are very desperate in your need to be loved, aren't you? But they don't love you like I do. And they are not your friends. Friends wouldn't have told me it was all your idea—"

"No," I ground out, refusing to believe him. My fingers searched for the friendship bracelet. But it was gone, burned in the fire. The greatest trick the devil ever played wasn't convincing others he didn't exist, but that your friends were your enemies.

"I'm not even sure they like you," he finished. "Let's try this again. Whose idea were the seeds?"

I crumbled, scrunched my eyes closed for a moment. Thought about what I should do. "It was all my idea. Planting and growing them by the creek."

"Where did you get the seeds?" His eyes changed, the shade darkening, the gaze of someone who knew they were powerful. Who knew they were in control. Who knew they had won.

I should have stopped there. I should have sacrificed myself. I should have fought. That's what we're supposed to do, isn't it? Never surrender.

Do you ever think about the tiny moments in time? The ones that take seconds? The ones you'd go back and do anything to unravel? This was my moment. The one I regret most, more than taking a piss in that abandoned parking lot, more than fighting with Danny. It's a tangled black ball inside me, always sitting in my gut.

I opened my mouth, ready to tell the truth, to take the fall. "Gabby found the seeds, but it was my idea to grow them. Please don't punish any of them—" I stopped abruptly, realizing the word, the name I'd let slip. The name I swore I would never utter out loud. Hope. I had said her real name, Gabby. A plea lodged in my throat as the lock on my door clicked into place.

Blink.

I woke to a door opening and slamming shut. Then a scream. A pain-filled cry.

"Please, David." Hope's voice was on the other side of the wall. I crossed the room and banged on the door.

"Hope," I pounded out. "Hope."

"You were my golden girl," he said.

"David," came Serendipity's wary voice. "She said she's sorry—"

"Shut up!" David yelled. *Thump.* The muted sound of a fist hitting flesh.

It quieted. I scooted my bed under the window and stood on it, peering over the ledge. They came around the corner. Michael's hand was locked around Hope's arm, dragging her. She fought back, but it was useless, like closing your eyes against a tidal wave. David followed with the dogs, their mouths foaming, malice rising. Serendipity knelt in the dirt, rocking and holding her face. I think she'd gone away like I sometimes did. My puppy Star trotted across the dirt and lay down near the bars. I curled my fingers around the cold metal, and Star licked the salt from my knuckles. "Hope," I said. Over and over again until they disappeared.

Then it was silent.

I banged my head against the bars. Star whimpered and ran away. I yelled until my shouts turned into nothing. Then I built a cave inside myself, crawled in, and prayed for forgiveness.

Blink.

Chapter

NINETEEN

THE INTERROGATION ROOM IS A windowless white-walled box with a two-way mirror. Chelsey takes her time settling in at the metal table across from Salt and his defense attorney.

"Mr. Salt," Chelsey starts. "Let's talk about Ellie Black."

Salt turns to his attorney, who gives him a subtle chin dip of permission. They'd spoken for twenty minutes before letting Chelsey in.

Lewis Salt shifts, chains around his wrists rattling. "Never heard of her."

Chelsey studies Salt's impassive face. "How about Gabrielle Barlowe?"

Salt taps his fingers against the table, bits of grime cling to the corners of his fingernails. "Doesn't ring a bell."

She flips open the file and withdraws a photograph of the University of Washington sweatshirt spread out on a metal table. "A week ago, Ellie Black appeared wearing this sweatshirt. The blood on it garnered a familial match to your dad. We're running your DNA right now—"

Salt sneers, leans forward as close as he can get to Chelsey's face. "It won't be a match. You ain't got shit on me."

A knock sounds at the door. Montoya enters, lays a piece of paper face down in front of Chelsey, and exits. Chelsey scoots the paper to the edge of the table and flips it up to read it like a poker hand. *Dogs didn't find anything.* She folds the note in half. No evidence of Ellie or Gabby on Salt's property. He could have a second property, she thinks, but feels less convinced now. If not Lewis Salt, then who?

"Bad news?" Salt's face oozes with a smile.

"I'm just wondering." Chelsey composes herself. A radiator against the wall clicks on, stirring warm air into the tiny room. "I'm just thinking . . ." she says aloud, allowing the guilty threads she'd bound up Lewis Salt with to unravel, trail away, lead her in a different direction.

The first time Chelsey's father brought her to the woods, they didn't do any hunting. They'd camped and spent their days driving logging roads, parking alongside clear cuts with binoculars to find deer or elk among the severed trees—a twisted version of *Where's Waldo?* Once, she'd even spotted a starving cougar panting in the underbrush. What is she not seeing here? She narrows in on Salt's hands, his fingers stained yellow from nicotine, then up to his wrists to a couple of tattoos. Music notes, a set of baby footprints with a date—February 1st, 2013.

All the hairs on Chelsey's arms stand up. "You got a kid, Salt? That didn't come up in your background check." She flips through his file to make sure.

Salt sneers at her. He tucks his sleeve back down in a protective gesture. "Her ma wouldn't put me on her birth certificate."

"*Her* mother?" Chelsey chokes out, her words bending the air. "You have a daughter?" Everything Chelsey was sure of quickly shatters, glass splintering to reflect a new distorted picture. What if . . . what if the blood on the sweatshirt *was* from another victim? Kinsley had said there was a mixture of DNA, female and male. She'd considered it once, outside of the Fishtrap, that there could be another vic, but then she'd landed on Lewis Salt. On his rural home, his barn with a cellar, and his blue station wagon.

Salt's gaze flickers. "I'm not talking until you tell me what this is all about."

Chelsey regroups and thinks for a moment. What is the best course of action here? How much should she divulge? Interrogation is a carefully choreographed fan dance of revealing and concealing the truth. "I'm investigating an abduction case. DNA from blood on a sweatshirt the victim was found in is a partial match to yours. I thought—"

"You thought like father, like son," he cuts in. "Because my daddy is a rapist, I'd be one, too."

Chelsey blinks and keeps her voice even. "You match a profile. Along with some other key evidence that fit." Salt squints his eyes, narrowing them at Chelsey. And now, Chelsey thinks about all the ways people can be wrong. A testament to assumptions. Lewis Salt is innocent. "When was the last time you saw your daughter?" Chelsey continues.

Salt turns a cheek and crosses his arms. "I haven't seen her for six years. I left her in the car to go into the casino"—he sticks up a finger—"once. I was only in there for an hour. Her ma didn't let me see her after that. She took me to court. I lost custody." He wags the same finger and pushes it into the table. "And a year and a half ago . . . a year and a half ago, cops showed up at my doorstep asking me all sorts of questions about Willa. If I've seen her. If I know where she is. Her ma reported her missing, I guess. So excuse me if I don't want to talk to any more cops. You all are the same. Harassing innocent men while the real criminals go free."

Missing. The word claws into Chelsey's brain. She works to stay still, even though everything inside of her is exploding. "How old is your daughter?"

"Willa," he says, "was seven when she went missing. She'd be nine now."

So young. Chelsey swallows hard. This is the first piece that doesn't fit. Why would Ellie's abductor take a seven-year-old? She focuses on the questions she can answer instead of the ones she can't. "If she's missing, why isn't her DNA in the system?"

Salt looks at Chelsey for a long moment. "My ex gave samples. Cops collected mine. You tell me why." Irritation floods his voice.

Chelsey nods, knowing all too well. With no suspect, DNA can take up to a year for a result. She pictures the racks and racks of rape kits in endless precincts that go unprocessed. Because of the cost. The manpower. Because she works for an institution that was not built for women or their interests. How much is a girl's life worth? "We can fix that." Chelsey fidgets with Salt's file. "In light of this new revelation, it's now my belief that your daughter may also be a victim of this man's."

"Finally, you're getting something right." He crosses his arms again and looks over Chelsey's shoulder at the wall. "I'm as innocent as the day I was born."

"Noted," Chelsey clips out. "Now, please, tell me about your daughter. Everything."

For a moment, the room is deathly still. "Not much to tell. Like I said, I haven't seen her since she was two. Her name is Willa. She was a sweet baby. Had a birthmark on her cheek. Red." He circles the upper part of his face and under his eye.

"What do you know about the investigation? What happened to her?"

Salt taps his fingers against the table. "She was out riding her bike and was snatched off the street. At least, that's what my ex told me. If you ask me, her ma's boyfriend had something to do with it."

Chelsey has heard enough. She does not need Salt anymore. She rises from the table. Thanks the defense attorney but does not spare Salt a second glace. Montoya is in the room next door. He's watched the whole thing through the two-way mirror.

"I'm going to need a photograph of Willa," she says.

"Already on it," he says, phone in hand.

Chelsey's heart beats double time. "And her DNA, whatever they collected when she first went missing. We need it pulled from the lab to compare against the blood found on Ellie's sweatshirt."

"I'll email over the case file soon as I have it."

Chelsey walks to the corner and presses her palms to her eyes until she sees stars. She is angry. Confused. A third girl. Why wouldn't Ellie tell her about Willa? What reason would she have to hide it?

She drives back to Coldwell in an agitated fog. Halfway there, Montoya sends two photos of Willa. Chelsey pulls over at a rest stop to stare at them. The first is a school picture. Willa smiles for the camera, red birthmark on her cheek scrunched like an un-bloomed rose. The next is Willa on a playground, hanging from a set of monkey bars, looking like the best days of childhood—blessed, beautiful, unbroken. Waiting to be carried home.

viii

I GUESS YOU'RE PROBABLY WONDERING about the next girl. Because there is always another girl, right? A girl waiting to be taken. To be swept away. I'll tell you about her. How she came after. In the winter. When everything was dead and cold. How she was blazing. Bright. Hope renewed. A reason to live. My path to salvation.

—

After David killed Hope, I was locked in my room all day. Right about sunset, keys jangled, and the door opened. Serendipity stood at the entrance. Her right cheek swollen and nearly black with bruises. She wore a holey sweater, yarn unspooling at the left cuff.

"I brought you some food." She stepped in, a piece of bread in her hands. The smell of yeast mixed with the scent of gasoline—a few hours before, David had burned the little patch of land where our Queen Anne's lace had grown. Tucked under Serendipity's arm was a stack of clothes. A University of Washington sweatshirt, jeans, socks, and a pair of running shoes half a size too big. Hope's things. "And these," she said, setting it all on the bed. "I thought you might like to have them."

I crawled across the bed and looked up at Serendipity. "Help me."

"The bread is fresh from a bakery nearby," she said, back rigid. "Michael brought it today."

I sat on my knees, beseeching. "Look at what he did to you."

She ghosted a hand across her cheek, letting it land in a nervous jumble at the back of her head where the hair was thinning and falling out. She smiled warily. "David hasn't been himself lately. You can't imagine the stress he's under."

"He's going to kill you someday. He's going to kill all of us." My stomach lurched. Tears bubbled. "Just close your eyes for a few moments, and I'll walk right out of here. You could come with me."

A flicker. "Oh, I couldn't leave." She lowered her voice. "You have no idea how much David has sacrificed for me, how much he needs me." She stopped, a thought crinkling her brow. "Sometimes I rehearse what I'm going to say to him," she quietly confessed. "You might try that." She clucked her tongue and shook her head. "Look at your nails." I'd raked them against the walls and broken them. "David won't like that."

Looking back, I understand now. It came down to cages. Mine was a forest, dogs, angry men. Serendipity's was dependence. But back then, I didn't get it. "Fuck you." Anger jumped in my throat. "You're just like him."

Serendipity's mouth slackened. "I'm not."

The air in the room changed, expanding with a third person. "Am I interrupting something?" David asked.

Serendipity shifted. "I was just bringing some food and clothes . . ."

David beckoned Serendipity forward. He whispered something in her ear. She collapsed in little sobs, and he held her, kissing her temple, smoothing her fine greasy hair. He cupped her cheeks, and she winced at the light touch. "I hate that I did this to you." He let her go. "Give me a moment?"

Serendipity nodded and scurried off. I watched David from the corner. He stared at the ceiling and sighed long. At last, he crouched in front of me and grasped my chin. A whine escaped from the back of my throat. Had he heard me ask Serendipity to help me escape? "This is a hard day for everyone." His eyes were cold and dark, like deep space. I could still hear Hope's keening. *Please, David.* "Hope was . . . well . . ." He dropped his hand and faux-grinned. A chastised schoolboy. "I have an illness when it comes to girls like her. All of you girls, actually, with your smiles like weapons, making promises and breaking them . . ." He trailed off. "It doesn't matter. I have much to atone for. I take full responsibility. I must be more careful. You all have me wrapped around your little fingers, don't you? What can I say? I'm just a boy, after all." He stopped. Sobered. "I have learned my lesson. And I hope you have learned yours, too. My love has limits. Do not forget." He shifted and squeezed my thighs. My skin tickled as if beetles were swarming it. "You can never rely too much on others. Hope was a crutch. I have set us both free. You'll thank me one day."

After he left, I held Hope's sweatshirt against my cheek. I could still smell her, see her. I slipped on the clothes—the jeans, the shoes, the sweatshirt. Outside, my body wouldn't stop trembling, but inside, I was still. That was what David did. He broke you down until you were nothing. Empty and waiting for him to fill you up. I forced pieces of bread into my mouth. The jeans had mud stains on the knees. Other than that, the clothes were in good condition. Clean and warm.

The bloodstains would come later.

—

I woke in the wee hours of the morning to a cry. My body was stiff. Weak. I listened. Nothing. I couldn't hear anything but the night—trees caught in the wind, chirping crickets, an occasional owl.

The cry came again. High-pitched. Unnatural. Human. My face turned automatically toward the thin wail in the distance. Again it came, a gentle keening. My fists clenched and unclenched and clenched again. My skin grew clammy. The voice was feminine. Young. One of the dogs barked. Far away, the girl cried. And I cried with her. Tears slipped down my cheeks. I let them fall into the grooves of the stained mattress.

David had abducted someone else.

———

Two weeks passed, and the cries faded. I tried not to think about why. I was almost asleep when the metal door opened. I backed to the corner and drew my legs to my chest.

Michael didn't say anything as he threw the new girl in. She huddled on the floor, a pile of bones with a mop of maple-colored hair, dressed in a purple shirt and pink corduroys.

"Hey," I whispered after the lock clicked. Her shirt had kittens on it. I nudged her shoulder. Her head turned. Hair hung in one of her eyes, big soft brown eyes. She closed them tight. Her nose was bruised and gushing blood. Underneath Hope's sweatshirt, I wore only a bra, but I slipped off the sweatshirt anyway and handed it to the girl, gently pressing it against her nose. Blood soaked the front of the sweatshirt. "What's your name?" She didn't answer me. She was so tiny, so much younger than I was.

I told her my new name.

Silence for a while. The bleeding waned, and I put the sweatshirt back on. She started quaking. Massive, uncontrollable tremors. "You've got to calm down," I told her. She did the opposite. The shaking grew worse, and then she started to hum. A soft buzz that reminded me of a beehive Hope had shown me once. She'd pointed out the female worker bees and explained that they were sterile. Their only purpose was to collect nectar and protect the hive. After a worker bee stung something, it died. Nature's suicide bomber.

"Listen, just breathe. You're going to make yourself sick. Please." I looked down at my hands, small and incapable. "You want to hear a story?" What stories did I like when I was that small? I couldn't think of any. But I was desperate to get her to calm down. And I guess I thought the more I talked, the more space I would fill up until there wouldn't be any more room for her sadness and fear.

I'd scratched constellations on my wall, thinking I could chart the stars and calculate the distance from the compound to home. Foolish thoughts. I told her about Ursa Major, the Great Bear, whose body in the heavens contains thousands of bright galaxies. "We're just a speck of dust among them," I said.

I explained how the Great Bear turned around the pole. How she was a watcher, a keeper, and the only animal the ancient Greeks believed could weather the solitude and the cold. The heaving of the girl's chest slowed. She grew still. I moved on to Ursa Minor, the Lesser Bear, the speaking constellation. Also known as Little Bear. This time I did touch her ear. She didn't flinch or move away. "She holds Polaris, the North Star, in her tail," I said. She looked up at me. There was a birthmark on her cheek, red and small, the kiss of a strawberry. I let my mouth curve up into a comforting smile. "Hey, there you are. How old are you?"

She held up seven fingers. Charity and Hope had never mentioned David abducting anyone so young before.

Big tears spilled from her eyes, carving tracks down her dirty cheeks. She dove into my arms. She smelled like urine and unwashed hair. I welcomed her and felt my world tunnel, my purpose change. She laid her head on my chest, right between my breasts, as if I were her mother. I asked her if she was tired. And she said yes. I helped her lie down on the bed.

I stripped off her socks and rubbed her feet, holding them against my belly to warm them. Then I carefully replaced her socks, giving her toes a gentle squeeze as I did. I tucked her head under my arm and called her "little bear."

Up until then, I'd still thought of escape. I didn't after that night. I made a list of things I would do to keep her safe. The list was short. It contained one word: anything. I didn't even know her name. But I knew she needed me. And need is such a powerful thing.

In hindsight, this was part of David's plan—to bind me to the compound with a string so tight it would cut off my circulation to the outside world. It worked.

The sun was beginning to rise when she finally spoke. Her voice was small and hoarse, a razor blade against my skin. "I was riding my bike," she said. "They called me Grace. But that's not my name. I'm Willa."

I squeezed her frail shoulders, then I fetched a file from the windowsill and began fixing up her hands. I told her how we were supposed to keep our nails, long but rounded. I told her Grace was a beautiful name. I told her to forget what she used to be called. We would never speak it again. We were a family now. We had so much to look forward to together.

TWENTY

IT IS DRIZZLING WHEN CHELSEY parks outside the Blacks' house. Kat's car is missing from the driveway. Jimmy's truck, too.

Willa Adams. The name tears through Chelsey. A little girl. Only seven years old when she was taken, nine now, if she's still alive. Willa is missing, could still be out there. Urgent isn't a strong enough word for what Chelsey feels. Chaotic. Desperate. Electric with fear.

Chelsey swallows back the taste of metallic dread. She is in unprecedented territory. Ellie is a victim. But she might also be a witness to crimes against other girls. The words *proceed with caution* blink inside Chelsey's mind. Gabby is dead and gone. But Willa is still out there. Willa could still be alive. Willa could still have a chance. Everything has shifted for Chelsey now. Willa is riding in the front seat. Ellie in the back.

Inside Ellie's home, a light is on in the living room, the telltale glow of a television—through the crack in the curtains. Chelsey texts Ellie: **I NEED TO SPEAK TO YOU. I'M OUTSIDE YOUR HOUSE. YOU HOME?**

The light clicks off, the television, too. Well, then. Chelsey's phone chimes. A text from Ellie says: **SORRY, NOT HOME. WITH MY MOM.**

Why do people lie? The reasons are varied and wide. To protect someone. To protect themselves emotionally or physically. To win something,

179

a reward of some type. To keep a secret. To avoid humiliation or embarrassment. To exert power or control. To earn admiration. Or to avoid punishment.

Chelsey fires up the car. Ellie might be withholding something on purpose. And it makes Chelsey suspicious. It makes Chelsey want to dig even faster. Faster and faster. Until the dirt has been wiped from these girls' eyes, purged from their mouths.

—

Over the years, Chelsey has uncovered many people's secrets. She has searched homes, mansions, and trailers; cleared out vehicles of all sorts, littered with garbage or polished with a cashmere cloth—all of it tells her something, but what tells her the most? Other people.

The sun is a pale slip battling storm clouds when she enters Dr. Cerise Fischer's office. She presses the button, alerting the therapist that someone is in her waiting room. A full five minutes pass, and Chelsey paces the small area. She's rubbing the leaf of a fake plant between her fingers when Dr. Fischer's office door finally opens.

"Detective Calhoun," Dr. Fischer says, surprise but also welcome in her voice.

"Sorry to barge in like this," Chelsey says.

"That's all right. I'm between clients. Come on in."

Chelsey follows Dr. Fischer into her office. It's an intimate-looking place. Soft couch. Breezy curtains. Subtle art.

"Do you mind if I eat while we chat?" Dr. Fischer pulls a salad in Tupperware from a small fridge.

"Of course not," Chelsey says.

"All right, then." Dr. Fischer sits behind her desk and drizzles dressing onto the green mess. Chelsey can't remember the last time she ate anything leafy. "So, what brings you here?"

"Elizabeth Black." Chelsey sits on Dr. Fischer's couch, perched on a lumpy edge.

Dr. Fischer's mouth tightens a fraction. "Chelsey."

"Cerise," Chelsey counters.

"I can't tell you anything—"

"Yes, I know, confidentiality." Chelsey waves it off.

Dr. Fischer arches a brow at Chelsey, spears some lettuce, and slips it into her mouth, chewing delicately. "I'm sorry you came all this way for nothing. I can't help you."

Chelsey considers her next move. The technique she might use. She opts for the truth, casting it out like a fishing line. Will Cerise bite? "I stopped by Ellie's house before coming here. I texted her to see if we could talk, and Ellie pretended that she wasn't home."

Dr. Fischer stills. "Oh?"

Chelsey nods slowly. She has Dr. Fischer's interest, notices something troubled in the doctor's gaze. "She doesn't want to participate in the investigation anymore."

"That's too bad." Dr. Fischer stabs at a piece of carrot. "But understandable, I suppose."

Chelsey nods. Lots of victims decline to help police. The criminal justice system is its own mountain to climb. For every one thousand cases of reported rape only seven lead to felony convictions. She gets it, she does, but . . . "Ellie's a bit of a cipher, isn't she?" Chelsey is missing something. A hunch again. She looks up at Cerise. "I can't put my finger on what it is. But something isn't right with Ellie."

Behind Dr. Fischer, the heat kicks on. Warm air stirs the room. "I wouldn't say that. I would say that she's a different person now. You cannot expect Ellie to be who she was before." Dr. Fischer's face is sympathetic. "Trauma changes people."

Chelsey glances down at her boots. She's tracked small bits of dirt onto the braided rug. She turns back to Dr. Fischer, showing some of her sorrow on purpose. Letting the worry darken her expression. The fan dance—that is what she is doing now. "There's been a recent development related to Ellie's case." Outside, there is the steady murmur of waves, of seagulls, of the coast. Ebbing and flowing. "The situation has become pressing. The sweatshirt Ellie was found in belonged to a girl who disappeared five years ago, Gabrielle Barlowe. Her body was discovered, strangled, about a year and a half ago." Dr. Fischer flinches. "There was blood on the sweatshirt. I assumed it was Gabrielle's, but it wasn't."

"It wasn't?" Dr. Fischer's expression becomes strained. Chelsey notes tiredness around the doctor's eyes, too. Chelsey isn't the only one worn down by her job. Why do women do this? Why are they conditioned to give and give and give? She thinks about those seven cases out of one thousand. Maybe one day it will be eight, then nine, then ten. Small bites are all she'll ever be able to take. And they will have to do. She'll never be full.

Chelsey shakes her head. She makes her voice as flat and smooth as polished wood. "No. The DNA isn't in yet but I strongly believe the blood belonged to another girl. A girl who is still missing. Her name is Willa Adams. She would now be nine years old."

Dr. Fischer's hand goes to her abdomen as if to calm herself, her swirling stomach.

"I believe Ellie has interacted with Willa. That she knows something about Willa and is hiding it, whether by fear or by design. Has Ellie mentioned other girls to you?"

Dr. Fischer glances at a file on her desk, the name ELIZABETH BLACK written on it. Chelsey can make out the edge of a paper inside, black crayon or charcoal scribbled on it. A drawing? "I hesitate to say anything, but in light of this news . . . She did draw something our last session . . ."

"Show me." Chelsey leans forward.

Dr. Fischer opens the folder and places the contents in front of Chelsey. She was right. They are drawings. Two of them. One of a field with holes in the ground. The other of four people. Girls, Chelsey thinks. One girl is smaller than the rest. Most likely Willa. "I'm sorry, I should have called you right away but I was going to discuss the drawing with Ellie next session and urge her to speak to you about it herself. If I'd known . . ." Dr. Fischer trailed off.

"It's okay," Chelsey says, but she keeps her eyes locked on the girls. On their open mouths. Locked in perpetual screams.

Chapter

TWENTY-ONE

DANNY LEANS AGAINST THE DOORJAMB, appraising Ellie and her bedroom. Piles of clothes. Crumpled pieces of paper. Bed stripped of linens. She sits crisscrossed on the bare mattress, frowning at the mess, the heaps of clothing like an infection spreading. She's wearing baggy sweatpants and a thin T-shirt. Not her own. Most likely Jimmy's.

Danny clears his throat. Ellie startles. "Sorry," he says. Danny is supposed to be working at the Fishtrap, a double shift. But Ellie called and asked him to come over. Time seemed to unwind itself then, and Danny imagined what it would be like to choose work over Ellie again. He will spend the rest of his life trying to not make the same mistake twice, so he called to tell his mom he was sick, couldn't come in.

"You doing some redecorating?" he says to Ellie now, gesturing toward the chaos and trying to lighten the mood.

She swings toward him, letting her legs dangle over the side of the bed. Her feet are bare, toes unpainted. "I tried on all my clothes this afternoon. Nothing seems to fit anymore. This whole room isn't right." Her mouth twitches, pinned somewhere between a laugh and a cry. "When did the world become such an unfriendly place?"

Danny deposits his keys on her dresser next to a postcard of birch trees. His eyes linger on the sleeve of a David Bowie record. At the man with cat

185

eyes, hand pressed to his chest, another hand gesturing up into the air. The first time he listened to that album with Ellie, they smoked weed. Brains cloudy and smiles stretched wide, they'd stared at the black-and-white cover and read the quote at the bottom over and over. *Tomorrow belongs to those who can hear it coming.*

"Bad day?" he asks.

She raises her eyebrows. "Is there any other kind?"

"I won't deny it. I've had more bad than good."

Ellie stares at the rain out the window. "You think it will ever get better?"

"Time heals all wounds."

"Bullshit." At last, a smile.

One side of his mouth curls up, too. He circles a pile of clothes and sits on his haunches in front of Ellie, careful not to touch her. "It's total bullshit. The wounds will always be there, won't they? They're like a boulder strapped to your back right now. Something that feels impossible to carry. But someday, they'll change shape. They'll become pebbles in your pocket. It won't be so overwhelming then."

"You read that somewhere?"

"My mom makes us put on *Dr. Phil* every afternoon at the bar."

"You don't believe that, do you?"

He hangs his head. "I think I have to." His foot is tangled on a sky-blue hoodie. Suddenly he is caught in the crosshairs of a memory. Ellie was wearing that sweatshirt, and they'd been walking around on Main Street. He'd just won her a stuffed elephant from the arcade when the sky opened up. They ducked into the Seaglass Museum. No one was behind the counter, and they wandered, hand in hand, far into the exhibits. In front of a case of blue bottles, he placed his hand on her hip, turned her to face him. A peck was how it started. But then she'd cupped his cheeks, and the kiss deepened. She'd pressed against him, and he'd been hard. They knocked into a display, rattling glass, and were invited to leave by the owner, a man who looked like he should be on a ship rather than stuck on dry land.

All of a sudden, Ellie's hand is on his knee. He stays still in that awkward squatting position. "Okay?"

"Okay," she says.

He shifts to sit, losing Ellie for a moment, but then she returns, slipping from the bed next to him. She places her hand on top of his. Tentative. Unsure. Slowly, he turns his palm upright. Ellie's fingers fall between his, and they interlace hands. "You sure this is okay?" he asks. Thinking about desire. How it changes. How the only thing he wants is not to hurt Ellie. Because you do not hurt someone you love. Or you try not to.

Ellie rests her head on his shoulder. "Tell me something good."

He's stiff, afraid to move. "Something good?" He feels her nod against him, the razor sharpness of her cheekbone. He looks out the window and starts to speak. He whispers to her every good thing he has ever seen. Sunshine. High tide. Elk on the beach. A pod of humpback whales. The sky right before the rain. Here right now. You and me.

"I wish you looked at me how you used to." The warmth of her skin seeps through his sweatshirt.

"How was that?" Everything inside of Danny is soft and quiet—still water. What a sad victory, he thinks. Touching someone and not being afraid.

"I don't know . . . like I was beautiful and unbroken. I want it to be the same, I guess."

He does not have the heart to tell her it is not the same. It will never be the same again. Just as the "Danny" Ellie knew is gone, so is the "Ellie" Danny knew.

"I just . . . I just miss the girl I was." She wipes her face and looks up at him, green eyes glassy sad pools. "Thank you for coming over." She squeezes his hand. "I wanted to ask you a favor. Would you take me somewhere?"

—

Night has come. The sun has set. The road is bumpy. Danny's and Ellie's bodies jerk with the movement of his car. Danny flips on the radio and scrolls through the stations, pausing and passing over a Christian gospel show—judgment day is upon ye. He settles on the blues and sets the volume low.

"You sure you know the way?" Ellie asks.

Danny nods. His hands tense around the wheel. He does not like this. *I want to go where I was found,* Ellie had said. And against his better judgment, he agreed to drive her. Her phone vibrates and she pulls it out. A glance shows Danny it's from Coldwell PD, probably Detective Calhoun. Ellie presses ignore.

"I saw her the other day. She came into the diner." He says the last part like a question with a million questions underneath it—what is happening with the investigation? Why does Calhoun want me to spy on you? What happened to you? Where'd you go? Ellie remains silent.

Danny takes out his frustration on the gear shift. He does not understand why she wants to do this, why he is helping her do this. The forest is thick and passes by in a gray blur. Danny starts to say something else but snaps his mouth closed.

He slows the truck. They have arrived. On the other side of the road is the mouth of the trail Ellie stumbled out from, blood-soaked and bruised. Yellow crime scene tape blocks it off. Some of it has detached and flutters in the wind. It is a reminder that after a while, everything is forgotten.

"I have a flashlight, I think." Danny cuts the engine and reaches to dig around in the backseat—clothing, camping gear, even a large fishing knife. He reemerges with a heavy-duty flashlight and hands it to her.

She gets out of the car, and he follows. The interior lights and headlights fade, and they are suddenly swallowed by night. It is so dark Danny can't even make out the tips of his shoes. Ellie clicks on the flashlight and points it toward the ground, at the faded white of her sneakers.

"I'd like to go by myself," she tells him.

Danny swears. "No, El."

"I'll text you every few minutes." As if it will help convince him, she digs her cell phone from her pockets and waves it.

He grabs the back of his neck, unsure and miserable. "I don't know . . ."

"I need this," she insists.

He sighs and studies her. Is this her way of coping? Of reconciling what happened to her? She is still an enigma to him. Still so stubborn. He sees a glimpse of the girl she was before. Head tilted. Arms crossed. Willing to die for something she thinks is important. He grinds out another curse. "Every few minutes, you'll text?"

"Cross my heart." She makes an X right over the center of her chest.

"Give me your phone. Let me make sure you have service." She rolls her eyes, murmurs something he can't hear, and hands it over.

Danny checks it out, pressing buttons. "Here." He places it in her open palm, screen absurdly bright and unnatural in the dark. "Full service."

She promises to be right back and darts across the street to the mouth of the trail. He stands, hands shoved into his pockets, and watches her. He paces back and forth, head down, and tries to talk himself out of it, but then he thinks fuck it and follows her.

He sets off at a jog into the yawning mouth of the forest, slowing when he nears her. She walks for a while and Danny creeps behind her, keeping pace at an even distance. Near a bend, she leaves the trail. His heartbeat accelerates when he finds her standing under a hemlock. She glances around, and he ducks out of sight. All this fresh air and Danny finds it hard to breathe, lungs constricting with apprehension.

The flashlight is on the ground, a cone of light illuminating the scene. Ellie crouches, touches a mound of dirt, and then starts to dig. In no time at all, her hands close around a small package. The contents are malleable as she pushes her thumbs into it, kneading. She stuffs the package into her waistband and covers it with her coat, checking to make sure it's hidden.

The wind picks up and howls. Danny uses the sound as cover and runs back to the trail. He jogs a ways down, then cups his mouth and hollers Ellie's name, hoping she'll believe he's just come this way searching for her.

The gentle pitter-patter of rain starts and increases steadily until it is a vicious downpour. Danny waits. Then Ellie is there. Hair plastered to her head. Danny's pulse beats heavy in his neck, and he's afraid. But of what? The dark? This trail? Ellie? He shakes it off.

"You're covered in dirt." He says it to see what she'll say.

"I fell."

A lie. The moon disappears behind a cloud, and it's hard to make out Ellie's face. "Did you find what you were looking for?" Water drips from his hair and catches in his long eyelashes. An image of her pops in his memory, Ellie in the forest, back bent, digging and digging.

"Not yet," she says.

His mind goes blank on what to do. How to handle this. It does not feel right to accuse Ellie of something. So he goes into default mode, does what he always wants to do with Ellie. Take care of her. Be a hero. He strips his sweatshirt off and puts it around Ellie's shoulders. "C'mon," he says. "Let me take you home."

The air in the truck is humid. They are a few miles down the road. "You warming up?" Danny reaches for the knob, turning the heat down. Ellie doesn't answer. She is softly crying. "What's the matter?" It's a stupid question, he thinks.

Ellie shakes and shivers. "It's nothing . . . I'm just . . . I'm so afraid," she chokes out.

"It's okay," he tries to soothe.

"It's not okay." The words roll out of her like a stomp of the foot. Everything is too jagged. Too sharp. "It's not okay, and it is never going to be okay. I sleep in a crawlspace. I carry around a rage that makes me want to hit people. I look for exits in every room I'm in; I make sure all the windows can be opened. I can't stand to be touched. I can't cut my fucking hair. And every time someone calls me Ellie, I want to tell them it's not my name. Where I was kept . . . they called me Destiny." A pause. "I shouldn't have said that. Forget it."

Everything Ellie has admitted is unfathomable. So heinous, what she has lived through. Danny has never seen such an ugly thing as survival. "Forgotten," he says, but files the name away. Destiny. Does it mean something? A hint at what kind of people stole Ellie? A cult? "It is okay, or it will be." He pauses, grips the wheel tighter. "If you want to sleep in a crawlspace, I'll build a bed there for you. If you want to hit someone, you can hit me. If you need exits, I'll open windows. If you don't want to be touched, I will sit next to you. If you panic, I will find a paper bag for you to breathe into," he vows.

A sob tears from Ellie's throat, the grief too much to hold on to. The pressure eases. "I'm scared," she repeats.

"Me too," he admits. "This is uncharted territory. But I'll hang on if you do."

Ellie doesn't say anything, but she does unbuckle her seat belt and scoot to him, resting her head on his shoulder.

TWENTY-TWO

IT IS CLOSE TO MIDNIGHT and Chelsey is in her father's office. She has cleared the walls of the animal heads, pictures, and plaques. And in their place, a giant map of Washington with little pins, sticky notes, and photographs. Thirteen pictures in total. All courtesy of Gemma Kincaid at the statewide Cold Case Unit. All unsolved missing persons. All girls ages fourteen to seventeen. All poor. White. Out of the thirteen, four bodies have been found, Gabby Barlowe included—all of them strangled and dumped in various state parks. One of the thirteen, Hannah Johnson, a foster kid, was last seen near a blue station wagon. Just like Gabby. Like Ellie. Two is a coincidence. Three is a pattern.

Chelsey turns to Willa. Still an anomaly. She does not fit. She has pinned her photograph to the side, away from the other girls. Why did he take her? What changed? Something happened. Gabby was the last body found. And Ellie magically reappeared. Chelsey thinks about Ellie's neck, the clean white flesh. Her nails filed neatly, unbroken. No signs of abrasions on her hands or knees, as if she'd jumped from a vehicle. Maybe she did not escape. Maybe she was not left for dead. What does that mean? It means something is off with Ellie. It means Ellie is not saying something.

Chelsey rubs her eyes and peers at the wall again. Is this crazy? To think that all these girls are somehow related? That Chelsey, this small-town cop, has stumbled into a case this large, a killer this prolific? That Ellie is somehow the key to it all?

If only these girls could talk. What would they say? What terrors would they whisper of? The half dozen Clif Bars Chelsey has eaten sit like tiny rocks in her stomach. At her shoulder, she feels the cold silhouette of Lydia. Her sister is suddenly all too present. Her laughter. Her scent. Her words: *Pinkie swear*. Then there are more shadows at Chelsey's back. A frenzy of missing girls. They do not give answers. They do not speak of what has come to pass. They whisper: *Find us. Please*. The words becoming a chant, a command. She tilts her head at the map, and silently says, *I will. Promise. Cross my heart and hope to die*. As if it is so easy. These childhood vows. Made when girls are young. When they slept under beds with fairy lights, ran through streets after dark, rode their bikes, and it was not dangerous to go far from home.

She scoops up her phone and dials.

The phone rings. "Detective Calhoun, it's after midnight," Kat answers.

"Sorry about the late call," Chelsey says, although she is not sorry. She feels like she's racing against a clock ticking twice as fast. "But I need you to bring Ellie to the station first thing tomorrow morning," she says, voice authoritative. She stares at Willa's photo. Chelsey is firm in her decision. Ellie isn't the only one to consider anymore. Hasn't been the only one since Gabby Barlowe. But then, Chelsey had felt time was on her side, Gabby long buried. Now, Willa could still be alive out there. Now, Ellie is stonewalling her, lying to her. Now, they are opponents. Staring down at each other from ends of a field.

"What? Why?" Kat is annoyed, slightly alarmed.

Chelsey feels as if she's about to wage a war with no winners. But what choice does she have? She will do what she must to find Willa. Even treat Ellie as a hostile witness. "I have some . . ." She pauses, lets the words bend on her tongue. ". . . wrap-up questions to close out the case."

"She has to come to the station for that?" Kat asks.

A ringing starts in Chelsey's ears. An alarm bell warning. "Yep, it's a formal process. Some of the paperwork has to be notarized." Here is Chelsey, feet perched on the edge of a very slippery slope. How far will she go? She does not admit it to herself, but she will do anything . . . anything to save a life. If only. If only. If only. It startles her a bit, realizing the depths she may go to catch this guy.

"Oh, okay. Sure," says Kat. "I'll bring her in tomorrow."

"Great," Chelsey says. They arrange a time, eight a.m., right when the station opens.

Chelsey leaves her father's office. In the hallway, she pushes the door to Lydia's room open. It smells the same. Baby powder and sunflower perfume. Like Lydia. Chelsey flicks on the light and sits on the bed on the white eyelet comforter. Above the door are seven bold bubbled letters, each filling a single page. Together they spell the word freedom. Lydia had made the sign herself. Chelsey had watched as her sister drew the outline of the letters, the smell of Sharpie light in the air—then filled each in with dots, stripes, or little daisies.

She wonders what Lydia might have become if Oscar hadn't killed her. She would have traveled, Chelsey is sure. Left home and attended music festivals, maybe Burning Man. But she'd always come back, road-worn and weary and thankful for their bulldog father, their fussy mother, her clingy sister. She would sit at the Lucite table with Chelsey and regale her with tales from afar while their mom, who is still married to their father, made dinner—chicken tetrazzini. Lydia has had pecan pie in Alabama, barbecue from Kansas City, crawfish in Louisiana, but her mother's cooking is still the best thing she has ever tasted.

A lump rises in Chelsey's throat, and she gulps it back. She won't allow the tears to come. All these girls. These bright, bold, beautiful girls. All that potential wasted. All those possibilities snuffed out. What could have been. The question stretches to infinity. She pulls one of Lydia's Beatrix Potter rabbits from the bed and screams into it with a shimmering, impotent rage.

ix

GRACE WAS A GIFT. A reminder that good things still existed in the world. Most nights, when it wasn't my turn, David let her sleep with me. I did not question it. I curled my body around hers and kept her warm through a brutal winter, pressing her blue fingers between my thighs and her head into my chest. The cold burned off, and in the spring, we chased snakes through the tall grass and found a rabbit's nest. Once we even spotted a fox sliding through the huckleberry bushes.

I taught her how to add double digits using a stick and by scratching numbers into a patch of dirt. We dissected owl pellets, too. I showed her the mouse bones like I'd been shown in elementary school. Summer came, and the compound reeked of rot. But we savored the heat and drank it up. In the evenings, we washed in the creek to keep cool. She'd hunch over while I cupped my hands and let the water flow down her spine, which I called a dragon's tail. We sang "Ring Around the Rosie" and played cat's cradle with twine.

And I remember being happy then.

Is that wrong? Is that bad? That I found the smallest seed of joy and nourished it? She was mine. And I wanted to be everything to her. Tried to be everything. Sister. Mother. Teacher. Savior. Anyway, what's that saying? The days were long but the months short? Is that how it goes? It's how it went for me. Time had less and less meaning. I'd finally given in to it, I think. Finally lost myself in the prism of David's world, trapped forever in the sentinel trees, cinder blocks, and plastic sheeting. I let the wilderness inside. Let the darkness swallow me up, and I smiled all the way down.

———

The edge of fall was in the air. The sky was a dark gray. I'd been watching the clouds all day as they grew over the mountains, more and more pregnant with ocean rain. Salmon were spawning in the creek. The water thick with blue-backed and bright red bodies. We reached right in and plucked one up. A female full of eggs that we cooked over the fire.

Grace picked at her plate. "I wish this was chicken nuggets," she whispered.

"Pretend it's chicken nuggets," I cajoled. The dogs lay around the campground, mouths open, breaths foggy. Star was next to me. She'd taken a liking to Grace, too. Always following us around, nipping at our heels. Chasing us through the trees.

I felt eyes on me. David watching.

"Take a bite," I told Grace, low.

"I'm not hungry," Grace said, loud. Too loud.

David rose from his chair. "Grace," he called, voice rolling across the compound like a bad omen. "Come to me."

A fluttering. Fear beating its wings.

"No." Grace wrapped her arms around my waist, pressing her nose into the softest part of my belly. "No."

When I was five and Sam was fifteen, she got a Life Saver stuck in her throat. Sam had charged into the kitchen from outside, her face red and sweaty, her breath wispy, like the air was passing through the tiniest pinhole. Mom called 911, all while rubbing Sam's arm, telling her how brave she was. My mother had this unique ability—she could stand in front of a moving train and say everything would be fine. Just fine. Don't you worry.

Anyway, she couldn't do the Heimlich because technically, Sam wasn't choking. Tears rolled down my face. I blubbered, *I love you, Sam. I love you so much.* Eventually, the Life Saver dissolved. Sam could breathe. But in those few minutes, when she had to fight for the slightest bit of air, I would have traded places with her. It was the same with Grace.

"It's my fault," I lied. "I brought up chicken nuggets."

David floated toward us, hands in his pockets. His lips twitched. He'd been in a mood lately. Spending more time in his room, watching television. Then bursting out to pace the compound, running his hands through his hair, jaw flexing, wounded eyes ringed in mania and mouth spewing nonsense. Like how the government was undergoing a dangerous and dramatic shift. It wanted authoritarian control. There was a whole new world order. He was being left behind.

"In some cultures, lying is punishable by death." He stopped feet from us.

I opened my mouth.

"Don't," Charity cut in on a whisper.

"Without discipline, there is disorder," David declared, creeping closer. "Those who do wrong must be punished."

I rubbed Grace's back, the space in between her bony shoulders. "I agree." I nodded. Then I started to pry Grace's arms from around my waist. Her grip loosened. I stood, a steel rod in my spine, ready to take her place. David's eyes flashed so subtly that I almost didn't notice. But I did. And it made my skin crawl.

The sky opened its gray mouth, and fat raindrops started to fall. Grace was yanked away from me. Michael had her by the waist. She kicked and screamed and cried out my new name, Destiny. She was kind of beautiful in her anger. Such defiance, so much spirit. I'd have to break her of it.

A clash of elbows, a well-placed knee, and Grace managed to break away. She latched back on to me. "Don't let me go," she said, arms like chains dragging me down. In that moment I realized, somewhere along the way, I'd become afraid to be angry.

David stood by. Patient. Calm. Waiting to see if I passed his test. If I huddled over Grace, her punishment would be worse. One by one, I pried her fingers from my hips. Her will was strong. But mine was stronger. I leaned down and put my mouth to her ear. "Go on," I whispered, tongue as dry as salt. I held back the tears. I didn't want her to see me cry. I didn't want her to cry more. "Pretend you're a Valkyrie. A brave warrior who gets her power from the lightning."

Charity nodded at me. I knew what I had to do. I pushed Grace away from me. "Nooo," she wailed. Michael lifted her in his arms. He carried her to the concrete bunkers. And the whole time, Grace called for me, her arms outstretched. I turned away from her and sat down, the rain pelting my back.

"You indulge her too much," Charity whispered, spoon near her mouth, eyes flicking over my shoulder to David, no doubt.

"I don't," I whispered back. My denial was thin. Maybe I did. Star nosed at me. She'd lost some teeth a few months back, and I'd made a little mobile out of sticks with them.

Charity managed a pale smile. "You do. It's better not to get too close," she said, her voice pounded down by the rain. We did not speak of Hope. Of what we'd done with the seeds before. Of what I'd done after. Or why we did it, to avoid getting pregnant, and that we might get pregnant now. I was terrified of it. I imagined all the scenarios. What if I did get pregnant? Would I try to get rid of it on my own? Or would I have the baby? What if David gave my baby to Serendipity, then killed me after he got what he wanted? I wish I could have talked to Charity about it. But she had tunneled into herself. Barely spoke. And she always seemed a little haunted, with ghosts in her eyes.

"You look at Grace like you hate her sometimes."

Charity remained silent. She didn't deny it. "You did the right thing," she said finally. "David would have made it worse."

I murmured my agreement. My love for Grace was in direct correlation to my fear. I was in a constant state of agitated worry. She was getting so thin, so frail. Most nights, while she slept, I placed my hand on her chest just to feel her lungs inflate and deflate. The only time I knew she was truly safe was when I could count her breaths. I dared to glance over my shoulder, at the bunker where Grace was locked away. My gaze snagged on David. He smiled a small, feral smile, something percolating in the depths of his expression. And then, even though my stomach ached, I ate every single bite of that salmon. All of it. Even the crunchy, burnt skin.

Chapter

TWENTY-THREE

THE FOLLOWING MORNING, CHELSEY WATCHES as Noah deposits a plate full of breakfast food in front of her at the table. Her hair is still wet as she chugs her second cup of coffee. Noah tilts his head at her as he sits down. "You okay? Tired? You got in late last night."

Chelsey flashes to her father's office. To the little holes she pierced through the plaid wallpaper to pin up the photographs of the lost girls. To calling Kat in the middle of the night. To fudging the truth. Ellie is due at the station in forty minutes.

"Ellie is coming in today. I want to be fully caffeinated," she says.

"Wow. You finally pinned her down for an interview? How'd you manage that?"

Chelsey's lips twitch. She focuses on her plate, on the scraps of eggs clinging to the rim. "With my sparkling personality, of course," she states dryly. She blows out a breath and slumps back in her chair. "I'm nervous," she confesses. "This may be my final shot at her and . . ." She sees Willa in her mind. She refuses to think Willa might be dead. Instead, she pictures a nine-year-old girl trapped somewhere, a looming shadow growing above her. She hesitates to tell Noah all of it. What might he think of Chelsey's theory? That other girls were kept with Ellie. That Ellie is withholding. And Chelsey's methods? That Chelsey is luring Ellie to the station today under false pretenses. But if Ellie is hindering the investigation deliberately . . . what does that mean? One word comes to mind. Complicit. Soon she'll be able to explain everything to Noah. Once she has all the facts. "Everything has to go right. That's all."

The corners of his mouth tug up. "You've done dozens of victim interviews."

Not like this, she thinks.

He reaches out, closing the distance between them, laying a hand on top of hers. "You've got this." He is so steady. Like one of those jagged rocks rising from the tide on Coldwell Beach, waves breaking against it. She turns her arm, so her palm is up. They interlace fingers.

"You're right," she says. She grips his hand. Holds on tight for a moment. Wishing she could give him everything he wants from her. She'll be able to someday, she thinks. After she settles the Ellie case. After she finds out the truth. Chelsey will be free.

—

"Thanks for coming in today," Chelsey says, leading Ellie through the station. Kat and Ellie had been waiting when Chelsey arrived. Kat had wanted to stay. To be with Ellie. But Ellie had shooed her mom off. Insisted she go run an errand, do *something*.

They arrive at the conference room and Chelsey opens the door wide, gesturing for Ellie to go in first. There's not much to look at. An old box television is in the corner. A whiteboard with an analog clock above it. A coffee machine that has not been cleaned since Chelsey has worked there.

Ellie shuffles in and folds herself into a chair. She's wearing the same oversized jacket she wore at the docks with her father.

Chelsey lifts a brow, hand curled around the door. "Do you mind?"

"No." Ellie straightens. "It's fine."

Chelsey closes the door with a quiet snick, muting the voices and ringing phones outside. "Like I said, I appreciate you coming here today." She pulls out a chair across from Ellie and sits, stack of papers in hand.

"My mom said I had to," Ellie says sullenly. "She said there's some paperwork I need to sign."

Chelsey sighs. "The truth is . . . the truth is I was slightly disingenuous bringing you down here."

Ellie lurches as if struck. "I'm leaving." She begins to stand.

"No. Wait." Chelsey stands, steps toward Ellie. "I need to speak with you."

Ellie pauses halfway to the door. She shakes her head. "I can't help you."

"Why can't you help me?" Chelsey studies Ellie. The way her mouth closes into a single white line. How her hands flex at her sides. She is hiding something. Ellie's eyes flick to the door. "Five minutes, that's all I need," Chelsey rushes out. "You don't have to say anything. Just let me talk to you."

Ellie melts back into the seat. "Five minutes."

"Thank you," Chelsey says, and lets a few seconds tick by, holding the stack of papers. "I'm sorry if I'm a little out of sorts," she starts. "I had too much coffee this morning, and I've been awake all night. And yesterday, I was in Lacey. We got a familial match on the blood on your sweatshirt. I mean, Gabby's sweatshirt." She clocks Ellie's wince as she lays Lewis Salt's photograph down on the table. "This is Lewis Salt. He lives in Lacey. On a large property with a barn and underground cellar. He drives a blue station wagon." Another wince from Ellie. Chelsey lowers her lashes. "I thought he might have been who took you."

"He's not," Ellie rasps out. "It wasn't him."

The corner of Chelsey's mouth tips up. "I know. He has a daughter." She plucks another photograph from the stack and places it in front of Ellie. "Willa Adams. Her blood was on the sweatshirt you were wearing." The result came in moments before Chelsey was due to meet with Ellie. Montoya had texted Chelsey on her way in: WILLA'S A MATCH FOR THE SWEATSHIRT. Ellie's fingers curl around the table. Chelsey goes on. "It's strange that whoever took you took her, too."

Chelsey stops. Waits for Ellie to deny it. But Ellie's gaze is stoic, and Chelsey reads it as confirmation. "In the past, he's taken teens. Girls your age." Chelsey starts laying out the thirteen photographs of the other girls—all pure conjecture, but she is beginning to believe she is onto something, that the scope of this is that wide.

Chelsey finishes with Gabby Barlowe's and Hannah Johnson's missing girl flyers, both vanished within the same year. She leans back in her seat, crossing her legs. "That's Hannah Johnson. Someone saw her get into a blue station wagon right before she disappeared."

Ellie closes her eyes, and tears stream down her face. A full minute passes, and Ellie doesn't respond. But she is still here, immobile and haunted, a gaunt shadow.

Chelsey goes on. "I don't think I've told you much about myself. What motivates me. What drives my sense of justice. My sister went missing and was murdered when I was in high school. I guess you could call that my cop origin story." Ellie opens her eyes and Chelsey gives her a wry grin. "We didn't know what had happened to her for two days. Where she went. If she was okay or hurting somewhere. I think about that a lot, the not knowing. I also think a lot about what I could have done differently. I was the last to see her alive," Chelsey gently admits.

The night comes back to Chelsey. Watching Lydia walk down the stairs and out of her life forever. Sometimes she replays it in her mind. Choosing differently. Instead of tucking herself back into bed, she should have shaken her parents awake, turned all the lights on, and chased Lydia out the door. In some ways she's doing that now, chasing other missing girls. Refusing to let another be lost because of her inaction. "I have so many regrets about that night. I wish I would have stopped her."

"Sounds like you'd do anything for your sister." Ellie's voice is thick with tears.

Chelsey nods. "I would. I would have done anything for her."

"I understand," Ellie says.

Chelsey thinks about Sam and Ellie. How Kat said they weren't close.

"I heard this anecdote once about how you can fight with your sister over a glass of water, but if she needed a kidney, you'd be the first in line," Chelsey says. There's a memory somewhere in Ellie's faint smile.

Chelsey leans in, elbows on the table. "Don't have regrets like me, Ellie." Chelsey's voice is soft. A plea in the dark. "Tell me something. Anything."

Ellie hesitates. She turns a cheek, chewing on the inside of it. Then she comes back, sweeping a hand over the first ten girls. "I don't know them."

"Okay." Chelsey turns the photographs face down, leaving Gabby, Hannah, and Willa face up, their eyes staring out at them. "And what about Gabby and Hannah? Did you know them?" Ellie dips her chin, a ghost of a nod. "Is Hannah still alive?"

Mouth closed, Ellie shakes her head.

"Hannah is dead?" Chelsey asks.

"Yes." Ellie cries and presses the heels of her palms to her eyes.

"Do you know where I might find her? I'd like to put her to rest."

Ellie cups her knees and squeezes, fingers turning white, then red, then purple. "I don't know . . . I don't know what he did with the body."

"That's okay," Chelsey says. "Perfectly fine. You've given me so much information right now, Ellie. You're doing so good. Forget about Hannah for the moment. That was a lot of blood on your sweatshirt. I am very concerned about Willa. Is she alive?"

Snot and tears run down Ellie's face. "She's alive."

The air rushes back into Chelsey's lungs. At last, she is inching toward the truth. But she has to keep steady. If she goes too fast, it might spook Ellie. "That's good, Ellie. That's really good to hear."

Ellie crosses her arms. "I kept her safe."

"I bet you did," Chelsey readily agrees, and a picture begins to form in her mind. A little girl alone in the woods, Ellie holding her hand. The two standing against a shadowy figure blocking their trail home. "It doesn't have to be just you anymore. I'm here now. I can help Willa. Can you help me help Willa?" Chelsey gently coaxes.

Ellie's chin trembles.

Chelsey shuffles the papers and pulls out the map of Washington State. She unfolds it and places it in front of Ellie. "Show me where, Ellie. All you have to do is point."

Ellie nudges the map away. "Can we take a break?"

Chelsey deflates. She smiles, but it does not reach her eyes. "Of course. Do you want something to drink? To eat?"

Ellie stares at the wall. "I want to go home. My stomach hurts."

"What about Willa, Ellie?" Chelsey almost adds *I bet she wants to go home, too* but digs her teeth into her tongue. She's made so much progress. She doesn't want to take a step too far.

Ellie looks down at the table. "I don't want to do this here. Just let me go." Her eyes skate around the conference room, landing on the door's small window as if worried someone is watching. "Come over tomorrow, and I'll tell you everything. I promise."

Chelsey squints at Ellie, trying to read her. "Sure," she says. "Tomorrow. I have your word?"

"Yes," Ellie says, rising to her feet. "I promise." She stops at the doorway, hand on the knob, and for a moment appears unbearably sad. But it is only a glimmer, here one second and gone the next. "The guy. The one who killed your sister, they ever catch him?" she asks, a storm in her eyes.

"Oh." Chelsey stands. "He . . . he died with her. His name was Oscar Swann. He was her boyfriend. Nobody thought he was capable of it. He was very charming. He killed her and then himself."

Ellie's gaze drops to the floor. "I'm sorry."

"We'll catch this guy." Chelsey's brow crinkles with good intention.

"Thank you," is all Ellie says.

"Thank *you*," Chelsey says as the door swings shut behind Ellie. She waits a beat, her promise hanging so thick in the air. *We'll catch this guy.* It is palpable. She swallows against the want. So close. So very close. He is nearly within Chelsey's reach. And in less than twenty-four hours, he'll be in Chelsey's grasp.

TWENTY-FOUR

KAT HAS JUST LIT A cigarette when she hears the squeak of the back door opening.

"Hey," Kat says as Ellie emerges.

"Hey." Ellie sits next to her mom in an ancient aluminum armchair.

Kat flicks ash off her cigarette. She always gets a tiny buzz on the first inhale. It's fading now. "Want me to put it out?"

Ellie hasn't said much since Kat picked her up from the police station. But Kat did notice the way Ellie sat in the car, still and quiet, wringing her hands. When she'd asked Ellie how it went, Ellie had said "fine," then disappeared into her room. Disappeared; Kat thinks of the word. All the different meanings it has. The way someone can be right in front of you but still be missing.

Kat checked on Ellie all day, pressing her ear to the door. The noises behind the wood were strange, sometimes a cry, sometimes a muffled bang. Maybe Ellie was angry again? Many mornings, Kat has woken to find that Ellie has destroyed some part of her bedroom—ripping up photographs, upending the mattress, and once, breaking a glass. But now Ellie seems calm.

Ellie shakes her head. "No. It's okay. I kind of like it." A pause. "It reminds me of the Fourth of July."

They'd had barbecues, back when Ellie was little. Kat invited the ladies from the beauty shop, Jimmy grilled. Once, this house had been a gathering place. Once, so many lives had been lived here. So much laughter shared. Kat smiles at the memory. "Maybe we'll have a party this year." Summer is right around the corner, but you wouldn't know it with the wet weather. There is the slight smell of ozone in the air. The scent of a storm brewing.

Ellie shrugs and plays with the zipper on her jacket. "That'd be nice."

Kat studies Ellie. This folded-up version of her daughter. She'd always thought Ellie was a touch dramatic. Howling when she skinned her knee. Screaming when she burned her mouth on a bite of macaroni and cheese. Acting as if the sky was falling. Ellie lived with such intensity. Why had she wanted to drill it out of Ellie? Why had she shushed her and told her to be quiet? But now she sees. She sees. The laughter. The fighting. The crying. It had all been a gift. All of it.

Kat drags on the cigarette again. "When Sam was pregnant, she refused to sit in these chairs because she was afraid they'd collapse beneath her weight. Your dad thought she was being silly. 'These chairs were built before you were born and will be here long after you're gone,' he said." She exhales. Smoke winds its way up, a vine curling into the night. "Anyway, he was sitting in one a few weeks later, and the legs gave way."

Ellie chuckles. Kat does too, but then her smile wavers. "It was the first time I laughed, really laughed, after you . . ." Another head shake. Her eyelids are hot, swelling warm with familiar tears. "I felt so guilty."

"It's okay for you to be happy." Ellie whispers the words like a final wish.

Kat nods vacantly, gaze lost in the brown grass. "I always wanted girls. Just daughters." She has said this before. Too many times to count. "They never leave you. Boys get old, have adventures, and then get married, and they're not yours anymore. Girls do all that, too, but they always come home."

A fat tear escapes Ellie's eye. "I'm sorry."

Kat's expression softens. "I wish there was something I could do. I want to fix things for you. When you were a little girl, all it took was a kiss on a scraped knee." She smashes her cigarette out.

"Mom," Ellie starts, then seems to reverse course. "You think I could borrow your car tomorrow?"

"Oh." Kat frowns, thinking about it. Thinking about letting Ellie go. Maybe before, Kat might have thought, What is the harm? What is the worst that can happen? Now, she wonders how to live with all this uncertainty. How to help her daughter dig out from where she is and not bury herself at the same time. "I could take you." Today she pretended to run errands when she dropped Ellie off at the police station, but really, she'd driven down the block and parked, waiting.

"I thought I'd go see Sam." Ellie stares at Kat.

Kat's features flare with surprise, and she immediately softens. "Yeah, sure, okay," she says. "That would be okay, I suppose." It is all she has ever wanted. For Sam and Ellie to be friends. The older she gets, the more worried she is about what she will leave behind. She'd like Ellie and Sam to be close, to have each other when she is gone.

"Thanks. I'm going to head up to bed." The chair's aluminum frame scrapes on the concrete as Ellie pushes it back to stand up. "Good night."

"Night."

Ellie pauses at the door. "See you," then even lower, she says, "Love you."

"Love you too," Kat says, but the door is already shutting. Ellie is already gone.

—

Jimmy makes a whistling noise when he sleeps. He is dreaming of the ocean and his girls—Kat, Sam, Ellie, Valerie, and Mia. They're on the deck of *Turmoil*. The day is clear, bright, and cold. Their cheeks are windblown, noses pink and smiles wide. They cast lines and laugh. They listen to Motown. The Beatles. A flash, and it's the same scene, only Ellie is younger, and it is the two of them. He's teaching her the fine art of gutting a fish. Another flash, and it's evening and he is drifting off on the deck, sun ripe and happy. Ellie is still there. Still with him. He feels her lips graze his cheek and opens his eyes.

He is awake now. At home. In his favorite chair and Ellie is a teenager. No, not a teenager. She is almost twenty. He keeps reminding himself that time has passed. That he needs to wander from the cave in which he's been living. "I didn't mean to wake you," she says. "I just wanted to say goodnight."

"Good night." His voice is gruff. "Where's your mom?"

Ellie jerks her head. "Follow the smoke."

Jimmy might say something about how those things are going to kill Kat, but he doesn't. He holds his tongue. He doesn't joke about death anymore. Ellie clicks off the television, folds a blanket, fluffs a pillow. "You want to go out on the boat tomorrow afternoon?" he asks.

Her brow furrows. A shadow passes over her face. "Yeah, I would. I'd like that."

He nods once. "It's a date, then." He stands. "I'm going to go wrangle your mom. Don't stay up too late."

He finds Kat in the backyard. She's lighting up another cigarette. Her tits are saggy under a thin sweatshirt. Knuckles warped and knobbed. Hair wiry and gray. She still looks like a dream to Jimmy. As beautiful as ever.

He sits, shakes a cigarette from Kat's pack, and clamps it between his teeth, lighting it.

"You see Ellie?" she asks.

"She's going up to bed."

Quiet then. They smoke together. "You never told me," Kat says. "That you went to see Detective Calhoun while Ellie was gone. I would have gone with you. Why didn't you tell me?"

For some reason, he remembers the schoolyard, the boys who made fun of his lisp, the budding terror that he eventually stamped down with stoicism. Then Jimmy wonders what makes a good husband. A good father. A good man. Sometimes he is not sure he knows himself. But he knows Kat.

"I wanted to spare you," he says. He thinks about how he loves Kat now. How he will always love her. More than the ocean. More than *Turmoil*. He makes a decision. "I've been doing some thinking." He curls his hands in. "I'm wondering if it's time to sell the boat and license."

"Yeah?" Kat asks casually, but there's a sheen in her eyes—hope.

"Yeah," he replies. "I'm sorry, Kat. It always made me feel like shit, you working when I couldn't earn enough." Inadequacy and anger rises in Jimmy again. Sometimes he feels like he missed out, that the world owed him something.

"I never minded that," Kat says.

He gazes at his wife. "You didn't?"

"No, Jim. We're a team. I was embarrassed, maybe, back then, but not now. Remember that Christmas with Sam? When we could only afford a box of crayons and a pad of paper from the dollar store. I was sad, but now when I think about it . . . I'm proud. We made it work. You understand?" she asks.

He does. If he is honest with himself, he hadn't loved Kat when they got married. And he knows it was the same for her. They'd only been dating a few months when Kat got pregnant. Jimmy was nineteen. Kat eighteen. It was a matter of practicality. Two against the world sounded better than one. But he'd fallen for Kat over the years, especially after having children. Yes, they'd been a team then. Operating on little money and less sleep. They'd earned each other's love.

He stares up at the stars. Even in a small town like Coldwell, there's too much light pollution. It would be clearer on the ocean. A part of him will always want the water. But he'll sell the boat. He'd sell everything he has for Kat, for Ellie, for Sam. His family.

TWENTY-FIVE

IT IS MORNING AND FAR too early for music. Especially this kind of music. Every time Sam's wife plays Jimmy Buffett, she questions her choice in women. Still, she watches with a half-smile as Valerie dances around and sings something about being a cheeseburger in paradise to their daughter, Mia. She gets why. It's a clear day. No clouds in the sky, and the sun is a bright yellow disc. A storm whipped through last night, fast and furious and gone by morning.

It is the type of day Coldwell lives for. Valerie too. She's from Florida and is constantly shivering in Coldwell. But today, she is smiling and playing Jimmy Buffett, and has ditched the thick wool sweater for a thinner shirt, still long-sleeved, of course. Sam leans a hip against the kitchen counter and yawns. Mia has been on a five a.m. wake-up schedule for a while, with a nap precisely at nine a.m. Sam does not mind. She has always been an early riser. It started when she learned seal pups were usually on the beach at sunrise. She'd wake up the whole house before dawn, banging pots and pans. Her mom would strap Ellie to her back, and her dad would make coffee. They'd sit on the dunes in the tall grass and watch the seal pups bark and roll around, coating their rotund bodies in sand. That had been a golden time.

A knock on the door. "I'll get it," Sam says. She sweeps through the living room, turning the stereo down as she goes.

"Ellie," Sam says. Mia waddles up and grabs her pants leg.

"Hey." Ellie jams her hands inside her pockets.

"Come in." Sam smiles wide, slightly manic. She catches Valerie's eyes across the room. Her wife nods encouragingly. They have spent hours discussing Ellie. How to speak to her. What to say and not say. How to love her best. Ellie shuffles into the room, stopping in the middle. "I hope you don't mind that I came by without calling."

"Of course not," Sam says. "You want to sit?"

"Um, sure. Maybe just for a minute." Ellie balances on the edge of the couch. It took Sam a whole year to decide which one to buy. She thought Valerie might divorce her then. Sam worries a lot about making the right choices. How one choice cascades into the next, like dominoes falling. The anxiety multiplied after having Mia. She could not sleep for fear her daughter might stop breathing. Spent hours scrolling blogs about infant formula and the best swaddles.

"So, what's up?" Sam settles on the floor near Mia, doing that thing all moms do, finding toys on the floor to keep her baby entertained while maintaining eye contact with the adults in the room.

"Nothing. Just came to say hi," says Ellie.

"Hi," Sam says. People used to joke about Sam being like a second mother to Ellie. She fussed over her little sister, fed her bottles, blew on her food to cool it, held her hand when she first learned to walk. She could tell when Ellie was hungry. When she was tired. Then later, when she had a bad day at school, just by the look in Ellie's eyes. When she lost her virginity freshman year to some kid named Will, when she stole Sam's license; she could always sense change in Ellie. Daylight coming. Storms brewing. A sister can always tell. That is how she knows now that Ellie is lying, but she also knows Ellie is sad. She decides not to push it.

Ellie casts a glance around the house. "This is nice."

That's right. Ellie has never been to this house before. Valerie and Sam purchased it after Ellie disappeared. Sam had sobbed the day they'd signed the papers. Ellie was not there to be a part of it. Sam was moving on with her life, and the guilt threatened to swallow her whole.

Mia grows fussy. "Hungry," Valerie says, swooping up their daughter. "Better feed her before things take a turn. I'll go make her something."

"You know what?" Sam says, smoothing her palms over her knees. "Let's go out to eat. Let's all go out to eat. What do you say?" she asks Ellie, rising from the floor. Her knees pop. Since having a baby, Sam feels very old. Every time her joints creak, it's her body's way of confirming it.

"Um, no thanks. I'm supposed to meet up with Danny," says Ellie. Valerie lugs a diaper bag over her shoulder, and Mia squirms in her arms. Ellie's gaze flicks to Mia, her niece. "Can I hold her?"

A beat passes, and Sam casts Valerie a heavy look. "Of course you can," Sam says finally.

Valerie deposits Mia into Ellie's arms, and she dips with the weight. Sam's eyes grow misty. "She's heavier than I thought." Ellie's nose skirts over the top of Mia's head, inhaling. Sam's daughter smells like old cereal. She put some lotion on her this morning to cover it up.

They file outside. Valerie opens the car doors, and Ellie deposits Mia into her seat but doesn't buckle her in.

"I'll do that," Sam says. "You practically have to be an engineer to use one of those."

"Okay." Ellie stays crouched in the door for a moment, staring at Mia. Then she pecks her on the cheek and touches one of her springy curls. "Hope you have a great day."

Mia is buckled in, and Valerie is behind the wheel. Sam stands outside of the car with Ellie. "You sure you don't want to ditch Danny and come with us?" She slips her sunglasses on her face. "Or Val and Mia can go out. I can stay."

"No, it's fine. Danny's waiting on me." She jams her hands in her pockets again.

Sam leans on the running car. The engine is warm against her backside. "We should hang out soon, have a girls' night. Talk."

"Yeah, that would be good." Sam notes Ellie doesn't promise anything. But that's okay. There will be time, she thinks. All this hurting cannot last forever. Ellie gives Sam a slight smile. "Hey, do you remember when you couldn't find your license?"

Sam raises her eyebrows above her sunglasses. "Yeah? Cost me twenty bucks to replace it."

"You accused me of taking it."

"I did," Sam states with a ghost of a smile—sometimes bad memories become good ones.

"I took it," Ellie admits.

Sam makes a face. "Duh." Inside the car, Valerie has turned on a playlist of nursery rhymes. The sound bleeds through the windows. Peter, Peter, pumpkin eater, had a wife and couldn't keep her.

"I'm sorry." Ellie squints against the sun.

"It doesn't matter."

Silence ensues. Sam is not ready to say goodbye. The sun shifts. The nursery rhyme changes. Mia lets out a cry. "I should go," she says finally. "Thanks for stopping by. You headed home?"

"Yeah," Ellie says.

Their mom's car is parked along the curb. And through the glass, Sam sees an overstuffed backpack. Unease prickles her skin. Suddenly, Sam is having an odd sense of déjà vu. Of time repeating itself. The world moving in a circle. She shakes it off and smiles at Ellie. The worry about Ellie switches to Mia, who is fussing. "All right, see you soon."

Chapter

TWENTY-SIX

MORNING BIRDS ARE STILL CHIRPING when Chelsey pulls up to the Blacks' house. Kat's car isn't in the drive, but Jimmy's truck is. She knocks on the door, and Kat swings it open wide. "Detective Calhoun," she says, surprised.

"Hey, Kat," Chelsey says with an amiable smile, even though she notes how Kat is using her title. No more first-name basis. "I'm here to see Ellie."

Kat's brow dips. The lines around her mouth deepen with a frown. "She's not here."

"She's gone? We were supposed to meet here. This morning."

Kat bobs her head. "She asked to borrow my car this morning. She wanted to visit Sam."

"What is going on?" Jimmy appears behind Kat.

"Detective Calhoun is here to see Ellie." Kat gives her husband a tight smile.

"We were supposed to meet today, first thing this morning here, to finish our conversation from yesterday at the station," Chelsey clarifies. Her skin prickles with worry.

Kat slips from the entrance. "I'll just call Ellie."

"Come on in." Jimmy opens the door wider, and Chelsey follows him into the living room. The windows are open. A once-white, now-

219

yellow curtain swishes in the breeze. The stirred air is soft and sweet, a little dusty.

Kat comes back less than a minute later, phone in hand. Concern grows on her face. "Ellie isn't answering."

Jimmy clears his throat. "Try Sam."

Kat nods and dials. "Hey, honey," she says. "Is Ellie with you? Detective Calhoun is here and needs to see her." Kat's brows edge together. "She's not?" Chelsey swallows hard and keeps her gaze steady on Kat. "She said she was headed to Danny's?"

"Ask how long ago," Chelsey prompts.

Kat does. "An hour?" A pause. "No, there's no need to worry. I'm sure it's all a miscommunication. I'll call you back, okay? Give Mia a kiss for me." Kat hangs up. "She stopped by Sam's an hour ago but left and said she was going to Danny's." Kat shakes her head. "I don't understand. She never said anything about Danny."

"Try Danny," Chelsey says.

Kat does and Chelsey listens. She listens as Kat asks Danny if he's seen Ellie. Listens to the disappointment in Kat's voice when he says he has not. Listens to the quavering of Kat's breath as she hangs up. "He hasn't seen her. He said they didn't have plans today." Kat's hand finds Jimmy's hanging in the air. And Chelsey does not miss how they squeeze each other.

Chelsey opens her mouth, and the phone rings, the sound shrill. Kat looks at the screen. "It's Sam." Kat answers. "Hi." Sam's voice is a murmur at the end of a line, and Chelsey cannot determine what is being said. But Kat's face whitens with terror. The air in the Blacks' home seems to grow thicker, the breeze a touch more stifling.

"What is she saying?" Jimmy asks.

Kat ignores him. "I'm sure it's nothing to worry about," Kat reassures Sam. "Let me speak to Detective Calhoun, and I'll call you back, okay?" Kat disconnects, looking as if someone has just walked over her grave. "Sam says Ellie had a backpack in the car."

Dread tightens in Chelsey's chest. A backpack? Why? To run away?

"I don't understand," Kat says. And she looks tired. Jimmy too. Both as if they've been staring into the sun.

"You're sure she didn't mention going anywhere else?" Chelsey asks.

"No," Kat says. "No." She rubs her eyes. "I don't understand. What is happening? Where is Ellie?"

Chelsey flashes to the night Lydia disappeared. Her toes flex in her shoes, feeling the carpet again. The urge to run off after Lydia. If only. It's quiet and Chelsey realizes Kat's and Jimmy's gazes have latched on to her, searching for answers.

"Something isn't right," Chelsey thinks aloud. Ellie is missing. Again. She glances at Jimmy and Kat. Where could Ellie have gone now? They've spoken with Sam. With Danny. Both had no idea. Where has Ellie been spending most of her time since she returned? Chelsey glances around the Blacks' house, up the shaded stairs. "Do you mind if I search her room?"

———

Chelsey slips on a pair of latex gloves in the middle of Ellie's room. Kat and Jimmy hover in the doorway. Jesus, the room is destroyed. Chelsey has been in here before. Two years ago. She sees her past self rifling through Ellie's things—tubes of flavored ChapStick, photographs of friends, a half-empty bottle of vodka on the top shelf of her closet. It was a different room then. Messy but still tidy. Now it is chaotic. This is a room with its hair torn out, with its face clawed, with its throat raw from screaming. A barren, ravaged place.

Chelsey starts slow, picking through the piles of clothes. Then she lifts a sheet to peer out the window. Opens Ellie's dresser drawers, sweeping the inside, then pulling them out to check the back. All clear. Next up is the closet; she uses a flashlight to search it. Nothing. She places her hands on her hips. She has no clue. "Is there any other place Ellie has been hanging out in the house?"

Kat and Jimmy share a heavy look. "I caught her sleeping in the crawl-space a few times," Kat says. "In Sam's old room."

"Show me," Chelsey says.

—

Chelsey crouches low and crawls into the space Ellie has been sleeping in. It's tight and claustrophobic, with enough room for a body to lie curled. Her eyes strain in the darkness. She kneels on a rumpled comforter and splays a hand on a lumpy pillow, the fabric smooth and cool beneath her fingers. Chelsey knows Ellie is not here, but she can sense her in the moldy air, in each dust particle. She flicks on her flashlight.

There. Something behind a wooden beam catches her eye. She reaches. Her hand closes around a brown package. There is also a pipe remnant and two crumpled pieces of paper. Chelsey pulls it all out and reemerges, laying what she found on the guest room's gray carpet. She sits back on her haunches and uncrumples the papers. They are postcards, all of the same photograph. A line of birch trees.

Jimmy makes a strangled noise. "I've seen that before." His face is white. "Ellie was holding one at the truck by the docks when you came to see us. I thought it was some flyer or something, left on my windshield randomly . . ." He trails off.

Chelsey flashes to that day. To Ellie, standing by the truck, white piece of paper in her hand, watching it flutter to the gravel. "What'd you do with it?" Chelsey's spine tingles.

"I threw it in the back of my truck. I'll get it." He turns and trots off.

While Jimmy is gone, Chelsey opens the package. It's empty, but there is residue in the corners and cracks. She fishes out a couple of specks. It doesn't smell, but she recognizes what it is. Gunpowder.

"You have any firearms, guns in the house?" she asks Kat over her shoulder. Chelsey's father used to make his own ammunition. And Chelsey remembers swirling the pool of gunpowder with her finger to make concentric repeating rings, like a Zen garden.

"No." Kat wilts in the doorway.

Chelsey turns away from Kat. She studies the plastic pipe. Rolls the gunpowder between her fingers.

The two main ingredients for a pipe bomb are in front of Chelsey.

Chelsey's mind fills with dark thoughts, things she does not want to think about, to believe. Could Ellie be planning to hurt herself? Others? A jolt of fear runs through her.

Jimmy returns, out of breath. "Here." He thrusts the postcard at Chelsey. She unfolds it. Same picture of birch trees. She lines the three postcards up, then flips them one by one. On the back are numbers. She uses one finger to slide them into order.

Three, two, one.

She glances up at Kat and Jimmy, feeling as if she is dissolving away, slipping into the void.

"What is it?" Kat asks.

Chelsey shakes her head. She lets the silence of the room wash over her. "I'm not sure." To her own ears, her voice is scratchy, far away. Her vision hazy. "But I think it's a countdown."

X

YOU ARE PROBABLY WONDERING WHY I did it. That's why you're reading this, isn't it? I can imagine this is all like a jumbled knot of jewelry to you. Unraveling one piece only to have another kink appear. Until it's all an impossible mess. It doesn't matter, I guess, when things started to tangle. Only the last snarl matters. If you tug too hard, the chain might break.

Or, if you're like me, you figure out a way to save the whole thing.

I sold my soul to the devil, and I don't regret it.

—

The air was near freezing. The sky was silver and purple, the color it turns right before snow. When all the light is sucked from the land. The night before, Grace had lost a tooth.

"Do you think the tooth fairy will find me here?" she asked, worming her finger into her mouth, prodding at the gummy hole.

We were sitting around the fire. Charity snorted and poked at the coals.

I smoothed Grace's hair back. It was getting long. I needed to find a way to keep it out of her face since David wouldn't let us cut it. "Of course," I promised.

Grace shifted to peer up at me. "Then why can't my mom?"

"Can't you keep her quiet?" Charity threw out.

I frowned at Charity and patted Grace's knee. "You know you're not supposed to talk about her."

I figured I'd find some twine and switch it out for the tooth. I'd planned all the ways I'd sell it to Grace. Oh, wow, the tooth fairy left you a piece of string? That is so cool. You must be really special. Say anything with enough enthusiasm, and you can convince people it's the truth.

A gust of icy wind tore at our backs, nearly dousing the fire. A door slammed. "Oh my god," Charity said, staring across the compound. I followed her gaze. The armory door swung back and forth. "It's open." She rose as if in a trance.

"Charity. No."

"It's our chance." Charity glanced down at me. Eyes glazed and bottomless, as if she was under a spell. She raced forward.

"Stay here," I commanded Grace, and ran after Charity. I found her in the armory. Sick pale sunlight streamed through a tiny opening at the top of the tower. Charity smiled, and it was a little wild, a little lost, too deep inside. "I'm going to kill him." She picked up a revolver and met my eyes.

We could be free. The unspoken words passed between us, skating on the frozen air. A dizzying sensation like biting into a warm, ripe peach in the middle of summer.

A shadow fell over us, blotting out the wisp of light. "Put down the gun, Charity," came David's voice. I could feel his body heat, the warmth from his chest. He inched forward and around me. "Be careful. You don't want to hurt anyone," he added, hands splayed. Calm. Too calm? Something felt off. The way he moved with certainty. As if he was sure no harm would come to him.

Charity placed both hands on the revolver and drew it up, David in the crosshairs. Seconds stretched into eternity. It began to snow, a quiet, sleepy dance. David's chest rose and fell with even, unhurried breaths.

He looked at me. "Destiny, take the gun from Charity."

Time moved slow again. Creeping down like molasses from a tree. Charity swung the gun back and forth between David and me.

David said my new name again. "Destiny, take the gun from Charity," he repeated. "Do it for Grace."

I whipped my head toward the compound. Michael's hands were on Grace's shoulders. An inch or two up, and he could ring them around her neck. Squeeze. Blot out the light. Her life.

It happened in a deranged blur. I rushed Charity, putting my shoulder into her midsection and slamming her into the armory's floor. The gun fell with a clatter. Charity pushed out from under me and shrieked. David swung a fist. Once. Twice. Blood came away on his hands, and little droplets sprayed onto the concrete, even outside. I see it when I close my eyes sometimes. Blood in the snow. He rose up, chest heaving. Charity lay crumpled, her face already swelling, already purple.

"You did it." He stepped over Charity and smiled, oddly giddy, a little breathless. "I had an inkling you might, after the other day at dinner." When I'd wanted to trade myself for Grace. "But I had to be sure."

"What?" I asked, ravaged. Bewildered.

"What, what? This was all a test." David swiped the gun from the ground. He pointed it at me and squeezed the trigger. *Click*. I winced, ready for pain. Nothing. No blow to the chest, no red stain blooming outward. David's smile doubled. "Empty. It was empty," he crowed. "You truly love Grace, don't you? I wanted to see how far you'd go to save her." I swallowed and searched out Grace. She was by the kennels, kneeling and poking her hand through the gratings to pet Star. My chin quivered. All a test? I'd hurt Charity because of a test? Breath sawed in and out of my lungs, scraping up my throat. A fog descended, and I started to hyperventilate and laugh at the same time. Was I as mad as David now? My fingers dug into my sides.

"Stop it," David said through his teeth. I didn't see his hand coming. It fell across my face. *Slap.* I sobered instantly, my fingers going to the sting in my right cheek. "You be quiet," he demanded. "Take Grace to her room," he called to Serendipity. I watched as Grace was ushered off. I'd taught her that—to do what she was told, to be silent, to not struggle. It was how we stayed alive, but it wasn't any way to live.

"I'm sorry. Please, I'm so—" I dropped to my knees, hunching over his feet. Sometimes I loved him. Sometimes I wanted his affection. Sometimes I craved his kindness, yearned for him to look upon me as if I was a treasure he wanted to keep.

David sighed and took me by the elbows to draw me up. My cheek screamed with pain, along with every other part of my body. "Poor girl," he crooned, folding me into his arms. We stayed like that for a moment. Swaying. A scream began at the base of my skull.

Then he stopped, pulled away so we were eye to eye. "Destiny." He smiled strangely and toyed with a lock of my hair. "Or should I call you Gilgamesh?" Above, two eagles circled. I'd watched one of them since it was a juvenile. It had mated now, and its nest was nearby. He kissed me on the lips. "I love you," he said.

I was all mixed up inside. Shapeless. Twisting and drifting until I was a speck of dirt on an infinite timeline. The sun exploding. A black hole consuming. "I love you too," I said. Is there a word for loving the thing you fear the most? He kissed my forehead. His touch spreading through me like a virus.

Chapter

TWENTY-SEVEN

CHELSEY STEPS FROM THE BLACKS' house and paces in the backyard, grass folding under her shoes, panic swelling in her chest. She fishes her phone from her pocket and dials.

"Detective Calhoun," Dr. Fischer answers after the first ring.

"Cerise, Ellie is missing," Chelsey says, voice somber.

"No," Dr. Fischer exclaims. "How? How . . . how are her parents?"

Chelsey looks at the house. "Not good." She sees Kat through the window, body rigid, arms crossed as if she is holding herself together. Chelsey swings around to face the street.

Dr. Fischer sighs. "I understand why."

Chelsey checks her watch. It is 10:15 a.m. now. She has started a new timeline. Ellie has been gone two hours and thirty minutes, give or take a few. She had with her a backpack and all the ingredients for a pipe bomb. Chelsey can get a warrant for the phone data, but that takes hours. And to do that means acknowledging Ellie is a threat to herself, to others. Chelsey needs to know why first.

She has a theory.

In her mind's eye, Chelsey sees the birch tree postcards. The thick felt-tipped numbers on the back. Evidence that Ellie was being watched after she came home. With that revelation, more puzzle pieces begin to fit together. Ellie had been acting cautious and vigilant—because she's had to be cautious and vigilant. She knew someone was keeping tabs on her. No wonder she hadn't wanted to talk to Chelsey to aid the investigation.

Other details slide into place. Chelsey thought Ellie had escaped or been left for dead. But there wasn't any physical evidence to support that theory. No fresh bruises. Neat nails. What if Ellie hadn't fought her way to freedom? What if she'd been . . . returned? It is ridiculous. Chelsey is a fool to even entertain the notion. But the idea sparks inside her, burning through her mind like wildfire.

"I'm hoping you can give me some more information. What you two talked about," Chelsey says to Dr. Fischer. Something in her chest tightens—a twisted knot of desperation and fear. "I believe Ellie's life is in danger. She was being followed by someone, and they could be tracking her now." And . . . and once Chelsey goes to Sergeant Abbott with this, Pandora's box will open. Any mention of a pipe bomb and the anti-terrorist unit will be involved. An all-points bulletin will be broadcast. Cops in every adjacent county will be searching for Ellie. Ready to rain down hellfire. "No detail is too small."

It is quiet on the line for a moment. A heavy silence. "Ellie is suffering from post-traumatic stress disorder. Our conversations were very introductory. We only had a couple of sessions. She said she felt like she was someone else, which is common with sexual assault victims," Dr. Fischer emphasizes. "We did some art therapy during our last session. And Ellie completed two drawings. I showed you those." Dr. Fischer stops. "Did I tell you she called the girls her sisters?"

It takes an enormous effort for Chelsey to stay upright. She slides back to yesterday. *Sounds like you'd do anything for your sister*, Ellie had said. *I would. I would have done anything for her*, Chelsey had replied. *I understand*, Ellie said, and her whole heart had been in that statement.

Anything? Like give up her life? Is Ellie trying to save someone? Willa, maybe. *I kept her safe*, Ellie had said. Is Ellie still trying to keep Willa safe?

"Her sisters. You sure?"

"Yes," Dr. Fischer says firmly.

Chelsey thanks Dr. Fischer and hangs up. Ellie was kept with other girls. She called them her sisters . . . Chelsey's mind races. Inside, the Blacks are waiting, and they will have to continue waiting. Tick, tick, tick. Chelsey feels the seconds dwindling. She flexes her hands, steadying herself. She reenters the house and tells Jimmy and Kat she will be back. That she has to go to the station. She has to report Ellie now. Put out an APB on Kat's car. The driver is armed. But dangerous? Chelsey isn't sure. It will kill Chelsey to place Ellie in the hands of others. Her only hope now is to find the girl first.

Please, Ellie, she thinks. Don't do something we'll all regret.

xi

A TINY RUBBER TIRE, A cracked headlight, and a plastic door—
what was left of the remote-controlled green truck lay in pieces around me.

I sat on the floor in the middle of the room with the plastic sheeting.
The weather was warm, and it was muggy inside the room. Spring was
coming. David was in short sleeves, his hairless arms throbbing with veins.
Sweat beaded on his upper lip. He had a particular look in his eye, a feral
gleam that wasn't quite right. I held two wires in my hands, one white and
one red—both harvested from inside the truck.

David crouched beside me. "That's it, Destiny," he said. My name in
his mouth was slippery, like oil. "Connect the wires to the tube." His
tongue darted out, licking the sweat from his upper lip. I did as I was told,
my hands shaking.

The tube had been prepared earlier. A hole had been drilled in it. Then
it had been filled with black powder and broken glass and capped. Vase-
line clung to one end of the tube, and it made my fingers slip, the wires
nearly connecting.

"Easy," David said. He petted my hand. His palms were moist. "Don't
want any accidents."

I set the tube and wires down, placing them far away from each other. I flexed my fingers, trying to steady my hands. I stared down at the red and white wires until the colors bled together.

David withdrew a watch from his back pocket. "Set the time and attach it." I took the watch from him. Gently, I opened the face. It was an old piece, beautiful, probably an antique. Such a shame. I set the time and attached the white and red wires. In two hours, they would cross, and then . . . BOOM.

Chapter

TWENTY-EIGHT

CHELSEY DRIVES TO THE STATION in half the time it usually takes her. She steps inside the precinct. It's the usual chatter. Phones ringing. Paper shuffling. Suzette at the front desk shoots Chelsey a smile, and she tries to reciprocate, her mouth grimly twitching. Despair gnaws at her guts. A flatscreen above the bullpen flashes with breaking news and catches her attention. **BOMB INTERCEPTED AT WASHINGTON GOVERNOR'S MANSION** is the headline.

Bomb. The word reverberates in her psyche. A bell with a terrible ring. Bomb. Bomb. Bomb. She draws closer to the television. Is it her, or is it suddenly hard to hear? To see? Her vision darkens around the edges, tunneling. Her throat constricts. She finds the remote on Doug's desk and turns up the volume on the TV. The gurgle of conversation dies down, replaced by the news anchor.

"Little information is known as of right now. But around eleven a.m. today, a security officer confronted a would-be suicide bomber. What is unusual about this case is that the perpetrator is a woman. Seen here in this security footage," Fox London says.

The screen shifts. A woman in a baseball cap, wearing an oversized jacket, hand pressed against her abdomen, darts across an expanse of green lawn. Chelsey recognizes that fucking jacket. It is Jimmy's, the one Ellie has been wearing. Chelsey's mouth goes bone-dry. *Ellie. No.*

"The bomber was waiting by the gates for the governor's motorcade, and it is by a sheer stroke of luck that her plans did not come to fruition. The governor was waylaid by a flat tire. The Department of Homeland Security would not confirm the woman's identity," Fox London says over the grainy footage. "But a docent recognized the woman."

The screen shifts to a gray-haired woman in a fleece vest. "Her name is Elizabeth Black. I'd seen her on the news. She's been missing, right?" The segment flashes to helicopter footage of the governor's mansion. A sea of police cars outside, men dressed in SWAT gear. All at once, the phones start to ring—the sound high-pitched and urgent.

Chelsey stumbles back. *Ellie, what have you done?*

Sergeant Abbott's office door springs open. "Chelsey," he barks, cutting through her fugue. "My office, now."

———

Heart pounding and a little dizzy, Chelsey stands in Sergeant Abbott's office.

For a moment, they exist in dumbfounded silence. Abbott's hands flex. A muscle in his jaw, too.

"Did you have any inkling of this?" Abbott sits up straight in his chair, appraising Chelsey like a hawk.

She shakes her head, terribly unable to speak. "No," she croaks out. "Actually, that's not true. I went to the Blacks to interview Ellie and found evidence that she might be intending to hurt herself or others. I was on my way here to report it. But I had no idea where Ellie was going. What she planned to do." *Ellie bombed the governor's mansion. Or attempted to. The semantics don't matter. How did this happen? This is Chelsey's fault. She missed it. She made a colossal mistake.*

The world falls away. Chelsey is lying belly down, rifle cocked, an elk trained in her sight. Sweat beads on her brow, and she moves to wipe it away. The elk's ears twitch. *Take the shot,* her father whispers. She pulls the trigger, and the bullet lodges into the elk's left flank. The elk is gone. *Dammit, Chelsey,* her father berates her. *That's your fault.*

"I'm sorry, sir," says Chelsey. And she hears the echo of herself that day in the woods, begging her father's pardon. She doubts herself. Her ability to do this job.

"This is a fucking mess, Chelsey," Abbott states.

Suzette knocks and pokes her head in. "Sir, apologies for the poor timing, but Homeland Security is on the line. I've explained the circumstances. They're insisting on speaking to you."

"Put them through," he says, and Suzette darts away into the muted chaos of the precinct. Through the window, cops are trying not to gawk. Chelsey hangs her head. How did she not see this? Ellie had been acting strange. Evasive, even. Chelsey had attributed it to trauma. But could she have been traumatized . . . and turned?

Abbott taps a button on his phone, and voices rise from the speaker. There are short introductions. Chelsey doesn't remember their names, Director and Special Agent something or other. Her stomach is unmercifully compressed as if she's been punched.

"We're going to need all of your case files on Elizabeth Black," the person on the phone says. "We're sending an agent to collect."

Chelsey's hand buzzes. She forgot she was holding her phone. Ellie's parents are calling.

"My detective will ensure everything is in order when your man arrives," Sergeant Abbott promises. He stands, placing his hands on his desk, his mouth close to the speaker. Chelsey sees the ghost of her father in Abbott's mannerisms. He'd acted similarly when Lydia had been murdered. Defaulting to some robotic state. She wonders what he's feeling. About his ex-wife nearly murdered. He'd said she was the love of his life. "What else?"

There are questions about Ellie. Who she's been visiting, who has been visiting her. Chelsey runs through all of her interactions with Ellie. She thinks of her now. The way she looked at Chelsey as if falling down a bottomless pit. Yes, Ellie was withholding, but a terrorist? A murderer? Chelsey cannot believe it.

Chelsey is told not to visit Ellie's parents. A federal agent will do that. Piece by piece, Chelsey is being removed from the case. Untangled from Ellie's web.

"Do you have any idea where she might be headed?" they ask.

Momentary relief floods Chelsey: If they're asking, it means Ellie got away. They have no idea where she is. But then worry slithers down Chelsey's neck. Ellie is on the run. Alone. Confused. Afraid. Dr. Fischer says Ellie doesn't know who she is anymore. Maybe Chelsey can find her, remind Ellie of the girl she was before. You are not lost. You are not gone. There is still so much for you to do in this world. I'm so sorry that you are hurting. But this is not the end of your story. Chelsey refuses to let it be.

"Detective?" Abbott barks.

Chelsey holds her body rigid. "No. I don't. She stonewalled me at every turn of the investigation."

"Makes sense, given what we know now," Abbott says.

"It does," the director agrees.

"Anything else?" Sergeant Abbott eyes Chelsey.

Chelsey smooths her hands on her thighs. She still can't believe this is happening. Finally, she shakes from her stupor. She has only one card left to play, one way to make them listen, stand down. "I believe Ellie is trying to save someone. Another missing girl. A child named Willa Adams." She talks urgently into the speaker, words darting from her mouth like tiny arrows. "Willa is young, just nine years old. She was abducted about a year and a half ago. The timeline lines up with Ellie's disappearance. I believe they were kept together. And I believe Willa is being used as a bargaining chip, and Ellie has been coerced by her abductors. I know it looks bad, but . . ." She draws in a breath, hoping her voice doesn't reveal her desperation. She needs them to take her seriously. "It's not her fault. Not her fault she did this," she pleads. "You cannot treat her like a traditional suspect. She's a victim here, too."

"We'll look into it," one of the special agents says, but it is evident in his voice that he will not. He does not care. How many times has Chelsey promised something that was technically impossible, used that flat intonation reserved for matters of procedure? "But for now, Elizabeth Black is considered armed and dangerous," he finishes.

Chelsey knows what that means. Shoot first. Ask questions later. She smooths her lips together. "I'd like to be involved. Let me help search for her. I can be in Olympia in sixty minutes, an hour and a half tops."

"We appreciate the offer," another agent drawls. The sound, the tone of his voice, is a pat on the head—you tried your best, let the men take it from here. "But this is a matter for Homeland Security now." A pause. "And given the nature of your department's personal relationship with the governor, it's best if you let us handle it."

Chelsey feels boneless as Sergeant Abbott thanks the special agents and promises the cooperation of his department. They hang up.

"I'd like to go to Olympia." Chelsey rises.

Abbott shakes his head, doesn't look at her. "No, Chelsey."

"But—"

"You're off the case, Chelsey. *We're* off the case," he states unequivocally, jerking his head up, eyes flaring a warning. "Do not push me on this. Get those files together and go home."

She stands but refuses to leave Abbott's office. "Sir—"

"It's an order, Chelsey. Go," he nearly booms. He softens. "I . . . I can't deal with this right now. I have some phone calls to make. My kids . . ." He rubs his brow. "Files and home, Chelsey."

Chelsey places a hand on the door. "The files are in my car. I'll get them." She opens her mouth to say something more, but Abbott's head is down, tapping something out on his phone.

Chelsey drifts outside the station and makes a call.

The phone rings three times. "Detective Calhoun," Montoya answers. "Good to hear from you."

Chelsey chews on her thumbnail and tries to regroup. "You seen the news?" Across the street, a group of teens laugh and elbow one another before heading into the diner.

"Yeah," he drags out slowly.

"You hear any chatter about her whereabouts, if they know where she might be headed?" Chelsey asks, recalling Montoya worked in the counterterrorism unit for a few years. Maybe he has some intel she can use.

"Nothing. She's in the wind. But they'll have copters in the sky soon. A statewide manhunt will be underway. They'll get a warrant to pull her cell records. You know the drill . . . they'll start pinging towers and zero in on her location. She won't be able to hide anywhere."

How long does Ellie have before she is found? Chelsey cycles through cases she's worked or has working knowledge of that involved bombs. Were there any similar to Ellie's? There was that man, a disgruntled contractor, who set up bombs around a concert and got to another state before being caught. How long did it take? Fifteen, sixteen hours? They'd found him hiding out in a salvage yard. Shot him in the spine. Now, he's paralyzed from the neck down.

"What will they do when they find her?" Chelsey asks Montoya, even though she has an inkling. She paces the sidewalk up and down, chewing on her thumb, eviscerating the skin.

"Honestly, I don't know. Tactics change fast. And I haven't been on the team in ten years, but when I was, our initiative was to negotiate first. Since Waco, the FBI has had a directive to avoid civilian tragedies. But . . . this is a Homeland Security issue. It's way different. If they think she's a danger . . . I mean, she could have more bombs."

Chelsey freezes, absorbing the information. "Thanks," she says. "That's helpful. Will you let me know if you hear anything?"

Montoya promises he will.

At her car, Chelsey plucks Ellie's file from the passenger seat. Her hands shake. Photographs of missing girls spill onto the asphalt. There is Gabrielle with her lips puckered for the camera, stack of friendship bracelets near to her elbow. Hannah, with her face turned, peering up at something far away. Willa hanging from a set of monkey bars. And Ellie on the beach, arms out, bracing herself against the wind.

Chelsey stuffs the photographs back into the folder. She waits a beat, staring at the precinct, quiet on the outside. Her father would tell her not to stop. He'd made her chase that elk through the woods. *Go after it*, he'd commanded.

Daddy, don't make me, she'd said, turning to her father. *Please don't.*

He'd been stern yet tender. *It isn't right to leave it like that. No good thing should suffer.* She tracked the animal's blood-soaked trail for six hours, her father on her heels, tears brimming in her eyes. The elk had collapsed in a nest of ferns. Again, she glanced back at her father. He nodded. *Go on.* She cocked her rifle and shot it square between the eyes.

She grips the folder and makes a decision right then, right there. Shrugs off the self-doubt. Knows what she has to do. She gets in her car, file with her, and heads off. No, she will not stop now.

Chapter

TWENTY-NINE

CHELSEY SCREECHES TO A STOP in front of her father's house. She bursts through the front door and makes a beeline for the office, dumping the contents of her file onto the floor. Her hands shake as she pins the map of Washington back to the wall.

Find Ellie. Find Ellie. Find Ellie. The words beat inside of her. She considers the idea of Ellie on a mission. Ellie returned.

The landscape begins to reconfigure. Boulders shift, mountains melt away, lakes appear as Chelsey mentally readjusts the topography of the case. She'd assumed Ellie had escaped—and that she'd been on foot. But what if she hadn't escaped or been on foot? What if her abductor was complicit in her return? What if she'd been driven somewhere? Dropped off? Yes. The puzzle pieces seem to fit. Ellie was returned. Ellie was supposed to carry out a mission on her abductor's behalf. Ellie botched the bombing . . .

So, what does Ellie do next? Where does she go? She cannot go home.

But maybe . . . maybe she is. Maybe Ellie is not going to the home Chelsey knows, the one with Jimmy and Kat, but the one she lived in these last two years. Willa is there. Ellie indicated Willa was still alive. Could Ellie be going back for her? To be with her?

Chelsey stares at the map, backing up a step, a missing girl flyer crunch-

243

ing under her heel. She glances down and plucks it up. Ten minutes later, she has them all pinned to the map. On the desk is a red marker, and Chelsey takes it into her hand, popping the cap off with her mouth. Cops can pinpoint someone's location by pinging their cell phones. The signals bounce off towers, and through triangulation, they narrow down an approximate location. Chelsey uses the same concept now. Tracing lines from one girl to the next.

It's a spiderweb with a clear center—the Olympic National Forest. Every girl she believes to have been taken by Ellie's abductor was within a three-hour driving radius of that clear center.

Chelsey inhales so hard and fast that she grows dizzy. The woods. More than woods. A national park near a million acres, sprawling across coastline, mountains, and impenetrable forest. Noah's folks have a cabin near there. She used to hunt there with her father. They'd spent two weeks one October backcountry camping, tracking black bears. One moment her father had been in front of her, and another, gone. She did not know to stay put. Instead, she wandered. She'd been lost, afraid, and forgot about the whistle around her neck. She remembered after a few hours and blew it. His whistle answered a beat later. Her father had found her shaking and snot-nosed, afraid of the trees that rose around her, like soldiers ready to shoot. He knelt in front of her. *Stop crying now. Nothing to be sad about. You did the right thing using the whistle,* he told her, rifle over his shoulder. *A man can get lost in here and never be found.*

It makes sense. Ellie had been kept somewhere far away. Without electricity. She'd smelled of campfire and vomit that day. Someone had made their own space in the wild. A farmer. A survivalist. A keeper of girls.

It is heady when a case splits open, and Chelsey feels it now. The certainty is almost intoxicating, luring her in with the promise of a fresh catch. To solve and be absolved. But the thrill is quickly diluted by a figure in the doorway.

Noah.

He stands for a moment, taking everything in before him. The house that has not been packed. The desk overloaded with case files. The map filled with colorful flyers and red lines. "What the fuck?"

"Noah. What are you doing here?" is all she can think to say. All she can do is stay still. Frozen.

"Seriously?" His mouth twists downward. "I've been calling you. I saw the news. I left school to be with you. I went by the precinct. Suzette said Abbott sent you home. You're off the case. But you didn't go home, did you? You're here." His cheeks flush, awful slashes of angry red. "And why are you here? You're clearly not packing the house." He gestures wildly at the office, at the wall, at the madness there. "What is this?"

"I'm working," Chelsey states plainly, drawing herself fully upright.

His jaw locks. "I guess your meaning and mine of 'off the case' is different."

"You don't understand. They're going to kill Ellie if they find her. I have to find her first."

Noah puts a hand to his brow, rubbing away what Chelsey presumes is a headache. Sometimes she fears she is too much for him. Her father used to hint at it, at women and girls being too complicated. Overly emotional.

"Whoever took Ellie has been doing this for years. Look at all these missing girls." Chelsey bolts into action. She begins unpinning their photographs, creating a pile that she thrusts at Noah. "I think Ellie was returned—and for a reason." She works hard to keep her voice even, but the mania seeps in. An edge of obsession. She will not rest until the last puzzle piece slips into place. "Look," she says again. She shakes the photographs. Her mind is filled with girls. Girls who wear University of Washington sweatshirts. Girls who listen to David Bowie. Girls who love *Into the Wild*. How the world let them down. How the world did not love them in the way it should have. "Look at them. They all fit a certain profile. Except for Willa Adams, but I think . . . I don't know what I think, why he took her, but I believe Ellie was forced to bomb the governor's mansion. That she may be going back for Willa—"

"Chelsey." The pity in Noah's eyes makes her flinch. "I could do that with any missing kid, anybody murdered. Put enough of them together, and you'll find commonalities. That's how statistics work. I sympathize with Ellie Black, with what she's been through, but this idea you've got that she was somehow turned? It's—"

"You going to call me crazy now?" Chelsey narrows her eyes at him. He closes his mouth. She feels herself folding up on the inside, away from Noah. She levels him with a fierce gaze. "You don't believe me."

He sighs, sitting with her words. "It's not a matter of believing you."

Disagree, Chelsey thinks. Belief is all that matters.

Noah places his hands on his hips and hangs his head. "Let's just go home, Chelsey." He draws his keys out, ready to walk, expecting Chelsey to follow.

"No," she says softly, firmly.

"No?" He turns back to her and arches a brow. "You're going to stay here?"

"I'm not going to stay here." She keeps her gaze steady on Noah. "I'm going after Ellie Black."

"No, you're not." He grits his teeth. There is a weird light in his eyes that Chelsey doesn't like. A fury she has not seen before.

"I am." She crosses her arms.

"Chelsey. Stop this. Come home." He swings out a hand to grab her, and Chelsey jerks away.

His face rearranges into a softer mask. "This case is over. You need to let it go. Let all of it go." He speaks quietly. "You have something going on beyond work. Something inside of you, Chelsey," he says. "Things with your dad—"

"This has nothing to do with my father."

"This has everything to do with your dad." He half laughs. "You really can't see it, can you?" He steps forward and addresses Chelsey directly, and it makes her want to recoil. The naked disappointment. "Your dad was a self-aggrandizing asshole who took you hunting instead of letting you grieve."

Chelsey's stomach lurches. Unforgivable tears rise in her eyes. She gazes at the plaid wallpaper, then shifts down to an outlet, a bare patch above it. Lydia had stuck a Lisa Frank sticker there, a neon tiger, when she was five. Their father had been so angry . . . She whips the memory away. "That's not true."

"It is. You're too scared to feel anything. You're too terrified to move on. You need to choose—Ellie Black, this case, this house, or me. Tell me now, Chelsey."

She hangs her head; her whole body burns with conviction. "I have to see this through."

"Fine. Maybe you should stay here for a while. I'm not sure I can be married to someone who is not as committed as I am."

She falters as she absorbs his statement. She shouldn't be surprised. Noah wants to be a priority in her life. A singularity. But Chelsey cannot revolve around him. *It's like living on another planet*, she remembers her mother saying after Lydia died. It's true. "Okay."

"Okay?" He blinks, stunned, lashes fluttering, and Chelsey fights a grimace. The urge to recant. But it is too late. She is far from Noah now. Has been far from him for a very long time. Drifting in open space. "That's it. Give me a call if you change your mind. But I'm not going to stand around and watch you self-destruct any longer."

He leaves, but she does not watch him go. She does not think about her marriage ending, how close she came to having it all.

—

Chelsey's chin trembles, but she refuses to cry. She hears a car door slam outside. An engine starting. Noah driving away. She walks back and forth in the office. Pacing instead of going after him. When her mother left, her father had holed up in his office. *Let her go*, he'd told Chelsey. And Chelsey had sat on his couch. Both of them tense and silent as her mother packed her bags. When she was gone, her father had placed both hands on his desk and stood. *Dinnertime. We'll go out.*

Her phone rings; the sound is like a lifeline, something she can grab on to. She wipes her nose and breathes deep, stale air filling her lungs. She doesn't recognize the number, but it says Coldwell. "Detective Calhoun," she croaks.

"Ellie didn't do this," Danny's voice explodes over the line.

Chelsey stares at the wall. At the photographs. "I agree," she says. She moves to the map, letting the green expanse of the Olympic National Forest blur her vision. "I believe Ellie was being watched—controlled." She traces the red lines she's made. "I'm going to find her before Homeland Security does. It's a long shot. I think she's headed to where she was kept, but the area . . . it's big."

"I'll come with you," he says.

"No," Chelsey says on reflex. It is too risky. Far too dangerous.

"I am coming with you," he insists. "The other night, she asked me to drive her to the trail where she was discovered. It was weird. I knew something was off. I turned on the Find My Friends app on her phone when I checked if she had service. I know exactly where she is."

At this, Chelsey jolts. Homeland Security will be able to track Ellie's phone, but before doing so, they'll need a warrant from a judge. Danny knowing exactly where Ellie is puts Chelsey and him a few hours ahead of them.

"She's outside of Olympia, heading north on I-5."

xii

WE SPOKE ONCE ABOUT REGRETS. Remember? How you implored me, Detective Calhoun? *Don't have regrets like me, Ellie.* I wish I could say I don't have any. But I do. So many. Little snags in the tapestry of my existence.

So, regrets. Yes, I have them. I'd like to go back and restitch so many things. I guess it was nice of David to let me come home a few days early to say goodbye. He let me have that do-over. Aren't goodbyes strange? Isn't it funny how you spend your entire life practicing saying it, but when it comes down to the real thing, it's near impossible?

—

My hand clenched around the bright red backpack hanging at my side. Inside it, I could hear the timer's seconds ticking down. David and I had been walking for a while. By my estimation, we had only a few minutes left. I glanced over my shoulder at him; he stood on the other side of the meadow, eyes on me.

I looked up at the birch trees stretching into the sky and picked at the peeling bark of the closest tree. I loved birch trees—their white trunks with long wistful branches tapered into serrated leaves. This one was old.

Even though the trunk was thin, it was tall, a sure sign of a long life. It was almost full, its leaves returning with the spring. It was surrounded by equally tall trees.

I laid the backpack at the base of the tree. I paced back, keeping it in my sight. When I was several feet away, I turned and broke into a run. Keeping my head down, I blindly headed in David's direction. David hooked an arm around my waist as I approached, stopping me. "Easy," he said into my ear, "we're at a safe distance."

My body went limp. He let me go, and I stood straight and stared across the grove. The red backpack an angry scar slashing through the green landscape. We didn't say anything else.

It came without warning—a sharp, quick bang. I could almost see the air ruffle with the sound. And then I felt it, pressure in my ears like the inside of a boiling teakettle. I covered them, but it didn't help. They felt as if they were bleeding. As if I had ruptured my eardrums. Orange flames and thick black smoke burned my eyes. I collapsed in a heap.

In a matter of seconds, it was over. The grove was eerily silent. Something pelted my back. Rain? I peeked from the cocoon of my arms. Wood and leaves and dirt fell around me.

Across the grove, my birch tree had collapsed in on itself. Cut off at the knees. The other birch trees were mangled and black as well. The scorched earth around the blast zone smoldered. Beside me, David was speaking, but I couldn't make out his words. The silence was lovely. I turned from him and got to my feet. We watched the forest burn until the fire went out, until the sky cleared, until I melted away to impermanence.

—

"You did well," David said. We were in his room. He flicked on the generator, heat flooding the room, and I flexed my fingers. "Sit, sit." David motioned to the edge of his bed.

My ears were still ringing. My steps were slow. The trees were dead.

Gabby was dead. Hannah was dead. I could see my path carved clear and deep, a trench in the blackest of soils—I would become like Serendipity, one of David's henchmen, unable to live without him. I looked at my hands, hands that were responsible for so much destruction. When you take a life, you lose a little of yours, too. I never thought it was possible to be alive and dead at the same time.

I sat tight on the edge of the bed. It hurt to speak. I'd inhaled some smoke and the inside of my throat felt like acid. I started to peel off my sweatshirt. The action involuntary and rote. David had never brought me to his room, but I knew what he wanted.

"We're not here for that." He pulled my sweatshirt back in place.

Through the window, I caught Serendipity hanging laundry on a line, surreptitiously glancing over her shoulder every now and again.

"I see so much potential in you." David moved about the room, slipping a newspaper from a stack. "You are a survivor. A fighter, like me. You care deeply for people, and it makes you strong, capable."

"I'm not," I said.

"You are," he insisted. "You will be," he insisted harder. He laid the paper across my lap. It was an edition of a local print. The words came together slowly. I hadn't read anything in years. GOVERNOR PIKE'S PLANS FOR THE FUTURE OF WASHINGTON. "It is my greatest desire that she no longer walk this earth." His voice tightened. "You want to do this for me, don't you? You will sacrifice yourself."

I squeezed my eyes shut. Tears leaked out. "I don't think I can." I was not like him. I did not want to be like him. A faceless husk that wished to rend the world in two.

His fingers bit into my flesh. He shook me, and my teeth clacked together. "You will do this."

Dread clawed at my insides. "I can't." I'd rather die on the compound. Let the dogs pick at my bones. "It's impossible."

"Nothing is impossible for the man who wills it. You can." He stopped shaking me and rubbed my arms, up and down. Up and down. "The weather is getting so nice. Little Grace loves to play in the water. I worry about her in the creek like that. She's so small. I'd probably only need one hand to hold her down. But then again, I'd hate to lose her. Only a few more years until she's fourteen. She'd be ripe then."

Fear spiraled around me. "No," I said. "Don't hurt her. Please."

"Do you love Grace?" He tilted his head.

"I do," I confessed, my stomach full of concrete.

When I looked at him, his eyes almost seemed a different shade, a darker blue, wet with triumph. "Tell me, what would you do for someone you love?"

"Anything," I said. "I would do anything."

Then he bent forward and whispered a sweet promise. "I'll let Grace go. Your life for hers." My only value was in relation to David. What I could do for him.

I flinched and then considered it. I was so tired of the pain in my chest, the numbness, the constant hurt. I had given Grace my shirts, my sleeping bag, portions of my food. The only thing I had not done was bleed for her. Grace still had dreams. For her the world was still wide and open. And my life? It was a mistake. A thread to be pulled, to be plucked. Discarded and worthless. I might not matter, but Grace did.

"Okay," I said, and it was a simple choice. "I'll do it. I'm ready." Then and there, I promised to give Grace all my tomorrows.

What is the price of absolution? Of forgiveness?

The answer was simple: a life for a life.

Chapter

THIRTY

"LEFT UP HERE." DANNY POINTS and Chelsey flicks on her blinker to veer onto 101. A sign reads OLYMPIC NATIONAL FOREST VISITOR CENTER, 68 MILES.

Her police radio is on, and it is heavy with chatter. An APB for a 1996 Corolla, Ellie's mother's car; a directive to not engage and wait for Homeland Security. The suspect is considered armed and dangerous. Chelsey blinks and imagines Ellie again, cornered by some cop with a sweaty trigger finger.

Danny holds his phone, map open, blue dot blinking with Ellie's location. She is moving fast. They're an hour and forty-seven minutes behind her. His lips are pressed together in a single fearful line.

"You don't have to come with me," Chelsey tries again. They haven't spoken much on the drive. Both lost in their own thoughts. But every few minutes, Chelsey feels a pinch of hot regret. She should not have let him get in the car. "You can give me your phone, and I'll drop you off somewhere. I can radio a local unit to pick you up."

A shake of his head. "I can't . . ." He scrunches his eyes shut, and tears squeeze out. It makes Chelsey shift in her seat, his sensitivity somehow unbearable. "I didn't show up for her once before."

His resolve, his remorse, is plain in Chelsey's ears. She thinks about

253

interrogating him at the station. Approaching him at the bar. How she could have handled both situations differently. Better. She is part of the dark shadow passing through Danny. "Listen, I'm sorry about the bar. I shouldn't have asked you to spy on Ellie. It's not how I usually operate—"

"Yeah, well, turns out you were right to want to keep tabs on her. This is some fucked-up shit." Danny stares out the window. It's pretty rural now. Houses set on acres of land with horses and cows and even some llamas. The occasional gas station. No hotels. "Look, I . . . I shouldn't have said what I said about your sister. It's not how I was raised. Throwing someone's personal tragedy in their face."

His words hover in the car, combining with the musty air, and Chelsey swallows against a scalding in her throat.

A red light on her dash blinks on. "Shit, we need gas," she says.

A mile down the road, she spies a gas station and turns in. Danny stays in the car. At the pump, she scrolls through her phone, checking various news websites.

They're still using the footage from earlier this morning. Screenshots of the governor's mansion, a SWAT team lining up behind shields, dogs straining on leashes. Chelsey can't hear, but she is sure the anchors are speculating on Ellie's motives, so she may be tried in the court of public opinion.

Chelsey's phone lights up with a text. From Noah: I'M WORRIED ABOUT YOU.

She deletes it. The passenger door slams, and Danny stands beside it. "We've got a problem," Danny addresses her above the car.

Chelsey nods at him. "What?" She removes the nozzle from the tank. "What's wrong?" She studies his grim face.

"I lost Ellie. She's out of service."

———

Chelsey parks the car in the gas station lot. On the hood, she spreads out a map of the Olympic National Forest. Danny has a second map up on his phone, too. With a black pen, she's circled Ellie's last-known location. An old logging road that splinters off in five directions, then splinters again and again.

"It will take us hours to search each one," says Danny. "Too long. This is impossible."

Chelsey nods. She scans the horizon. Looking at the tangerine and blush-pink sky. She keeps waiting to hear the thump of a helicopter. For the radio to announce that they've found Ellie. She puts her hands to her hips and hangs her head. What is she not seeing? What question is she not asking? What string has she not yet plucked?

"Why the governor?" she says aloud. She conjures an image of Pike. What she's seen on television. Polished and glossy haired, waving to the cameras, standing at a podium, lip curled, fervently promising women's rights. Chelsey remembers the precinct picnic. Back to when she was a kid. To when the governor was not the governor. To when she was Abbott's wife. Chelsey sees her. Sitting in the bleachers, baseball game in progress, a weird pained smile on her face, body wound tight, a tether about to snap.

"What?" Danny asks at the prolonged silence.

"Nothing," Chelsey says. "My boss used to be married to the governor. A long time ago."

"Your boss used to be married to Regina Pike?"

Chelsey shakes her head. "That wasn't her name then. She changed it after she divorced him." Discarded her first name for her middle, traded in her last for her maiden. "She was Destiny Abbott when I knew her."

Danny's face goes ashen. "Ellie told me they called her Destiny."

"What?" A bony-fingered chill runs up her spine.

"Whoever took her called her Destiny."

The memory reemerges. Destiny Abbott perched on the metal bleachers. Back straight, hands gripped between her thighs clad in pedal pushers. The picture pans out. There is Abbott next to her, standing, hand balled into a fist, rooting one of their kids on. Is that right? How had Chelsey forgotten this part? One of Abbott's kids stumbles, botches a play. Abbott launches himself from the stands, stomps onto the field to scream at his child, at Doug. Yes, Chelsey remembers the flop of Doug's hair, how it covered his eyes. How Destiny popped up from the bleachers, the barest quiver in her lip, and marched right onto the field to draw Doug away from Abbott. A few terse words passed between Destiny and Abbott. Abbott stomped off. Then Destiny sat with Doug in the stands, hand under his shirt, using her nails to rub comforting circles on his back.

Fast-forward, and Chelsey sees herself in the precinct, in Abbott's office. When he professed to still loving his ex-wife. Did he hate the thing he loved the most? Could Abbott have taken these girls? No, Chelsey thinks sharply. It couldn't be Abbott. She cycles through the crime timelines. Who went missing and when. She'd been with Abbott. No way he could have orchestrated this. But . . . doubt lingers. "See what you can pull up about Patrick Abbott. He's my sergeant, the governor's ex-husband."

"You think he had something to do with this?"

"I don't know." Chelsey's mind is spinning. "But whoever did this, it's personal for them. Very personal. Abbott and the governor's marriage didn't end well."

Danny's thumbs move over his phone. "There's a bunch about Abbott. Mostly career-related stuff. He has three kids. Two sons and a daughter . . ."

"West, Douglas, and Annie," Chelsey fills in. "Look up the kids. Start with West Abbott," she tells Danny, feeling a rush, the sensation of water breaking over rocks. *Maybe mommy issues*, Noah said, and Chelsey had laughed it off. But now she thinks of her own mother. How angry she'd been when she left. How she'd wanted to punish her. She flicks the thought away.

Instead, she joins Danny in researching Abbott's kids. Information is sparse. Not much online. Chelsey switches and logs into DMV records using her police credentials. West Abbott's last-known address is an apartment building in Seattle, long ago demolished, an upscale grocery store in its place. Annie lives in Coldwell, same as Doug. His vehicles are listed. Vehicles? A Prius she has seen him drive to work. And another car . . . a 1995 blue Ford station wagon.

Chelsey tightens with alertness. "Doug owns a car like the one seen at Ellie's and another girl's abduction sites." She thinks of Doug. Seeing him sporadically at the station. He could have done this, but not alone. "West Abbott, we need to find West Abbott," Chelsey hurries out. She is letting the wave carry her, certain she will end in the right place. Certain she'll wash up near Ellie, at Doug's and West's feet.

"A Sunshine LLC is registered under his name." Danny casts Chelsey a bright-eyed, feverish look. "Ellie . . . we listened to music one night. I put on the song 'You Are My Sunshine,' and she nearly broke the record in half." He squints at Chelsey, keen assessment in his eyes.

Chelsey inhales. She digs into Sunshine LLC. Two businesses are listed: a farm co-op and a kennel. Chelsey stops. The dog hairs found on Ellie. The bite marks imprinted on Gabby's bones. "Sunshine LLC operates a kennel. Here. It's a property in the Olympic National Forest—an old World War II bunker the government auctioned off." She punches in the address, forty-three miles away.

"We found them," Danny says.

Chelsey can only nod. The whoosh of the discovery winds her. West and Doug Abbott, two men she knows. How deeply it cuts. How good it feels, this brutal certainty. Finally. Finally.

"This could be really dangerous," she says once they're in the car, her hands on the wheel. "We don't know what these two guys have, what kind of arsenal." She pauses. "We might not come back."

"I'm coming," Danny says. There is stark fear on his face, but something else blazes in the depths of his eyes—all the love he carries for Ellie. He is desperate to sacrifice himself.

Chelsey backs the car out of the parking lot and takes a right, heading toward Doug and West Abbott. Toward Ellie. Toward whatever they might find.

"Why is she going back there?" Danny finally says once they're down the road. He's tapping his thumbs against his jeans. Afraid but undaunted.

Chelsey nods, acknowledging his question and remembering Danny doesn't know everything about Willa, the other girls. She thinks about herself. About Danny. What they are risking. Why they are risking it. Her thoughts flip to Ellie, the way she touched Willa's photograph, a tenderness to it, a mother cradling her baby's cheek. Love can push you to make the ultimate sacrifice. "I think she's going back for someone she cares about."

They travel on. And Chelsey thinks about her sergeant and his sons. How they'd been right under her nose. How smart they must have felt. Like they'd won. Playing hide-and-seek. But Chelsey wasn't really in the game before. Now, she is. Now, the tables are turning. Come out, come out wherever you are.

THIRTY-ONE

WILLA'S ARMS ARE TIRED, HER eyelids heavy. Even though Destiny always told her not to, she can't help herself; she sucks her thumb and rubs the sleeping bag between her fingers. The fabric is cool and soft. It makes her feel better.

Ever since Destiny left, Willa has been sad—even sadder than usual, and lonely. She huddles deeper into the covers. Her feet are cold. If Destiny were here, she'd rub them. She used to like it when Destiny would use her thumbs on her big toes and arches. She would always say that it helped the nightmares stay away. *It is a kind of magic*, she remembers Destiny saying.

Now, the door creaks, the lock clicks, and Willa scrunches her eyes shut. It might be him. He is called David, but she calls him the boogeyman in her head.

She hasn't seen him that much since Destiny left, but he comes to check in on her every so often. She hates it when he looks at her; it makes her feel itchy inside.

Now, a hand skirts over the sleeping bag and cups her shoulder. "Hey there, Sleeping Beauty." Willa wiggles from the safety of her nest. It's Destiny! She's back!

Willa grins and leaps, wrapping her arms around Destiny's waist.

Destiny jerks and throws her head back, laughing. Willa rubs her cheek against Destiny's abdomen. She is real. She is real. She is real. Then, Willa feels Destiny's body tremble, feels a kiss drop into her hair, tears too. Destiny pulls away and cups Willa's cheeks with both hands, her touch warm and reassuring. "Destiny," Willa says. Happy. She is so happy. Everything will be okay now.

"My name isn't Destiny, it's Ellie, and yours isn't Grace. It's Willa."

Willa feels light, and she smiles. "My mom called me Willy. She thought it was funny." She stills. She should not have talked about her mom. She waits to be shushed.

But Destiny—Ellie, she tells herself—smiles and kisses her forehead. "It suits you." She leans down so they are almost nose to nose. "Listen," she says, and she is serious. As serious as when Willa gets too close to the fire. "We don't have very much time. We need to get out of here. You need to stay close to me and do everything I say. Got it?"

Willa nods, a little frightened. "Where are we going?"

"I'm going to . . . I'm going to try to take you home."

Home. "Yes," says Willa. "I want to go home. Can I take my rock collection?" This morning, she found a white stone by the creek. It is smooth with tiny black marks, like a ribbon is woven through. It is her new favorite. She pretends it is a zebra.

"No, there isn't any time," Ellie says. "We have to go now." And already she is shoving Willa's feet into shoes, a sweatshirt over her head. "C'mon." They grasp hands, and Ellie pulls Willa into the dank hallway that is more like a cave. Willa does not like the way it smells, like bad food.

"I'm so glad you came back," Willa says.

"Hush," Ellie says. "Quiet voices now."

Willa drops her voice. "I'm so glad you're back," she repeats. "Charity never plays with me, and she doesn't share her food."

Ellie stops short, and Willa nearly runs into her. They are almost at the entrance now, near the steps that lead up into the compound. Ellie grips Willa by the shoulders. "Charity is here? I thought she was dead."

Willa nods at the room farthest down the hall. You can't see the door in the pitch black. Willa hates how it is always night in the bunker. "She cries a lot. I can't sleep sometimes."

Ellie reverses course and walks so fast that Willa needs to jog to catch up. "Where are you going? I thought we were leaving?" She peers up at Ellie.

Willa does not hear the first thing Ellie says, but she does catch the end. "Not without her."

———

An hour after sunset has always been Hannah's favorite time of day. It is the prologue to night, the beginning of endless possibilities. She used to dance. She'd go to the underage clubs and loved how the bodies pressed against hers, all writhing together—a hot sticky mess. It made her feel less lonely. Even here, dusk is still her favorite time of day. She does not dance anymore, but she does know one hour of peace when David retreats to his room to watch television. This is her sixty minutes without fear. It is what she lives for now. And she is alive. Barely.

Here is the thing about Hannah: She grew up in the system. One of her foster moms used to call her "little wolf" because of the way she skulked around the kitchen and table right before meals. Hannah is accustomed to not having things. She has gone without food. Without clothes. Without bedding. She is a survivor.

After she pulled a gun on David, Michael dragged her into the woods and held her there until David came. He spouted off some bullshit about loving her. She wobbled. Something wasn't right with her left leg—it hurt to put weight on it. She spat at his feet. Red slashed his cheeks, and he throttled her again. She opened her mouth to speak. He shook her and pressed harder, crushing her windpipe. *You wish to beg*, David said, and he released her. She fell down, gasping. *Beg me*, he had said, inordinately pleased. David's favorite thing was women at his feet. *I'm . . .* she started, unsure what to say. How to save her life. Then two words came, squeezing through the folds of her subconscious. *I'm pregnant.* It is what David wants more than anything. A child.

He'd thrown her back in the bus but fed her. Then brought her back, and Ellie was gone. Hannah assumes Ellie is dead. Soon, Hannah will be dead, too. Because she is not really pregnant. She has played a trick on the devil, and he will collect twofold when he learns of it. David will not abide being made a fool.

Now, there is movement outside of her room, and Hannah throws herself back against the stone wall. Coldness bleeds into her clothing as the metal door opens. And because she was just thinking of it, she imagines David has learned the truth. That instead of strangling her, he has something far more insidious planned. Fear makes her vision hazy, and she is unsure what she sees. Two figures before her, small and hunched . . . Grace? Destiny?

"Hannah." Hearing Destiny speak jolts Hannah from her trance.

Hannah crawls to the edge of the bed. "Destiny? Is it really you? How—"

"Ellie. My name is Ellie." Destiny—no, *Ellie* swipes under her nose. "I could ask you the same thing." She shakes her head. "But there's no time. Can you walk?" She eyes Hannah, her stiff movements, the way she drags her left leg behind her.

Hannah nods eagerly. "I can. I mean, I will. David—"

"I don't know where he is." Ellie moves forward and loops Hannah's arm over her shoulders. They glance at each other, and Ellie's eyes are wide and white, like a frightened horse. What is lurking out there? Michael. David. Serendipity. The woods seem just as hostile. Cold sweat breaks out along Hannah's hairline as they shuffle into the hall. Hannah leans against Ellie, and Grace comes around to grip Hannah's hand. "My name isn't Grace. It's Willa," she states.

"That's good, kid," Hannah grinds out. They are in the hall now. Water trickles down the walls.

"A mile or two from here, I have a car parked," Ellie whispers, the effort of supporting Hannah clear in her voice. "If we get separated . . . follow the creek north. You remember how to find north?"

"Polaris. The North Star," Hannah says, sagging against Ellie. When she'd first arrived at the compound, Ellie had taught her.

As they continue on, a sharp pain shoots through Hannah's leg, and bile rises in her throat. She might be sick. God, the pain. She tries not to think about the odds against them. What they'll have to accomplish. How a mile might as well be twenty. She won't focus on that. One foot in front of the other, she decides, that's what she'll concentrate on. Keep moving until you cannot anymore. Because she is a survivor. This will not beat her.

"That's right," Ellie says. "Follow Polaris and stay along the creek. I left the keys on the tire. You know how to drive?"

Hannah nods. She does not have a license. David snatched her before she could get one. But she'll figure it out. It's the least of her worries.

They trod along and stop at the bottom of the stairs. Hannah's eyes travel up. There are fifteen steps in total. Sometimes David skips down them, two at a time. Hannah shakes, and Ellie grips her tighter. Does she remember it, too? Gazing at the stars with Hope. Mending woolen socks. Rabbit meat. Hauling cinder blocks. Fists. Blood. Betrayals. "What about the dogs?" Hannah asks.

"They're in their kennels. But . . . I let one out. Star," Ellie whispers. Hannah remembers Ellie feeding the puppy. "Ready?"

"Ready," Hannah replies.

"No more talking," Ellie says to Willa, and Willa mimes zipping her lips shut.

Hannah ducks from Ellie's hold and uses the wall as support. But Ellie catches her hand. Willa takes Ellie's other hand. Together they embark. Each step, their breaths grow shallower—out of fear, out of pain. But they are together again. That is all that matters. Hannah knows after a life of nothing, it is the small things that count. At the top, Ellie smiles at Hannah, half encouraging, half victorious. Hannah listens and scans the compound—

empty, the whir of the generator, Michael's blue station wagon, but then she notices David's window is dark. Did he go to sleep? No, it is too early. They need to move. And quickly.

"Well, well, well," a voice says.

Slowly Hannah turns, bringing Ellie and Willa with her. David is behind them, hands balled into fists. They huddle together. The three girls wrap their arms around one another.

David sticks his fingers in his mouth, and a high-pitched whistle splits the air. Michael follows close behind, a gun in his hand, venom in his eyes. The two men stand over the shaking trio, rising like giants from the dry grass and dirt.

If this were a movie, Hannah might strike at David and tell Ellie and Willa to run. But this is real life, and she doesn't have the strength. The girls hold tighter to one another, cowering. Because no matter what Hannah believes, what she thinks . . . she is not a survivor. She is just a girl. A wolf without teeth.

THIRTY-TWO

IT IS PITCH BLACK, AND the logging roads are dark and bumpy. Inside, the car is silent. Chelsey white-knuckles the steering wheel, hyper-aware of the trees rising around them, of how small they are in comparison. Finally, her headlights catch on a familiar vehicle.

"Kat's car." Chelsey dips her chin to the side of the road, where the Corolla has been haphazardly abandoned.

"Yep," Danny says, tight-lipped. The tense air in the car ratchets up a notch. Ellie is out here, somewhere in these woods. I am coming, Ellie, Chelsey keeps thinking over and over again. Hold tight. Hold on. Her chest fills with longing.

"I'm going to turn my lights off."

Danny shifts uneasily. "Okay."

Chelsey clicks off the headlights, the cab darkens, their cheeks instantly awash in the ink of night. Slower they move on. Cell service went out a few miles back. But they drew a map on a napkin. Danny is holding it, the paper limp from sweat. The moon reflects off a white post: mile marker eight. Chelsey eases to the side of the road. This is it. Chelsey makes out an old, rusted gate marking the entrance. From there, it is about a mile trek. "I want you to wait in the car."

Danny sighs. "No—" Barking nearby rends his refusal. "What is that? Wolves?"

"Dogs," Chelsey says. Wolves don't bark. Not like dogs. They make a huffing noise. Plus, wolves have been extinct on the peninsula since the early 1900s, killed by farmers because they threatened livestock. "I can't have you come with me. You're a liability. And I need someone on the radio." She flicks it on, relieved the scanner still works. "If I'm not back within an hour, you drive away and call for help." It is not the best plan. But it is the only plan. She shows him how to work the radio.

Danny takes the radio and pinches his lips together. "One hour." He glances at her, a plea in his gaze. Please bring Ellie back.

"One hour," Chelsey confirms. She exits the car, closing her door with a barely audible click. She pops the trunk and fishes out zip ties and a hunting rifle, tucking them away on her body, keeping her hands free. She rounds the car again and nods at Danny once before slipping into the woods.

The air smells like wet dirt, and it is cold against her hot cheeks. Ferns and salmonberry tickle her ankles. She waits a half second and tips her head to the canopy, to the starless sky. It is so familiar here. A second home. She understands this land, has stroked its boulders and bark, skirted her fingers against its unforgiving underbelly. Shoulders tight, she lowers her body and creeps forward in a crouch, keeping to the right-hand side of the road, using the brush as cover.

She inhales. Exhales. The natural scents beginning to mingle with the unnatural—campfire, rot, decay. Up ahead, the road widens and splits, a pair of dark wings opening. Concrete buildings, suffocating in ivy, rise from the dirt-packed earth. Each structure radiates a hostile energy— meant for fear, for destruction, to kill. Garbage piles dot the landscape, stink oozing from them. There's a crumbling wall made of concrete blocks. Her stomach squeezes, and adrenaline somersaults through her veins. She assumes at least Doug and West are on the compound. But there could be more. Chelsey could be walking into an ambush. Ellie might already be dead. She shakes off the panic. The chill creeping up her spine.

How to proceed? Chelsey calculates the best route. Wind rustles the trees, and surfing on it, a moan. A female whimper. Chelsey's muscles tighten, ready to run. But no. She cautions herself. Hears her father as they army crawl through the brush toward a doe and her fawn. *Don't give up the advantage of surprise. Wait for it.* Listen. Another cry. From the east, Chelsey surmises.

She circles a building sunken halfway into the ground, chasing the thread of that whimper. The windows are barred, and a horrific stench rises from them. Beyond that is a row of kennels. The shape of dogs crouching, baring their teeth, gnawing at the metal bars of their cages. One of the kennel doors is open. The paw prints outside the kennel are fresh. She lopes past the dogs to a blank patch of concrete wall and peers around the corner.

Three girls huddle together, a sad, quivering lump in the dirt illuminated by moonlight. But also a beacon to Chelsey. She recognizes Ellie. Her ratty hair, that oversized jacket. Above them, two men rising like giants. One holds a gun, a red bandana covering his face. She recognizes the firearm. Police issued. Doug Abbott, then. The other is West. The years show on his body—fleshier, saggier.

She cocks her rifle and steps into the clearing, keeping Doug and West in her lens. "Coldwell PD. On the ground," she yells over the barking. The dogs are wild now. Slamming their bodies against the kennels.

West raises his arms; Doug, too, gun still in hand. "Chelsey Calhoun," Doug says. His eyes are wide, spooked. "How'd you find us?"

She edges forward. "I'd love to tell you, Doug. Why don't you put the gun down, and we'll talk about it?"

"You told me no one would ever find out," Doug addresses his brother, a tremor in his voice. "Oh my god. Oh my god. Oh my god. You promised." He yanks the bandana down, visibly heaving, then puts his hands to his knees, gun jangling in his palm.

West snorts. "Get a grip, Dougy." His hands are still up but loose, unconcerned. "Look around. There's no one with her. She's alone. Kill her."

Doug straightens, body inflating with hope. "That true? You here without backup?"

The girls huddle closer together, bodies and eyes squeezed tight.

Chelsey's hands are shaking terribly, but she keeps her voice even. A drop of sweat falls into her eyelashes, and she blinks it away. "You going to do your brother's dirty work, Doug? Is that what you've been doing this whole time? Catching girls for him, disposing of the bodies? I bet you're like one of those dogs in the cages, aren't you? Can't think for yourself?"

"I'm not like him," Doug explodes. "Tell her," he speaks to the girls. "I fed you on the bus. I never touched you."

The girls stay put, lost in a haze of terror.

"I believe you." Chelsey creeps forward a little more. "Give me the gun, and we'll talk about it," she croons. "Would you like to see your dad? I can make sure you do."

"Kill her," West commands. "She's lying. All women lie. She's just like Mom. Promising you one thing then doing another."

It happens so fast. A blur of motion. West drops his arms, pushing Doug forward, and at the same time, Doug raises his, gun in hand.

Boom.

Birds startle from the trees. The girls scream. The dogs howl. Chelsey's ears ring, and when she comes to, Doug is face down on the ground, blood pooling around him—dark red, thick, steam rising.

West's lip lifts in a sneer. "You're going to pay for that, you bitch!" He charges Chelsey, and she fires off a shot. Her heart drops as she misses. It clips West's arm and lodges in a concrete tower. She aims again, but too late.

West plows into Chelsey, pinning her beneath him. Her rifle clatters to the ground, out of reach. His hands are around her throat, squeezing. Chelsey grips his wrists, but he is too strong.

Distantly, in some muted past, she hears her father's voice. Other cops throughout the years. *How will you defend yourself against someone bigger, someone stronger, in hand-to-hand combat?* Black edges her vision. Now is the time. She only has seconds, she understands, before passing out.

She releases his wrists and gouges his eyes with her thumbs. For one pulse, West loosens his hold, and Chelsey brings her knee up into his groin. He doubles over, and Chelsey claws her way from underneath him. Oxygen coming as if through a pinhole. She emits a strange whistling sound as she rises to all fours. Saliva gathers and drops from her mouth. Chelsey peers at Ellie, eyes and throat burning. "Run," she grunts out.

"You fucking cunt." West is on the ground, on an elbow. *Click.* He has Doug's gun aimed at Chelsey.

"Go," Chelsey chokes out to Ellie, pain searing her throat. "Go."

Ellie just shakes her head. All three girls are still paralyzed.

A low growl coasts across the compound, and a dog appears at the tree line, hackles raised, teeth bared. West laughs, full-bellied. "This is perfect. I'm going to let it eat you." Chelsey clocks the distance to her rifle. Ten feet. She scrambles for it just as West sticks two fingers in his mouth and blows. The whistle is high-pitched. A savage call to arms. The dogs in the kennel bay, then whine. Rabid to do their master's command.

But the free dog stays. Chelsey grips the rifle. West raises his gun again.

Ellie shudders, hugs Willa a little tighter. She props her chin on Willa's shoulder and stares at the free dog. "Star," she whispers, then whistles low, the sound soft like the final words of a lullaby.

Like a crack of lightning, the dog jumps and tears at West's arm holding the gun. Shredding flesh from the bone. West shouts, a combination of pain and outrage. He thrashes, gun sliding out of reach while he tries to dislodge the canine.

Shaking wildly, Chelsey rises to her feet and staggers to West. The dog is still in a frenzy, gnawing at West, who is curled in a ball. Chelsey raises the butt of her rifle, hitting West square in his temple. He goes limp.

The dog ceases, backs up, whines, then lopes away into the forest. Chelsey kicks the gun far from West, then drops to her knees. Feels his neck. Still a faint pulse. She wheezes and takes the zip ties from her back pocket. She rattles off his Miranda rights, although she is certain he does not hear. She feels disconnected from her body. Floating. Calm. She zip-ties

West's hands. His ankles. Thinks about how small he looks now. How weak.

Rifle still in hand, she checks Doug. Nothing. Gone as the leaves in fall. She steals his bandana and wraps it around West's arm to staunch the bleeding. She wants him alive.

That done, she approaches the girls. They tremble and hold one another, lost in fear, begging for asylum.

"Hey," she says, soft and slow. The sudden calm is unnerving. "I'm going to get you out of here." Shaking and moaning. All of them are still terrified, still trapped in their memories, lost in this hellscape. "Come on now." She gentles her voice even more. It hurts to speak. Hurts more to look at all of this. The carnage. What one human can do to another. Vaguely, Chelsey understands this will be something she will never get over. It will follow her. This ghost, a new haunting. As long as these girls have demons, Chelsey will too. Ellie begins to rise, stiffness in every inch of her body. Then another girl. Chelsey recognizes her. Hannah Johnson. Beaten and bloody but breathing. And last, Willa, who clings to Ellie's hand. All of them here, standing, makes Chelsey want to drop to her knees and weep. She found them. She found them.

A door slams, the sound echoing, bouncing off the trees. Chelsey whips around as a slim, lithe figure darts into the woods. "Who's that? Another girl?" she asks.

"She's not one of us," Hannah says, words dropping from her mouth like acid. "That's Serendipity. She's with them."

Chelsey inhales. Could it be Annie? The third Abbott child? She wipes wetness from her upper lip. Blood comes away. Her face is numb. Her nose might be broken. "Got it." Chelsey grips her rifle. "Wait here," she instructs the girls. She sprints away, body aching, every muscle protesting. By sheer force of will, Chelsey continues on.

The woman leaves an obvious path of trampled brush for Chelsey to follow. She catches up to her near a creek. "Stop," she shouts over the rushing water and cocks her rifle. "Stop!" Chelsey screams. Adrenaline courses through her veins. One last charge. That is all that is left in Chelsey before she shatters. Already, she can feel herself coming apart. Ready to disintegrate into nothing.

The woman keeps running. Thirty seconds and she'll be in the trees and harder to track. Chelsey has no choice. She cocks her rifle. Presses the trigger. A third shot cleaves the night. She sees the woman's left leg buckle, then watches her fall emitting a grunt of pain.

Chelsey stomps through the creek, cold water soaking up to her knees, shocking her even more awake. She's no longer numb; she's aware of the pain in her body, like a vise is tightening each limb. "Hands on the ground," she barks. She can't see the woman's face; it is obscured by limp, blond hair. The woman places her hands flat, fingers digging in the dirt. Chelsey starts to read the woman her Miranda rights. "You have the right to remain silent." The woman begins to tremble. Chelsey whips zip ties from her back pocket. "Anything you say can and will be used against you in a court of law. You have the right to an attorney—" Up above, the thump of a helicopter can be heard. Danny must have called the police.

Chelsey kneels. The woman lifts her chin, and Chesley goes slack—dark brown eyes, straight eyebrows, a sculpted nose. Fair hair. Milk skin.

Surprise dusts the woman's features. "Fox face," she says to Chelsey, and the truth registers, locks into place as sure and swift as a deadbolt.

Not Annie but Lydia. Aged fifteen years. Resurrected. Her long-lost sister. Not a victim but a captor. Alive.

xiii

THE DAY I WAS RETURNED began like any other.

I woke up with the dawn, light streaming through the barred window, blanketing the dirt floor. Willa slept heavily next to me, sweetly oblivious. I took a moment to savor everything—her sticky breaths against my neck, her tangle of hair between my fingers, the threadbare kitten shirt she still insisted on wearing.

David opened my cell door and motioned for me to follow. I stroked her forehead and pulled the moldy sleeping bag over her shoulders. Then I hesitated. How could I leave her?

Willa cracked open a sleepy eye. She sat up, hands rubbing her face. "What's going on?"

I slipped off the bed and pulled on Hope's sweatshirt. Willa's blood still stained the front. "I'm going somewhere," I said.

"Can I come?" Sometimes I still hear her little voice in my sleep. The slight lisp, the way she depressed her R's.

"No." I moved to the door.

"When will you be back?" she asked.

I couldn't face Willa. My lips parted. I didn't have the words. I won't be back. She scrambled from the bed and latched on to me. "Come back soon. Promise?" She peered up at me, her chin resting on my chest.

I nodded solemnly. Then I fetched a windbreaker from the corner and wrapped her up in it. "It's going to be cold tonight. There's a surprise in the pocket." A brown agate I'd found by the creek.

"Remember, you promised," she said as I stepped over the threshold.

I didn't say anything back.

———

David led me through the narrow hallway, passing Hope's door, then Charity's—both rooms empty. Both girls gone.

We hit daylight, and I squinted even though it wasn't particularly bright. I searched for the position of the sun. The wagon was parked near the break in the trees. Star whined in her kennel, wanting to follow me.

David opened the back door and gripped me by the shoulders. He stared into my eyes. "Have I ever told you my story about the boat?"

I shook my head.

"My parents divorced when I was young. My mother never had a maternal instinct. Not like you." He half-smiled. "I was angry after. How could she leave us? After all we'd given her. My father was drinking more and more by then. He had a boat, and I took it without his permission. The water was rough, angry, and I didn't know what I was doing. I wasn't out for more than half an hour, not too far from shore. The boat started to take on water. I didn't know what to do. Steering it was impossible, so I hid in the bathroom."

David exhaled and leaned against the car. "There was this little light in there, and I remember watching it as the water rose above my knees. Finally, the whole damn thing capsized. The light shattered. It was dark. But I managed to right myself. The boat was upside down, and I was floating in that tiny bathroom, with only enough space and air for my head. I begged for my life. Called out to my mother. I was so scared. I was stuck in there for the whole night, enough time for my skin to soften and begin to slough off. Right when I was on the very edge of giving up, divers came and rescued me. My father waited on the dock, and I ran into his arms, this shaking broken mess." He flexed out the tremors in his hands.

"I got fixed up and was home within a day. While I rested, my father came to my room. He told me he knew I had taken the boat. He had seen it capsize from the dock. He heard my cries and knew I was alive in there, but he waited to call for help. Then he asked if I would take the boat out again without his permission. I said no, of course not. I had learned my lesson." He stopped. A crow cawed in the distance.

"I'm sorry," was all I could say. I didn't know why he had told me that sick story. It made me angry. I thought about David on that boat. How scared he must have been. How his fear had turned into anger. Rage. Hurt. Hate. Torment. I kind of pitied him.

"It wasn't my father's fault," David said. "He was out of his mind. Losing my mother. She should have been there. She should have stayed." A pause. Sometimes David seemed so fragile. Afraid. Like he knew he was always destined to come up short. To be forgotten. David drew closer to me. He placed a blindfold over my eyes. "Make me proud." Serendipity tied my wrists together. The engine of the wagon revved. Michael behind the wheel. I listened to the wind in the trees and the babble of the creek.

David repeated the terms of our deal. "I'll be watching you and sending you messages. You won't know where I am. But I will know where you are. I'll let you know when it's time. I want to see it on the news. I want to see she's dead. Then I'll let Grace go." He paused. "If you breathe a word of this to the police, I will kill Grace. Do you understand?"

I nodded so fast and hard, I thought I might break my neck.

"No one would believe you anyway," he added. He shoved me into the backseat.

"Wait," I cried out, my fingers digging into the fabric seat. Panic inched up my spine. "Please take care of Grace. Please." No answer. *Whoosh*—the door slammed shut.

The wagon started and lurched forward. Pressing myself into a corner, I counted to five, ten, twenty. Inhaled. Exhaled. I slipped my arms under my feet so that my tied hands were in front of me. Then I waited. For the wagon to stop. For Michael to backhand me. We kept driving. I brought my hands up, thumbs hooking under the blindfold to raise it just enough to see under the edge if I laid my head back at a certain angle. Then I looped my feet through my arms, so my hands were behind me again. We were going fast, flying down a gravel road. I'd lost some time—a few minutes. The clock read 10:21 a.m. I noted the speed on the speedometer—needle hovering over forty miles an hour.

Michael sat at the wheel, bandana in place. He reached up and pushed the rearview mirror down so he could gaze into the back of the wagon. I hunched over but counted the right and left turns, glancing up occasionally to catch the time. David may have wanted to stay hidden, but I wanted to know where I'd been kept.

By one o'clock, we were on a main road. Cars whizzed by. I thought about opening the back door and letting my body roll into traffic. But I dug my fingers into my back instead.

After two hours, we entered another park. Michael barked for me to lie down, but before I did I spied a family gathered around a camping van. Forty-six minutes later, Michael swerved into an abandoned dirt lot—Bear Canyon Trail, #888, closed for maintenance. The wagon stopped, and I was thrown back again.

"End of the line for you," Michael said, opening the door. He yanked the blindfold from my eyes. With a callused hand, he untied my wrists. From the front seat of the wagon, he produced a package wrapped in thick paper. "Everything you need is in there. Bury it in the woods. Remember where you buried it. Come back in a few days, when the attention dies down. This trail is lightly used, but someone should come along and find you. Wait at least an hour. You got all that?"

I nodded and took the package from him. Inside was a watch, wires, gunpowder.

He grabbed my chin. "What are you going to do with the package?"

"Bury it in the woods." I wondered what it would be like to die. Would it be painful? Probably. But I hoped it wouldn't be. I hoped it would be over quickly. That it would be gentle. Soft. I decided I'd think of my mother when I did it. Willa too.

"How long are you going to wait before finding help?"

"At least an hour."

He forced my chin up. "Until then, hide. You got that?" he asked again.

"Yes."

Michael watched until I disappeared into the woods. Package in hand, I darted off the trail and let the trees swallow me whole. While I waited for an hour, I repeated the information I'd gathered. We drove approximately forty miles an hour. We turned left at 10:35. Right at 11:55. And so on.

I squeezed my eyes shut, and I imagined Willa. That the love I had for her would transcend the confines of my body. That one day, she would run wild across a meadow toward a bright future. And I'd be a distant memory. Those days on the compound like a bad dream.

This was the only way to set us both free.

THIRTY-THREE

EAST OF COLDWELL IS BURNING. Fire season has come to the Pacific Northwest. An immolation of red and orange. Smoke hangs in the air above the Washington Corrections Center for Women. Chelsey sits in her car in the parking lot, a sob wracking her body, her hands tightening around the steering wheel.

Over the last seventy-two hours, the entire tapestry of her life has unraveled. She visited the hospital not as a detective but as a patient. Doctors wanted to keep her overnight, but she'd insisted she was fine and caught a cab back to her father's house. Then she'd slept. Fourteen hours without dreams, only to wake to a splitting headache, a burning in her throat. She looked in the mirror, at the black-and-blue bruises, and had her first flashback. Of zip-tying Lydia, leaving her in the woods, unable to look at her sister.

She could not process it. The knowledge Lydia was alive vibrated through Chelsey, hitting her stomach, heart, lungs, and liver like an ugly percussion. On autopilot, she had cleared the compound. Sweeping the rooms—a loft with a television and generator and a king-size mattress on the ground, another building stocked full of weapons and ammunition, and then, the bunker. The rooms underground, with metal doors and padlocks and crumpled sleeping bags. One had stars scratched into the wall, and a mobile made from sticks and dog teeth strung together with fishing wire. Then, after Homeland Security and the police arrived, after Ellie and the girls had been draped with trauma blankets and loaded onto helicopters, Chelsey had followed a marked path into the woods. There she'd found the bus. Opened the hatch. Jesus. The stink that rose up— human waste. It burned the inside of her nose. Days later, she could still smell it and vomited into the sink.

Next came the phone calls from Homeland Security, from Noah— whom she ignored. Because she felt so out of control. The sadness came in waves, giant swells that toppled her while she was showering or trying to sleep or eat. She was vulnerable, confused, as naked and slippery as a newborn baby. Terrified to be seen this way.

Sergeant Abbott resigned and has been calling. She does not answer. But she listens to his long, thick-voiced messages—Abbott had started drinking again. *I had no idea, Chelsey. You have to believe me. I don't understand how this could have happened. My boys, my boys . . .* Crying, sobbing. *Please call me back. There is more we need to speak about. Things you don't know . . .*

Chelsey knows enough. She sees Abbott clearly now. A man who could not cope with his own fears, so he drove them into his wife, his children. Chelsey has created a timeline in her father's office. You cannot even see the plaid wallpaper anymore, the patch with the Lisa Frank sticker. She worked backward, aligning dates.

Regina Pike wins the popular vote and becomes the gubernatorial elect. Willa Adams is abducted while bike riding. Regina Pike becomes the frontrunner for governor. Ellie Black is stolen from a gravel parking lot. On it goes. Each time Regina succeeded, West took another girl. Most striking is Douglas Abbott joining the force when his mother remarried. Chelsey has put together that Douglas helped kidnap the girls, then tracked their missing cases on behalf of his older brother. It shows a careful calculation on West's part. A Machiavellian effort. But Chelsey still has many unanswered questions. That is why she is here. Today. To see her sister, to seek the unknown.

She flips the visor down, dabs under her eyes, and does her best to clean herself up. She gets out of the car. Press vans are parked along the curb, and Chelsey is transported back to the night Ellie was discovered when she went to the hospital. Then, Chelsey had been anonymous, but now they recognize her and swarm. She keeps her head down, dodging microphones and questions. "Are you here to see your sister? We'd love to have you sit down for an exclusive interview." Media have been at the police station and outside the gates of Paradise Glen. Chelsey has even gotten a call from a documentary crew.

Acrid wind whips up from the east, and the press fall away as Chelsey enters the visitor area. "Who are you here to see?" a female officer asks behind a desk.

"Lydia Calhoun," says Chelsey, voice quiet with disuse.

"No press," she states.

"I'm not press. I'm her . . . I'm her family. Her sister."

The female officer eyes Chelsey. And Chelsey is reminded that she does not look like Lydia. She hands over proof. Her ID.

Chelsey is checked in, searched, and asked to leave personal items in a locker. It is not busy in the waiting room. A dad with a toddler. A woman with tired eyes. A television behind scratched Plexiglas is on, and Chelsey settles into a seat farthest from the other people. Fox London, the silver-haired anchor, is at a table with two pundits—a black woman in a navy suit and a white man in a tweed blazer.

"It is something you might find in fiction," Fox London says. "But this is all too real. We've been covering this since last Saturday, when an attempt to bomb Washington Governor Pike's mansion was botched. The suspect? Elizabeth Black. If that name sounds familiar, it should. Elizabeth Black went missing a little more than two years ago and mysteriously reappeared only recently. After Elizabeth Black allegedly bombed the governor's mansion, a statewide manhunt ensued. But it was a small-town detective, Chelsey Calhoun, who tied Elizabeth to her abductors—none other than Governor Pike's estranged sons, Douglas and West Abbott—

and in a stunning showdown, killed one, arrested the other, and shot and found her own sister, Lydia Calhoun, who disappeared in 2007." Fox London pauses, whiplashed. "Several bodies of missing girls recovered at various state parks have now been attributed to the brothers."

Chelsey ducks her head, but she can still hear the broadcast.

"Honestly, I'm not sure where to start with this," Fox says.

"You didn't mention Oscar Swann," the man in the tweed blazer says.

"Yes," Fox says. "Oscar Swann's car and body were discovered at the bottom of a cliff at a popular lookout point fifteen years ago in 2007. There was damning evidence that Lydia had been with him. Lydia Calhoun's clothing, even a part of her scalp and hair, was nearby. It had been assumed Oscar killed Lydia, then himself, that her body had been washed away in the tide. But questions have arisen whether this was some elaborate setup on West Abbott's part." Chelsey knows there are all sorts of conspiracy threads cropping up online. "For years, Oscar Swann has been criminalized as a murderer. And his family is speaking out with a desire for his name to be cleared posthumously."

"You know what I want to talk about?" the woman in the navy suit interjects. "I'd like to discuss what we think Governor Pike will be doing regarding Elizabeth Black."

"Rumors are swirling that the governor is urging charges be dropped against Elizabeth Black. Which would make sense, given the circumstances," Tweed Blazer says.

"I believe that's the best course of action. It's interesting, too, that Governor Pike is refusing to resign, given this scandal. Unlike her ex-husband, Patrick Abbott, the boys' father, who resigned his position almost immediately as sergeant of Coldwell Police Department," Fox mentions.

"Why is there an expectation she should resign?" the woman in the navy suit slashes in. "She's a victim here, too."

"Lydia Calhoun," an officer announces, swinging open a metal door. Chelsey jumps up. As she slips through the door, Fox London's voice reaches her ears. "Tonight, join me for a special about the Abbott brothers. Raised in a small town, both had good grades and a solid family life. How did two men with such promising futures go wrong?"

Of course, Chelsey thinks, there is the obligatory effort to excuse Douglas and West. Their alcoholic father will be blamed. Their absent mother. But Chelsey saw West on that compound. He was in control the whole time. "We'll also be discussing Lydia Calhoun, who lived with the brothers for near two decades. Was she complicit? Sources say the DA is considering charges."

Chelsey is led to a larger room resembling a cafeteria. Tables and chairs are scattered about. It's completely empty, except for Lydia in the corner. Chelsey gives her sister a nod and walks over. The officer stations himself against a wall underneath a mural of an ocean.

"How are you?" Chelsey asks as she pulls out a plastic chair. It's a stupid greeting, and it sounds strange. As if Chelsey hadn't shot Lydia. Pinned her to the ground. Arrested her.

"The food in here isn't very good." Lydia perches on the edge of her seat, her hands gripping either side. "But it's usually warm, and I can see a nice patch of forest from my window." At last, Chelsey studies Lydia in the light. The years have been mean to her sister. Lydia's face is hard, all the softness of youth gone. Her knuckles are bony, skin scaly, badly chapped. At Chelsey's examination, Lydia curls her hands in.

"What about your leg?" Chelsey glances at Lydia's thigh. Her gunshot had been a flesh wound. One night in the hospital, eight stitches, and then Lydia was transferred here.

"Barely feel it," Lydia says. She smiles. "I'm happy to see you."

Chelsey can't help but smile, too. "Yeah." She remembers them as little girls, nights spent laughing, whispering secrets, sleeping in the curves of each other's hollow spaces. They had not been two halves of a whole but extensions of each other.

"You look tired," Lydia says.

"I haven't . . ." Chelsey starts. "I don't sleep very well."

"Me either." Lydia leans in. "I've missed you," she whispers with honest ferocity.

Chelsey's hands shake. Her eyes water. All these years, she'd been so lonely without Lydia. Nothing seemed right. "I've missed you, too."

The corners of Lydia's mouth turn up with pride. "My sister, the cop. Just like Dad. He must be proud." There is a slight edge to Lydia's words.

At the mention of their father, Chelsey dims. "You should know that, um, Dad, he passed away about a year and a half ago. Throat cancer." Is it terrible that Chelsey is glad their father is dead? That he does not have to see this is what has become of his children?

"Oh." A shadow crosses Lydia's face, and she turns a cheek. Her head bobs. "That makes sense. He used to smoke so many cigars. Was there a funeral?"

"It was really nice. A lot of his old co-workers came. He's buried on a hill . . ." *Next to you*, Chelsey almost says. A memory emerges from the cramped corners of her mind. Chelsey is watching Lydia's casket as it is lowered into the ground. Her empty casket. They decided to have a funeral even though there was nothing to bury. Lydia's body was never recovered. It is the real reason Chelsey hates the beach. Why she won't walk it. Too afraid she'll find the remains, brought in by the tide. Another memory crops up. Her father by the gravesite muttering, *Such a waste*. A waste of life. Money. Time. All of it. "But Mom . . . she's still around," Chelsey hurries to say. "She lives in Arizona. She's on her way. And she's going to visit you first thing." Chelsey had been quick to relay the news and hang up. "But I kept the house. After Dad died, I mean. I've been staying there, and your room is the same. Everything is the same."

Lydia screws up her nose. "I always hated that house."

"What?" They'd been so happy there, high on the hill.

Lydia guffaws. "I hated living there. And Dad, he was so mean to Mom." Chelsey blinks and feels the air stir around her, the start of a veil being lifted. "Remember that time he threw a pen at her?"

Chelsey's natural reflex is to defend her father. He'd always been stern. That was his way. "He was working a case—"

"She was bringing him dinner." She shakes her head.

"I don't remember that." The air continues to shift around Chelsey, faster and faster. A memory whips by on a gust. When Lydia had put the Lisa Frank sticker in his office. Their father had yelled, and Lydia had balled up in the hallway, rocking back and forth. He'd sent Lydia to bed without dinner.

"You're married," Lydia exclaims, pointing to the gold band on Chelsey's finger.

Chelsey is grateful to pull back from the memory, unsure what to do with it. Where to place it on the wall of her father's accomplishments. "I am." Time seems to be moving slowly now. It is all surreal. Speaking to Lydia as if the years haven't passed. As if they are still little girls confessing secrets to each other. After Lydia, Chelsey didn't confide in people. No one measured up to her sister. "His name is Noah."

"Maybe you could bring him to visit, and I could meet him?" She beams. "I'm married too, you know," Lydia says, as if telling a secret. A gentle forbidding floods Chelsey's veins. "To West. We had a ceremony in the woods. Douglas officiated . . . I insisted." She drops her voice. "I didn't want to . . . do it unless we were married. Did you wear a white dress when you got married? I didn't get to, but it was still romantic."

Chelsey studies Lydia, feeling suddenly unsettled. "How did you two meet?" It's the detective in Chelsey speaking now. Asking questions.

"At the picnic," Lydia throws out.

Chelsey wants to vomit. At the precinct picnic. So much had been set into motion then.

"I'm lucky I found West," Lydia goes on, undeterred. "He never lays a hand on me unless he's truly angry. The first time was the worst." She lifts her hair up to reveal a bald patch.

Chelsey curls her hands into her fists. "West do that to you?"

Lydia hums. "It wasn't his fault," she says. "It was years ago. I went out with Oscar to make West jealous." She drops her voice. "West doesn't share his girls. I should have known better. West was angry. He bashed in Oscar's head." Chelsey blanches, and Lydia rolls her eyes. "He didn't suffer."

"Then West pulled out your hair?" Chelsey asked.

Lydia smooths her hand over her hair. "We had to make it look like I died with Oscar. His dad said—"

"His dad?" Patrick Abbott, Chelsey's former sergeant?

Lydia nods. "He said we had to leave some evidence behind. He told West it was the last time he'd cover for him."

A flush of adrenaline courses through Chelsey at the knowledge Sergeant Abbott was involved in all of this. How long has he been covering for his sons? She remembers Abbott denying her the resources to track down the blue station wagon. Had he known then? Or before?

"It's been so difficult for West, not being able to see his father. So sad."

Does the affection in her sister's voice mean Lydia would do anything for West? Even help him steal and keep girls? How did this happen? Why did no one ever tell Lydia that the most dangerous thing in the world isn't natural disasters or wars or weapons? It is unremarkable men with beautiful smiles and even bigger promises.

"Lydia," Chelsey says quietly, "do you know what's happened? What West has done?"

Something shutters across her sister's face. "He said it was my fault. I couldn't have a baby." She opens her hands. "I got pregnant once." Her eyes shimmer with tears. Each word falls, heavy and absolute, a barrier between the sisters. "He wanted a family. One that couldn't leave him like his mom did."

Chelsey shakes her head, realizing Lydia has not grown up. She has warped. Twisted. And is very much still fifteen in some ways. "I can't hear this," she says, but then she thinks of Gabby. Of Willa. West isn't speaking, and Chelsey needs to know. "Why did he take Willa?" she forces herself to ask.

"Who?" Lydia's face screws up.

"Grace. You called her Grace."

"Oh, that? He wanted someone younger. I think he wanted to mold her. The other girls could be very rebellious. He wanted someone who would be devoted. And since I couldn't have a baby . . ." She trails off, her eyes sad, then changes the subject. She puts a hand near her mouth as if whispering a secret. "But then he saw how Destiny loved Grace and figured he'd use that instead. He can be so impatient sometimes." She grins. "Do you want to know about the rest of them? Charity got into the car with Doug. All he had to do was offer her a ride. And Hope . . . West loved her and then hated her so much. She broke his heart—"

"That's enough." Chelsey's face is a rictus of revulsion. She wonders how it is possible to still love someone who has done such horrible things.

"Right," Lydia says. "Sorry, I forgot. The trial. Hey, do you think I might be able to see West? Have you seen him? Is he okay? He doesn't like sleeping alone. Also, I need a nail file. West hates ragged nails. He likes our nails rounded. Smooth. Like yours but a little longer."

"Lydia," Chelsey says, hesitating, unsure how to handle this. "Don't you get it? What West has done? To those girls? To you?"

"He loves me," Lydia says. Then, more harshly, "He loves me."

For one second, Chelsey hates her sister, but the feeling is gone in a flash, replaced by pity. The tide is coming back again, threatening to sweep Chelsey away. She stands, the chair scraping and nearly toppling over. "I have to go. Mom will be here to visit tomorrow, and I'll come back soon." Without another word, Chelsey walks away.

Chelsey drives from the prison but pulls over a few minutes later, skidding to a stop on the shoulder. She inhales, screams, beats the wheel, then collapses in a sob. She thinks about the subjectiveness of memory.

She reaches for her phone and presses dial on her most recent missed call.

"Chelsey." Noah's voice is like a hand reaching for hers.

"I'm sorry." She half ventilates the words, lost in a whirlpool of reckoning and awakening. "I've been wrong about so many things."

THIRTY-FOUR

ELLIE DRUMS HER THUMBS AGAINST the leather-bound notebook in her lap.

"You finished it?" Dr. Fischer nods to the journal.

"Yes," she says, gazing out the window. The view at the psychiatric hospital is not nearly as nice as the view from Dr. Fischer's office. A parking lot with some maples evenly planted along the sidewalks. Tall lampposts. A fence with barbed wire.

Ellie has been caged again. This time in an inpatient program for three weeks. She'll be out soon. A matter of hours. Doctors say her medications are working now. The prosecution declined to press charges. And Ellie has written her full confession, to be delivered to Detective Calhoun. She scribbled the last line mere hours ago. *I squeezed my eyes shut, and I imagined Willa. That the love I had for her would transcend the confines of my body. That one day, she would run wild across a meadow toward a bright future. And I'd be a distant memory. Those days on the compound like a bad dream. This was the only way to set us both free.*

Dr. Fischer has come nearly every day. Sometimes for a session. Other times just to visit. Today she is here for a proper session. Ellie can tell. Because her yellow notepad is out.

The first few days, Ellie just sat across from Dr. Fischer. Mute.

Dr. Fischer says it's okay. Walking through the door is enough. Everything is her choice now. To speak. To stay silent. To scream. Sometimes she hates Dr. Fischer's positive affirmations—Dr. Fischer says that's okay, too. But finally, Ellie began to tell her story. Writing it down and speaking it aloud to Dr. Fischer. How she disappeared. The friends she had. The friends she lost. The deal she made to save Willa. She'd been so terrified when she was returned. It had been like walking on shards of glass. Michael left the postcards at David's behest. She was never far from his reach, Willa even closer. But when it came down to it, Ellie couldn't kill anyone. She botched the bombing and fled. Because she knew David would be watching, she'd felt her only choice was to go back to the compound and try to rescue Willa herself.

Now, Ellie is inordinately tired and a little pissed off.

She crosses her arms. "It's been weeks. I've done everything they've asked me to. When do I get to see Willa?"

"I don't know," Dr. Fischer answers evenly. "She has her own work to do, just as you have yours."

Ellie's jaw locks. "Yes, but I need to see her."

"You've received updates," Dr. Fischer says. Letters arrived from Willa's mother, along with pictures.

"It's not the same," Ellie gripes. It is not the same as touching her, feeling her. Making sure she is breathing. "Did you remember to tell her mom that she's been learning to tie her shoes? That I taught her that song about bunny ears? Oh, one of her teeth got infected once, and I had to pull it out. She probably needs to see a dentist. Sometimes she has bad dreams, and she likes to be sung back to sleep—"

"Ellie," Dr. Fischer says calmly. "We've spoken about this. You don't have to protect her anymore. She is safe, and it is time for you to think about your own future."

A shake of her head. Ellie throws up her hands. "I can't . . . I'm not sure how to live with this . . . missingness." She feels like an ellipsis, trailing off into nothing.

"It is a difficult thing, to find hope again."

Hope. At the word, Ellie crumples. Things she doesn't like to think about jump the barricades of her mind. Eating bitter seeds. Screams in the night. Muffled cries.

"You're thinking of her?"

"It's *all* I think about." Gabby. Willa. Hannah. "I couldn't save them."

"You were willing to sacrifice yourself for them. You went back to the compound, drew the police there. Now Douglas Abbott is dead, while West Abbott is awaiting trial . . . that is all very heroic in my book."

Douglas Abbott. Michael. She remembered long after that he'd been the narcotics cop who'd come to the school the day she'd been arrested for pot in her locker. That's how he'd found her. The other girls. Through his job. Social media. Gabby had followed him, liking his stupid videos. Anger rolls again in Ellie's stomach. It's doesn't matter what Dr. Fischer says. What dragon has been slain. The pain remains. Dr. Fischer leans forward. "I was thinking . . ." She glances down at her pad. "That maybe we could do an exercise."

"What kind?"

"I'd like for us to go back together in your mind and free Gabby and Hannah and Willa. Humor me?"

Ellie laughs, even though she has learned to trust Dr. Fischer. She'll follow Dr. Fischer wherever she leads. Here in this white room, they pass through the borders of Ellie's pain. "Yeah, okay, sure."

"All right, then," Dr. Fischer says, then drops her voice an octave. "Go ahead and close your eyes for me."

Ellie does, feeling a bit silly.

"Good," she croons. "Now, let's go back to the compound. Let's rescue Gabby."

It is not that hard for Ellie to sink into the memory. To feel as if she is there again, among the concrete structures. She inhales, and there it is, the campfire and dogs and the forest after the rain.

"Are you there?" Dr. Fischer asks, and Ellie nods. "Okay, now go to a day when you were all together. You, Hannah, and Gabby. Do you see them?"

It is fall, near winter. The day when the girls whispered their real names to one another. Their cheeks were warm from the fire. Their hands itchy from harvesting the seeds. "I'm there with them."

"Do you see yourself, too?"

A knot forms in Ellie's throat, and she swallows against it. "Yes." She is there, sitting on a log next to Gabby. Knees touching. So warm. So alive. "Okay. Now, include Willa. Can you do that?"

Willa came after Gabby, but it is easy to put her near the fire, too. Because it is what Ellie wants, for them to be together, to be safe, to have each other.

"Take each one of them by the hand. Tell them that they don't have to stay there anymore."

Ellie's eyes water. In her mind, she reaches out and lifts them one by one—Hannah, Gabby, and Willa—from the logs. *Come with me.*

"Are they with you?"

"Yes."

"What about David? Is he there?"

"No," says Ellie. "He's in his room. He can't hear us."

"Do you want to do anything to him?"

"What do you mean?"

"Kick him. Hurt him. Send him into space. Whatever you want."

Ellie laughs. "No. We just want to go."

Dr. Fischer says okay. She tells Ellie to walk Gabby, Hannah, and Willa from the compound. "No one will stop you."

So, she does. For a long time, they travel through the woods with near-freezing rain soaking their clothes, crossing a burned patch of land where Queen Anne's lace once grew, over the top of a rusted bus. They arrive at a clearing, and it is day now. Summer, too, and they are not desperate for warm clothing. Their teeth are no longer chattering. Their lips are no longer blue.

The fear slowly peels away. They turn to one another and dare to grin. Suddenly, all of their mouths are bursting with laughter. Ellie cups her hands over her mouth and shouts her real name. Then Gabby does, too. Then Hannah. Then Willa. It feels good to be as loud as they want. They are not worried about being quiet. Being called ungrateful or watching for a swinging hand. They unravel themselves against the sun and sky and rolling open fields. Giddy and happy.

"You still with me, Ellie?" Dr. Fischer's voice pierces the bubble.

Ellie nods. She tastes salt on her tongue—her tears have run into her mouth. "I'm not ready to leave yet." She wants to stay in this golden place forever.

"It's time to come home. But you can bring them with you."

"How?"

"Take them to your house. Knock down a wall and make rooms for them."

Throat thick, Ellie builds a room next to her own for her friends. A place with a bed and a window that opens. The air is fresh and does not stink of garbage and animals. This is what she wanted all along. For them to be free. Together. They strip the clothes from their bodies and replace the garments with cashmere. Then they lay down in sheets that smell of lavender. And Ellie whispers promises she knows she can keep. *We'll never eat dandelions or huckleberries again. No one will touch you without your permission. There will be no more plants that make you bleed.* Hannah and Willa drift off to sleep. And there is no need to think about touching their chests to measure their breaths. Ellie knows they can rest, and when they wake up, all will be well. Gabby turns to Ellie, and they rub noses, stroke each other's hair, bask in it all.

"What would you like to say to Gabby?" Dr. Fischer asks.

"I'm sorry." Ellie is sorry she could not save her. She is sorry that Gabby will never know the joy and agony of tomorrow. The feel of a gentle hand. The touch of her children. The spray of hot water. The first bite of a good meal.

"What does Gabby say?" Dr. Fischer asks.

"I want her to say that I don't have to be sorry."

"It is not your fault, Ellie," Dr. Fischer says. "Do you believe that?"

Ellie opens her eyes. Tears track down her cheeks. She opens her mouth and closes it. "I'm trying to."

"We'll keep working on it. Until tomorrow." Dr. Fischer stands.

They say goodbye. They'll see each other the same time the next day but in Dr. Fischer's office. Because Ellie is going home. Her parents are waiting in the lobby.

"Hey," her dad says, slipping the bag from her shoulder. "You ready?"

Her mom smiles. "Okay?"

Ellie nods and climbs into the car. They set off, the rocking of the vehicle soothing Ellie as she fingers the pages of her journal. Soon enough, they are at the Coldwell precinct and asking for Detective Calhoun.

Chelsey rounds the corner. "My favorite family," she says, shaking Ellie's dad's hand and hugging her mom. "That for me?" She nods at the journal.

"It's all in there." Ellie hands it off.

"Good, this will help with the trial," Chelsey says. "We're going for the maximum sentence, a lifetime in prison."

West Abbott is pleading not guilty and has rejected a plea deal. Ellie wishes he would plead guilty. That he would go away and never come back. But he wants his day in the sun. And Chelsey has assured Ellie it will be his last. Ellie shakes Chelsey's hand again and says goodbye. She loads back up into the truck with her parents.

"I forgot to tell you." Her mom turns from the front seat to speak to Ellie. "Sam and the family are coming over for dinner tonight."

Ellie's lips tip up. "Sounds good," she says. Her mom turns back around, and Ellie looks out the window. She sees her reflection in the glass and touches her profile. Reminds herself that she is here. She is here. She *is*.

She places her hand back in her lap, touches her wrist with the other. Sometimes she thinks she can still feel it, the friendship bracelet Gabby gave her, and she wonders how she is still hanging on. If she will always be living life as if staring down the barrel of a gun. Her thoughts turn to Dr. Fischer. To their conversation an hour ago. Ellie still has a hard time believing it wasn't her fault. What happened to Gabby. To Hannah. To herself. Often, she thinks of what she might have done differently. Will she ever let go of the blame? She is not sure. But she hopes she will someday. Just as she hopes that someday the smell of campfire will not make her sick. That someday the sound of a dog barking will not take her away. That someday she will not be afraid.

That someday she will unlock the doors. Leave the crawlspace. Sleep in a bed. Cut her hair. Call an old friend. Kiss an old love. Hold her niece. Laugh with her sister. Hug her mother and father. Run headlong into her future, carrying the loss in one hand and hope in the other.

Yes, Ellie thinks. I will live again. I will be a bird and I will sing.

THIRTY-FIVE

LYDIA'S WOODEN HAIRBRUSH, HER PAISLEY robe, her ragged Beatrix Potter bunnies, her white iPod, her *Into the Wild* poster, her dried roses tied with twine, her toy VW bug car—Chelsey places all of it carefully in a box and closes it. Last, Chelsey stands on a chair and unpins the FREEDOM sign from above Lydia's door.

Noah appears in the doorway, hefting a box. "Almost done? It's almost five. We have to get going if we want to drop off the keys to the Realtor before they close."

Chelsey nods, swallows. "Just finished."

"I'll meet you outside." He carries on down the hall. "I saw another reporter hanging around the gates earlier. You'd think they'd have given up by now," he throws over his shoulder.

Chelsey does not answer. It has been three months since she found Ellie in the woods. Since she killed Douglas Abbott, arrested West and Lydia. Trials will start within the year. But the media interest has lingered. Chelsey still will not comment. Even though she knows exactly what she would say. She would not speak of West, Doug, or even Lydia, nothing about her sister's guilt or innocence—the truth lies somewhere in the middle. She would say nothing about the governor or Chelsey's former sergeant, who has also been arrested and will be standing trial, too. Abbott confessed to tampering with a crime scene, framing Oscar for Lydia's murder.

But he swears that he did not know what his sons were doing in the woods. A jury will decide if he's telling the truth. Chelsey would speak of none of that. Instead, Chelsey would talk about the girls. All of them. She would say their names. Brittany, Theresa, Gabby, the ones who did not make it out of the woods. Willa. Hannah. Elizabeth . . . the ones who did. Even though they lived, even though Ellie didn't face charges, something has irrevocably been lost. She would ask the media, the world: When will it be enough? How society accepts women dying at the hands of men. Chelsey mourns girlhood.

She drifts through the house, clicking off lights as she goes, taking her time. This is Chelsey's final goodbye, a wound closing—sometimes these things heal naturally, sometimes they must be cauterized. At last. At last. Through her parents' bedroom, she goes. Nothing is left here. Just a bed frame, the mattress leaning against the wall. In the bathroom, she sits on the edge of a pink jetted tub. For a moment, she is five again. Lydia is six. Water trickles from the faucet, and bubbles float in the water. They're giggling. The memory sucks the air out of her lungs. Her throat rushes with anguish, and Chelsey does not push it down. She allows it to come. She lets the grief roll through her and crest. A foamy burst. Because what is grief but the other side of love?

She wanders from the bathroom to her father's office at the very end of the hall. The room is empty now. Once, she took comfort in this space, and now . . . now she is not sure. Sometimes she is angry at her father. Lately, memories have morphed, good into bad, bad into good. She sees him clearly now. Chief Calhoun, a man who destroyed his own marriage because he could not recognize his own faults.

She shuts the door to her father's office. It does not escape Chelsey's notice: the similarities between Sergeant Abbott and her father. Both of them cannibals, devouring their wives, children, themselves. Or how similar her story is to West and Doug's. Lionizing their fathers. Vilifying their mothers. But West and Doug became adults worse than their father. And Chelsey . . . better, she hopes. She thinks about the choices people make. The paths we carve of our own free will. The one she is about to forge. A new home in a new city. She stayed with Coldwell PD long enough to close the Ellie Black case. Then she'd quit. Chelsey and Noah are moving to Olympia. She doesn't have a job yet but has applied to a few police departments. She will see. The past is unchangeable. But the future is uncertain, and Chelsey is ready.

She travels down the stairs and feels the ghost of fifteen-year-old Lydia beside her, skipping out the door, full of girlish dreams, to be free of this house, in love and in danger. Chelsey flicks the final light off. She closes the front door and locks it. On the stoop, she stares at the lighthouse for a moment. Sees her and Lydia as children. In the past, the sun is near setting, but the air and concrete are still warm. Little girl Chelsey runs through the streets, up the stairs of the lighthouse, hangs from the window, cups her hands over her mouth, and shouts, *Olly olly oxen free.*

"That trash?" Noah cuts into Chelsey's thoughts and nods at her hands where the papers are cradled, the bubble letter F on top.

Chelsey shakes her head; she thinks about putting one life down in order to embrace another. "It's going with us." This is a thing she will carry. This is a thing she will keep. This single word. Freedom.

This is how it ends.

ACKNOWLEDGMENTS

I am not sure it's possible to thank everyone who brought this book to life, but I will do my best.

To that end, I'd like to thank my editor, Carina Guiterman, for showing such faith in me and this book—I am so grateful to have you in my corner. Also, thanks to Tim O'Connell and the rest of the team at Simon & Schuster, who have worked on this book from typesetting pages to singing its praises far and wide: Sirui Huang, Wendy Blum, Sophia Benz, Amanda Mulholland, Lauren Gomez, Zoe Kaplan, Morgan Hart, Beth Maglione, Hannah Bishop, Danielle Prielipp, Crystal Watanabe, Andrea Monagle, Helen Seachrist, and Sara Kitchen.

Thanks to Erin Harris, the best agent in the biz and a true guiding light—here's to a decade of working together and hopefully many more decades to come. Also, thanks to Joelle, Josh, and Sara—you three are magic makers.

Thanks to Yumi and Kenzo; you make me happy.

And thanks to Craig for all the reasons.

ABOUT THE AUTHOR

Emiko Jean is a *New York Times* bestselling author of young adult and adult fiction. Before she was a writer, she was a teacher. She grew up in the suburbs of Portland, Oregon, and now lives in Washington with her husband and kids.